The Ghost and Mrs. Mewer

Krista Davis

CENTER POINT LARGE PRINT
THORNDIKE, MAINE

This Center Point Large Print edition
is published in the year 2015 by arrangement with
The Berkley Publishing Group,
an imprint of Penguin Publishing Group,
a division of Penguin Random House LLC.

The text of this Large Print edition is unabridged.
In other aspects, this book may vary
from the original edition.
Printed in the United States of America on permanent paper.
Set in 16-point Times New Roman type.

ISBN: 978-1-62899-559-6

Library of Congress Cataloging-in-Publication Data

Davis, Krista.
The ghost and Mrs. Mewer / Krista Davis. — Center Point Large Print
edition.
pages cm
Summary: "Holly's Jack Russell, Trixie, and kitten, Twinkletoes, find a
young woman drowned in the Wagtail Springs Hotel's bathhouse—the
spot of the town's most infamous haunting. The crime scene is eerily
similar to the creepy legend, convincing Holly that the death wasn't just
accidental"—Provided by publisher.
ISBN 978 1 62899-559-6 (library binding : alk. paper)
1. Hotelkeepers—Fiction. 2. Haunted places—Fiction.
3. Murder—Fiction. 4. Large type books. I. Title.
PS3604.A9717G48 2015
813'.6—dc23
2015003692

To Buttercup, Queenie,
and Little Miss Sunshine

Acknowledgments

People often ask if I do any research for my books. I learned a lot about ghosts for this book. It was fascinating to hear about ghosts that people have encountered. Thanks to all of the lovely people who shared their ghost stories with me. It was equally interesting to learn how some people have manipulated situations to make us believe in ghosts. The Apparition Apprehenders took me into the believers' side of the paranormal, and Eva's position led me to examine the scientific position. I have learned a great deal, mostly that there is no grand conclusion.

Special thanks to Shawny Darby for answering my questions about ghost hunting. And also to Kathleen Joyce, who suggested the name Apparition Apprehenders. As always, I couldn't do this without my editor, Sandra Harding, and my agent, Jessica Faust. I thank Susan and PJ Erba for taste-testing the recipes for me. And my dear friends Betsy Strickland and Amy Wheeler for always being so supportive. I can't forget my mother, my first reader and biggest fan. As always, any errors are my own.

Dogs love their friends and bite their enemies, quite unlike people, who are incapable of pure love and always have to mix love and hate.

—Sigmund Freud

APPARITION APPREHENDER GHOST TEAM
Felix Fischbein and Casper (Weimaraner)
Brian Anderson
Mr. Luciano and Gina (bulldog)
Eva Chevalier and Mrs. Mewer (Siamese cat)
Grayson Gatewood
Mark Belinski
Mallory Gooley

OTHER SUGAR MAPLE INN GUESTS
Lillian Elsner
Parker Colby

SUGAR MAPLE INN STAFF
Liesel Miller
Holly Miller
Zelda York
Casey Collins
Shelley Dixon
Mr. Huckle
Marisol Rodrigues
Gingersnap—canine ambassador (golden retriever)
Trixie (Jack Russell)
Twinkletoes—feline ambassador (calico kitten)

RESIDENTS OF WAGTAIL
Doc Kilgore and Siggie (black Labrador)
Officer Dave Quinlan

Clementine Wiggins
Rose Richardson
Holmes Richardson
Aunt Birdie Dupuy
Val Kowalchuk

GHOSTS
Elmer Dupuy
Dr. Ira Wraith
Becca Wraith
Dr. Hiram Montacue
Obadiah Bagley

One

"There is no such thing as a ghost." Eva Chevalier turned her pointy nose up in the air and chortled. "It's preposterous. Nonsense, folderol, fiddle-faddle."

No sooner had she spoken than the automatic sliding glass doors to the parking lot whooshed open. A gust of wind blew in, bringing dried leaves with it.

A grey Weimaraner with startling blue eyes stepped away from the doors and growled. Ginger-snap, the Sugar Maple Inn's canine ambassador, simply wagged her tail. In typical golden retriever fashion, she continued kissing the guests gathered in the reception area.

The doors closed again as if a person had passed through. I felt the chill of a late October wind pass by.

"I bet there's a ghost in here now," Casey Collins whispered, gazing up at the ceiling and shoving his glasses to the bridge of his nose with his index finger. Casey worked at the inn as a desk clerk but seemed more like a little brother than an employee. At twenty, he still looked boyish and reminded me of the young Harry Potter, with similar glasses, a shock of dark hair that always

13

fell over his forehead, and sweet, innocent eyes.

Five guests who were part of the Apparition Apprehender ghost hunting team had arrived a few minutes ago and were waiting to check in. They had come to town to shoot what they hoped would be a pilot episode for a potential TV show about ghosts. Wagtail had plenty of them, but the most well-known allegedly haunted the creepy old Wagtail Springs Hotel. At the mention of a ghost, the guys dived into their luggage and pulled out assorted handheld machines. The chatter behind Eva stopped as they concentrated on their gizmos, apparently trying to prove the ghost's existence through technological devices.

I raised my voice a little to get their attention. "Welcome to the Sugar Maple Inn. I'm Holly Miller. If you need anything during your stay, please let me know." I smiled broadly, but they were intent on their machines. Oh well.

Eva turned her eyes toward the ceiling and shook her head in amused disbelief. The doors were automatic, but I had to admit that opening on their own had been odd. Probably the result of that gust of wind.

Only the day before, I had moved to Wagtail Mountain permanently to join my grandmother, Liesel Miller, as her partner in running the Sugar Maple Inn. Halloween was nearly upon us and the first thing I had seen at the outskirts of town was a huge orange banner over the road that proclaimed *Welcome to Howloween in Wagtail, where spooky things are afoot!* A cat with an arched back adorned one side and a howling dog decorated the other.

The inn's Halloween decorations only added to the fun. Pumpkins clustered at the base of the doors on both sides. Spiderwebs clung to the walls with a parade of faux spiders marching along them. The sinister figure of a grinning vampire hanging upside down in a black cape was enough to give anyone a chill. Two skulls lay at rakish angles on top of the registration counter, and vultures peered at us from the large antler chandelier overhead.

My grandmother, whom I called *Oma,* German for *grandma,* had flitted off to a meeting of some sort, leaving me to keep an eye on the Apparition Apprehenders when they checked in.

Not that I minded. I welcomed any excuse to leave my apartment on the top floor. Boxes upon boxes cluttered my quarters. My entire life was still packed, except, of course, for my calico kitten, Twinkletoes, and my Jack Russell terrier, Trixie, who sniffed around the back of the reception desk in search of the treat jar.

Zelda, another desk clerk, had called me when the ghost hunting crew arrived. I hadn't expected any major problems, but here I was, already thinking that I would have to have a little talk with Casey about arguing with guests. After all, Eva was paying to stay with us, and if she didn't believe in ghosts, that was her business.

"That was *not* a ghost." Eva took a deep breath and watched the antics of the guys behind her. She turned back to Zelda and me. "I'm a university professor and have students like them. What frightens *me* is not ghosts, but the fact that my students and people like these ghost hunters believe ridiculous claims of spirit sightings. If these gentlemen would think it through, they would understand the absurdity of believing in ghosts."

Eva wore thick glasses in pink cat-eye frames that accentuated the odd paleness of her skin. Clearly vintage, a boxy coat of drab green wool hung on her, at least two sizes too large. A wide pink hairband pulled her dark hair back—very 1960s. She was thirtyish, like me, I guessed.

A Siamese cat on a leash jumped onto the registration counter, startling Trixie. She yipped at the cat and danced around to the lobby side. When she saw the open bags, she lost interest in the cat and buried her nose in a duffel bag.

I glanced at Eva's reservation. She'd been booked as part of the Apparition Apprehenders group. Obviously an error on our part. She should be in the cat wing. An easy fix.

"I'm sorry. It appears we've made a little mistake. I have you down as one of the ghost hunters. But no matter, we can—"

16

"Your confusion is understandable. My reservation was made by Mr. Luciano, the producer who is in charge of the ghost hunting expedition. I'm the ghost debunker whom he hired."

Ghost debunker? She definitely shouldn't be staying near the ghost hunters. Her cat would be happier in the Cat's Pajamas, our cats-only wing, anyway. I made a quick room assessment based on her apparent love of vintage clothing. "Zelda, let's put Ms. Chevalier in *Pounce*." Unless I missed my guess, she would love the pink cabbage drapes and the old-fashioned feel of the room. "Ms. Chevalier, what is your cat's name?"

"Mrs. Mewer."

"Like *The Ghost & Mrs. Muir*? That's cute."

Eva smiled. "Thank you. It's M-E-W-E-R, of course. I have a fondness for both 1960s TV shows and puns. The name came from Mrs. Mewer's tendency to talk."

"Mrs. Mewer will enjoy *Pounce*, I'm sure."

Zelda nudged me. "Where should I put Mr. Fischbein?"

"Move him to *Hike*."

"What peculiar names for rooms. Do you have an aversion to numbers?" inquired Eva.

"Like the town of Wagtail, the Sugar Maple Inn is pet-friendly, so we've changed all the room names to reflect pet-related activities," I explained.

A small man whom I'd barely noticed separated

himself from the other ghost hunters, stepped closer, held up his forefinger, and murmured softly, "I . . . I'm Felix Fischbein. I . . . I brought my dog? I was told that was okay?"

Eva turned to him with a devilish expression. "Mr. Fischbein, we meet at last."

Fischbein's Adam's apple bobbed. He stuck out a stiff hand to shake hers, his shoulders pulling tight as though he was cringing inside. He forced a smile, one corner of his mouth twitching with doubt. "I've heard a lot about you." Fischbein shot a glance at one of his friends, a pudgy man who glared at Eva.

Fischbein shoved hair out of his forehead with his palm in a nervous gesture. "Your reputation precedes you." Even his Weimaraner backed away from Eva.

Eva cast a critical eye at the pudgy guy. "I imagine it does." She turned to us again. "I love it when ghost hunters quiver in my presence."

Uh-oh. Did I sense tension? *Hike* is a terrific room, Mr. Fischbein, and we're very happy that you brought your dog." That worked out well. He must not have informed us that he was bringing a dog. No matter. Problem solved. Plus we had moved away from the argument about ghosts.

And then Casey returned and had to go and say, "It was definitely a ghost."

Zelda, who fancied herself a pet psychic, whispered, "Bet she doesn't believe in psychics, either."

Oh no. Not what we needed right now.

"There's nothing wrong with my hearing," Eva announced. "But you are quite right. Psychics prey on those who haven't the intelligence to know better. They're nothing more than modern-day snake oil salesmen." Eva gathered her cat into her arms.

Zelda stiffened. "Mrs. Mewer wants you to know that she's afraid of the vultures."

Eva glanced up at the antler chandelier before frowning at Zelda. "Which way is my room, please?"

Mrs. Mewer hunched her back and dug her claws into Eva's unfortunate wool coat, ducking and twisting her head so she could keep an eye on the vulture decorations overhead.

I hoped Zelda and Casey wouldn't high-five in front of Eva. I hurried to change the subject. "Would you like a GPS locating collar for Mrs. Mewer's use during her stay?"

Eva pondered for a moment. "No. She's very good at walking on a leash."

I didn't dare trust Zelda or Casey to show Eva to her room. They were bound to argue with her about ghosts and psychics.

"Would you keep an eye on Trixie?" I asked them.

I handed Eva her welcome packet. "This way, please." I picked up her bags and led the way into the main part of the inn, past the large sitting room and the grand staircase. Someone had gone overboard with the decorations. A mummy stood guard on each side of the staircase. Candles flickered on assorted black iron stands, and a trio of faux, oversized black cats hissed at us.

I pointed at the busy tables in the dining area. "We serve breakfast, lunch, and afternoon tea, as well as light dishes by room service on request. There's a menu in your room, and a cat menu for Mrs. Mewer. I believe Mr. Luciano has made special arrangements for most of your meals. Breakfast is here at the inn at your convenience, and there's a welcome reception for you at five o'clock this afternoon in the Dogwood Room." We walked through the library and into the newly built cat wing.

I unlocked the door and switched on the overhead light, gesturing for Eva to enter. If she was distressed by the conversation regarding her disbeliefs, she showed no sign of it, but I still debated apologizing for the staff. I probably should.

She lowered Mrs. Mewer to the bed and turned around in the center of the spacious guest room, taking it in with a dreamy expression. "This is lovely. Thank you for changing my room. I have no idea what the other room looks like, of course, but it couldn't be any more perfect than this."

Pink and red cabbage roses on a soft blue background graced the drapes and the goose-down comforter. The walls had been painted the palest blue and the wood floors had been whitewashed, a nice match with the white headboard, white tufted bench at the foot of the bed, and cozy white armchair near the fireplace. Over the top of the bed, in between paintings of cabbage roses, hung a framed quote in an artful gold script: *"If man could be crossed with the cat it would improve the man, but it would deteriorate the cat." ~Mark Twain.*

An antique mahogany dressing table with a huge mirror and the delicate crystal chandelier that hung from the ceiling offered additional feminine touches.

Mrs. Mewer wasted no time in leaping to the catwalk that ran along the walls near the ceiling. She viewed us from above with haughty pleasure.

I strode over to the sliding glass doors and demonstrated how to lock the cat door to the porch. When I opened it, Mrs. Mewer zoomed through, evoking a cry of distress from Eva.

"She's fine." I unlatched the sliding glass door and walked out to the porch with Eva on my heels.

"It's securely enclosed with cat-proof screening."

Mrs. Mewer had already climbed to the highest point of the tree that had been installed inside the porch just for feline guests. She rested on a branch like a panther, purring so loud that we couldn't mistake her contentment. A gentle wind blew, no doubt carrying the scents of squirrels and other woodland creatures.

"This is amazing. Luciano told me that the Sugar Maple Inn offered special quarters for cats, but I never imagined anything like this. Is there a litter box?"

"In the bathroom. And I must apologize for Casey and Zelda. I'm terribly sorry about their behavior."

Eva shrugged. "I'm used to it. Three out of four Americans believe in ghosts or some sort of supernatural activity. To do otherwise would destroy their hope in an afterlife. It's understandable that they wouldn't want to give up that dream, hence the continuing search for evidence which does not exist." She sighed. "I can't complain. I'm augmenting my teaching income by proving it's all nonsense. The believers keep me employed."

"Thank you for being so understanding. Give me a call if there's anything you need." As I left the room, Eva was examining the contents of her gift basket. Mrs. Mewer would be thrilled with the locally made toys and treats, and after her less-than-welcome reception, Eva would probably enjoy the bottle of Fat Cat wine.

I hurried back to help Zelda and Casey, but when I rushed into the registration lobby I stopped short.

A perfectly round, white circle was traveling slowly across the wall.

Two

Trixie broke the hush by barking and chasing the orb, while Gingersnap and the Weimaraner pranced after her.

Someone whispered, "I've got it on my camera!"

Then it vanished.

"Too bad Miss Chevalier wasn't here for that," breathed Casey. "Amazing!"

"What happened?" I asked.

Zelda held up her plump hands and shook them nervously. "I never would have believed it if I hadn't seen it myself. That thing entered the room and floated around."

"That *thing* was a spirit. Probably the ghost of someone who died here at the inn." The speaker hadn't been there earlier. Straight coppery hair swung across her back when she scanned the ceiling as if she expected to see more ghosts. Pale skin peppered with freckles pulled tight across her high cheekbones. A lavender dress skimmed her boyish figure, ending in an asymmetrical hemline, cut high in the front but mid-calf in the back.

Felix Fischbein appeared skeptical. "I don't know about that one. It *could* have been a reflection of something. The sun might have beamed on a shiny surface of some sort that bounced the light."

The woman swung around and glowered at him. A fashionable necklace of teardrop-shaped lavender stones set in silver draped around her neck. Matching earrings dangled near her jaw. Anger edged her tone. "I don't believe we've met. Mallory Gooley. Perhaps you've heard of me? I wrote *Haunting Horrors of Wagtail*."

Felix blinked at her. "I thought Mark Belinski wrote that."

It seemed he caught Mallory by surprise. "We worked on it together. I'm his girlfriend."

Felix reached out his hand to her. ". . . I'm Felix." When she showed no sign of recognition, he added, "Mark's college roommate?"

"Oh," she said, clearly unimpressed and disappointed. "He's here somewhere looking for you. Too bad he missed the orb."

The orb appeared suddenly and then vanished? And my grandmother was absent? Hmm, I smelled a rat. A silver-haired one with a German accent. I couldn't help wondering if my grandmother and Mr. Luciano had cooked up the ghostly welcome.

Mallory kept her eyes trained on the walls.

In their rush to find their ghost hunting cameras and paraphernalia, the Apparition Apprehenders had strewn the contents of duffel bags, backpacks, and suitcases all over the floor. Trixie and the

Weimaraner sniffed everything, their wagging tails showing how thrilled they were.

To my horror, Gingersnap had snagged something. She lay near the love seat and methodically nibbled the seam of a stuffed dinosaur. "No, Gingersnap!"

I rushed toward her intending to take it away, but that drew Trixie's attention. When Gingersnap dropped the dinosaur, Trixie grabbed it and wildly shook her head left to right. Wads of white stuffing flew out like soft snowballs.

Gingersnap grabbed a part of the dinosaur that extruded from Trixie's mouth and pulled, starting a game of tug-of-war.

I dared to grab the small exposed section of the dinosaur between their mouths. "Drop it!" I jerked it upward while they tugged sideways. They paid no attention. I tried again. "Drop it!"

Gingersnap reluctantly released her end, and I had a better grip on it than Trixie so I finally prevailed. I held up the dinosaur and said, "I'm so sorry! Whose is this?"

Felix flicked his hand as though it didn't matter. "Mine. I, uh, brought it along for my dog."

"We'll replace it, of course. My apologies." What a way to start their visit.

"That's okay. I'm just glad *my* dog didn't grab anybody's shoes and chew on them. He's forced me to be tidier at home. If my shoes aren't in a closet, he thinks they're fair game."

Too late. The Weimaraner trotted by carrying a black sneaker in his mouth. I pointed at him. "Is that your dog?"

"Aww, Casper!" Felix snatched the shoe and held it up—one of the other guys claimed it.

Smiling brightly, I said, "Well, let's get you all checked in, shall we? Felix? What is your dog's name?"

He concentrated on Mallory while his buddies stuffed their belongings back into bags. "Hmm? Oh, Casper."

I handed him a Sugar Maple Inn collar. "This is for Casper's use during your stay. It has GPS in it so we can track Casper down if he should get loose."

"Cool!" He snapped it onto Casper and removed the leash.

"This way, please."

Felix looked at me for a moment, his eyebrows creating a deep furrow over his nose. "Holly . . . why does your name sound familiar? Oh!" He pulled a wrinkled letter from a pocket in his jacket. "Holly Miller?"

"Yes?" I felt apprehensive. There wasn't a single good reason for him to have anything in his pocket with my name on it.

"A woman in Wagtail said you could show us the way to her house. A Birdie Dupuy?"

Zelda snickered.

My Aunt Birdie was a pill. My mother's sister,

she disapproved of everything. It was a good thing my grandmother had trained me from childhood to be nice to the guests. I might have had some choice words about Aunt Birdie. How could she have known I would be here when Felix arrived? I smiled sweetly. "Of course. I'll give her a call and set something up."

"Great. Just tell me when."

I started up the stairs to his room. "Why are you going to see Birdie?"

"She wrote to me when she heard we were coming. She thinks she has ghosts in her house."

"Most of the people in Wagtail think they've seen ghosts."

"We find that a lot in old communities."

I showed Felix and Casper to their room on the second floor of the main building. Each room had been furnished differently, and *Hike* was one of the most masculine, in browns and blues. It wasn't as large as the newer rooms in the cat wing, but it ranked right up there for coziness. I swung open the door. "The stone fireplace dates back to the 1800s, when the inn was built as a country home."

Felix nodded. "You must encounter a lot of ghosts here in the inn."

"Actually, I haven't." I wasn't going to insult him by saying I didn't believe in ghosts. I quickly added, "But others have." Or thought they had. Frankly, I agreed with Eva. But I had learned long ago not to spoil everyone else's fun. Besides, it

27

was Howloween, the time of year when it was fun to suspend disbelief and imagine ghosts and goblins prowled the world.

"Nice room. I like the plaids. They make me feel like I'm way out in the mountains on vacation, not working." His expression soured. "The lights made from deer antlers are a little creepy, though."

I got his meaning right away. "No deer were harmed. They shed them every year."

"Oh! Good to know." He tilted his head and considered them. "Now I kind of like them. Sort of a rustic elegance, and when you think about it, they're recycled and good for the environment. It's not as though I'm a vegetarian or anything, so I guess that makes me an awful hypocrite, but I'd hate to think they were killed for their antlers." Felix brushed back his thick, wavy hair with his hand.

An eager man poked his head inside the open door. "Is that you, Felix?"

He startled me, not by showing up, but by his appearance. Intensely serious blue eyes dominated his face. Over each eye, the eyebrow ran straight across, barely hooking downward at the outer edges. Neatly cropped, dark blond hair framed his forehead, giving him a serious appearance. He hugged Felix in a fond, masculine manner, pounding softly on his back. Nearly a foot taller than Felix, he towered over him.

Felix grinned at his friend. "Mark, you old dog, I thought I'd have to find your house. Or are you staying at the inn with the rest of us?"

Mark laughed. "I was tempted. At my house there's no maid service, and I have to do the cooking."

A second man swung into the room. Average height with brown eyes, he wore a dark brown mustache. He might not have been tall or built like a Greek god but his square chin with a dimple in it was guaranteed to make women swoon. Vaguely reminiscent of a young James Garner, he lit up the room with an easy charm. "Let's get this party started!"

Mark nodded. "Grayson, this is Felix, the guy I was telling you about. Grayson is our star. You probably know him from the reality TV show he was on." He eyed me as though he had just noticed me. "I'm sorry. I don't think we've met. Mark Belinski."

"Holly Miller."

"This must be Casper," he said, bending to pet Casper and Trixie.

Grayson reached a hand toward me. "Your grandmother told me you were coming here to work with her. I think that's so cool."

"Thanks. You've been here a few days?" I asked.

"I came up early to help Mark get ready and take a little time to relax. I did some hiking. It's a beautiful area."

Felix gushed, "I can't believe we're here together."

Mark opened his arms wide as if he were proud of himself. "You didn't think Luciano put this group together by accident, did you? He came to me and asked for the best of the best." He gestured toward the man with the mustache. "Grayson is our headliner. Brian and Eva should be good for some fireworks, and you and I are the brains."

"I wouldn't tell Brian that you set him up," said Felix. "He's still licking his wounds from his last encounter with Eva."

I interrupted briefly to disengage myself. "Excuse me. Mr. Luciano has arranged for a welcome reception in the Dogwood Room at five o'clock. It's down the grand staircase and to the left. Let me know if you need anything, Felix."

Mark held out his hand to stop me. "Won't you join us for a drink at the reception?"

"Thank you for the kind invitation. I might be there, but I'll be working."

"Stop coming on to her, you old wolf." Felix laughed. "I just met Mallory downstairs. New girlfriend?"

Mark rolled his eyes. "Hey, I'm looking out for *you,* buddy. Otherwise the welcome reception will be borrr-ing."

Trixie and I left, passing Casey, who was showing the remaining ghost hunters and crew to their rooms. We trotted down the back stairs into the newly built addition that housed the reception area.

Zelda grabbed my arm as soon as she saw me. "Is he cute or what?"

"Do you mean Mark or his buddy, Grayson?"

"Neither one. Mark is taken, and I remember all the scuttlebutt about Grayson from the TV show he was on."

"What scuttlebutt?"

"Oh, Holly. Don't you read the gossip magazines? One of the girls on the show accused Grayson of getting rough with her. It was a big scandal. I'm surprised that Mark invited him to join the Apparition Apprehenders."

"You do know that those reality shows are fake, right? They probably did it for ratings."

"I wouldn't be so sure. But it's Felix I'm after! He's so adorable. I just want to cuddle up with him, like a puppy! Besides, Mark has a girlfriend. You saw Mallory. He's a local celebrity of sorts because he wrote a book about Wagtail."

"I thought you swore off men."

"Felix isn't like my good-for-nothing ex. Casey says he's some kind of genius." Zelda let out a squeal. "I'm so glad you're back." She hugged me and did a little dance, seemingly unable to stop grinning. "Welcome home, Holly."

"Thanks." I peered into my grandmother's office behind the reception desk—our office now, I supposed. "Where *is* my grandmother?"

"Big session to replace the mayor," said Zelda. "The village elders are meeting to appoint an interim mayor until they can hold an election. She should be back anytime now."

"Did you get everyone else checked in okay?"

"No problems, but I *was* a little spooked by that ghost. I'm glad Casey's working here tonight, and not me."

"You're a psychic and ghosts scare you?" I couldn't help giggling.

She tossed back her long blonde hair and pumped her fist on a well-rounded hip. "I'm not a people psychic. It's just that I can communicate with animals. That's a lot different than being able to connect with ghosts. And animals are always nice."

I had serious doubts about her abilities, but Zelda was a wonderful person, full of life and kindness. I would never want to hurt her feelings. She did get a few things right, like Mrs. Mewer's fear of the vultures. Of course, any observant person might have noticed that. Still, I asked, "You've never encountered a growling dog or an angry cat?"

"Well, sure. But those are their defense mechanisms. Most of the time *they're* the ones who are afraid. Either people have treated them badly in the past or something has upset them. Animals don't usually *want* to harm anyone. It's people who will hurt you."

The sliding doors opened again, but this time my lovely grandmother marched through them. Her cheeks were flushed from the cold like red apples. She raised her arms for a hug. "Holly! I apologize for leaving you alone so soon." She hugged me and patted Trixie. "It could not be helped." Oma hated that she still spoke with a German accent after fifty years in America. She tossed her short sassy hair in an exaggerated manner. "You are looking at the interim mayor of Wagtail!"

More hugs ensued, from Zelda, and Trixie and Gingersnap, too. Casey returned just in time to hear the good news.

"Congratulations, Oma!" I said. "I had no idea you were interested in being mayor. I thought you intended to take a long cruise."

"A mayor can take a vacation, no? While I am gone, you will handle anything that comes up."

I was pretty sure that there were no rules of familial succession when it came to governing, but I figured we'd take that up when the time came. After all, she was only an interim mayor, and I had a hunch that while she liked the idea of a cruise, it might be difficult to talk her into actually leaving Wagtail, even for a few weeks. The woman was as stubborn as I was.

"You are settled in, Holly?" she asked.

"I wouldn't exactly call it *settled*. But now that I'm here, I can take my time unpacking. I think a few pieces of furniture will have to go across the hall into the storage attic. Is that okay?"

"Yes, of course." She gazed at Trixie. "I cannot get over the change in Trixie."

"You mean her fur?" I asked.

"It is so soft now. And almost white!"

I knew just what she meant. When Trixie adopted me, she had been abandoned and living outdoors, eating what she could scavenge. Her fur had been yellowish and harsh to the touch. I thought her fur was becoming silky, but it was hard to tell because I was with her every day.

Her sweet, dark eyes reminded me of a seal. Trixie often wore an earnest look, like she was worried. I assumed that was the result of being homeless and fending for herself so long. Her black ears flipped over in a very sweet way. Other than her ears and cute little nose, a black spot on her rump that went halfway up her tail was the only other bit that wasn't white. No one had docked her tail. About ten inches long, it usually curled upward.

Zelda knelt to pet her. "It's amazing what a difference decent food can make. She says she feels better, too."

I tried hard to hide my grin of amusement when Zelda relayed Trixie's thoughts. I imagined she did feel spunkier though. If her fur had improved, it only stood to reason that her general health had, too. "Should I help Shelley with the welcome reception?" I asked Oma.

"That would be good of you. She is a pro and probably needs no help, but check with her, yes? And I would appreciate your assistance tonight at the bonfire."

"We're having a bonfire?"

"Not the Sugar Maple Inn, the whole town. It's one of our Howloween events, along with a hayride through the haunted woods. You've arrived at just the right time, liebchen. There are events planned every day to draw visitors to our Howloween celebration. Rose is in charge of it."

That explained a lot. Rose Richardson was Oma's best friend and like another grandmother to me. If she had planned the Howloween events, Oma and I would be right there by her side, helping out.

"It gets bigger and bigger each year," Oma continued. "All the rooms and rental cottages are sold out this week. Isn't that wonderful? Do you have a costume?"

"You mean like a Halloween costume?"

"Of course." She smiled at Trixie. "I have just the thing for you, my little one." Oma led the way into her office, pulled a costume out of a bag, and held it up.

It took me a moment to figure it out. Longish white ruffles flared from both ends. The center was a deep brown with white lettering. "A Tootsie Roll?"

Oma laughed. "Isn't it cute? It would never work for Gingersnap, but it is perfect for Trixie's body shape. Do you have a costume, or should I help you put something together?"

Until my move to Wagtail, I had worked in fund-raising and had attended more than one costume gala. "I have some things. It's just a matter of finding them in all the boxes."

I left to help Shelley, pleased to see that Trixie and Twinkletoes alternately followed and raced ahead of me, feeling quite at home. But when I neared the grand staircase, Mallory of the coppery hair, coauthor of the ghost book, intercepted me.

"This would be such a perfect place for a wedding!"

"We host quite a few of them."

She gazed at the grand staircase, her face lighting up with bridal euphoria. "He would love a Halloween wedding. No lights, just candles. At midnight! The witching hour, when spirits are the closest. I could walk down these stairs in a long ivory gown. Oh! A pumpkin wedding cake with cream cheese frosting, and martinis with olive eyeballs in them. Wouldn't that be fantastic?"

"Would you like to book the inn for next Halloween?"

"Hmm?" She swung toward me. "I'd like to do it *this* Halloween."

"That's not much time. It's only days away."

She gazed past my ear at the stairs. Blotches of red flashed up on her face, and I thought she stopped breathing. The corner of her mouth twitched. "Well, maybe next Halloween would be more realistic, but I'd rather not wait that long."

Felix, Mark, and Grayson ambled down the stairs with Casper in the lead.

Mark headed for us with a distinctly unhappy look. "Excuse us, Holly." He gently touched Mallory's elbow and ushered her a few feet away.

"Sweetie," she cooed in a tone that even I knew was saccharin-fake, "where have you been?"

There was no sweetness in his tone. "Knock it off, Mallory." He lowered his voice to a whisper. "I thought I made it very clear that you are not involved in this project."

She batted her eyelashes at him. I almost laughed. Who did that? Had she watched too many old movies?

Mallory's eyes strayed like she sought an escape hatch. They landed on Grayson and floated to Felix. "Felix!" She skittered over to him. "You don't mind if I come along for dinner, do you?"

Felix blinked in surprise. "Uh, sure. It's okay by me, but I . . . I'm not in charge."

She flashed a pleased look at Mark.

Eva arrived from the other direction with Mrs. Mewer on a leash. Her mouth open, she stopped dead.

Mark lowered his head, but I could see his jaw twitching with anger. Clearly annoyed, Mark hustled after Mallory. "It's not fair to put Felix on the spot. I'm sorry, but this is a private reception and dinner afterward. I'm not footing the bill. We have reservations, and I can't just start adding people. I was very clear about this with you, Mallory."

"You're such a doofus sometimes." She pecked Felix on the cheek. "I'll see *you* later, Mark." Mallory started for the front door. She stopped mid-step at the sight of Eva. "Well, isn't this interesting?"

Mark barked, "Mallory!"

"I'm going," she sang. With a wicked smile and a twist of her shoulder at Eva, she finally left the inn.

Eva appeared paler than when she checked in. I rushed to her side. "Are you all right? Can I get you anything?"

"I'm fine, thanks. Just a little shock at seeing a ghost from my past." She flicked an angry look in Mark's direction. "Excuse me. I'd better hurry over there to meet Mr. Luciano." She picked up Mrs. Mewer and made her way to the sitting room, her head held high.

I kept wineglasses filled while Shelley circulated with miniature salty Virginia ham biscuits, herbed goat cheese crostada topped with caramelized red and yellow peppers, and cheese-straw witches' fingers with almond-slice finger-nails at the tips.

Most of the conversation revolved around ghost hunting. They swapped stories, and I heard them exclaim as they discovered they had mutual acquaintances.

When the ghost hunters left for dinner, I helped clean up and finally trotted upstairs to my apartment.

An hour later, it looked like it had been ransacked. I thought I'd been careful about marking all the boxes when I packed them, but evidently not.

We developed a ritual. I sliced a box open with Trixie sniffing it. As soon as I determined that it wasn't the correct box, Twinkletoes jumped inside it to investigate. I had never seen such a snoopy cat. She was adorable, hiding in boxes and raising her head just high enough to peer out. Inquisitive green eyes dominated her white face. Just above them, it looked like she had shoved sunglasses up on her head with one lens of dark chocolate and the other of caramel. Her body had the typical calico pattern of dark chocolate and caramel patches on white. Even though she was still just a kitten, her tail bushed out in a fancy dark plume.

I did manage to place a few items on the bookshelves and fireplace mantel, but I didn't have time to unpack each box. Maybe when the Apparition Apprehenders had left, and I had become accustomed to a daily routine at the inn, I could focus on unpacking in an orderly manner.

A shriek of glee escaped me when I located my flapper outfit—a heavily beaded red dress with a black feather boa and a red headband adorned with more black feathers. Hah! I had even packed the bead necklace with it. Perfect.

Twinkletoes grabbed the boa with determined claws, as if she thought it the best toy ever. It wasn't easy to remove it from her clutches. In the end, she escaped with a black feather, and I tucked the boa neatly in a drawer for safekeeping until I dressed.

At seven thirty, I followed Oma's instructions to prepare for the bonfire. I loaded one of the inn's electric golf carts with lanterns, urns of hot cider, chocolate bars, marshmallows, graham crackers, three carved pumpkins with candles, and a flashlight. Dressed as a flapper, I took my wagging Tootsie Roll companion and drove through the quiet streets of Wagtail to the opposite end of the pedestrian zone. The golf cart barely hummed, but dried leaves crackled under the wheels as I drove up to the creepy Wagtail Springs Hotel—the perfect backdrop for a Howloween bonfire. Many of the leaves had fallen, and as though it had been ordered, a not-quite-full moon shone through gnarled tree branches. No one else had arrived yet.

I was a little spooked just looking at the two-story hotel. Moonlight gleamed on the white building. Front porches ran across both levels. I could imagine people rocking on them in the hotel's heyday, much as they did at our inn. Chimneys shot up the side on each end. Dark and forbidding, the windows of the old place almost begged for stories of ghosts. No wonder the Apparition Apprehenders would be investigating it.

A large white gazebo off to the side and set back on the lawn seemed eerie alone in the dark. It housed one of the original mineral baths from the days when Wagtail had been a spa resort. In the 1800s, Wagtail had thrived on visitors who came for the waters.

I tried to shake off the dismal feeling and hopped out of the golf cart, but Trixie wouldn't come. She sat on the golf cart seat, fixated on the old hotel. And then she barked like crazy.

Three

I had only heard her bark with such intensity once before. That time, someone appeared out of nowhere. I scanned the hotel but didn't see anything unusual.

She kept up the wild barking. I seized the

flashlight, turned it on, and aimed it at the hotel. On the second-floor porch, the beam caught a movement. I held the light steady.

An older man with silvery hair rose slowly and disappeared into the building. I double-checked my cell phone. Did it work here? Wagtail was notorious for poor signals. Only one carrier worked at all, and reception was sporadic at best.

One bar. That was better than nothing.

The man emerged from the front door. He walked toward us leisurely but with an able gait. I trained the flashlight on him. He wore jeans, a red plaid flannel shirt, and heavy boots. I put him in his seventies. As he approached, I realized that he was laughing and was actually fairly attractive. A black Labrador followed him, almost hidden in the dark.

He patted Trixie. "I've heard about *you*. Bet you're a great hunting dog." He reached a calloused hand toward me. "Doc Kilgore. Sorry if I spooked you. I was waiting for my scout troop to arrive with wood. They're building the bonfire."

My heart was still pounding, but I relaxed a little bit. "Who is this?" I asked, stroking his dog, who wagged his entire rear end as though I was his new best friend.

"Siggie. Named after Sigmund Freud because I think he calms my patients."

"So you're a people doctor, not a veterinarian."

"Exactly. Some folks 'round these parts think I

should retire because my hair isn't black anymore, but I've still got my wits about me. Can I give you a hand here?"

"That would be great! There's supposed to be a table set up somewhere." I gazed at Trixie. It wasn't going to be easy to unload everything with her on a leash.

"What's wrong?"

"Trixie hasn't been to dog school yet, so I was debating whether to let her off her leash."

"She's got a GPS collar on her. I bet she'll be fine. Siggie will keep her around." He spoke with such confidence that I wanted to believe him.

With some trepidation, I unlatched the leash. "Stay close by. Do you understand?" She wagged her tail, but I knew that was meaningless. Maybe Doc was right and playing with Siggie would keep her from roaming.

Doc Kilgore and I set the lanterns on the table and lit the wicks so we could see better. The scouts arrived just as we finished setting up the last urn.

I thanked him for his help and watched as the young boys crowded around him, each one shouting for his attention. They obviously adored him.

Trixie and Siggie danced among them, sniffing the wood they piled into a pyre and snatching particularly enticing pieces to drag away.

I finished setting out the marshmallows, graham

crackers, and chocolate bars. I placed pumpkins at intervals along the table and lighted the candles. "Hey, Doc," I shouted. "Did the scouts bring branches for the s'mores?"

He had them build a small campfire for cooking so no one would get too close to the bonfire. The scouts arranged a lovely heap of branches near the end of our table.

Visitors to town drifted over to see what was going on. Before long the bonfire blazed. Oma and her best friend, Rose, joined me to hand out hot cider laced with cinnamon.

Just behind us, a tractor pulling a hay wagon rolled away. People and their dogs sat on hay bales for a nighttime hayride by the cemetery and along a road through the woods.

"Will there be ghosts on the hayride?" I asked Rose.

She laughed. "Of course. And maybe a vampire or two!" Rose made a darling Miss Marple in a dowdy gray wool hat with a short brim. Her hair fluffed out beneath it. She wore a heavy tweed jacket over a fussy lace blouse with a large cameo brooch clasped at the throat. I felt as though Miss Marple had walked off the page and into Wagtail.

I studied Oma for a moment. Tidy blue suit, white button-down shirt, sturdy shoes, a magnifying glass hanging around her neck. Had she cut her hair or was that a wig? I didn't want to offend her by asking what was going on. Her taste usually ran a little more to what she called country elegant.

It wasn't until a man said, "Thank you, Mrs. Fletcher," that I realized she was in costume. She had always loved mysteries. I should have known.

I watched the bonfire and the happy people in costume, most of them with dogs or cats in costume, too. I recognized Mr. Luciano and his bulldog, Gina, and waved to them. Mr. Luciano always made me think of the movie *The Godfather*, no doubt due to his deep, gravelly voice and prizefighter build.

Felix, Mark, and other ghost hunters milled around him. The glow from the fire reflected on Mallory's coppery hair. She tossed it back seductively and appeared to be flirting with Felix. Eva, on the other hand, stood apart, looking lonely.

I excused myself and brought her a cup of cider. "Where's Mrs. Mewer?"

"Oh, thank you! How thoughtful of you." Eva sipped the cider. "I took Mrs. Mewer back to our room. I loved taking her to the restaurant. They even had a feline menu. I thought she might be too nervous to eat but she snarfed their salmon. Still, she's never been anywhere except the veterinarian, and I thought the big fire might scare her, so she's taking a catnap to recover from all her new adventures today."

A yellow lab with three heads dipped her

middle nose toward Trixie, who pinned her ears back and edged away toward the safety of my legs.

I did a double take myself. Eva and I exchanged a look and giggled.

The lab's owner had attached an additional head made out of felt to each side of her collar. No wonder Trixie was confused. The three-headed dog appeared very real.

I bent over to reassure Trixie. "It's okay. Two of those heads are fake."

Casper, the Weimaraner, buddied up with Trixie like they were old pals. Emboldened by the presence of Casper, Trixie joined him in sniffing the mysterious extra heads of the yellow lab, who waggled happily at all the attention.

Flames from the bonfire licked up at the velvety night sky. In the mountains, the stars always seemed closer, and tonight was no exception.

In the distance, a glow-in-the-dark skeleton walked a large dog wearing a glow-in-the-dark dog-skeleton outfit.

Eva had turned her attention to Mallory, who clung to Felix, laughing and flirting.

"Everything okay?" I asked.

"If I had known she was going to be here, I never would have come."

"If it's any comfort, I gather she's not part of the Apparition Apprehenders."

Zelda joined us. "If Mallory is with Mark,

would someone please explain to me why she's flirting with *my* Felix?"

Eva gave a jolt, spilling her cider. *"With Mark?"*

"Didn't she say they were an item?" asked Zelda. "They wrote that book about Wagtail's ghosts together."

"Ughhhh." Eva closed her eyes and pressed a palm on the top of her head. "I am so stupid."

"I don't get it," said Zelda.

Eva adjusted her glasses. "Once upon a time, Mark and I were a couple. When he invited me to join this group we exchanged e-mails and talked on the phone, and it"—she sighed hard—"it seemed like old times again. He was charming at dinner, but now I see why he wanted to include me. That devil."

I shot Zelda a questioning glance.

She shrugged.

Eva caught our moment of confusion. "Sparks! Fireworks! If Mallory and I engage in a cat fight it will boost the ratings of the show."

Now I saw where she was coming from. I would have been furious, too. How dare he dupe her that way? "But wait—Mallory isn't part of the show."

Eva peered at me over her glasses. "Then what is she doing here? Why is she hanging around? No, no, Holly. It's the same reason Mark put Brian and me together. He knows we'll have some disagreements."

"What if you don't?" asked Zelda.

Eva snorted. "Impossible. Brian always pulls childish tricks. I'm bound to catch some of them." She eyed Mark. "But two can play this game." Eva smirked at us. "Give me a few minutes, Zelda. I'll lure Mallory away from Felix so you can move in on him."

Eva strode toward Mark and Grayson.

"I like her!" Zelda fluffed her hair. "Now all we have to do is fix you up with someone."

"No, thanks. I'll sit this one out."

"Aww, pining for Ben?"

It was my turn to snort. "That relationship is dead in the water."

"How can that be? He asked you to marry him."

"In a text, Zelda! That's not a real proposal. Besides, once I decided to move here, he was so miffed that he acted like I was already gone. I'd hardly call that love."

"Look, look," Zelda whispered.

I couldn't tell what kind of magic Eva had worked, but sure enough, Mallory abandoned her grip on Felix to hurry toward Mark and Grayson.

Zelda was already moving in on Felix. I chuckled to myself, happy for Zelda. I hoped Eva was wrong about Mark's motivation for including her, though. Inviting her so she and Mallory would spat seemed even worse than a texted proposal. I returned to my job of handing out cider.

"Wow! Great costume!" Felix's friend was as animated as a kid who'd eaten too much candy on

Halloween. A little on the tubby side, he held a half-eaten chocolate bar in his left hand. He straightened his baseball cap that said *I'd rather be ghost hunting,* leaned toward me, and reached out his beefy hand. "Brian Anderson. Holly, right?"

"Right. Are you enjoying Wagtail?"

"Sure am. What a dinner! Luciano is pulling out all the stops for us. And everybody has been so nice. Like they're excited to have us here."

I filled a cup of cider for him. "They probably are. It's not every day that someone makes a TV show in Wagtail. What do you think of the ghastly old hotel?"

Brian accepted the cider. "I can't wait to get inside that place."

"Does Casper go with you?"

Brian nodded vigorously. "He's our ghost dog. Weimaraners are called ghost dogs because of the gray color of their fur. Sometimes in the dark, Casper looks kind of like a ghost. We even call him Ghost as a nickname."

I laughed. "That's an appropriate breed for a ghost hunter. Has he ever sniffed out a ghost?"

"Yeah! Dogs see things we can't see. Or maybe they smell them. They don't close themselves off to possibilities of another realm. They just react to what's there. Casper is pretty good. He's not much of a barker, but he senses things and alerts us to their presence."

Brian reached down to stroke Casper's back. "I wish you had alerted me to Eva's presence," he grumbled, looking toward the fire where Eva chatted with a group of ghost hunters.

Felix and Zelda had drifted over for cider.

"Don't let Eva get to you." Felix sighed, then said to me, "Brian had a little run-in with Eva last year."

"Oh?"

Brian yanked at his ear. "Aw, she's a pill. If I had known she was coming, I might have reconsidered."

"No, you wouldn't have!" Felix clucked at him. "There's no way you would have missed out on this."

Brian grinned. "Yeah, you're right. But I would have known what I was getting into. Catch you later, Holly."

The three of them wandered off to gaze at the old Wagtail Springs Hotel. Casper sprang ahead of them looking a bit ghostly as they left the glow of the fire. I was very pleased that Trixie chose to stay by my side. She was probably worn out.

We closed down at eleven. Oma and Rose helped me pack the food service items into the golf cart and rode back to the inn with Trixie and me.

After unloading, I headed straight to my grandmother's private kitchen—not the tiny one in her apartment near the registration area or the professional restaurant-style kitchen for the inn, but the big kitchen next to the dining area. Off-limits to guests, it was our private retreat in the inn and doubled as a private dining and sitting room. When I was growing up, my parents had shipped me off to Oma and the Sugar Maple Inn every summer vacation. I had spent many happy hours in that kitchen.

Unless I missed my guess, Oma's fridge would be packed with leftovers from breakfast and lunch. Trixie bounded ahead through the pet door that led to the kitchen. I pushed open the door to the dark room. My hand was on the light switch when Trixie growled at the ominous shadow of a person at the door that led to the garden.

Four

Metal scraped against metal. I could only make out the shape of a head and shoulders through the window in the door.

My first thought was that someone was trying to break in. My heart pounded, and I could hardly breathe.

Fortunately, my second thought set me straight. A guest had probably gone for a walk and couldn't find an open door on the lake side of the inn. I had lived in the city too long. It was time to reset my thinking and realize that I ran an inn and that people sometimes did peculiar things like try to open a locked door instead of walking around to one of the two open entrances. At this hour, the front door and the registration entrance were both unlocked. Any guest could come and go as he pleased.

I flicked on the kitchen lights.

The shadowy head jerked up. In an instant it was gone.

I froze. A chill ran through me. Wouldn't a guest have knocked, glad to be let in?

That could only mean one thing. The person must have had sinister reasons for trying to break into the kitchen. The only reason I could think of to enter the back way was to avoid being seen.

Casey! What if the intruder entered through the registration doors? I had to tell Casey. I phoned him from the wall phone in the kitchen and told him to lock the doors.

When I hung up, I peeked out to the main lobby of the inn where the front door led to Wagtail's pedestrian zone. Quiet as a mouse. Still shaking, I darted to the door and locked it. Using the house phone, I called 911.

While I was on the phone, a blonde woman walked down the stairs. She appeared to be concentrating and didn't notice me. She strode toward the cat wing but soon returned and passed me going in the other direction. Oma and Gingersnap greeted her warmly as they walked toward me. She must be a guest.

"What is going on?" asked Oma. "Casey says we have an intruder?"

"Someone was trying to break into the kitchen door. He bolted the second I turned on the light."

Oma frowned at me. "You are certain about this? Maybe it was just a guest . . ."

"Then why did he run away?"

She cupped her right hand to her cheek. "This makes no sense. Anyone could walk in the front door at this hour. Why would someone break in the back?"

I didn't want to offend her, but the truth was that she had created an unsupervised lobby when she remodeled and moved the registration desk to the side entrance. "Oma, do you think it might be time to put a camera on the front door so the clerk in registration can keep an eye on it?"

She sank onto a bench. "No, no. This should not be necessary. We are a small operation. During the day Shelley is working in the dining area and keeping an eye on things. Maybe we should hire someone to be the concierge from five to midnight?"

A knock on the front door spooked us. I peered out the sidelight and recognized Dave Quinlan—*Officer Dave* to locals. I opened the door. "That was quick!"

Dave had served in the navy and it still showed

in his posture. His police uniform fit perfectly, suggesting that he made time to work out. "This time of night, I hang around the pedestrian zone because that's where the action is. What's up?"

I filled him in, ending with, "You didn't happen to see anyone running away from the inn, did you?"

"Can't say I did. Let's have a look at that door."

I led him into the kitchen. Oma and the dogs followed us. He unlocked the door, turned on the outdoor light, and pulled out a flashlight, which he shone on the lock.

"Ladies, I recommend installing a deadbolt." He flashed the light toward the stone terrace outside. His eyebrows rose but his mouth pulled into a grimace. "Not much to see. No footprints. This stone wouldn't show much unless it was snowing or muddy."

He stepped inside, and I locked the door behind him.

"I'd leave the outdoor light on back here at night. Someone could break the bulb or unscrew it, but if you're right, and he didn't want to be seen, it might be enough to discourage your would-be intruder."

"Why would anyone want to sneak inside?" asked Oma.

"Oh, Liesel. You're not new to this. Most people who travel carry cash. You have any particularly flashy guests right now?"

"No," she said. "No one like that. A ghost hunting team—"

Dave flicked his eyes toward the ceiling. "Oh, swell."

"You don't believe in ghosts?" I asked.

"Can't live in Wagtail without experiencing some weird stuff. I'd say I'm on the fence. But there's something about Howloween that makes people kick up their heels and play pranks. That's more work for me." He groaned.

Oma still frowned. "We have two guests who are not part of the ghost team—a businessman and a sweet lady."

"Is that the woman who just walked by?" I asked.

Oma nodded.

"I'll take a hike around the outside of the inn whenever I'm down this way," said Dave. "Call me if anything else happens."

I locked the front door behind him. Gingersnap and Oma went to tell Casey what had transpired, but Trixie and I headed straight for a snack. As I had suspected, the fridge offered an amazing selection. I helped myself to turkey chili, which I promptly stuck in the microwave. I added a bowl of fruit salad, and grabbed some butter for the loaf of rustic bread I spied on the cornflower blue island.

A bottle of wine called my name, but I decided against it. I wanted to stay awake long enough to eat. One bowl was labeled *turkey stew for dogs*. "Turkey for you, too?" I asked Trixie.

I spooned a portion into a bowl and nuked it just enough to warm it. Trixie ate much faster than I did, then parked herself next to me and watched with hopeful eyes while I ate at the island. I broke off a few small pieces of the bread crust and popped them into her bowl. She ate them like a canine vacuum cleaner.

Twinkletoes shot through the pet door and screeched to a halt at the sight of us. Arching her back like a Halloween cat, she danced sideways for a few steps, then changed direction and flew out the pet door. Trixie scrambled after her. At least they were having fun.

Twinkletoes had shown up at the inn on her own before I adopted her. She was probably happy to be back where she had room to roam. My house in Arlington, Virginia, was tiny compared to the inn. Thanks to the booming real estate market there, I had rented it out for an amount that covered the mortgage and left me with a little stream of income.

After washing the bowls, I took Trixie outside for a quick stop at the doggy bathroom. Back inside, I spied the blonde woman pacing the second floor hallway. I considered asking if she needed something but she disappeared into a room.

We trudged up the stairs to our quarters but

Trixie had stopped bounding ahead of me. We had both run out of steam.

In my own little kitchen, I spooned shrimp supper into a bowl for Twinkletoes, slid into a nightshirt, and snuggled happily under the down comforter on my bed. Trixie turned in a circle three times before plopping next to my hip, and Twinkletoes soon bounded onto the bed and settled near my head.

The phone rang in the dead of night. I groped for it in the darkness and mumbled, "Hello?"

"Holly, is that you?"

My Aunt Birdie. I closed my eyes and lay back on my pillow. "Yes."

"Dear, I need help."

I rolled over enough to peer at the clock. "Birdie, it's four in the morning."

"I'm sorry. Have I inconvenienced you? I'll just lie here in pain. What's a better time to call?"

Aargh. Guilt surged through me. I sat up, rubbing my eyes. "I'll call the ambulance."

"No! Don't do *that!* I'm in my nightie."

"Aunt Birdie, I'm sure they've seen nightgowns before."

"Not mine, they haven't. And they're not going to, either."

I slid my legs over the side of the bed. "Okay, I'm on my way."

"Thank you, dear."

Grumbling under my breath, I pulled on jeans and a turtleneck, and grabbed a jacket and my purse, in case I had to go to the hospital with her.

Trixie and Twinkletoes followed me to the door. "You guys better stay here this time."

I locked the door behind me and trotted downstairs through a silent inn. As I passed through registration, I told Casey where I was going just in case a trip to the hospital was involved and I wasn't back by breakfast.

I fired up one of the inn's electric golf carts and headed for Birdie's house. Wagtail slumbered. A breeze scattered dried leaves, and the moon cast a strong beam through bare branches. Porch lights and a few pumpkins glowed in the night, but no lights shone in houses yet. Except at Aunt Birdie's, where the windows were ablaze.

Two black witches' brooms rested upside down on her front porch. Pumpkin-colored pillows created an inviting vignette on the white wicker settee until I noticed that a faux bat hung upside down in the black birdcage on the table next to it. Huh. I never knew Birdie had a sense of humor.

She had clustered pumpkins around a chair that held an elaborate flower arrangement containing sunflowers and wickedly wild grapevines that jutted out in odd directions. And right next to it, a faux skeleton perched on a closed coffin. His legs were crossed, as though he were simply taking a break.

I walked up the steps and it dawned on me that her door was probably locked. How ironic that I might now be the one trying to break in. I knocked as a formality, then tried the doorknob. The door readily swung open.

Birdie stood in her foyer wearing bright red lipstick that matched a chic dress. Years ago, she would have been called a handsome woman. Her face was attractive, almost beautiful, but the sour expression she always wore took it down a notch. She was painfully thin. The skin on her face clung tightly to prominent cheeks and a nose that might be a bit too pointed. A streak of white hair sprang from the middle of her forehead, emphasizing the darkness of the rest of her hair. Her complexion seemed too pale, and frighteningly close to being witchy.

"How nice of you to bother to come, Holly. I understand you've been in town thirty-six hours," she sniffed.

"You're up. And dressed. And your hair is done."

"What? No hug?"

Was she kidding? I glared at her. "Is that a stop-watch in your hand?"

"Eighteen minutes. You're going to have to work on that."

Had she lost her mind? "No, I'm not. Because *you* are never going to pull a stunt like this again." I pointed my forefinger at her. "If you do, then you can forget about me *ever* coming to your rescue." What a moronic trick. A woman in her sixties ought to know better. Unless . . . unless she wasn't thinking straight anymore.

"If your mother had taught you any manners, you would have come by to visit immediately."

"Oh, but it's good manners to wake a person in the middle of the night and haul her over here on false pretenses?"

She slapped a manicured hand to the base of her throat. "No one speaks to me that way."

"Maybe it's time someone did." I turned on my heel and marched out, fuming. I didn't look back until I reached the golf cart.

Birdie stood in her doorway, holding the door frame with one hand, looking forlorn. Her sad expression cut through my anger. I had never lived near relatives as an adult. Maybe I *should* have dropped by to say hello the second I hit town. I drove away with guilt creeping over me. But I shook it off. Maybe Birdie was the loon my father had always claimed she was.

The golf cart was rolling slowly through a residential neighborhood in Wagtail when a little white Jack Russell terrier darted across the street in front of it. *That couldn't be Trixie. It sure looked like her, though.* When a calico kitten sped along behind the dog, I turned the golf cart at the next corner. How could they have gotten out?

I called them, trying not to wake sleeping Wagtailites. They ran through yards, evading me.

I would glimpse them, and they would disappear again.

I turned to the right, toward the pedestrian zone, and spied them happily scampering along. I parked the golf cart, hitched my purse over my shoulder, stepped out, and ran. Where had those little goofballs gone?

The scent of burning wood hung heavily in the air. I cut through the parklike middle of the pedestrian zone and stumbled on a piece of a shattered pumpkin. I hated to think that some drunk had damaged the pretty carved pumpkins that lined the walkway.

In the clearing near the Wagtail Springs Hotel, I was shocked to discover that the bonfire had started again. It wasn't blazing yet, but it would be soon. The scouts must not have put it out properly. It didn't appear to be spreading, thank goodness, but I pulled out my phone and called 911 immediately. The dispatcher promised to send Officer Dave over to check on it.

I spied Trixie on the other side of the fire, much closer than I thought was safe. "Trixie!"

She clamped her teeth on a heavy branch and pulled it.

"No!" I ran toward her, knowing perfectly well that was probably the wrong thing to do. But I had to stop her from dragging around a limb that was burning on one end. If she didn't hurt herself, she might set something on fire. The Wagtail Springs

Hotel loomed nearby. That place was probably a tinderbox. If she dropped the branch on the wood porch, I might not be able to stop the fire from spreading.

She saw me coming. I sighed with relief when she dropped the branch and sniffed the ground. I grabbed the limb and tossed it onto the fire.

A moment later, she picked up something else that I couldn't quite make out. "Drop, Trixie."

She danced just out of my reach. Happily a scent must have interested her, and she dropped what she held in her mouth. Trixie's nose took her in a circle around the bonfire. I followed her as fast as I could without running, trying to be calm, so she wouldn't sense my desperation to catch her. Just as I bent over and reached for her, she took off, her nose still to the ground. Ugh. Undoubtedly on the scent of an evil squirrel.

I didn't dare leave the fire, but on the other hand, I didn't want to lose sight of my two rascals, either. Trixie was getting farther away. She zoomed by the Wagtail Springs Hotel. In the night with no one else around, it looked unbelievably spooky. No wonder people thought they saw ghosts in the eerie windows.

Frantic barking started. It had to be Trixie. I listened carefully for a clue to her whereabouts.

I jogged a few steps. "Trixie? Trixie?"

The furious barking continued. Where was Dave?

Like magic, he strode up, dressed in his uniform—an oasis of calm in the night. I waved at him and ran after Trixie. I would explain as soon as I had Trixie and Twinkletoes safely in my arms.

The light from the street lamps didn't stretch far as I rounded the hotel. I slowed down, stepping through the grass carefully while my eyes adjusted to the darkness away from the fire. Without the light of the moon, the expansive lawn in back of the hotel would have been treacherous. The huge gazebo shimmered faintly. The barking grew louder. But where were they? I squinted and scanned the lawn for any sign of their white coats. "Twinkletoes! Where's my pretty kitty?" I tried to sound relaxed so they would come to me.

Meep. Twinkletoes didn't speak much, but that sounded like her cute little mew.

Were they in the gazebo?

Twinkletoes darted out at me and swiped a paw at my leg as I neared the structure. I wasn't quick enough to grab her.

She scampered into the gazebo.

"Trixie!" I called. "I have treats." At this point I would have said anything to get them to come to me. But they didn't.

Trixie hadn't stopped barking, either. *Yap, yap, yap.*

Built at ground level, the gazebo contained a mineral spring in the middle. I had played there as a child, joyfully splashing my cousin. Shallow water covered ancient stones, worn to smoothness. Simple wood stairs led from the decking into the pool.

As I approached, Trixie ran around the deck of the gazebo, yipping. I sighed. This would be an aggravating exercise in futility because she could simply scamper around in a big circle, always keeping out of reach.

She would sense my desperation. I tried to be calm and called her softly. She backed away, and backed away.

I stepped onto the decking and squinted in the darkness. Why hadn't I brought a flashlight?

Trixie's white coat gleamed in the moonlight. She whined at the water—and at the person floating in it, facedown.

Five

Trixie stopped barking when I screamed.

My purse dropped to the floor. The contents clattered as they spilled onto the wooden deck.

I yelled for Dave.

There was only one thing to do and no time to think about it. I had to turn the person over. I plunged into the cold water. It came up just over my knees.

A filmy white dress floated around the body.

Long silvery hair caught the glow from the light of the moon. I flipped her and dragged her to the side, but even though she was a slight woman, I couldn't lift her out of the shallow pool. The gauzy white fabric caught on her arms and mine, wrapping us like mummies. After several tries, I managed to maneuver her shoulders up against the edge of the deck. Where was Dave? I yelled his name again.

Minutes mattered. I couldn't allow her head to drop back into the pool. Pinning her with my shoulder to keep her from sliding down, I hoisted her legs up enough to roll her over onto the deck, dislodging the wig she wore.

Copper hair fell to the floor. Mallory! Shock flooded through me. The young woman who dreamed of her wedding didn't appear to be breathing.

I tried to recall the first aid classes I had taken years ago. I leaned Mallory on her side so water could drain from her mouth. She needed CPR right that moment. I started it but was having no success. "Dave!"

It broke my heart to have to stop, even for a second. I rushed to the entrance. No wonder he couldn't hear me. In the quiet of the night, the bonfire crackled loud enough to drown my cries for help. I ran toward it, waving my arms. "Dave! Dave! Help!"

When he turned toward me, I waved frantically

and jogged back to the gazebo to start chest compressions again, wondering what else I could possibly do to revive her.

When I saw the beam of a strong flashlight I jumped up. "Here! We're over here!"

Dave aimed his light at Mallory.

"Is she alive?" Dave flashed the light on her face.

"I don't know. I found her floating facedown. I've been doing compressions, but there's been no sign of . . ." I couldn't bring myself to say it.

Dave kneeled beside her and felt for a pulse. "I'm not getting anything." He handed me the flashlight and resumed the chest compressions. "Call 911 and have them send an ambulance."

Twinkletoes scampered down the steps that ran into the water. She reached out, patting a dark ring on the water with her paw.

I squinted at it. A wreath of black roses. Mallory must have been dressed as the ghost of Becca Wraith. According to local legend, Becca's ghost always wore a circle of black roses in her hair.

"Your cat's here, too? What's going on?"

I called 911 before answering him. Only when the dispatcher assured me that an ambulance was on the way did I hang up and explain to Dave how I came to be there. "I have no idea how Trixie and Twinkletoes managed to get out of the inn."

My wet clothes clung to me and the night was cold, but I ran in search of the ambulance anyway.

I flashed Dave's light at them and shouted. Three amazingly calm EMTs crossed the lawn to the gazebo and peered at Mallory.

One of them checked for a pulse. "Are you a relative?" He took over the chest compressions.

"No. I just happened to find her."

Dave stepped aside so they could work. He snagged Twinkletoes. Handing her to me, he said, "You better put on some dry clothes. I'll come to the inn if I need more information."

"Thanks." I hoped they could resuscitate Mallory. Carrying Twinkletoes in my arms, I called Trixie. She came with us but dodged off to the fire again. I was far too cold and wet to play games. I called her again and again. She raced toward me carrying something in her mouth. Ugh. I hoped it hadn't been alive at one time.

I reached for it but she ran from me each time I tried to grab it. She willingly hopped into the golf cart, though.

Dawn hadn't broken yet when I returned to the inn. Safely inside, I finally released my grip on Twinkletoes. She leaped from my arms and immediately started grooming her fur, no doubt miffed that it was wet.

Trixie still carried the thing in her mouth. But indoors, I could see it clearly. I grabbed a treat from the cookie jar at the registration desk and tried to barter with Trixie. The scent of the treat must have been powerful because she finally gave in and traded me a faux fur black cat for the cookie.

I rocked back on my heels laughing. A toy. The cat's back was arched like a Halloween cat. Some dog had probably dropped it at the bonfire. I handed it back to her.

"What happened to you?" asked Casey.

"I jumped in a mineral bath to pull Mallory Gooley out."

"What? Is she okay?"

"I don't think so. Is she a friend of yours?"

"No. I've seen her around town, though. She doesn't live here. At least I don't think so. You better get cleaned up. Aren't you freezing?"

I nodded and shuffled away like I was one hundred years old.

"Hey, Holly. How's your aunt?"

Huh? I was still so shocked about finding Mallory that I hadn't given Birdie another thought. "She's fine. Thanks for asking, Casey. She's absolutely fine and dandy."

Trixie refused to take the elevator, but I was in no condition to climb two more flights of stairs. She met me at the door to our apartment. It was locked tight.

I opened the door to find Twinkletoes resting on top of a box, cleaning her fur and looking so innocent that if I didn't know better, I would have thought she'd been there the whole time. "The cat door." In my haste to leave, I'd forgotten about it. I hobbled to the dining room of my quarters. Way down on a bottom shelf the cat door was open. It led down hidden stairs to Oma's private kitchen. I wedged heavy books in front of it so there would be no more escapes for the time being.

I took a long, hot shower but it didn't wash away the events of the night. Wrapped in a fluffy Sugar Maple Inn bathrobe, embroidered with my name, I had just stepped out of the bathroom when a muffled cry alarmed me. Someone was in my apartment!

Six

I stumbled around the boxes in the hallway and craned my neck to see into the kitchen.

A stooped man wearing white gloves and a butler's uniform placed a tray on the counter. He turned and his thick gray eyebrows jumped up at the sight of me. "Miss Miller! I'm so sorry to have disturbed you. I stubbed my toe on a carton. I must say, it's a bit of a mess in here with boxes everywhere. Shall I unpack them for you?"

"No. Thank you. That won't be necessary." I peered at the tray. A carafe of something, sugar, cream, a dog treat, a cat treat, and a chocolate croissant. This man was definitely friend, not foe.

I studied him. Why did he seem vaguely familiar? "I'm sorry, I don't know your name. You weren't here last month, were you?"

"Niles Huckle, miss. I remember you. You played with Miss Clementine when you were just little girls. Your grandmother has hired me to help Shelley five mornings a week. Mrs. Miller likes hot coffee and exactly two, no more, no less, honey cinnamon graham crackers, and a biscuit for Gingersnap at six a.m. sharp. She ordered this for you. If you should prefer something else, please let me know. I shan't let on if you don't like what she sent."

"It's lovely, thank you." What a luxury. This certainly beat rushing around to leave the house and then sitting in traffic to get to work.

Twinkletoes wound around his ankles, marking him with the side of her face.

"Now go on, you little scamp. You'll get white fur all over my trousers."

I locked the door behind him and asked Trixie, "Why didn't you bark at him?"

She wagged her tail but wasn't divulging her secrets. Either she was all barked out or he bribed her with a dog biscuit.

Feeling quite guilty about indulging in a pre-breakfast chocolate croissant, I ate it anyway, and shared the other treats with Trixie and Twinkletoes. Steaming hot tea with milk and sugar first thing in the morning was living the high life for me. Room service *and* someone to clean my quarters? It was almost too heavenly to contemplate. I would be thoroughly spoiled forevermore.

Cold to the bone, I lit a fire and sat on the hearth with my hands wrapped around my hot mug of tea. The image of Mallory's gown floating around her was burned into my mind. How could she have drowned in so little water? Why didn't she sit up? Or stand up? Could the long gauzy material have tangled around her legs? Two feet of water! Short as I was, it hadn't even reached my hips. It was like drowning in a bathtub.

I stretched my bare toes toward the crackling fire and thought about the previous night. Something had been going on with Mallory. She'd talked about marrying Mark, yet he had been cold as ice toward her. And she upset Eva, who'd said *two can play that game*. Goose bumps popped up on my arms. I wanted Mallory's death to have been an accident. But wishes wouldn't make it so. Something untoward had happened to that poor young woman last night.

I'd heard of people drowning in shallow water before. But why was she in a costume? The last time I'd seen her was at the bonfire. She wore a dress with fashionable costume jewelry. When had she changed clothes?

She didn't have family around that I knew of, and if Mark and Eva were any indication, not much in the way of friends, either. The least I could do was make some discreet inquiries. Dying alone in a strange place was bad enough. I couldn't desert her. She needed someone to be her friend now. Especially if she had been murdered.

I finally blew my hair dry. When I turned off the blow-dryer I heard voices. More than one. I was beginning to feel like my new home was Grand Central Station.

In a hurry, I found khakis and a long-sleeved periwinkle blue V-neck tee in a suitcase, pulled them on, and ventured into the sitting area. The voices came from the TV. Trixie sat in her favorite toile armchair, and Twinkletoes lay sphinxlike on top of a big packing box. Both of them were watching the news.

"How did you turn the TV on?" I searched for the remote, thinking one of them must have accidentally pounced on it. They probably knew where it was, but in the chaos of boxes, I didn't see it anywhere.

Relieved that no one else had entered my apartment, I navigated between boxes back to the bedroom, slid on a belt, and added gold hoop earrings. As I passed the French doors, I paused for a moment to step out onto the balcony that overlooked the heart of Wagtail—the pedestrian zone. Many of the leaves had fallen off the trees, exposing gnarly branches, but creating a charming mosaic of reds, oranges, and golds across the grass. Corn stalks and pumpkins decorated the expansive green between the wide sidewalks. It reminded me of a long park with a walkway winding through it. Benches offered places to rest. Lively dogs could run off some energy in one of the fenced play zones.

The lack of traffic noise still amazed me. Wagtail had become a golf cart community, allowing precious few vehicles through on the residential streets. Tourists parked at a large facility just outside of town. Electric golf carts, locally known as Wagtail taxis, transported them into town.

Beneath me, early risers strolled and jogged with dogs and an occasional cat. A couple of the coffee shops and bakeries appeared to be open but most of the stores were still closed. To the left and right, the roofs of Wagtail made for a charming scene. And beyond it all, mountains rose in the distance like a beautiful, undulating quilt of fall colors.

Returning to the Sugar Maple Inn was like coming home again. My parents had moved away when I was very small, but they had sent me back to Wagtail and Oma every summer. Oma put my cousin, Josh, her best friend's grandson, Holmes, and me to work at the inn. We had learned everything from the bottom up. We washed dishes, whitewashed fences, checked guests in and out, and made beds, yet there had always been plenty of time for swimming and playing in the woods. They had been wonderful times, away from the issues of my divorcing parents. Even though my father and his sister had left Wagtail, the Sugar Maple Inn was the family homestead. It was more of a home to me than any place I had ever lived.

I gazed over my new hometown with joy. There was something special about new beginnings and starting fresh—leaving old problems behind. In my case, my old boyfriend, Ben, and a horrible problem at my previous job. They were in my past now, and wonderful new possibilities lay ahead.

And then I remembered Mallory. Maybe they had resuscitated her. I would hate to think that her future had been snuffed out. She was so young and so full of happiness about her wedding. I would have to check with Dave. I closed my eyes and hoped for the best.

The cool morning air brought on shivers, prompting me to dig through my suitcase again, where I found a lavender-ish fleece vest that coordinated with my top.

"You guys ready for breakfast?" I asked, returning to the kitchen. I spooned some chicken bits with sauce into Twinkletoes's bowl. In the small dining room, I dropped to my knees and opened the cat door in case she wanted to return later for a snack or a quiet nap. Trixie was still watching TV. I discovered an *off* button on the TV set and pressed it, thinking Trixie and Twinkletoes were far smarter than me because they knew where the remote was.

I nabbed Trixie's leash in case I needed to coax her away from the meals of other dogs, and the three of us were out the door. Trixie and Twinkletoes sprang down the grand staircase far faster than I could go.

By the time I reached the dining area, Twinkletoes was watching leaves blowing outside the window. The muscles in her shoulders jerked as if she meant to leap after them.

Trixie had her front paws on Oma's lap.

I said good morning to Oma and latched Trixie's leash on her collar. "We'd better make a potty stop first."

We passed the registration desk on our way out. Zelda was arriving for her shift. She looked like a movie star with a hangover. Huge dark sunglasses shielded her eyes. She was massaging her temples.

When Casey and I chimed, "Good morning," Zelda placed a finger over her lips. "Shh. Not so loud, please."

"Rough night?" I asked.

"The night was fine, but morning has been pretty grim so far." She yawned. "I'm getting too old to stay out half the night and go to work the next day."

Trixie and I walked outside. We were back in a flash.

Zelda held a bottle of aspirin in her hand.

"I'll be having breakfast if you need help."

She nodded.

Trixie ran ahead of me to the dining hall.

When I sat down at Oma's table, I leaned toward her and whispered, "Has Dave called you, by any chance?"

Oma rested her hand on top of mine. "I'm sorry, liebchen. Dave said they tried very hard to save her but it was too late. He called me early this morning because he had to notify the interim mayor."

"Noooo. Oh no." I slumped in my chair. "How awful. I didn't have much hope, but still . . ."

"It is very sad. She was only twenty-nine. Now tell me, please—what were you doing out there in the middle of the night?"

I explained about Birdie's call. "What I don't understand is how Trixie and Twinkletoes managed to leave the inn. The cat door was open in my apartment, but Casey would never have allowed them to leave through the registration doors."

"Holly, did you lock the kitchen door last night?"

I thought back. "I'm pretty sure I locked it when Dave was here."

Oma pulled her hand-knitted sweater closed as though she felt a chill. "It wasn't locked this morning."

"Maybe a guest went out that way?" But even as I offered that explanation, I knew it didn't make sense. Why would someone go into the private part of the inn and leave through the back door?

"The front door wasn't locked, either. I fear you are correct. I have made a mistake by moving the registration desk to the side entrance, thus leaving the front door unobserved."

Shelley bustled over to our table, tucking a strand of light brown hair firmly into her bun. "I'm so glad you're back, Holly. Chocolate chip pumpkin pancakes with maple syrup and maple glazed bacon for breakfast this morning? We have a doggie version, too—chocolate-free, of course."

Oh, the guilt! I had allowed myself to gobble all the rich food on my last visit, but now that I was here for good I really shouldn't. I spied the remnants of maple syrup on Oma's plate, and the scent of bacon from another table wafted by. Trixie lifted her nose, no doubt catching the aroma. Maybe just this once we could indulge . . . "Sounds wonderful. Trixie and I will both have the pancakes. Thanks!"

I gazed at Trixie. "We're going to have to do a lot of walking to work off those calories." She didn't seem to be at all concerned about that.

"Did you take her to training?"

"Not yet. She saw the vet and was spayed, but otherwise it was all I could do to rent my house, pack it up, and move. Besides, there are probably more trainers here in Wagtail. I'll make arrangements as soon as I get organized."

A guest walked out to the terrace, and Twinkletoes jumped back in alarm when a gust from the door shook a spray of decorative bats that were flying across the huge window. She stalked them carefully from below, periodically jumping up to try to reach one.

"By the way, nice job last night with the ghost orb and the lights in registration. You had the ghost hunters going."

Oma raised her eyebrows. "Casey told me about that. He was quite impressed. But you are giving me credit for something I did not do."

I tilted my head at her. "Really? Why don't I believe you?"

"I admit that it would have been great fun to greet the ghost hunters with such an event, but I had nothing to do with it. I was at the meeting about the mayor."

"Then it must have been Mr. Luciano."

"He's been here a week already, but quite busy. I don't imagine he would bother to make up such a thing."

I doctored my second cup of steaming tea. "So what's with Mr. Huckle?"

"He is delightful, yes? He worked for the Wiggins family for many, many years, but Peaches, the last wife, kicked him out. I could not bear to see him suffering without a job. He is not very fast or strong anymore, but guests have raved about how considerate he is. He acts as though he is everyone's personal valet—shining shoes, walking dogs, delivering flowers and packages to rooms. He's an excellent dog and cat sitter, I'm told." Her head wobbled from side to side a bit. "And I must say that I love the indulgence of coffee waiting for me when I rise in the morning. I miss him on his days off."

Down to business. I wasn't quite sure what my responsibilities would be at the inn. Oma wanted more time to enjoy life, and running the inn was a 24/7 job. "What's on tap for today? Should we make a list of the things you expect me to do?"

"Yes, this is a very good idea. Perhaps we can work on a list later on? It should be fairly quiet. We have a full house, but almost all of them are ghost hunters." She lowered her voice. "The lady eating alone is Lillian Elsner, the widow of the famous Congressman. She arrived a few days ago. Lillian is one of the two guests not affiliated with our ghost hunters. Her little Yorkie is GloryB."

Aha. The woman who had paced the hallways last night.

Lillian was what my mother would have called a femme fatale. I put her near fifty even though she appeared younger. I had met a lot of well-heeled women like her in my days as a fund-raiser. Blonde tresses curled just below her shoulders in a breezy, just-rolled-out-of-bed style that had been carefully cut by a clever hairdresser. The blonde probably hid the beginnings of gray, but it didn't hide gentle laugh wrinkles around her eyes. The sleeves of her oversized white shirt were rolled up, exposing tanned arms that sported gold bangles. A sweet Yorkshire terrier sat in the chair next to her, behaving better than some of the children I'd seen in restaurants. A rhinestone-encrusted collar circled the little dog's neck. At least I hoped they were rhinestones. Large bejeweled rings enhanced Lillian's fingers.

Except for dark mascara and eyeliner, her makeup seemed nonexistent. A clear gloss shimmered on her lips.

Altogether, a look calculated to appear casual and devil-may-care but, in reality, carefully planned.

I whispered to Oma. "You told Dave we don't have any wealthy guests right now."

Oma blinked at me. "So I did. I forgot all about Lillian's jewelry. Let's get that bolt on the door. Maybe you can take over the morning walk-through to make sure all is in order? And when you have finished that, could you go to the hardware store, Shutter Dogs? Have them make a set of master keys for you, and pick up a deadbolt lock for the back door."

"I'd be happy to."

After breakfast, armed with an old-fashioned

clipboard, I toured the public hallways and rooms of the inn, starting from the far end of the cat wing. I paused in the library to be sure it was tidy and had been cleaned during the night, eyed the floor in the dining area, and peeked out on the terrace. The day had warmed a bit and diners had flocked to the outdoor tables for breakfast in the sunshine, overlooking the lake.

Down by the water, Lillian strolled with GloryB, who raced happily along the shoreline. Watching her, Lillian massaged her hip as though it was sore.

Back inside, I stopped in the old lobby, where the foyer must have been when the inn was a private residence many decades ago. I examined the grand staircase, which had clearly been vacuumed, and chuckled at the fabulous life-sized mummies and scaredy-cats. Tall candelabra held black candles, with faux flames that flickered even in daylight. I did a 180-degree turn and stepped out on the front porch.

It ran across the front of the original building. Every single rocking chair was occupied. Dogs and cats lounged happily while their people lingered over mugs of hot tea and coffee. Before them, the pedestrian zone was coming to life.

Gingersnap already occupied her favorite spot on the porch. I reached down to stroke her soft red head.

Her tail swished across the floor.

I returned indoors to the sitting room, also known as the Dogwood Room, because the floor-to-ceiling windows overlooked Dogwood Lake. I ran a finger across the fireplace mantel. Clean as a whistle under the faux spiderwebs. The night housekeeper was doing a great job.

The lights on two black five-armed candelabra flickered. In between them, the large painting of Dogwood Lake had been replaced by a mirror with a chipped black frame that revealed flecks of platinum underneath. The mirror itself was crackled with the patina of age, the silver missing in spots, leaving a haunting dark gray underneath.

Oma had embraced the season with gusto. It was fun, even if the mirror was a bit on the creepy side.

Twinkletoes lay upside down in a sunbeam.

I paused and joined her at the window, thinking of Mallory. How could she have drowned in so little water? Why hadn't she pulled herself out? I knew nothing about her, yet she haunted me as I walked through the inn. Her life had come to such an abrupt end. She was planning to be married, for heaven's sake! Her family must be devastated. Mark must be crushed. Especially after being so miffed with her last night. If we knew we would never have another chance, we'd all probably be a lot nicer to one another, especially our loved ones. I forced myself to focus on my job and move on.

Trixie accompanied me through the inn and

around the grounds off-leash. She paused to greet GloryB. They sniffed each other politely.

Meanwhile, I introduced myself to Lillian.

She wore a broad-brimmed straw hat and held her hand out to me. "I heard you were coming. Your grandmother is so pleased that you moved to Wagtail. I hear you lived in the Washington, D.C., area like me."

"Arlington."

"I know you won't miss the traffic. I love it out here with the birds and the chipmunks. It's so peaceful. And GloryB is having the time of her life."

"How did she get such a cute name?"

"My husband and her breeder came up with it. Her sister is a fancy show dog. They intended to breed GloryB, but my husband talked them into letting us buy her."

GloryB scampered back to us, sat down, and stared at Lillian, who laughed.

"She's such a bossy little girl. I believe she's ready to move on. Excuse me." Lillian walked on, with GloryB running ahead.

Trixie roamed but never lost sight of me—a relief after last night's chase. I called her as a test. She perked her ears and ran to me, planting her bottom on the ground before I could ask her to sit. I rewarded her with a crunchy three-calorie blueberry treat.

We returned through the reception area.

Zelda had shed the dark glasses. She crooked her finger at me and shuttled me over to the tiny inn gift shop. "Officer Dave is here," she whispered. "They're going to think I killed Mallory!"

Chill bumps rose on my arms. Oh no. Not Zelda! "What happened?"

"I'm in so much trouble. I don't remember a lot about last night, but I'm pretty sure I said some choice threatening things to Mallory." She must have seen the horror in my eyes because she hastened to add, "Well, she was being a real pest. Felix invited me to go to Hair of the Dog with the Apparition Apprehenders. We were having a great time"—a wisp of a smile crossed her mouth—"I think Felix really likes me, and then a couple hours later, Mallory waltzed in and acted like she owned Felix. I'd had a couple of drinks by then, and my tongue might have been a little bit loosened up."

I relaxed. "Oh, Zelda. That was stupid."

"Hey, I didn't know someone was going to kill her! The cops must suspect us. Why else would Dave be here to see Felix?" Her eyes darted wildly about the room.

"You think Felix is a suspect?"

"He walked us home," she said glumly.

"Us?"

"Felix and Mallory dropped me off at my house first, and then Felix walked her over to Mark's place."

"Zelda." I wrapped a reassuring arm around her. "Then you have nothing to worry about. Even if someone did kill Mallory, you have an alibi. Felix!" Of course, he had a serious problem, but I didn't mention that. "It's not as though you were the last person to be with her."

Her top lip slid inward, and she chewed on it. "Yeah, you would think so, wouldn't you? Except I was snockered and didn't trust her, so I might have just happened to sneak out and follow them."

"Zelda!"

"Well, it seemed logical at the time. If they were, you know, sleeping together, I didn't want to be chasing him."

"Did he stay at Mark's?"

"No. He kissed her on the cheek and left." She turned huge eyes toward me. "But I didn't kill her." Her hand shook when she briefly covered her mouth.

"Of course you didn't. Where did you go?"

"Home." Her voice dropped to a whisper. "But I can't prove it."

"Maybe you won't need to." I hugged her and tried to be upbeat, but I was worried for her.

Zelda went back to work.

I collected my purse and a set of master keys, snapped a leash on Trixie's collar as a precaution, and walked along the pedestrian zone. I stopped by the front porch and asked Gingersnap if she wanted to come with us. She was far too busy kissing two little girls who were giggling and hugging her.

The merchants had outdone themselves with Howloween decorations. In addition to pumpkins and cornstalks, they had added cute Halloween signs like *Watch Out for Flying Bats* and *Black Cat Society Meeting Here*. Store windows featured witches, ghosts, and ghastly goblins. Animatronic skeletons at Pawsitively Decadent stopped their dance and seemed to peer at us! Trixie yelped in alarm and backed away.

I located Shutter Dogs just around a corner on a side street. The hardware store must have been a home once. It was painted a fresh gray with white trim. The merchandise had overflowed to the sidewalk, including colorful wagons that looked like toys but were clearly useful around Wagtail. The front door was set back between two glass showcase windows. A ghost holding a pitchfork ogled customers on one side, while a zombie with a chainsaw glared out of the other.

I found someone who could duplicate the keys and shopped around while he replicated them. Upstairs I discovered an amazing assortment of cat, dog, and horse hooks and drawer pulls that forced me to dawdle and admire. I made note of the lamps that featured all sorts of creatures, like ceramic bunnies and bronze horses, thinking I would have to stop by again when I had actually unpacked and found that I needed a lamp.

To my complete surprise, I discovered a rack labeled *Shutter Dogs* mounted on a wall. I had no idea that was the name of the metal scrolls that held shutters open. Trixie pulled me along to the rear of the store, where they stocked a large assortment of food and treats for cats and dogs. "Your nose always finds the food, doesn't it?"

Not that I faulted her for that. I was a little bit too fond of food myself, and I had never starved like she had.

Trixie gently pawed at a package of bat-shaped cookies made in Wagtail. I acquiesced and picked up one of the cellophane bags. "But you can't eat one until we pay for them."

She jumped up, placing her tiny front paws on my knees and cocking her head.

"Good try, sweetie. You still have to wait."

Back on the first floor, I collected the keys and waited in line to pay for them, the treats, and the bolt lock.

The woman first in line at the counter must have clipped up her long blonde hair in a hurry. The barrette had gone askew. Her tresses hung lopsided and tousled as though they hadn't been brushed. A fashionable sleeveless white dress clung to her thin frame. More appropriate for summer than fall, it appeared oddly out of place in the hardware store, as though she were heading to a cocktail party. The snazzy high heels had to be designer, and a hefty gold bracelet of linked horse snaffle bits hung on her thin wrist.

I edged to the side for a better look at her face. "Clementine?"

Her fingers, busy in a quilted leather Chanel wallet, froze. She winced. Sucking in a deep breath, she turned toward me. Her entire frame appeared to sag with relief. "Holly! Uh, just a sec."

She paid for three cans of cat food in quarters and dimes, thanked the clerk, and took her bag before stepping aside and reaching out for a hug. "Gosh, it's good to see you. I'd heard you were moving to town."

We had played together as children when I came to stay with my grandmother during summer vacations. Clementine had grown up with all the luxuries of wealth. Her father was well known as the richest man in Wagtail. They bred beagles and horses on a gentleman's farm just outside of town. But horse-crazed Clementine had never played the princess. She mucked out stalls, was always present when a horse gave birth, and could handle just about anything on the farm.

She winced at the sound of a crash in the back of the store. "I've got it," she yelled to the cashier as two young boys dashed by her. She reached out and grabbed the collars on their shirts. They squealed but she reeled them in. "Say hello to Holly."

"Hello, Holly." They choked out the words with

complete disinterest and wriggled out of her grasp to pet Trixie.

"Where's your sister?" she asked them.

The boys looked at each other. They appeared to be twins and a handful of trouble.

"I'm so sorry. The D-I-V-O-R-C-E"—she spelled the word—"has been hard on all of us, and I'm afraid I've been too indulgent." Speaking to the children, she added, "I thought we weren't going to act like wild monkeys anymore."

They giggled and ran down the aisle.

"I'm sure they're very sweet. How's your dad?"

"Off to a major dog show with Babylicious and her last litter. He's convinced that Baby is a star. I think your grandmother's Great Dane, Dolce, is at the show, too."

She winced at the sound of another crash. "If you'll excuse me, I believe we have a mess to clean up in the back. We'll have to get together for lunch sometime."

"I'd like that." I watched as she rounded up her little boys and hustled them toward a girl about the same age. Triplets? Her daughter was trying to rebuild a pyramid display out of cans that were rolling on the floor. She carried a stuffed dog, old and threadbare in spots, that looked exactly like one Clementine had had when we were kids.

Clementine set the boys to work picking up cans and did her best to restore the display.

A tall, seriously good-looking man roamed past

their aisle, distracting me. Short hair the color of coffee beans had outgrown its cut just enough to be charmingly ruffled. He wore the haven't-shaved-in-a-couple-of-days look. Boots, jeans, T-shirt, green army jacket—he could have walked out of an ad for cowboys.

He pretended to study some bins of nails, but it appeared to me that he was actually watching Clementine and her children.

Seven

Clementine spotted him, too. Her eyes widened in fear. She wasted no time grabbing the hands of the two boys. "Emily, let's go." She dodged out the other end of the aisle and through the store to the entrance, where she beat a hasty exit.

The good-looking guy ambled toward the front and exited the store a beat behind her.

I set my items on a display rack and dashed outside with Trixie to see if Clementine needed help. Holding the boys' hands, she ran as well as anyone could in those shoes. Her daughter raced ahead of her.

The man pretended to window-shop. When Clementine and her troop turned the corner, he picked up his pace. Trixie and I did, too.

By the time we reached the corner, they had all

vanished. I paused and listened for any sound of distress. If the guy had nabbed them, surely he wouldn't be able to keep those two boys quiet.

A pebble shot toward us on the sidewalk. Trixie sniffed it, but I looked in the direction from which it had come.

A darling one-story shingled house was set back a bit on a heavily landscaped lot. The sign near the sidewalk identified it as Pampered Pet Portraits. A large show window at the front of the house displayed stunning paintings of animals. Trixie and I strolled toward it.

"Don't come over here." It was little more than a frantic hiss.

"Clementine?" I peered behind a row of manicured boxwoods.

Clementine crouched with her children, holding a hand over each of her sons' mouths. "Is he gone?"

"I think so."

"Make sure."

I casually returned to the sidewalk and gazed around. If he was hiding, I didn't think *he'd* toss a pebble my way.

We doubled back, and I pretended to admire the portraits in the window. "I don't see him, but he could be hiding."

"Ouch!" Clementine stood up. "What did I tell you about biting?" She grabbed the boys' hands. "Thanks, Holly." Her eyes canvassed the area so fast that it made me dizzy.

"Clementine, do you need help? Maybe you should come to the inn."

"No, no! We're good, thanks." She took off down the street with her three children.

"That was strange, wasn't it?" I asked Trixie as we walked back to the store. I didn't know what Trixie was thinking, but I pondered what I had seen. If the man had been her husband, surely the children would have run to their dad. Was her ex the type who would hire someone to spy on her?

I would have to ask Oma if she knew anything about Clementine's domestic problems when I returned to the inn. I paid for my purchases and stepped outside, keeping an eye out for the mysterious man.

It dawned on me that Hair of the Dog wasn't too far away. It wouldn't hurt to nose around a little bit for Zelda's sake. "C'mon, Trixie. Let's ask a few questions."

Trixie wagged her agreement and happily sniffed everything her nose could reach on the way to the pub. Located in a Tudor-style building with outdoor tables in the front, the pub was a source of aggravation for some townspeople who hated the noise when it closed at two in the morning. We stepped inside. It took a minute for my eyes to adjust to the dim light.

A chalkboard advertised Bewitching Brews, Spooky Spirits, and Monster Burgers.

The woman behind the bar pushed back hair the

color of Kahlúa. She tilted her head at me. "What can I get you, Holly Miller?"

I didn't remember her from my recent visit. It seemed like I would have. She had a girl-next-door face and a don't-mess-with-me attitude. She wasn't much taller than me, but she oozed energy. "Do I know you?"

"You do now." She stuck out her hand. "Val Kowalchuk. Everybody knows *you*. Up until this morning, your arrival back in Wagtail was the hot news in town. Guess they're still talking about you, but in a slightly different way now"—her voice dropped to a whisper—"since you found the body." She slapped the bar. "What will you have?"

It was probably the height of impoliteness to barge into a bar for information without ordering anything. "How about a sparkling water for me and plain water for Trixie?"

"Sure thing." Val slid a frosty glass toward me and poured water into it. She pulled a small stainless steel dog bowl from under the bar and filled it with cold water.

I lowered it to the floor for Trixie, who lapped at it.

"So, Val," I said casually in a hushed voice, "were you here last night at closing?" I gulped the refreshing water, more thirsty than I'd thought.

Val squinted at me. "You're the third person today to ask me that. I'm here every night at closing. Comes with the territory." She took a breath. "Our girl Mallory was very big on Zombie Brains. They're sweet, so they go down easy, but they pack a wallop. We make 'em small for that reason. But I have a strict policy about cutting people off when we think they've had too much to drink. Mallory was what I'd call giddy. Not stumbling, not slurring words, just talking loud and being silly."

"What was she talking about?"

"I didn't pay much attention. Men and ghosts, I think. But then, all the ghost guys were here. Mark, Grayson, the whole gang of them. Mr. Luciano bailed early but the rest of them closed the place down." She leaned her elbows on the bar. "I'll say this, though. She was flirting with every single one of them. I'd say she left the whole lot of them in confusion about who might go home with her, if you know what I mean."

I knew exactly what she meant. "Was Eva here?"

Val smiled. "Is she great or what?"

"Was she upset about Mallory?"

Val raised an eyebrow, and I knew I'd phrased my question wrong. "No. But there was something going on. Eva kept an eye on Mallory, for sure."

"So who else came in here asking questions?"

"Started with Officer Dave, then Doc, and now you. Is Mallory a friend of yours?"

I shook my head. "Barely knew her. I just feel terrible. She was all alone in a strange place and something really awful happened."

Val's eyes widened. "I know what you mean. Everybody is asking how she could have drowned in shallow water like that. Of course, I have a vested interest in hoping she didn't drown because she was loaded. I just bought this place. Don't need that kind of reputation." She leaned toward me again. "Is it true that she was wearing a ghost costume?"

I nodded. "Did she ever come in here before?"

"Oh sure. She was a talky sort. Had all kinds of plans to marry Mark. Rumor had it that she wanted to move in with him but he put the kibosh on that and sent her packing."

"So she didn't live in Wagtail?"

"Far as I know, she came up now and then to try to win over Mark but he wasn't interested. This is what I want to know. She left here at two in the morning wearing a nice dress with chunky jewelry. One of those bib necklaces that are so popular. Why did she change into a ghost costume in the middle of the night? Why would she do that? Was there a party somewhere in town? I must be getting old, because when I close the bar, I go upstairs and fall into bed. The last thing in the world I would do is put on a Halloween costume and run around."

I laughed at her reference to being old, because

Val was probably in her mid-thirties. If memory served, though, Hair of the Dog was open for lunch, so she probably didn't get much sleep. I pulled out my wallet and paid. "Val, if you hear anything, give me a call, okay?"

She smiled. "Sure thing. We girls have to stick together." And then she was off, tending to something in the kitchen.

Trixie and I walked home, enjoying the beautiful fall day—only to find chaos in Oma's office.

We sidled past the little cluster of people crowding the room. Wearing his uniform and appearing quite official, Dave leaned against Oma's desk, his arms resolutely crossed over his chest. Rose appeared worried. Her fingers were curled into tight balls. Mr. Luciano was speaking with her.

To my utter dismay, Aunt Birdie showed up. I had to give her credit for dressing well. She wore a narrow black pencil skirt with a red top and a matching shawl-collar sweater belted at the waist. A prominent red and silver necklace hung on her neck, and silver earrings peeked out from under her black hair.

Birdie sniffed and nodded in cool recognition when I said hello. She headed straight for Mr. Luciano and Rose.

Three other people whom I didn't know mingled in the room.

"What's going on?" I whispered to Oma.

"I am so relieved that you have returned. Would you mind helping Shelley put together a little buffet lunch for us in the office?" Oma wrung her hands. "My first big problem as interim mayor—whether to call off the ghost walk because of Mallory's death. It's such a popular tradition. And it's only two days to October thirty-first. The visitors who are here came for our Howloween events."

"Call it off? Because she was murdered?"

"Holly! Not so loud. This is what I need to determine. Most Wagtail residents live off tourism one way or another. Howloween is always a big draw." Oma lowered her voice to the tiniest whisper. "After all the news about the recent murders, we're having to put our best paws forward to recover."

I had been there during that time and understood how the murders might have discouraged tourists. Before then, residents like Zelda hadn't even bothered to lock their doors.

Oma clapped her hands. "Will everyone please take a seat?"

I slipped out quietly to help Shelley. As usual, she already had everything under control.

"Today's lunch special is pulled pork. If you could set up these chafing dishes and drinks on the buffet in your grandmother's office, that would be a huge help. I'll be along shortly with the food."

I pushed the cart to Oma's office, glad to have an excuse to listen to the discussion.

One of the men was saying, "I don't think there's a thing to worry about. Mallory was probably soused. It wouldn't be the first time in history that a drunk fell into water and drowned."

"Officer Dave?" asked Oma.

"The police are still searching the area as we speak. They're going through the Wagtail Springs Hotel as well. It will take some time."

"The hotel? Don't tell me we have to cancel the costume gala!" Rose's voice escalated to a shrill pitch. "What are you searching for?"

Dave took a deep breath. "Evidence."

"You don't think this was a tragic accident?" asked Oma.

I held my breath, thinking of Zelda.

Dave seemed uncomfortable. *"I"*—he placed such emphasis on the word that I wondered if he might be alone in this opinion—"don't believe so."

Oh no.

Rose gasped. "Dave Quinlan, you better be wrong. Wagtail can't take another murder so soon after the previous ones!"

One of the men whom I didn't know chimed in. "I'm speaking for all the merchants when I say that we will ruin the reputation of Wagtail if we cancel the ghost walk. People came here from great distances and at quite some personal expense. They expect to be entertained."

Another man spoke up. "I'd like to point out that the merchants spent a lot of money in advertising and inventory and special events for Howloween."

The first man spoke again, quite angrily. "Are we going to cancel everything? I don't see why we should single out the ghost walk."

Shelley rolled in a cart with food, and we arranged it on the buffet while the others gazed at Rose.

She ticked items off on her fingers as she spoke. "There's the apple bobbing relay to see if dogs or their owners can bob faster. Canine and feline trick-or-treating at homes throughout Wagtail. Hayrides, the cemetery celebration, dog and cat costume parades and contests, Howloween portraits, the cornfield maze for dogs, the ghostly feather agility games for cats, and the grand costume gala at the hotel—not to mention the unofficial contests and specials being held by individual stores and businesses."

A costume gala at a deserted hotel? Had I heard that correctly?

The merchant shook his head. "We can't call everything off. They don't do that in other towns. Can you imagine any big city that would cancel everything because one person died? It might be different if we had a madman on the loose, but"—he glared at Dave—"what we've got on our hands is the very sad drowning of a drunken young woman. I say we sweep it under the rug as quickly as we can."

My eyes met Shelley's. She appeared as horrified as I felt.

"Let's not make light of this," said Oma. "Mallory's death is a terrible tragedy."

Luciano cleared his throat. "Look, I'm as upset about this as everyone else, but I'm footing the bill for an entire TV crew. What are we talking about realistically? Will we be able to get inside the hotel tonight to shoot the show?"

"I still don't understand." Rose frowned at Dave. "Didn't she drown in the gazebo? Why are you searching the hotel?"

"It's just a precaution. Some people reported seeing . . . someone . . . in the Wagtail Springs Hotel last night."

"Who?" demanded Rose.

Dave exhaled. With a sheepish expression, he said, "Becca Wraith."

The merchant snickered. "A ghost? What are you expecting to find? Ghost fingerprints?"

The other man exclaimed, "Oh, for cryin' out loud! My wife says she saw Becca Wraith's black panther walking along the street last night. People have gone Howloween crazy. They're seeing ghosts everywhere."

"It's not *that* ridiculous," Dave protested. "Mallory was dressed as Becca Wraith when she died. She might have been inside the hotel with someone."

The door opened, and Doc Kilgore peeked in. "Sorry I'm late." He tucked a pair of glasses into the pocket of his blue plaid flannel shirt and took a seat next to Oma.

Aunt Birdie sat up straighter and primly crossed her thin legs.

"Doc," she said, "Dave has just told us Mallory's death might not have been an accident."

Rose gazed at Doc Kilgore hopefully.

Doc scratched the side of his face and winced. "Well now, Dave was one of my scouts. Always was a smart little fellow."

I glanced at Dave. Doc was talking about him like he was twelve. I felt for him. People like Doc still saw him as a little boy.

"Gotta say I'm right proud of him. But this time," said Doc, "I'm afraid it's just a very sad accident. I've seen a lot of drownings in my time. There's no evidence of foul play. No sign of a struggle. Mallory has a hematoma on the back of her head. There are particles of bark in her wig, so it appears that she fell and hit her head before she made it into the gazebo. It all fits together. She was drunk, which caused her to fall, then she became disoriented or confused, and that accounts for her being in the gazebo and unable to save herself when she hit the water. We're sending her to Roanoke to the medical examiner's office, so we won't know anything more for a few days. I expect they'll find water in her lungs and evidence of intoxication."

In spite of my own doubts, Doc's position on the matter came as a relief. He made it sound so simple. Maybe it was.

"Shameful!" Birdie spouted. "It's simply shameful that we have young women carousing about at night in Wagtail."

"Then I don't see why we have to call off the ghost walk," said Rose. "I'm as sick as everyone else about Mallory's death. She was a lovely young woman. But we can't shut down the town every time someone dies. Dave, you just tell those men to be through sweeping the hotel by eight o'clock tonight. That ought to be plenty of time for them to know if anything untoward happened in there. The walking tour doesn't take people into the gazebo anyway. We flash a light on it, but that's all."

I left the room before they took a vote, but I thought I could see where it was going. Zelda would be as relieved as I was by Doc's findings. Poor Dave needed to do his job, but he was under a lot of pressure from the merchants to keep up appearances and follow through on the advertised Howloween activities. Mallory could very well have been intoxicated. Val said the Zombie Brain drinks packed a punch.

I called Trixie and found Gingersnap out on the front porch, as usual. I laughed aloud when I realized she had settled next to a sign written in a bloody Halloween script: *Beware of dog . . . kisses!*

"How about we get some lunch, Gingersnap?"

She readily accompanied us. It was late enough for the noontime crowd to have dwindled. I settled at the corner table near the pass-through where Shelley picked up food.

The cook opened it and saw me. "Pulled pork for all three of you?"

"Yes, please!"

Shelley deposited a tray of dishes to be washed, hurried over to my table, and slid into a chair. "Is it true?"

"Is what true?"

"That you found Mallory's body?"

"I'm afraid so. Was she a friend of yours?"

"I didn't know her. She came and went, I think." Shelley fidgeted with the salt shaker. "I know we're not supposed to speak ill of the dead, but she was a little bit high on her horse."

"What do you mean?"

"Well, just about everybody knows and loves Mark. He's outgoing and friendly, and he's been talking to a lot of us about the ghosts we've seen over the years. He fit in real well. Then when Mallory came, she acted like she thought she was some kind of rock star or something and ran around town taking credit for Mark's book. I think it put folks off, you know?"

The pass-through opened, and the cook slid three dishes onto the counter. "Y'all enjoy!" The window snapped shut.

Shelley and I rose to collect the dishes. They looked like food for Goldilocks' three bears. The platter with a bun, coleslaw, and hush puppies was the largest. A smaller one was meant for Gingersnap, and the tiny one belonged to Trixie.

"Hot tea or iced?" asked Shelley.

"Hot, thanks. I think I'm still a little chilled from last night."

She brought a mug for me. "It must have been awful."

I nodded. "I was so focused on trying to save her that it didn't really sink in at that moment."

Shelley studied her fingers for a second.

"What's wrong?"

In the softest whisper, Shelley asked, "Was she really murdered?"

"Where did you hear that?"

"People talk. Several reliable people reported seeing Becca Wraith's ghost at the Wagtail Springs Hotel this week."

I laughed aloud. "Oh, Shelley. I'm sure that was some kind of advertising stunt for the tourists. You're so silly."

"Really? Why would they advertise at two in the morning the night of Mallory's death?"

No wonder Dave had the cops searching the hotel. Had Mallory managed to get inside and wander about? Why would she do that? I tried to make light of it so the rumor of murder wouldn't spread. "That place is spooky just because it's empty. I'm not surprised that people think they see ghosts in the windows."

"Holly Miller, one day you'll see a real ghost and sing a different tune. Just you wait. Wish I could sit and chat longer. I still have a few customers, though."

I ate my lunch while Gingersnap and Trixie watched me with hopeful eyes.

"There you are!" Oma said, bustling over with Rose. "I need a strong cup of tea. How about you, Rose?"

"Make mine strong coffee, Liesel. I have a long night ahead of me."

Oma disappeared into the kitchen while Rose sat down with me. "I'm so relieved that the ghost walk won't be cancelled. Honestly, you'd think it would be easy to set up a ghost walk, but there are always complications."

Oma returned with mugs of coffee and tea, as well as sugar and cream, and a platter of pumpkin whoopie pies with shapes cut out of the tops so that the white filling showed through like a ghost. "This is much more relaxing than eating at the meeting."

"I thought your first meeting went very well, Liesel." Rose doctored her coffee with cream.

"Overall I can't complain. Everyone was most cooperative. It's you who has the problem now."

"Liesel! Don't bother Holly with our headaches. For heaven's sake, she just arrived." Rose ate a bite of whoopie pie, taking great care not to look at Oma.

Oma poured cream into her tea. "It wouldn't interest Holly anyway."

"Exactly. It's not her sort of thing," said Rose.

I could smell a plot afoot. "You do realize that I'm right here?"

"Of course we do, liebling." Oma smiled at me. "We'll work something out, Rose."

I took a deep breath. Why did they feel they had to bait me? "Why don't you just tell me?"

"You see, Mallory was going to help us with the ghost walk." Rose placed a hand on her chest and heaved a huge sigh. "It's tonight, and it's important that we pull it off well because we've been advertising it just everywhere, and now, at the last minute, I have to find a replacement for Mallory."

That didn't sound too bad. "What was she supposed to do? Maybe I can fill in for her."

"Nooo." Oma sipped her tea.

"If only so many people hadn't gone to the dog show," Rose complained.

Oma lifted her hand in a gesture of hopelessness. "Maybe one of my employees could do it?"

I sucked in a deep breath but couldn't hold back my grin. "You two are terrible actresses. What do you want me to do?"

With feigned innocence, Oma said, "You know, maybe Holly *is* the right person for this. She

106

doesn't believe in ghosts, so she wouldn't be afraid."

"That's right. I forgot all about that." Rose smiled at me sweetly.

Forgot, my foot! They knew exactly what they were doing.

Rose reached for the shopping bag and handed it to me. "You are the sweetest person in the whole world to volunteer, Holly." She met my eyes. "I should warn you, though—there are ghosts haunting the Wagtail Springs Hotel."

What a show they had put on. They had everything ready and waiting for me. I peered in the bag. A long white wig and a crown of black roses lay on top. "Becca Wraith? You want me to dress as the ghost of *Becca Wraith?*"

Eight

"It's easy, sweetheart," said Rose. "You'll have fun. You just flit up to the windows like a ghost when you hear me talking about Becca. There's nothing to it."

I had to yank her chain a little bit. "You're afraid real ghosts won't show up for the ghost walk, so you have to ask people to pretend to be ghosts?"

Rose answered sincerely, "You just never know about ghosts. Sometimes they show and other times they don't! I'll leave the bag with your costume in the Wagtail Springs Hotel, upstairs in room ten. That way, you can go on part of the ghost walk with us." She bestowed another sunny smile on me. "But don't blame me if the real ghost of Becca Wraith shows up for tonight's performance."

Yeah. Like that was going to happen.

After they left, it dawned on me that I hadn't asked Oma about Clementine. I was on my way to find Oma when I met Eva in the lobby walking Mrs. Mewer on a leash. "We had the best time this morning," she raved. "I took Mrs. Mewer to the cat park. It's so clever the way they set it up with moving mice and pretend birds. She absolutely loved it. Then we had brunch at a darling café. I thought the poor baby would be locked in my room all the time. I couldn't have been more wrong."

Felix, Casper, and Brian were just coming down the grand staircase.

"Are you headed for Mark's house?" Felix asked Eva.

She adjusted her glasses. "I don't believe I was invited."

"There aren't any invitations," Brian blurted. "We're going to pay our respects."

Eva frowned at him. "Respects? Who died?"

"Mallory," said Brian.

Eva stared at him. "That's not funny."

"I'm afraid it's true, Eva," said Felix. "She died last night—or early this morning, I guess."

Eva blinked hard. And then she crumpled into a heap on the floor, landing on Mrs. Mewer's tail.

Mrs. Mewer yowled and raced down the hallway, dragging her leash behind her.

I knelt beside Eva and said her name softly. She didn't respond and appeared to be out cold. I tapped her cheeks. "Eva?"

Additional ghost hunters clustered behind Brian and Felix, asking what had happened. The dogs milled around their legs, sensing the tension. Shelley must have seen Eva faint, because she broke through the little crowd to hand me a wet cloth.

I dabbed Eva's face. She blinked several times and groaned.

"Can you sit up?" I asked.

She reached out one hand. I slid my arm around her and helped her to a sitting position. For a few minutes, she remained on the floor, refusing all assistance.

Trixie reached her head toward Eva's and licked her nose.

"Okay, okay. Thanks, Trixie. I think I'll be fine." Eva was wobbly when she stood, but managed to make her way to a sofa in the sitting room.

I leaned over to her and asked very softly, "Would you rather I helped you to your room?"

"Good heavens, no. Please don't fuss. To tell the truth, I'm thoroughly embarrassed. I've never fainted before. I'm quite sure I'll be fine. Thank you, Holly."

She adjusted her glasses using both hands, her fingers extended. The worry in her face made me want to reach out to hug her.

She jolted forward and jumped up unsteadily. "Where's Mrs. Mewer?"

Felix came to the rescue. "We'll look for her. She can't have gone far. Everybody, spread out and look for a Siamese cat."

Eva stumbled toward the front door, frantically chanting, "Mrs. Mewer! Here, kitty, kitty, kitty."

Felix murmured, "Oh, man. She's lost it."

"You'd probably do the same for Casper. You go that way, and I'll look upstairs."

"Deal."

Ten minutes later, I was back in the dining area, but we still had no clue where Mrs. Mewer had gone. "Can you find the kitty?" I asked Trixie. "Do you know where she is?"

Shelley was setting up for tea. "Do you hear something? What is that?"

We tiptoed to the lobby. Eva was in the Dogwood Room bawling.

I sat down next to her on the couch and let her cry on my shoulder.

"It's my fault. I never should have let go of her leash. I never should have brought her here. I never should have come at all! This is all my fault!"

I could understand her distress. I didn't think it was quite so hopeless, though. Chances were pretty good that Mrs. Mewer was still inside the inn somewhere. But I let Eva cry because I had a strong suspicion that it wasn't just Mrs. Mewer that had upset her.

She sniffled and pulled away. "I'm so sorry. You're really a stranger to me. Thank you for being so kind."

I didn't know what to say. *You're welcome* seemed so wrong. "Do you want to talk about it?"

"I want to find Mrs. Mewer!" The torrent of tears began again.

Grayson, Felix, and Casper appeared in the lobby. Felix held up his hands and shrugged.

"Of course you do. I bet she's hiding somewhere in the inn. She was probably scared when you fainted." I avoided mentioning that she fell on Mrs. Mewer's tail, fearing that would set off more guilt and tears.

Felix inched closer, evidently feeling awkward. "Um . . . you know, Mark is a friend of mine, too."

"He is?" she sniffled.

Grayson took a seat, his elbows on his knees, his face turned toward the floor.

Felix sat down near Eva. "We were college roommates. He's a great guy. I can't believe Mallory is dead. Mark must be flipping out."

Eva nodded. Was she holding her breath?

111

"Did . . . did you work with Mark?" asked Felix.

"Sort of. We met when he was investigating some haunted manor houses in England."

Felix's eyes widened in surprise. "Cool. I've done a few of those. Did you know Mallory?"

"This is so tragic. Do you know her family story?" Eva sniffled and knotted a tissue. Her face screwed up. "It's so sad!"

Grayson wiped his eyes with his fingers. "When Mallory was fourteen, her father and brother died in a boating accident. You can imagine how horrible that was. Her mother couldn't take it, and a month later, Mallory came home from school to find her mother had intentionally overdosed."

"She was shipped from relative to relative," said Eva. "I can't believe that their family saga ended this way."

"It's like they were cursed," said Grayson.

Felix seemed at a loss. "I talked with her last night. She was so happy." Felix rubbed his face with both palms. He looked at me when he said, "Mark is a trust fund baby from an Oklahoma oil family. You'd never know it. He acts like a regular guy, but he's filthy rich."

"Must be nice," said Grayson. "My grandfathers were missing in action."

"Both of them? Vietnam?" asked Felix.

"That's not what I meant. They were just absentee. We never saw them. My parents went through a nasty divorce when I was just a baby.

My mom took my sister and me, started a new life, and in the ensuing bitterness, cut off all contact with my dad's family. Then my dad died."

"Good grief!" said Felix. "Your life sounds like a Greek tragedy."

"It wasn't that bad." Grayson grinned. "My mom remarried, and my stepdad adopted us. But my mom's dad had alcohol issues that brought on an estrangement between them, so I never knew my grandfathers." He shrugged. "Standard family dysfunction, you know?" Grayson thought for a moment. "Funny, I've known Mark for a few years, but he's never driven a fancy car or been a flashy kind of guy."

Eva nodded. "He's so grounded. Not at all pretentious."

A smile briefly twitched over Felix's lips. "His grandfather wasn't happy with the laziness and financial demands of his own children, so he set up trusts for the grandchildren that they would get on whichever event happened first—they got a doctorate or turned sixty. I always thought he must have been a pretty sharp guy. Of course, they all did graduate work to get their money, so he had a bunch of grandchildren who were very well educated."

I smiled. "Pretty clever of Gramps."

"Mark is a physicist," said Felix, "which is great, because he thinks about ghosts in a different way."

"Was Mallory a physicist, too?" I asked.

Felix shrugged. "She was a psychic. She said something about being an assistant manager of a store. A girly kind of store, accessories or something."

"A psychic?" asked Grayson.

Eva tilted her head. "Not a very good one. She relied on a lot of guesses and mostly parroted back what people wanted to hear."

"I don't get it," said Grayson.

Eva sniffled, but raised both of her hands, palms outward. "I'm getting the letter M. Who had someone pass over with that initial? Ah, it's a grandmother, or possibly an aunt."

Grayson sat up straighter. "Okay, now you're freaking me out. My aunt's name started with an M."

Eva sighed. "She loved you very much. She's telling me what fun she had reading to you."

Grayson gasped.

"And I'm seeing cookies. Chocolate, maybe?"

"How could you know that?" asked Grayson. "It was our thing to bake chocolate chip cookies. And she always read to me. Are you psychic?"

Felix laughed. "In most groups of people, it's a good bet that someone has lost a grandparent. Eva expanded that by adding an aunt. She used one of the most common initials—M. Other likely initials are A, C, S, and J."

"But the cookies and the reading," protested Grayson.

Eva shrugged. "A good guess. That's what a lot of aunts and grandmothers do. And everyone wants to hear they were loved."

Grayson sat back. "Aww. Now you've taken the fun out of it."

"I called Mark this morning," said Felix. "They're sending Mallory for an . . . an autopsy, so he doesn't know when she'll be buried. Luciano is giving everyone the opportunity to withdraw from the show. But . . . everybody is here, and we signed contracts and everything." He heaved another big breath. "It sounds so uncaring for life to go on." He rubbed the back of his neck. "That really bothers me. But it's not like calling off the ghost hunt would bring Mallory back."

I was glad Grayson had taken Eva's mind off Mrs. Mewer. It wouldn't be long before she remembered, though. "Why don't you three talk while I take care of a few things?"

As I walked away with Trixie, Eva asked, "Felix, what happened? How did Mallory die?"

Trixie and I walked from one end of the inn to the other, starting on the top floor and ending in the basement. Unless someone had invited Mrs. Mewer into a guest room, which was always a possibility, she had either escaped the inn or was curled up somewhere. When I reached the reception desk, I took a few minutes to print notices that said *Do Not Let Cats Out*. I taped one on the glass door in reception and another on the front door.

We took Casper along with us when we walked around the outside of the inn. Mrs. Mewer wasn't on the porch with Gingersnap, but Grayson had moved outside. He sat in a rocking chair staring at his hands.

"You okay?" I asked, perching on the chair next to him.

"Yeah. It's just . . . wow. You don't expect things like this to happen."

"You knew her well?"

"No, but I just spent the last couple of days with her and Mark. She liked to hang out with ghost hunters. It's just mind-boggling that she was fine a few hours before and then she drowned."

"Mr. Luciano would probably let you go home."

Grayson nodded. "I know. But I can't let the other guys down. A TV show is probably the biggest thing that ever happened to them. And there's the possibility of a series. I can't walk out on it." He massaged Casper's ears.

"Let me know if there's anything I can do."

"Did you find Eva's cat?"

"Not yet. I was just going to look outside the inn just in case she managed to sneak past someone."

We left him to his thoughts of Mallory and walked around the property. Mrs. Mewer wasn't lounging in the sun on the back terraces. If she had

116

climbed a tree or nestled somewhere, the dogs showed no sign of noticing her.

When I returned, Grayson had fetched Zelda.

All eyes were on her as she rotated a hand under her chin. "I see her. Mrs. Mewer says she's scared. She found a place to hide."

"Where is she?" asked Eva eagerly.

I couldn't help wondering what had happened to the woman who didn't believe in psychics. Now that *her* cat was lost, she certainly had a different attitude toward Zelda's alleged powers.

"All I see is white walls," said Zelda. "Maybe a closet or a corner someplace?"

"Doesn't she miss me? Tell her I want her to come back!"

Zelda smiled at Eva very kindly. "She loves you, too. But right now, she wants to hide for a little bit."

"Eva," I said, "if you want to go with the guys to pay your respects, I'll stick around and keep an eye out for Mrs. Mewer."

Eva sucked in a sharp breath of air. "No! Oh, no, no, no. I'll stay here. Maybe Mrs. Mewer will come out of hiding when everyone is gone and it's quiet."

Felix took the cue, collected the ghost hunters and herded them out the front door. In mere seconds, the inn fell silent.

Shelley very thoughtfully appeared with a tray bearing a cup of tea and a platter of the pumpkin whoopie pies. She set it on the table in front of Eva. "Let me know if there's anything you need, sugar."

Shelley, Trixie, and I left Eva sitting in the Dogwood Room. I looked back at her as we walked away. She heaved deep breaths and stared at the floor. The hand that clutched a tissue shook slightly.

Shelley whispered, "I hope that cat shows up soon. The afternoon tea crowd will start trickling in before long. The noise and commotion might scare her even more."

I spent the next few hours installing the new deadbolt on the kitchen door. Trixie stretched out on the floor for a nap, and Twinkletoes curled up on the fireplace hearth. Neither of them appeared to be one bit disturbed by the annoying sound of the drill or the battery-operated screwdriver. I hoped the noise wasn't keeping Mrs. Mewer away.

At five o'clock, dogs, cats, and people in costumes gathered in front of the inn for a Howloween Yappy Hour. Although the inn didn't serve cocktails at Yappy Hour, the town permitted people to bring their drinks to the porch of the inn to watch the parade. Oma insisted I join in with Trixie, dressed in her Tootsie Roll outfit, and Gingersnap, who wore a big furry ruff around her neck that made her look like a lion.

It didn't take a dog psychic like Zelda to know that the dogs were having fun. They pranced around, wagging their tails and showing off their finery. A black-and-white mutt wore a skunk jacket, a Doberman had donned a vampire cape, and a boxer was dressed as a pirate, complete with a live parrot riding on his hat! I recognized a cairn terrier dressed as Dorothy, a host of doggy witches, a ladybug, a bee, and several little devils with red horns.

Lillian marched in the parade with GloryB. They wore matching witches' hats and black capes adorned with flashy rhinestones and black feathers.

The cats held their own too, though many of them were being carried in the parade. They wore witch hats, pumpkin outfits, mouse getups—one even came wearing Cleopatra hair with a faux asp attached to her collar.

As silly as it seemed, I thoroughly enjoyed it. There wasn't a single person in the parade who didn't smile or laugh. For that short time, I didn't think about Mallory. I chatted with people about their cats and dogs, and my mouth muscles hurt from grinning.

When the costume judging began, I beat a hasty exit lest Trixie or Gingersnap should win. After all, we were locals. The prizes should go to visitors. We returned to the inn, where the ghost hunters watched from the porch, cocktails in hand.

Brian and Grayson caught me coming up the steps and applauded.

"I'm sorry Felix missed that," said Brian. "It would have brightened his day."

"Where is Felix?" I asked.

"He's skipping dinner tonight," said Grayson. "He wasn't hungry. Eva, either."

I didn't want to be a pain in the neck, but decided to take them something to eat anyway. It was the least I could do. After helping Trixie and Gingersnap out of their costumes, I loaded up a room service cart with piping hot macaroni and cheese, a bowl of Oma's goulash, fruit, and our onion-free goulash doggie dinner for Casper, the ghost dog.

I knocked on Felix's door.

"It's open." He said it in a weak, resigned tone, but I was certain I'd heard him.

I rolled the cart inside. Mark was slumped in the chair by the fireplace, staring at the blaze. Felix straddled a desk chair that he had turned around. Casper jumped to his feet and strolled over to greet Trixie.

I shoved the cart next to Felix's chair. "I brought you some dinner."

He glanced up at me. "We're not really hungry."

"I'm so sorry for your loss, Mark."

"Thanks. I hope you don't mind, but I'm hiding out here with Felix for a while. People keep coming to my place."

"He's got enough food to feed the whole ghost hunting team for a week," said Felix.

Mark ran a hand through his hair. "Mr. Luciano is dedicating the show to Mallory."

"That's a very thoughtful gesture."

He didn't respond.

"I can understand if you're not hungry. I brought dinner for Casper, too. Just let me know if you need anything." I turned to leave.

Felix jumped up and said, "Holly?"

"Yes?"

He followed me to the door and gestured toward the hallway. We walked out of the room, and he closed the door.

Nine

Unsure what Felix wanted to talk about, I thought it best to wait and let him fill the dead air.

He chewed on his lower lip. "Mark says the place where Mallory drowned isn't deep."

"It's not."

Felix gazed around uncomfortably. "Then . . . then how could she have drowned? Why didn't she stand up or sit or something?"

I wasn't sure how much to say. "Doc thinks she was too drunk."

Felix nodded and studied the floor. "We all

drank too much last night. I guess that could explain a lot of things. Mallory flirted with me."

"I noticed that. Seemed odd to be so obvious in front of Mark."

A worried V formed between Felix's eyebrows. "Mark insists they broke up ages ago."

"That's odd. Wasn't she staying with him? She was asking about having their wedding here."

His eyebrows squeezed tighter together. "That doesn't jibe with what Mark says." He squinted at me. "Why would she be interested in me if she was planning to marry Mark? I'm not the kind of guy women chase. I don't have Brian's ease and jolliness or Mark's cool-guy flare or Grayson's fame."

"Fame?"

"He was a heartthrob on one of those reality TV shows. I never saw it, but he acts like it was a big deal." He shrugged. "I guess it was. A couple of people recognized him last night."

Ben, my last boyfriend, had been a geeky guy, like Felix. Although Oma didn't like him, and he hadn't even bothered to call since I decided to move, he had his good sides. "Don't put yourself down. You're very charming."

He finally looked over at me, a half smile on his face. "Yeah?"

"Absolutely. Zelda is quite taken by you."

"Really?" His face lit up.

"I hope you'll come to the ghost walk. Casper

probably needs to get out for a bit, and I know Zelda will be there."

Felix scuffed the toe of his shoe against the floor. "It feels wrong to do anything fun, you know? Is it just me, or does something seem not right about all of this? Do you think Mallory was murdered?"

My breath caught in my throat. I looked him straight in the eyes. "Why would you ask such a thing?"

"Officer Dave woke me up this morning. I don't think he would have done that if he didn't suspect someone killed her. He came to my room and asked me questions about Mallory and what happened last night. I guess it could have been in the regular course of business, but he didn't give me that impression."

Conflicting thoughts ran through my head. The official verdict was that Mallory's death had been accidental. Even if I had my doubts about that, shouldn't I stick to what I'd been told, rather than spout my own suspicions? "Doc Kilgore says it was an accident, probably due to intoxication."

Felix nodded his head and studied his shoes for a moment. "Thanks for the dinner, Holly. I'll see you later." He returned to Mark while Trixie and I headed back to the kitchen.

But Felix's words lingered with me. *Does something seem not right about all of this?* It was exactly what I had been feeling.

I fetched another cart with mac and cheese and goulash and pushed it through the library to the cat wing. Surprisingly, Eva's door hung open. I rapped on it anyway. "Eva?"

Like a mirror image of Mark, she sat in the chair by a blazing fire, but she jumped up when I said her name. "Have you found Mrs. Mewer?"

"Not yet. I'm so sorry. I brought you dinner. You really should eat something."

Her shoulders drooped, and she dropped into the chair. "I apologize. I'm usually not such a quivering mess. Mrs. Mewer is everything to me. She's like my baby."

"I understand completely. Trixie was lost the last time I was here, and it tore me up."

She plucked at the fabric of her skirt. "Holly, you're the only one I can talk to about this. You don't believe all that nonsense about ghosts, right?"

"No, of course not."

In a voice so tiny I could barely hear her, she asked, "Have you ever had complaints about odd lights in this room?"

"Not that I'm aware of." I hastened to add, "This is a new addition. It's not as though anyone died here or anything." *At least not that I knew of.* "Did something happen?"

"There was a light in the room last night. I'm used to orbs in photographs, of course. They're usually just insects or particles of dust and people want to imagine that they're something more. But this was a round light. It *must* be some kind of reflection. I can't figure out where it came from. It wasn't my imagination. Mrs. Mewer saw it, too. I'm usually adept at finding the source, but this time I couldn't."

Oh boy. I didn't know whether she needed my assurance that it must have had some earthly origin, or if she wanted confirmation that it could have been something else. Probably the former.

"I walked around outside," said Eva, "thinking it must surely be a light from a neighboring building, but there isn't anything back there. Just a clearing for bird feeders and then woods. There has to be a rational explanation. There just has to be!"

Her voice rose in agitation, alarming me.

She seized my hand. "You were there. Do you think Mallory was . . . murdered?"

I drew in a sharp breath and pulled my hand back. They all thought the same thing! "Why do you ask that?"

She sagged back against the chair. "Mallory didn't need a pointy hat and a broom to be a witch." She snorted in derision.

A rustling sound caught my attention. I turned to see that Twinkletoes had jumped into a huge Vera Bradley tote. She dug deeper until only the tip of her fluffy black tail was visible.

I was about to dart over to her when Eva reached

backward and caught my arm. "Have you heard anything? It *was* an accident, right?"

Her questions caught me off guard. Here I was again, stuck between Doc Kilgore's official line that Mallory's death had probably been a terrible mishap and my own instinct that it wasn't accidental. What if Felix and I were right, and she had been murdered? Obviously I wasn't the only one with doubts about a vibrant young woman drowning in shallow water. "Are you saying that someone wanted to kill Mallory?"

I watched her reflection in the mirror. Her eyes rose slowly to study me in the mirror. She released her grip. "No. No, I'm not saying that at all."

I wanted to like Eva, but at that moment, I knew without a doubt that she was lying. She nearly burbled in her haste to change the subject. "I'm being absurd. I have to find the explanation for that light in the room."

"I don't think you're being ridiculous at all." I shot a glare at Twinkletoes, not that it mattered, because she had already left the bag and now prowled through the room, her tail high like a waving flag.

"If you see the light again, why don't you call me and maybe the two of us can figure it out?" I offered.

"All orbs have logical, rational, earthly explanations. I'll find the source. Thank you for bringing me dinner and setting me straight."

"You're so welcome. I'll see you at the ghost walk?"

"Yes." She closed her eyes and leaned her head back against the chair.

It was the perfect opportunity to catch Twinkletoes. She pawed at something under the dressing table chair. I tiptoed toward her, bent over—and like a flash of white lightning, she flew from the room with something clenched between her teeth. Oh great.

I hurried after her but hadn't even made it to the door when Eva said, "Holly? Leave the door open, will you? I'm hoping Mrs. Mewer will come back."

Leaving the door ajar just enough for a cat to pass through, I dashed into the library. Twinkletoes was lying on the window seat, but jumped up when she saw me.

It was a standoff.

I knew perfectly well what would happen next. She understood that I was after whatever she had stolen. As soon as I neared, she would seize it and scamper off again. I edged toward her slowly, trying to see what she had. A turquoise catnip mouse. For heaven's sake, she'd stolen a toy from Mrs. Mewer.

No problem. I could replace *that*. I chuckled under my breath as I passed her and headed to the kitchen for yogurt to sustain me while I played ghost.

• • •

By eight thirty that evening, the sun had vanished behind the mountain. Orange and purple Howloween lights decorated stores and restaurants. People, dogs, and cats walked along the pedestrian zone under the streetlights and gathered on the plaza in front of the Sugar Maple Inn. The moon cast a golden beam strong enough for me to make out scary goblins and cute dogs waiting to go on the ghost walk.

I watched from the front porch with Trixie securely attached to a leash so she wouldn't wander. Zelda shooed us to the plaza. Her bawdy serving wench costume should certainly get Felix's attention. Her curvy figure filled it out perfectly.

"Rose is about to begin," she whispered before she hurried off.

Framed by garlands of fall leaves, Rose stood on the lighted porch at the top of the steps. Clusters of pumpkins and purple mums added cheerful color to each side of the stairs. Giant crows perched on the pumpkins that decorated the porch. I chuckled at two skeletons happily seated on rocking chairs. One of them held a leash that led to the faux skeleton of a dog. Spooky bats dangled from the porch roof and appeared to flit around in a light breeze.

Without warning, the porch lights went out. A small beam glowed just beneath Rose's chin, giving lovely Rose a haunted appearance and emphasizing the green cast to her makeup. The stars on her kinked witch's hat glowed in the dark, as did the horizontal stripes on her tights. In a crackly voice, she said, "Welcome to all! But beware! For Wagtail is home to many ghosts." She pointed a crooked forefinger at someone in the crowd. "You dare to snicker? This tour is not for the feeble or the easily spooked."

Ten

Zelda pushed a cart across the plaza in front of us, handing out lanterns and lighting the candles inside them. Felix, Mark, Grayson, and Brian wedged next to me to take lanterns. Felix's eyes met Zelda's, and they both grinned.

A spark! But why was Mark on the ghost tour? I guessed that people grieve differently. Maybe Felix coaxed him to come along, just to distract him for a while. After all, he was presumably Wagtail's foremost authority on ghosts. He might have even helped Rose prepare for the ghostly happenings in Wagtail.

I glanced down at Trixie. Casper nuzzled her like they were already old friends.

"The year is 1885," said Rose. "In the dark of night, the only lights in Wagtail come from gas lamps." She pointed her finger toward the sky as if casting a spell.

At that moment, the streetlights dimmed, and if I hadn't known better, I would have sworn they had gas flames. The crowd gasped.

"Follow me, my dears—if you dare!" Rose cackled so wickedly that a chill shivered through me. Who knew that sweet Rose could sound so devilish?

Carrying lanterns, we fell in behind her as she led the way through Wagtail, stopping at various houses to tell ghostly tales. The residents of the homes along our route had agreed to play the game by turning off most of their electric lights.

Menacing pumpkins leered at us. Chains rattled and eerie moans issued from some houses. Ghosts peered out of windows and witches guarded porches. Dogs barked everywhere—not surprising in Wagtail—but some howled, and at one house, an organ played music worthy of an old Christopher Lee movie, accompanied by a mournful howl that elicited sympathy howls from the dogs in our group, including Trixie and Casper. Dry leaves rustled underfoot and a gust, as though prearranged, kicked them up now and then.

In between two locations, I noticed Mark walking with Eva, and I found myself with Lillian and GloryB, Grayson, Felix and Casper, and Brian.

"Thanks for the dinner, Holly," said Felix. "That was really nice of you."

I was afraid to ask if Mark was feeling better. How could he be? Mallory's death had to be a shock to him. I changed to another subject. "Are you supposed to hear all this? Don't you go to haunted houses cold, without knowing the background?"

Felix shrugged. "We usually do research before we visit a haunted building. It's not like we're psychics who are supposed to figure out what happened. We're just checking for paranormal phenomena."

Felix squinted toward a cat on a fence. "They've done a great job here. Seriously, I can't tell if that's a real cat or a prop. This must be incredibly scary for kids who trick-or-treat."

The cat meowed as we walked by, but I still wasn't sure if it was real, either. In any case, it wasn't a Siamese.

"Wagtail has to be a hotbed of paranormal activity." Brian spoke eagerly, as though he could barely contain himself.

"Have you been here before?" I asked.

Brian shook his head. "This is all new territory for us. But Luciano hit it right this time. We're bound to find something."

"People used to come here for the mineral springs, right?" asked Felix. "It only stands to reason that a good number of them were sick and died here."

"These streets are probably teeming with spirits right now." Brian held his lantern higher as though he thought he might see them.

That creeped me out a little bit. Outside of the Halloween decorations, I didn't see anything unusual, though. "Do *you* see them?"

"It's not like that. Most of them are going about their business. But once in a while, one might touch your shoulder, or you'll feel a cold whiff of air. That's a ghost brushing by you."

I shivered again in spite of myself, even though I knew a whiff of cold air was easily explained by something as common as a breeze.

"Our main focus is the Wagtail Springs Hotel." Brian peered at me. "Know anything about it? Maybe we could have a drink later tonight and you could fill me in?"

I might not believe in ghosts, but the Wagtail Springs Hotel could send chills down anyone's spine. "It's definitely creepy—like most unoccupied buildings."

"You're a skeptic, aren't you?" asked Felix.

"I'm sorry." It was just as well that they knew. I wouldn't have to keep up pretenses.

"Don't apologize," said Felix. "I was, too."

"What changed your mind?"

"A few years back, I was staying in an English castle with very aristocratic and stiff-upper-lip sort of people when the cook rushed out of the kitchen in a panic. Naturally, we hurried *into* the kitchen, and it was the strangest thing I've ever seen. Cookbooks were hurling through the air. The cook had a roast in the oven, but that kitchen was as cold as a freezer. Naturally, I assumed the flying cookbooks were a setup for the benefit of the guests and the kitchen was cold because castles aren't insulated. All that stone, you know? But I went back in the morning to look around in daylight. The temperature was perfectly normal."

"Did you check to see if the cookbooks were rigged?"

"Naturally. I'm a scientist by training, so I'm not prone to believing every silly thing. But I examined those books very carefully. They were perfectly normal. No strings attached, no holes or weights or evidence of, well . . . anything. That was the event that triggered my interest."

"So you think because you couldn't see any other mechanism, that meant a ghost was throwing the books?" I couldn't help being doubtful.

Felix grinned at me. "That's the old argument. How do we know it was a ghost if we don't have tangible evidence of one? We can't blame everything we don't understand on the paranormal. I get that, which is why I find it all so fascinating."

I liked Felix. He wasn't defensive about his position on ghosts. He clearly gave it a lot of thought and wasn't prone to jumping to conclusions.

I excused myself and pretended to fall back to

speak to someone else. When everyone gathered to hear the next ghost tale, I sprinted away with Trixie and cut through the streets to the dark and gloomy Wagtail Springs Hotel.

On the front porch, I held up my lantern to see where I was going. The door screeched when I opened it. The hotel had fallen into disuse a long time ago, so I expected the worst.

Candles flickered in the lobby.

I shrieked at the sight of another person, and felt incredibly stupid when I realized my own reflection in a strategically placed mirror had scared me. The glass bore veins of age and a creepy film. It probably frightened everyone who entered.

Rose's committee had done a splendid job of decorating the old inn for Howloween. I guessed it was for the upcoming costume gala. Cobwebs hung where they would brush the tops of some heads. Spiders crawled up the registration desk. Scary hands reached out of the old-fashioned cubbies where keys and mail would have been held for guests.

In spite of all that, the thing that surprised me the most was the perfect condition of the building. Behind the decorations, the walls didn't appear to be dingy or ruined at all. The ornate registration desk had been carefully restored. Walnut, I guessed, with six beautifully carved panels across the front depicting deer.

Someone had cleaned it up quite nicely. In daylight, I bet the old hotel wasn't one bit scary inside.

Trixie tugged toward a hallway that led to the back. The group would be arriving soon, though. "No time for exploring now, Trixie."

We hurried up the stairs and easily found room number ten. Exactly as promised, the bag with the Becca Wraith costume awaited us. I closed and locked the door, just in case other faux ghosts were roaming the hotel for the show, and set the lantern on a dresser, wondering why there would even be a dresser and a plastic-covered mattress in the room. It was as though someone had planned to open the hotel.

I unsnapped the leash so Trixie could sniff around.

Rose must have had the dress custom-made by someone in town. Had Mallory sewn her own costume? Maybe Becca had become so popular that they could be bought off the rack in Wagtail.

Panels of gleaming satin comprised the skirt of the white gown. The top had been studded with sparkles that caught the light. But over the top of the dress, a gauzy fabric had been made to appear dirty. The sleeves were lightly shredded, as though it had been buried underground for a long time. I coiled my milk chocolate brown hair into a loose bun on top of my head and wiggled the long white wig over it, much as Mallory must have done the night before. I assumed I was to apply the white makeup in the bag. I smeared it on, checking my progress in the mirror over the dresser. It caused the skin around my eyes to appear dark and haunted. The ring of black roses turned out to be real. Where on Earth did they find black roses to dry? I set it on my head carefully and finished the costume by pulling on white gloves.

The dress dragged along the floor when I walked, which I imagined was the look they had wanted. Through the glass door to the upper-level porch, I could see the lanterns of the ghost walkers nearing in the distance. Leaving Trixie safely in the room, I stepped out onto the porch.

A mist rose around me, and someone in the approaching crowd screamed. I assumed it was because of me. How would a ghost walk? Stiffly, perhaps? That didn't seem right. Maybe they floated gracefully. I drifted along the length of the porch slowly, barely picking up my feet. Taking a cue from Rose, I carried the lantern low, hoping the light would diffuse, making me seem more ethereal. My other hand hung limp.

As they gathered below, I disappeared into room ten again.

Rose probably should have given me cues so I would know when to appear in the windows. No matter, I would just have to wing it. I opened the door to the hallway and peered down the corridor.

I assumed I was supposed to show up in different windows. Thankfully, I could hear her speaking.

"The most famous haunted structure in these mountains is the Wagtail Springs Hotel. While you may wish to think there are no such things as ghosts, no matter what you believe, the facts of this tragedy remain historically accurate."

Faux candles suddenly switched on in the corridor behind me.

Rose spoke in a slow, calm voice. *"During the civil war, Dr. Ira Wraith converted the Wagtail Springs Hotel into a hospital for the few lucky souls who managed to survive the long trip up the mountain. Dr. Wraith's daughter, Becca, was known far and wide for her astonishing beauty."*

Aha! My name. I should probably make an appearance. I stumbled over the long gown in my hurry to appear on the porch.

"Raven locks tumbled down her back, and her eyes were said to be bluer than the twilight sky of the harvest moon. Suitors came and went, none winning the hand of the lovely Becca until the day Hiram Montacue came to Wagtail to study medicine under the tutelage of her father. Becca and Hiram fell in love immediately and soon planned to marry."

I faded away by walking backward and nearly tripping again. Picking up my skirt, I walked to the far room, planning to appear on the porch when it seemed appropriate. But it dawned on me that no one was screaming when I appeared. Maybe I was supposed to go downstairs? In a low voice, I called Trixie.

She was digging for something between the mattress and the wall.

"Leave that alone," I hissed. "Come on, Trixie!"

Lifting the skirt, I tried to glide down the stairs. A good move. The front door hung open and a machine spewed a mysterious fog. I heard people gasp outside.

Rose's tone became ominous. *"But the devil arrived in Wagtail—in the guise of snake oil salesman Obadiah Bagley."*

I raised my arms to seem like I was misty, and peered out a window. This time someone screamed.

Oddly enough, while I had heard the story of Obadiah Bagley as a child, I never gave any thought to its authenticity. Had these things really happened in Wagtail? Maybe the core of the story had, but the ghost part must have grown out of folklore as it was repeated. I backed away again and headed for another room.

Rose continued. *"Obadiah quickly made a name for himself when his magical elixir cured the snakebites of several hunters. People flocked to him to buy his potion as a cure for all that ailed them. But Dr. Wraith cautioned them and denounced Obadiah as a dangerous quack. Unfortunately, Obadiah set his sights on the doctor's beautiful daughter. He went to Becca's father and asked for her hand in marriage. The angry and distraught doctor refused. In a stormy argument, Dr. Wraith threw Obadiah out exactly where I stand right now!"*

Eleven

There wasn't another sound, as though everyone was entranced.

Rose continued the story. *"Embarrassed and humiliated, Obadiah disappeared. Naturally, everyone thought they were done with him."*

A tremor tinged Rose's voice. *"Two days later, on All Hallows' Eve, the day of her wedding"*— undoubtedly my cue, I walked to the window— *"Becca perfumed herself with lavender and wore a ring of pink roses in her hair. That morning, a black panther guarded the door to the bathhouse. Dr. Wraith shot over his head to frighten him and the animal ran to the woods. The doctor discovered Obadiah's lifeless body floating in the mineral bath behind the Wagtail Springs Hotel. Becca rushed to see him and broke through the crowd of townspeople that tried to detain her from the grisly sight. Before their very eyes, Becca's raven locks turned completely white from the fright."*

This time I slammed into the window and was

rewarded by several screams. I pulled back and searched for another window.

"In spite of the horrific death of Obadiah, Hiram insisted the wedding proceed. It was the social event of the year in Wagtail. Everyone had turned out dressed in their finest."

She paused. *"Everyone but Becca. The bride never showed up to her own wedding. Becca left Hiram standing alone at the altar, broken-hearted."*

Rose let the impact sink in before she continued. *"While townspeople gathered for her wedding, Becca returned to the site of Obadiah's death, where she discovered a brass button with the shape of a man and his dog on it—a button she knew to be from one of Hiram's coats. Everyone in Wagtail thought Hiram had drowned the odious Obadiah, including Becca, who declared that she could never marry a man who had it in his soul to murder. Hiram pleaded with her, but Becca turned a cold heart to Hiram. Now, you might think that Wagtail was finished with Obadiah. After all, he was dead. But that didn't stop Obadiah's ghost from returning a few days later with a dozen rattlesnakes."*

I waltzed through the lobby again and peered into a room in time to see someone holding up writhing snakes.

I screamed at the same time as the crowd outside. I backed up fast, my heart pounding.

140

Surely the snakes couldn't be real. Trixie barked and dashed into the room where someone was pretending to be the ghost of Obadiah.

"Trixie," I whispered. "Trixie!"

She turned and ran toward me, wagging her tail as though she was having fun.

Rose continued the story. *"He brought them to the Wagtail Springs Hotel. Obadiah tossed half the snakes in the lobby and carried the remaining snakes to room number three on the first floor, where Hiram was tending a patient. The guests, Dr. Wraith, and his horrified family fled outside."*

Screams rose from inside the hotel. Where were they coming from? They must have been recorded. The front door slammed shut. I peered into the lobby but didn't see anyone. How did they do that? As long as it wasn't the snake guy, I would be fine. If those snakes were real, I didn't want to meet him.

"But the door to room number three slammed on Hiram when he tried to escape, trapping him there."

A woman outside screamed. More screams arose in the crowd. I called Trixie and headed upstairs in a hurry, assuming the main part about Becca was over.

"Try as he might, Hiram could not open the door. He pressed himself against the window"—she paused, and I could hear banging somewhere

inside the hotel—*"and begged for help. A few sympathetic townspeople brought hammers and axes, but no one could break the glass. They tried to enter the hotel, but the black panther returned and sat exactly where I stand at this moment, preventing anyone from entering the inn."*

Trixie and I reached the top of the stairs. I wondered if I should make a brief appearance on the upper balcony.

"Hiram screamed as the snakes bit him. Without Obadiah's magic elixir, there was no hope of saving him. Dr. Wraith stepped forward to say, 'Repent and confess or the devil shall take thee to him for thy evil deed.'

"You would think Hiram might have done just that to save his life, but Hiram cried out, 'There is no evil in my heart. I curse thee, Ira Wraith. Ye and thy progeny shall never know true love, and all that ye gain in life, ye shall lose. Misfortune and misery shall be the lot of the Wraiths until the day the truth be known.'

"His pleas and cries for help grew weaker as the venom consumed him. A local hunter arrived and shot the panther, who ran into the woods to die. They were finally able to enter the inn and found the door to room three unlocked, with Hiram dead on the floor."

The dim lights inside the hotel went out, leaving Trixie and me in the dark again, except for the lantern.

"Becca Wraith could not bear the sorrow or the guilt that two men had died because of her."

I opened the glass door and waited. A scratching noise drew my attention. I raised the lantern. Trixie was digging at something near the mattress again. "Stop that!" I hissed.

"She became a recluse in a small cottage near the cemetery, in the place now known as Wraith's Hollow. The black panther found her there, and she was able to heal his wounds. She was known for her herbs and poultices, and many called her a witch. The panther never again left her side. There are some who believe that Hiram or Obadiah's spirit inhabited the panther. Becca lived a long life, and the panther lived an abnormally long life, dying minutes after Becca did.

"To this day, Becca's ghost can be seen in the hotel"—I drifted outside on the porch, trying to appear light and airy—*"and walking through Wagtail, wearing a ring of black roses in her white hair. Many have heard the rattle of the snakes in room number three. But it is Hiram who is most often seen about town, searching for his beloved Becca. And on rare occasions, Becca's father, old Dr. Wraith, has been seen roaming the grounds of the Wagtail Springs Hotel."*

After a moment of drama-filled silence, Rose said, "And now, please join us in the center of town where we'll be bobbing for apples. The merchants have some special treats for the kids!

And we have tarot card readers waiting to tell you *your* future!"

I hustled inside, closed the door, and hastily changed back to my own clothes. Ugh. How would I get the white makeup off? A roll of paper towels in the bathroom had probably been left there by Rose exactly for the purpose of removing makeup. The lantern cast eerie shadows, making the hotel seem ghoulish, but the truth was that someone had spent a lot of money on refurbishing the place.

The bathroom was designed in an old-fashioned style with a claw-foot tub, but there wasn't anything old about it. Everything seemed new and unused.

Trixie returned to the mattress. She struggled to wedge her paw between the wall and the mattress. When that didn't work, she dug on the mattress again.

"Stop that!"

She went back to pawing the spot next to the wall. I finally shoved the mattress over an inch. An odd orange ball clung to the wall. Trixie pulled and pulled, wagging her tail. I didn't think she could hurt it, so I let her have her fun.

I managed to wash off most of the makeup. I was packing the dress and headgear in the bag as Rose had when I heard a *pop*. Trixie wagged happily, carrying the orange ball in her mouth. It sprouted a concave part that looked like it was intended for suction. She'd managed to pull it off the wall.

Hmm. We probably shouldn't exit through the front door. Even though most people probably realized everything was staged, it seemed preferable to exit where we wouldn't be so obvious. Proudly carrying her orange trophy, Trixie led the way through a narrow corridor to a kitchen that was obviously intended for restaurant use. I lifted my lantern and turned around. No freezers or refrigerators. No ovens, either, but I spied a fancy grill. Whoever was renovating the kitchen hadn't finished the job.

I couldn't get over how good the interior of the hotel looked. It was almost ready for business.

Trixie ran to a back door, her nose to the floor. I opened the door, and we exited onto a small stone patio that led to a steep stairway with confining walls on both sides.

No one had bothered to update this area of the hotel. An ominous feeling overcame me that I couldn't shake off. The stairs looked like something out of a horror movie.

Trixie turned and barked ferociously at something behind me. The door slammed open, and in the dark shadows, I made out a man raising snakes in the air.

My scream must have echoed all the way down the mountain.

Twelve

I staggered backward. Trixie quit barking to wag her tail and jump on the man.

He lifted off his mask. "Gotcha!"

I slid down the wall to the cold stone landing, my heart pounding. "I hate you, Holmes Richardson."

In spite of my current feelings, his laugh was music to my ears. Holmes had been part of my summertime trio when I was growing up. Along with my cousin, Josh, we had worked at the Sugar Maple Inn every summer as kids. Truth be told, I'd never quite outgrown the crush I had on the first boy who ever kissed me. But Holmes lived in Chicago now and was engaged to be married. Still, one good look at his crooked grin, and I was hooked all over again.

He ruffled his sandy hair with the snakes. "Ugh. That mask is hot."

"Please tell me the snakes aren't real."

He laughed again and shook one hand, causing the snakes to dance. "Naw, they're pieces of plastic attached to gloves. Amazing how lifelike thcy seem from a distance."

Trixie barked at him and jumped up to examine the snakes more closely.

He offered me his hand to help me up.

"I'm not touching that!"

He grinned at me and slid the glove off. "When did you turn into such a city slicker? What happened to the girl who ran through the woods without a care and chased her cousin with a live crawdad?"

I scooped Trixie's orange toy off the ground, grasped Holmes's hand, and stood up. I dusted myself off, laughing. "I'd forgotten about that! Too many years in the city, I guess."

He tried the door. "Aw, rats. We're locked out." He took my lantern. "Well, come on then. Heard you were the one who found Mallory last night." He bent his head forward. "I didn't really know her, but Mark's a good guy. I feel terrible for him."

"Everyone has said very nice things about him." *Not so much about her, though.* I didn't say it out loud. But it did strike me as odd. Usually people only said flattering things about people who had died.

We rounded the hotel to the pedestrian zone. Orange lights that looked like flames burned in the street lamps, casting an eerie aura over Wagtail.

"There they are!" cried Oma. She, Rose, and Doc appeared to be waiting for us.

"That was a very nice performance," she whispered when she hugged me. She reached her arms out. "Holmes! I'm so happy to see you!"

Rose, Holmes's grandmother, still wore her

witch outfit. She marched over to him and hissed, "What are you doing out here with the mask and snake gloves? Tuck them away so no one will notice! Quick!"

Holmes had no place to put them. He removed his jacket and draped it over them. "Better?"

Rose wasn't fooling me. Holmes could do no wrong in her eyes. "Why didn't you leave them there?" she demanded.

"We got locked out."

Rose's eyes narrowed. "Did you see anything weird in the hotel?"

"No! Why would you even ask that?" I asked.

"Because the police felt it necessary to search the hotel. Not to mention that it *is* a bit of a coincidence that Mallory died exactly where Obadiah did. I'm relieved that the hotel wasn't involved. The big gala will be there, and I don't need Dave throwing up any obstacles."

Doc smiled at her. "Rose, don't worry so much. I told you nothing untoward happened there. The death of that poor young woman has us all on edge."

"The hotel surprised me inside. I thought it was run-down," I whispered to Rose.

"Parts of it are. A good portion has been completely renovated. People keep buying it, but it's cursed."

"The renovations cost more than they expected, and they run out of money?" I could imagine how expensive it would be to refurbish an entire hotel, even a small one.

"No, it's the curse. All the owners go broke," said Doc. "Hiram cursed it."

I sucked in a deep breath. Rose believed in curses and ghosts and things that went bump in the night. "Oh, right," I chuckled. I wasn't sure, though, if Doc believed that. Was there anyone in this town who didn't believe in ghosts and curses?

A few of the ghost-walking participants still lingered. Rose and Holmes answered their questions about Obadiah and Becca. Evidently, visitors didn't believe the story could be true.

Felix, Casper, and Brian made their way over to us.

"Cool story!" said Felix. "Sad—but most ghost stories are. I can just imagine every one of their ghosts roaming the hotel and trying to set things right."

"We lost you," said Brian. "I couldn't find you in that crowd."

I scrambled for a response. They evidently didn't realize that I had played the part of Becca. "There *were* a lot of people."

Brian stared at the dark inn. "I can't wait to get inside. This is going to be terrific. Hey, Holly, wanna come with us tonight?"

"I think I'll pass. It's probably not good to have too many unbelievers present."

Brian locked his eyes on mine. "Scared? I'll protect you."

"Thanks, I'm sure you would."

"Knock it off, Brian. She clearly has a boyfriend." Felix cocked his head toward Holmes. "Sorry, Brian has a thing for you."

Like a schoolboy, Brian slammed his friend in the arm.

"Oh." If he thought Holmes and I were an item, maybe that was a good thing. It might discourage his interest. "Thanks for inviting me, Brian." Time to change the subject. "So you'll be hunting for the ghosts of Becca, Hiram, and Obadiah?"

Felix closed his eyes and muttered, "Oh man. I hate snakes."

I tried to be upbeat for his sake, even though I shared his aversion. "Ghost snakes," I teased. "They can't bite. And if they could, I'm pretty sure they wouldn't have any venom."

Felix laughed and nodded. "I hope not. With any luck we'll see Becca. I think I'd rather deal with a panther than snakes, ghostly *or* real."

"Will you be taping the rattling sounds in room three?"

"Absolutely. It's amazing how many people in Wagtail have told us they heard them. Some have seen Obadiah or Hiram, but it seems like everyone has seen Becca or Dr. Wraith."

"Is Eva going with you tonight?"

Brian pointed his nose up in the air and

mimicked her. "I must observe the Apparition Apprehenders at all times lest they use subterfuge to perpetrate a hoax."

Even Oma laughed.

"We better head back to the inn to get our stuff. It's getting close to our witching hour." Felix waved as they ambled away.

Officer Dave leaned against a street lamp watching them. He strolled over to us, his hands in his pockets. "Evening, Liesel, Rose, Doc. That went very well, I think."

"Yes, I am quite pleased," said Oma. "And our careful timing seems to be working, too. People are heading for the center of town. They'll be going to restaurants and bars for dessert and drinks. The merchants will be very happy."

"Dave," I said, "could I have a word with you somewhere private later on tonight?"

Oma raised an eyebrow at me. Quite loudly she announced, "Rose, aren't we due at the Blue Boar?"

I wanted to crawl into a hole. "Maybe you could come by the inn whenever it's convenient?"

If Holmes had the same reaction as Oma, he didn't show it and gladly walked back to the inn with Trixie and me.

It was silent as a tomb when we entered the Sugar Maple Inn. With the TV crew and the Apparition Apprehenders out for the night, it felt as though the place belonged just to us.

Twinkletoes raced down the stairs, mewing nonstop.

I swung her up into my arms. "Too quiet for you? I think you like all the attention the guests give you."

Holmes built a fire in the sitting room to take off the chill, and Twinkletoes stretched out to her full length in front of it. We found a bottle of white wine and leftover roast beef in the fridge of the private kitchen. Holmes and I worked side by side making sandwiches with a touch of horseradish. While I popped one in the panini maker to heat it, Holmes hit the refrigerator again.

"I miss rooting through this fridge to find good stuff," said Holmes. "Most of the time my refrigerator only has leftover takeout and stale bread in it."

"Did you learn nothing from Oma? Never keep bread in the refrigerator. Something about the cool temperature crystallizing the starch makes it stale."

"That explains a lot."

"Either eat it or freeze it."

"Yes, ma'am. Hey, I found something that looks like pumpkin cake with cream cheese frosting. This is definitely on our menu tonight. And there's a salad with shrimp and avocados. Nice appetizer." He brought them to the island. "You have it made living here. I hadn't thought about the food angle."

"When are *you* coming back to Wagtail for good, Mr. I-have-to-visit-every-month?"

He rubbed the back of his neck. "I'm proud of you, Holly. It's a big step to leave your job and your life in D.C. to move back here. How's that guy you were dating?"

"Don't know. Haven't heard a peep from him since I moved. That ought to tell me something, huh?" I slid the second sandwich into the panini maker.

"You deserve someone who loves you. I'm surprised he didn't load up and move here himself."

"Move? Are you kidding? He couldn't even bring himself to call me. For all he knows, I slid off the side of the mountain into a ravine."

Holmes leaned against the counter. Trixie stretched up and placed her front paws on his thighs. He massaged her ears gently. "I wish I had a dog. You know what I miss the most? We get a lot of snow in Chicago, but I always loved walking through Wagtail at night in the snow. It's so clean and quiet and magical. Like walking in a snow globe." He snorted. "That sounded stupid, didn't it?"

I shook my head. "No. It didn't. There *is* something special about Wagtail. It's quaint and intimate. I hardly knew my neighbors in Arlington. We passed each other once in a while, but everyone was always in a hurry to go someplace. Life is more relaxed here."

"It would be hard to give up my job."

"You could develop the land that your family owns."

His head snapped up. I spied an eager glint in his eyes. "Every time I come to Wagtail I wonder if . . . What am I saying? I can't see my fiancée living here. She's not the type. It's complicated."

"What do you mean?" I held my breath, hoping against hope that his relationship was cruising to a swift demise. Not that I would ever wish him ill. But I wouldn't mind if Holmes were officially available again.

"Aw, nothing. She's just a city girl. Is that ready yet?"

"Load up the tray. I'll bring the wineglasses and Trixie's dinner." What else could I say? Maybe I could weasel more out of him later.

We settled by the fire. I tore a piece of roast beef into tiny pieces for Twinkletoes and offered Trixie a bowl of cheesy chunky chicken that I had nuked to take the chill off. It looked like chunks of chicken with carrots, barley, and tiny bits of cheddar cheese and apples.

She wolfed it as fast as she could and trained her eyes on me.

I accommodated her with a little piece of roast beef.

"So what happened with your job back in D.C.?" asked Holmes. "You never told me why you quit. You were a fund-raiser, right?"

"Have you ever heard of Ron Koontz?"

"Nope." Holmes bit into his sandwich.

"I guess he didn't make the headlines everywhere. Ron set up a Ponzi scheme and stole millions from people. Retirement funds, college funds, family fortunes. I knew about him because some of our donors were impacted."

"That must have been rough on them."

"It's kind of a double whammy. Not only do they lose their money, but they feel, well, kind of stupid for being taken in. Anyway, my boss had been working with an anonymous donor for a while."

"Anonymous? I thought most people liked to be recognized for their generosity."

"You'd be surprised. A lot of philanthropists keep a low profile. My boss kept the name close to his vest, which was fine. But one day, a communication crossed my desk with a big old *RK* as the signature. All kinds of red flags jumped up in my head, so I did a little sleuthing and, sure enough, Mr. Anonymous was none other than Ron Koontz of the Ponzi scheme."

Holmes set down his sandwich and stared at me. "He stole so much money that he *gave* it away? That's so twisted!"

"No kidding. So I confronted my boss, who made it clear that he wasn't going to do a thing about it, so I quit. He would have fired me anyway. It was a huge ethical problem. I felt that

155

the people who received the money should know it was tainted."

"Exactly. And the people who lost their money through his fraud deserved to have it back!"

"I might have, uh, dropped a hint with someone a little higher than my boss."

"Good for you."

"They had to know! It could have put the whole company in jeopardy. Koontz was quite a character. Now that he and his coconspirators are in the pokey you'd think the saga would have ended, but they planned ahead and bought a bunch of rare collectors' items. His wife had most of them stashed at their house, but they can't find some diamonds. They're called ghost diamonds because they've been missing and sold underground for so long that no one knows for sure if they're real or fictional. Can you imagine? They're supposed to be worth a few million dollars. If they exist!"

Holmes moaned. "Guys like that are slick. I wouldn't put it past them to have made up ghost diamonds to put investigators off the trail of something else. Hey, you forgot the best part of that story."

"Huh?"

"That they fired your boss and offered you his job." Holmes toasted me with his wineglass.

I smiled at the memory. Holmes had been in Wagtail with me when I received the good news.

"That was icing on the cake, for sure. But you know, as much as I liked that job, I don't think I'm going to miss it one bit."

Footsteps approached in the hallway.

Trixie perked her ears. Twinkletoes turned her head. The four of us waited for the person to appear.

Dave walked right by us.

"Want a snack?" I called.

"You two look pretty cozy." Dave gazed at us in surprise. "Hope I'm not interrupting anything."

"Don't be silly. Are you off duty? Can you drink wine?" I asked.

"I think I'll stick with water for now. It's pretty quiet out in the pedestrian zone, but that can turn on me fast as people get loaded."

I clambered to my feet, heated another sandwich in the panini maker, and brought it to the Dogwood Room with a tall glass, a bottle of ice-cold water, and extra plates, napkins, and forks.

Dave sat by the fire talking with Holmes. I handed him his sandwich and water.

"Thanks, Holly." He poured water into the glass. "So what's up?"

"I wanted to talk to you about Mallory's death."

Holmes sipped his wine. "What's to talk about? I thought she drowned."

"Doc Kilgore has pretty much put this to bed." Dave's lips mashed together. He spoke softly as though he didn't want anyone to accidentally overhear. "I've always liked Doc. He's a cut-and-dried kind of guy, and I appreciate that. He tells it like it is. But this time, I don't agree with him."

Thirteen

"I know Doc Kilgore has seen a lot of drowning victims over the years. He's an old hand at this," said Dave. "From what I understand, drownings are often tough calls if there aren't any signs of a struggle to indicate the victim was attacked."

"Attacked? I don't get it. If there's water in her lungs, she drowned. What's difficult about that?" Holmes bit into his sandwich.

"Why was Mallory there in the middle of the night to begin with?" I asked.

"Wasn't she drunk?" asked Holmes. "That's what Grandma Rose said."

Dave swallowed a bite of sandwich. "I saw Mallory at the bonfire. She was hanging all over that guy Felix. Then she joined the ghost hunters at Hair of the Dog. Val said Mallory put away some pretty powerful drinks. The ghost hunters finished up the night at Hair of the Dog. They closed it down at two in the morning. No one remembers Mallory being obnoxious or having trouble walking. I'm not saying she wasn't intoxicated, but I'm not convinced she was falling down drunk, if you know what I mean."

"Val told me Mallory drank quite a few Zombie Brains," I added. "She didn't watch her carefully, but Val didn't think Mallory was staggering."

"Oof! I've had those Zombie Brains. They're potent! But not everyone shows it when they've had a lot to drink," said Holmes. "I had a friend in college who could swill all night and didn't even have the decency to sway when he walked."

"Doc did say that Mallory fell and hit her head, so she might have been confused," Dave pointed out.

"Okay, then answer this," I said. "The bar closed at two. I found her around four twenty in the morning. Where was she for two hours in the middle of the night? And why was she dressed like the ghost of Becca Wraith?"

Holmes had stopped eating. "Hold everything. Are you two suggesting someone murdered Mallory?"

Dave raised his eyebrows and tilted his head.

"Oh, come on. Doc and the EMTs realized that she'd drowned. Wouldn't they have been suspicious if they saw anything incriminating?" asked Holmes.

"Of course they would. Of *Holly!*"

I nearly slid out of my seat. "You're not serious." It came out in a whisper.

Dave rolled his eyes. "Cut them some slack. It was peculiar enough that Mallory was there, but you were with her in the middle of the night for no good reason."

I jumped up. "I had a very good reason. Trixie and Twinkletoes were running loose. It's not like I'm in the habit of sneaking around in the dark of night! Nor am I in the habit of having late-night rendezvous with strangers. I'd only just met Mallory. Did they think I was going to discuss wedding plans with her in the middle of the night?"

"Calm down, Holly. You're not really a suspect," said Holmes. "Is she?"

"Not in my book."

"Thank you for believing in my character." My entire body shook with indignation. I sat down, still breathing heavily.

"Don't thank me. Thank your Aunt Birdie. She forced me to have coffee with her this morning, but she confessed her little scam to see how fast you would come to her aid."

So much for my stellar character.

"The way I see it, you might have had time to drown her, and you were certainly wet enough to have done it yourself"—Dave shook his head—"but by all accounts, I honestly believe that you barely knew Mallory."

Holmes met my eyes. "I suppose it's not likely she stopped to visit a friend. If she was drunk, maybe she fell asleep somewhere or was unconscious after she hit her head."

"She probably went back to Mark's to change clothes. She was dressed in that Becca Wraith getup when I found her. She sure wasn't wearing it at the bonfire."

"How long would that take? Fifteen minutes?" asked Dave.

Holmes laughed. "None of the women I know can change clothes that fast."

I punched him playfully. "Wasn't she staying with Mark? I don't know where he lives, but she would have had to walk home, change, and walk back. Why would she do that? Why didn't she just go to bed? Why dress up as a ghost in the middle of the night? If she had done it earlier in the day I would have thought it was some kind of promotional thing. You know, wandering around town in the hope that a few people might see her."

Dave set his water glass down. "Maybe she was supposed to meet up with someone who was playing the role of Hiram or Obadiah. It wouldn't surprise me if you're right about it being a promotional stunt. Luciano or Rose would know who she was supposed to meet if that's the case. Or maybe someone was with her."

I held my breath. Dave's expression was grave. I had a bad feeling I knew who he meant. "Such as?" I asked as casually as I could.

"Aw, come on, Holly. You know as well as anybody that she left with two people—Zelda and Felix."

"Zelda?" spouted Holmes. "Not a chance. Zelda wouldn't kill a housefly."

"That doesn't change the facts, Holmes. I have to deal in facts. Cold, hard truths."

"Where was Mark?" I asked. "Did he call anyone to report her missing?"

"He acted pretty surprised when I knocked on his door this morning."

Holmes cut a piece of the cake. "I'm confused. Can't you just declare a murder investigation?"

"We *are* investigating. We didn't find anything of interest in the hotel. It doesn't help, of course, that Doc is the medical examiner and doesn't think anything criminal happened. He claims she might have gotten tangled in that gown she was wearing."

"That's not implausible," I said. "It coiled around me when I was trying to pull her out of the water. But even if it did, it seems like she could have sat up or stood or done something to lift her head out of the water."

Dave had stopped eating. While he was respected in the community, he had some issues with Wagtailites who remembered him as a cute little boy and didn't give him the deference he deserved.

"They're fighting you on this, aren't they?" I helped myself to a piece of pumpkin cake, which I was certain I now deserved, if only to calm my frazzled nerves.

"Mallory's death doesn't pass the smell test for me. I could use your help, Holly. Not yours so much, Holmes. Somehow I don't think you'll hear about this back in Chicago. Holly, would you keep an ear to the ground? You're liable to overhear the ghost hunters talking about Mark. Sounds like a few of them know him pretty well."

"You think Mark killed Mallory?"

"Don't go jumping to conclusions, but we always look at husbands and boyfriends first."

"Then how about that Felix guy Mallory was hanging on that night?" asked Holmes. "Maybe he wanted more, and she refused."

"Nooo," I whined. "Not Felix. He's far too nice."

Holmes laughed at me. "What is it with you and nerdy guys? I thought women liked tall, rugged cowboy types."

"That counts you out, doesn't it?" I teased. "Sure, Dave. I'll pass along anything that I hear." But as I spoke, I couldn't help wondering if he was really asking me to spy on Zelda.

When Holmes and Dave left, Trixie and I went up to bed. As usual, the TV was blaring in my quarters. But this time there was no sign of Twinkletoes. I turned off the TV and heard hissing. Hiram must have been on my mind, because the first thing I thought of was snakes.

I stopped cold. Did rattlers hiss? I thought they

only rattled. Oh, what did I know about snakes? Less than nothing.

Trixie barked in my little dining room. The hissing grew stronger and more frequent. Staying a good distance away, I kneeled on the floor thinking this was exactly how a person could be bitten on the nose. Twinkletoes nestled by the hidden pet door, hissing at something that flicked through it.

A low rumbling sound spooked me. It morphed into a high-pitched yowl.

I stumbled to my feet in a hurry and grabbed Twinkletoes's favorite toy—a stick attached to a string with a pompom hanging on the end. I wiggled the pompom in front of her to lure her away from the door. Jiggling the stick to make the pompom dance, I slowly backed up.

Twinkletoes couldn't resist. She pounced on it and claimed her pompom, seizing it in her mouth and marching off with it, as proud as if she had caught a mouse.

Without warning, Mrs. Mewer flew through the door. That explained all the hissing. Clearly, Mrs. Mewer had found her way into the hidden stairway, an excellent and quiet hiding place, but Twinkletoes had prevented her from entering our apartment. The proverbial catfight!

At least Mrs. Mewer wasn't lost. I glanced at the clock. Almost midnight. I hadn't gotten much sleep the night before, so I didn't relish the notion of trekking over to the Wagtail Springs Hotel to tell Eva the good news. Maybe she had taken her cell phone. I called Casey at the reception desk for Eva's number and dialed. Just my luck—Eva didn't answer. Either the Wagtail Springs Hotel was one of Wagtail's dead zones or they had turned off their phones so they wouldn't disrupt the ghost hunt.

I rubbed my eyes, no doubt smearing my mascara. I had to tell Eva. She'd been so distraught. If I were in her shoes, I would want to know. There just wasn't any way around it. I had to walk over and tell her. My glance fell on the overstuffed armchairs. I longed to sink into one and put up my feet. But that would be wrong, wrong, wrong. I collected Trixie's leash and a jacket.

Mrs. Mewer watched me carefully but I was able to step on her leash so she couldn't dash away from me. Picking it up, I cooed gently, "I'm going to take you back to your room, Mrs. Mewer. And in a few hours, Eva will be back for a long nap with you. How does that sound?"

She walked with me willingly, pausing now and then, as cats do, to sniff something of particular interest. At Eva's door, I paused to pull out my newly minted master keys but found the door had been left open. Although I knew Eva was at the Wagtail Springs Hotel with the ghost hunters, I knocked anyway and called out her name. She didn't answer, so I switched on a light.

Trixie accompanied Mrs. Mewer and me inside. I locked the cat door to the balcony and made sure Mrs. Mewer had food and water. Trixie made a beeline for Mrs. Mewer's food dish.

"No, no, no. That's not yours." I snapped Trixie's leash on her and removed the leash from Mrs. Mewer's collar.

"Eva will be back in a few hours," I told her. "You be good and stay here."

She was probably worn out from her day on the lam in the inn. Chances were that she would eat and then take a long nap.

I locked the door behind us and tried the knob to be doubly sure Mrs. Mewer would be safe. As we walked though the inn, I pulled on my warm jacket.

We swung by the registration desk, where I updated Casey about Mrs. Mewer. In minutes, Trixie and I were out in the cold, strolling along the pedestrian zone, which wasn't nearly as quiet as I had expected.

A number of restaurants were still doing a lively business. Music blared from one. Another was packed with quieter patrons sipping from large mugs. Dogs and cats lounged comfortably at their feet.

Trixie tugged at the leash to give a wide berth to a giant, leering pumpkin. I couldn't blame her. Witches and vampires gazed at us as they went about their business.

At the end of the pedestrian zone, I paused to look up at the foreboding Wagtail Springs Hotel. I had expected some lights to be on. Why hadn't I brought a flashlight? Would they all be upset with me if I walked inside and shouted? Probably.

Downstairs on the right, in the room allegedly cursed by the locking door and the sound of rattlesnakes, a white image shimmered briefly in the window. I blinked, and it was gone. Probably one of the ghost hunters.

A voice in the darkness said, "That was Becca Wraith. I saw her, too."

Fourteen

Trixie pulled on her leash in her eagerness to sniff the speaker.

"Hi, puppy!"

In the darkness, I could barely make out Mark Belinski crouching to pet Trixie. "Your white fur makes you look like a little ghost in the night."

"I'm so sorry about Mallory."

Mark stood up and peered at me. "You took over playing Becca Wraith's ghost for Mallory."

"That's right."

"You did it quite well. It's a pity they can't schedule the real Becca to appear like she just did for us."

How was I supposed to respond to that? "It was probably one of the ghost hunters."

"With long white hair? I don't think so. Not even Brian would go that far. We just saw Becca's ghost."

Oof. I should probably pretend to believe him. Or just not disagree with him, at any rate. What was he doing out here anyway? "Are you waiting for the Apparition Apprehenders?"

"No."

He didn't offer more information. But then, he had just lost Mallory. He probably couldn't sleep. Maybe he didn't want to be home alone. Or maybe he just wanted to walk. It *was* sort of soothing to be out in the night air.

"I should be in there with them, but Mr. Luciano very kindly gave me some time off."

Of course. How stupid of me. No one would expect him to work yet.

"I need to speak to one of them. Would they be upset if I went inside to find her?"

Mark's head swiveled toward me. His tone was even and calm when he spoke. "Eva? You can go inside. C'mon. I'll go with you. I'd rather be working than thinking about . . ."

He led the way up the steps.

The door screeched like one in a horror movie when he opened it. Trixie readily entered, and I followed.

Did we dare turn on a light? Or would that scare

away the ghosts? *What was I thinking? There were no ghosts.* But they would blame the absence of ghosts on me if I did the wrong thing. "Can we turn on a light?"

"Better not."

I listened for the sound of footsteps. Where were they?

The beam of a flashlight landed on my face. "Holly!" It was a loud whisper. Casper's fur almost shimmered in the dark. I could see why Weimaraners were called ghost dogs. Felix ambled toward us. "Mark! I'm glad you came after all. What are you doing here, Holly? I thought you weren't interested."

"I found Mrs. Mewer. I thought Eva should know so she wouldn't worry."

"Hey, that's great! She'll be really happy. Come on upstairs with me."

We followed him up the steps. He led us along a corridor to Eva and Brian, who were clearly surprised to see us.

"Eva, I bring good news. Mrs. Mewer has been found and is safely in your room, waiting for you to come home."

Eva launched herself at me and hugged me as though I were a long-lost friend. When she released me, she held her hand over her nose and sniffled. "Thank you, thank you! I'm so grateful. Would you guys mind if I took a little break to check on her?"

"Sure, go ahead," said Felix. "We'll take care of things."

Eva started for the stairs and Mark followed.

"Holly! Come quick," Brian hissed at me.

I looked back at Eva just in time to see Mark slide his hand into hers. Uh-oh. That didn't seem like a bereaved boyfriend to me.

Trixie and I returned to the ghost hunters. They clustered in a dark room.

"Obadiah," called Brian in a loud voice, "if you are here, turn on the light."

We waited in silence. Even though I didn't think Obadiah or other spirits were in the hotel, I had to admit that it was creepy standing in the dark room of the old building. After all, there must have been a nugget of truth to the tale about Obadiah. And even if there wasn't, many people had slept there, and given that it belonged to Dr. Wraith at one point, patients had probably died there, too.

And then, a flashlight on the floor flicked on.

I jerked in surprise. No one was touching it. I didn't see any strings or other gizmos attached. The light went out.

"Hiram," Brian intoned, "if you murdered Obadiah, turn the flashlight on again."

We waited in silence. Nothing happened. Just when I had given up, the light flicked on briefly. But there was no mistake that it had flashed on for a few seconds.

Brian picked up the flashlight and spoke to the

camera in hushed tones. "I can feel the evil in this room. There's no question that Hiram haunts this hotel. Looks like we finally have proof that Hiram killed Obadiah. After all these years, Hiram has confessed. To clear his conscience? To make his peace? Only Hiram knows that."

Okay, that was a bit of a leap. I didn't think anyone would consider the flashlight undeniable proof. Still, the flashlight *had* turned on and off all by itself.

Brian looked over at me. "Do you know why the room with the snakes is locked?"

I grinned. *Probably because he locked it.* "Haven't a clue."

"Shh," said Felix.

There was no mistaking the sound of footsteps downstairs.

"It's probably Mark."

But before I finished speaking, the ghost hunters tore out of the room and hurried downstairs, leaving Trixie and me in total darkness without a flashlight. Swell.

I felt my way along the corridor. By the time we reached the top of the steps, Felix had thoughtfully returned with a flashlight. "Sorry about that. C'mon Ghost, we're heading this way."

"Was it Mark?"

"No, I don't know where he went. But it will be interesting to hear if we got anything on the EVP recorder."

"The what?"

"Electronic Voice Phenomena recorder. It picks up sounds."

I bit back a grin. "Really? Ghost sounds?"

"You'd be surprised what you can hear some-times."

"Felix, you're a reasonable guy. How can a ghost make a sound?"

"Haven't you ever heard footsteps when you know no one is there?"

I chose my words carefully. I didn't want to be rude. "That usually means someone *is* there."

His chin lifted, and he smiled at me. "Not always."

Back at the inn, I snuggled under my down comforter, glad to finally get some rest, but at three in the morning, Trixie started jumping on and off my bed, whimpering. She trotted in restless circles. I groaned, but quickly felt guilty. If she had to go, she had to go. I should be grateful she didn't leave me an unpleasant surprise in the apartment.

I slid on my plush Sugar Maple Inn bath-robe and opened the door for Trixie. She and Twinkletoes bounded down to the second floor faster than the speed of light. By the time I got there, Trixie was running along the corridor with her nose to the ground.

I paused, wondering if she really needed to

relieve herself. Why had she stopped at the second floor?

Someone screamed.

Trixie turned around, raced past me, and scampered down to the main level with Twinkletoes hot on her heels.

I dashed along behind them as fast as I could and came to an abrupt halt. Eva stood at the bottom of the stairs. Her hands covered her nose and mouth in horror.

I followed her line of sight. In the ancient mirror over the sitting room mantel, a face shimmered. It was a weak image, but there was no doubt in my mind that it was Mallory.

Fifteen

Mallory smiled as she had only days ago in this very room. Lavender earrings dangled from her ears. Her face morphed to anger and grew much larger.

Eva grabbed my arm, and Mallory disappeared. "Did you see it?" she asked breathlessly.

"I did. Eva! You're shaking!"

The poor woman quivered. Surely she must have seen things like that before. It couldn't be real. Besides, if Mallory's ghost had really made an appearance, wouldn't Twinkletoes and Trixie have noticed? The two of them sniffed the Halloween decorations as though nothing had occurred.

I led Eva to a sofa in the sitting room. She sat down, her chest heaving with each breath.

"I'm sure there's a logical explanation."

She nodded. "There must be. It just caught me by surprise." She twisted and studied the mirror. "Is that the same mirror that was there before?"

"I think so." Looked like it to me.

The edges of Eva's mouth pulled back. She stood up, still somewhat shaky, drew a deep breath, and walked to the mirror. Reaching up, she touched it gingerly. "You don't see anything in the mirror now, do you?"

"No."

Eva tilted her head to examine it from the bottom and the side. She turned toward me, licking her lips, and demanded, "What did you see?"

Somehow I hated to tell her. I had a feeling she wouldn't have been quite so upset if the image had been of Becca Wraith. "Mallory," I murmured.

Her eyes narrowed, and she peered at something over my shoulder.

I whipped around. I didn't see anything unusual, just Halloween decorations and the stairs. Trixie sniffed merrily at the bases of the pumpkins. "Did you see her again?"

"No. I'm looking for another mirror, something

that might have thrown the reflection this way."

She scanned the room. "It's easy to manipulate a video to create a ghost image in a mirror. Any average kid can do it. But it had to project from this area."

Eva strolled through the sitting room, eyeing everything. She finally sat down next to me. "I don't know why I'm so terribly out of sorts about this. I've seen a lot of strange things, and they always have explanations. Sound, reasonable, concrete explanations. Well, mostly they do."

"Maybe it's hitting too close to home this time?"

Her head jerked up. "What do you mean by that?"

I spoke as soothingly as I could. "Mallory was someone you knew. It's more unnerving to see her face."

"Oh. Yes, I suppose you're correct."

"Have you ever seen a face in a mirror before?"

Eva tsked. "Oh heavens. It's the most common schoolboy trick you can imagine." She turned her eyes toward the mirror. "Except that mirror doesn't look like it has been tampered with." She rose and walked to the bottom of the stairs.

"What are you doing?"

"I'm trying to recreate it. Maybe I can trigger it into appearing again."

I joined her.

Eva moved around and waved her arms but nothing she did brought the ghostly image of

Mallory back to the mirror. We tried recreating the event. I jogged up the stairs and rushed down. Still no Mallory.

"Eva, could I make you a cup of tea? Maybe that would calm your nerves."

"It's not my nerves that are the problem. Someone monkeyed with that mirror"—her eyes grew wide—"on purpose." Suddenly she switched gears. "Goodness, look at the time. I have to get some sleep. I'm so sorry to have disturbed you, Holly."

We said good night, and I watched her walk toward her room. "Trixie!" I called in a hushed voice. "Let's go out while we're down here."

She sped ahead of me toward the reception area to play with Casper. Casey chatted with Grayson and Felix.

Suddenly painfully aware that I was wearing a bathrobe, I hustled Trixie outside. She complied quickly, and I had no choice but to walk by the ghost hunters again.

"How did it go tonight?" I asked.

Felix smiled at me. "Great!"

I coaxed Trixie away from Casper and up the back stairway from reception to the second floor. We walked through the silent hallway but heard hushed voices as we approached the large stairwell in the middle of the building.

I peeked over the railing in time to see Eva opening the front door for Mark.

"Did he follow you?" she asked.

"I think I ditched him."

She seized his hand and pulled him toward the bottom of the staircase. I knew I shouldn't eavesdrop, but I did anyway. I picked up Trixie so she wouldn't give me away and stepped back, hopefully out of their line of sight.

In a soft voice, Eva told Mark about seeing Mallory's image in the mirror.

"Hey, you're the one who doesn't believe in this stuff. You think she came back to haunt us?" It sounded as though he was gently teasing her.

Their voices faded, and not a minute too soon, because I heard footsteps on the back stairway at the other end of the hall. Probably Grayson and Felix.

I set Trixie on the floor and hurried down the grand staircase and over to the library. Peering through the archway I wondered what I would say if Mark and Eva caught me spying on them. I needn't have worried. The door to Eva's room had just closed, and the lock on the other side slid into place.

As Trixie and I started back up to bed, I caught a glimpse of Grayson scurrying to the other end of the second floor. We arrived too late to see where he had gone, but we heard a door close softly.

In the morning, I was up at dawn. I wasn't much of an early riser, but I didn't want to be a slacker.

Besides, I hoped to have a word with Casey before he left after his long night shift.

Low clouds clung to Wagtail. I hoped they might burn off, but the view from my French doors was gloomy. In a way, it suited my spirits, because Mallory's death weighed on me.

The only bright spot was finding piping hot tea, a chocolate croissant, and treats for Trixie and Twinkletoes in my kitchen. I shuddered to imagine what Mr. Huckle thought on finding my boxes had erupted. It was getting worse by the day as I ripped open boxes to look for things but didn't bother to unpack them. Maybe I could steal a few hours to get some serious unpacking done today.

In the spirit of the season, I dressed in a bright yellow top, black trousers, and a scarf the colors of fall leaves. A little bit corny, but I thought it worked.

Twinkletoes followed me as I dressed, winding around my ankles and jumping up on everything I approached.

"I get it. You're hungry." I tickled her cheek, and she rubbed her head against my hand. "What will it be this morning? I walked into the kitchen with her dancing ahead. "Chicken delight or roast turkey?" She looked up at me, the tip of her tail undulating in anticipation. "I hope you're in the mood for turkey." I spooned turkey chunks in a creamy gravy into her bowl.

Twinkletoes dug in, lapping the gravy first.

Trixie inched closer, her little black nose quivering.

"Trixie," I cautioned. "Come on, let's go." I carried Trixie's leash in case I needed it.

The aromas of coffee and bacon wafted all the way up the stairwell to the third floor. Trixie scampered downstairs much faster than I could. In spite of the early hour, a sprinkling of visitors and their dogs had found their way to the dining area. Most had settled near the panoramic window overlooking the lake and the mountains. A mist rose off the water. A few brave souls had taken their coffee mugs out to the terrace.

The spectacular view of the lake and the mountains, not to mention the fabulous food, drew visitors who were staying elsewhere, as well as our in-house guests.

We turned left and headed for the registration desk.

When the door opened for an entering guest, Trixie took advantage of the situation and flew out the door.

I dashed after her. "Trixie!" But the sweet little girl had gone straight to the doggy restroom. She trotted right back to me, happy as could be. "Thanks for being a good girl." We had only been in Wagtail a few days, but she was catching onto our routine. Not that we had much of one yet.

She followed me inside. Luckily, no guests were

around, so I could speak privately with Casey. Nevertheless, I used a hushed tone.

"Casey, do you remember the ghost hunters coming back to the inn the night before last?"

"Sure. I love those guys. They're really funny. Did you know they invited me to go with them? Rotten luck that I have to work the midnight shift."

"That's too bad. Let me know if they invite you again, and I'll cover for you for a few hours."

"Gosh. Thanks, Holly!"

"Think they were drunk when they came back that night?"

"I thought I wasn't supposed to rat on guests."

"You're not. But this is private between the two of us."

"Maybe a little bit. They were pretty loud."

"Were Mark and Mallory with them?"

A cloud of sadness passed over Casey's face. "Only Mark."

"Did he say anything? Like where he was going?"

"No. He went upstairs with the ghost hunting guys. Why are you asking me these questions? You sound like Officer Dave."

"Just one more. Did you see him leave?"

Casey cocked his head at me like an adorable puppy. "Come to think of it, I didn't see Mark leave. He must have gone out the front door."

"He must have," I said, but I wished I knew what time that was. He could have departed right away and ambushed Mallory or he might have spent the next two or so hours right here in the inn. It seemed very odd to me that he wouldn't have reported Mallory missing.

"Hey, Holly," Casey said, shooting me a mischievous look, "you forgot to ask me something."

"What?"

"Dave asked if they all came back to the inn together."

"Did they?"

"Nope. Felix stumbled in about forty-five minutes after the rest of them."

Sixteen

No wonder Dave woke Felix to question him the next morning. That didn't look good for Felix at all. But he was so nice. He couldn't be a killer!

Contemplating the implications, I headed for breakfast, Trixie by my side.

She ran straight to Shelley. My smart little girl knew exactly who served the food at the inn. Shelley laughed. "All the dogs remember me because I'm the lady with the food. Tea?"

"Yes, thanks! Is Oma up yet?"

"She ought to be here any minute."

I pulled out a chair at a table and sat down.

Trixie came to me when I called and tempted her with a mini treat.

Shelley paused as she walked by. "It's a little slow today. I guess the ghost hunters are sleeping in."

"They were out late last night."

"Country ham and Asiago cheese omelet is our special this morning."

That sounded almost healthy. "Wonderful. Do you have the same for dogs?"

Shelley eyed Trixie with a sly grin. "Of course."

Trixie wagged her tail. I blamed her insatiable appetite on her weeks alone, lost and hungry.

Shelley brought my tea immediately. Steam rose from the Sugar Maple Inn mug. "People all over town are still reporting seeing Becca Wraith's ghost in the Wagtail Springs Hotel this week."

I leaned toward her. "Shelley, that was me. I dressed as Becca for the ghost walk."

Shelley nodded her head but squinted at me. "Oh really? I suppose it was you they saw the night before the ghost walk, too?"

I whispered so no guests would overhear. "They're just trying to pump up business for the town by spreading silly rumors."

"You go right on believing that. I'm telling you, honey, you're in for a big revelation. Something will happen that will change your mind about ghosts."

She winked at me and grinned, so I knew we were good. But she was wrong.

I poured milk in my tea and stirred in sugar.

Trixie roamed a bit, her nose to the ground. Twinkletoes danced over to her and, after a quick investigatory sniff of the floor, playfully smacked Trixie, who promptly chased her through the pet door that led into the private kitchen.

Had Mark left the inn that way the night of Mallory's death, leaving the door unlocked? Was he the one who had let Trixie and Twinkletoes out? They might have zoomed past him underfoot. But why? Why not leave through the front door of the reception area? His behavior that night seemed peculiar. Wouldn't a normal person have departed by the door in the registration area where he came in? Why search through the inn for an alternate exit? Had he gone straight home? Was that why he never reported Mallory missing? Because he didn't go home? I was being silly. He could have returned home and fallen asleep, so he didn't notice her absence. Or not . . . He definitely spent some time with Eva last night.

Oma arrived as I ate my first bite of savory eggs with salty ham. What a perk to have a gourmet breakfast fixed for me every day. And no dishes to do, either!

Oma patted my shoulder and sat down. Gingersnap deftly avoided Trixie, who was snarfing the omelet in her bowl. The sweet golden retriever approached me from the other side, wagging her feathery tail. I stroked her broad head and cooed good morning greetings.

"I'm surprised you are already up. It was a long day for you yesterday. How is the unpacking coming?" asked Oma.

"I'm hoping to find a few hours for unpacking today. Eventually all those boxes will irritate me, but right now, I'd rather jump into my new job."

She rewarded me with a big smile. "I'm so glad you took me up on my offer. It is a very big weight off my back to have you here. Thank you for buying the lock yesterday. I'm quite impressed that you knew how to install it."

I gasped. *Clementine!* I'd forgotten all about her!

Oma frowned at me. "Is something wrong?"

"I saw Clementine yesterday."

"Yes? I always liked Clementine. You should invite her for lunch."

Shelley poured coffee for Oma, who took one look at my omelet and asked for the same.

"I will. She mentioned getting together. Do you know anything about her ex-husband? A man seemed to be following her."

"What?" Oma's spoon clanked against her coffee mug. "You are certain about this?"

"She hid from him and asked me if he was gone."

Oma gripped the mug. "I do not like this at all.

Her father is away at the dog show. You should go out to Fireside Farms this morning to check on her."

"I *could* just call. Excuse me." I rose from my seat and hustled to the office. The Wigginses' telephone number was in the Rolodex. I dialed and waited. No one answered. Not even a machine.

Shelley was serving omelets to Oma and Gingersnap when I returned.

Trixie raced to Gingersnap's meal to eat again. That was a good way to get bitten. I quickly fastened the leash on Trixie. She would have to learn to stay out of other dogs' food. "Be glad that Gingersnap is so nice. If you do that to the wrong dog, you'll be very sorry." I turned to Oma. "There's no answer at the Wiggins house."

Oma shook her head. "Go to see Clementine. On the telephone it is too easy to deny anything is wrong."

"What do you know about her husband?"

"I never met him personally, but I understand that they were very well off. Now I am worried about her alone out there on the farm. Perhaps you should check on her as soon as you finish breakfast."

A scant half hour later, I took off in one of the inn's electric golf carts. Orange and gold leaves still dotted the woods in between trees that had already shed their foliage. I recognized Fireside

Farm right away. The white fence with long crossed rails seemed to go on forever. The paddocks and sprawling fields were impressive. Even as a child I had been in awe of the massive white horse barn with a chandelier visible through a lofty window. Four white cupolas lined the long peak of the roof.

The Dutch Colonial manor house sat back off the road, surrounded by ancient oak trees. Double white pillars on either side of the front door soared up two stories. Clementine and I had loved playing on the second-floor balcony. I recalled the view between the pillars. The red brick sidewalk stretched almost out of sight between dogwood trees and perfectly manicured box-woods. Clementine's home had seemed like a palace to me, insulated from everything else in the world.

I turned down the long drive to the house, clutching Trixie's leash tightly in case she was tempted to leap off the golf cart and chase a rabbit or a squirrel. I parked, and we walked up to the white front door. It seemed to me that the boxwoods weren't quite as perfectly trimmed as I remembered. I banged the door knocker.

No one answered. I didn't hear footsteps inside. I tried again. Still no answer.

I turned and gazed at the sprawling farm. She was probably in the barn tending to the horses.

We walked around the side of the house and

across to the horse barn. Fallen leaves crunched under my feet.

"Stop! I have a gun, and I *will* shoot you."

I stopped in my tracks and shouted, "Clementine? Don't shoot! It's Holly!" I glanced around. "Where are you?"

Clementine peered over stacked hay bales. She stood up, let out a huge breath of air, and dusted off her trousers, holding a revolver by her right leg. "Sorry about that." Dark bags hung under her eyes, unmistakable against her delicate complexion.

"Is everything okay?"

"Yeah, sure. What brings you out here?" Her eyes darted around, as if she expected someone else to suddenly appear.

"Oma and I were concerned about you. Was that your ex-husband following you yesterday?"

Clementine stared at me blankly for a moment, as though she didn't know what to say. "Oh, that." She flipped her hand casually. "It was nothing."

It didn't look like nothing to me. "I see. That's why you're hiding behind hay bales with a gun."

Her mouth pulled to the side. "I don't know who he is." She heaved another sigh. "He just seems to turn up everywhere I go."

"Have you told Officer Dave? Maybe he can talk to the guy."

As soon as I mentioned Dave, Clementine appeared panicked. She waved a thin forefinger.

"No, no, no. Not Dave. I'm fine. I can handle this."

I was getting a little peeved with her. "Clementine, what's going on?"

"Okay, look"—she brushed her long ponytail back with her free hand—"he's someone I dated in college. He heard I was divorced and simply wouldn't take no for an answer. I thought he'd give up when I moved back to Wagtail, but he found me."

I crossed my arms over my chest. "You're such a lousy liar. If you dated him, why do you need a gun?"

"And you're a pill. Haven't you ever dated someone who seemed obsessed? I have kids to protect. What if he flips out?"

Hmm, okay. I could buy that. I didn't hear any wild children, though. "Are the kids in school?"

"I'm homeschooling them this year. Maybe next year too. I'm not sure yet. But I know my limits—they're in Wagtail, learning French this morning. Kids pick up languages so fast. I'd hate to miss this window of opportunity when it's easy for them. Outside of menus, my French is pretty limited."

I knew that feeling. "How about lunch at the inn today before you pick up the kids? Oma would love to see you."

Her expression softened. "Really? I would like that. You have no idea how much I would enjoy that."

"You sure you're okay out here alone? It's so quiet without any dogs around."

"No kidding! I'm used to them setting up an alarm if anyone comes on the property. Don't worry about me. I'm getting ready to muck out stalls. No one will mess with me if I have a pitchfork and horse poop at my disposal."

At least she hadn't lost her sense of humor.

Trixie and I drove back to the inn. I parked the golf cart and strode toward the reception entrance. The doors whooshed open automatically, and Trixie ran inside, but I stopped, stunned. I could hardly believe my eyes. Zelda was twirling a lock of long hair around her finger, coyly looking up into the face of the very man who had followed Clementine.

Seventeen

Trixie didn't share my hesitation. She ran to him, all wiggles and wags. He stooped to pet her, telling her what a cute dog she was.

I wanted to rip her away from him. Couldn't she sense that he was an enemy?

Zelda called me over. "Holly, this is Parker Colby. He's staying in *Swim*."

He was a guest at the inn? I reluctantly offered my hand, forcing a cheerful innkeeper's smile.

"Holly Miller. I hope you're enjoying your stay."

He still wore the day-old beard. He must have one of those shavers that leaves stubble on purpose. He'd ditched the army jacket for a brown leather one, though. Had I been asked, I would have said he needed a haircut, but given the stubble, I suspected he wore his hair tousled and tumbled intentionally.

"I certainly am. Everyone in Wagtail has been friendly and welcoming."

Really? Clementine's gun hadn't been exactly welcoming. I played innocent, though, and changed the subject fast. "What brings you to Wagtail?" This ought to be interesting.

He smiled, revealing white teeth that seemed a little too perfect. "I'm looking for a town to locate the headquarters of a new dog magazine. Wagtail seems like just the place."

I hadn't expected *that* response. Then again, who would admit that he was chasing an old girlfriend? Especially when he appeared to have been flirting with Zelda? He'd said it so smoothly. He hadn't stammered as though I'd caught him by surprise. He must have had that line prepared. I looked around. "Where's your dog?"

"I'm on my own this trip. But I hope to bring them soon." He flashed the pretty grin at me again. "Tell me, who would I speak with about real estate in Wagtail?"

Zelda jumped in, rattling off names and handing him a brochure.

Meanwhile, I was thinking that he played his game very well. I'd bet he had suckered everyone in town. A con man, perhaps? We needed to be wary. Would I be betraying Clementine somehow if I mentioned Parker to Dave? Of course, Dave was so busy with Mallory's death that . . .

I gave a little jolt that Parker noticed. What if Parker had something to do with Mallory's demise? I had no reason to think Mallory had any connection with Parker, but there was something smarmy about this guy, no matter how gorgeous he was.

With Clementine on my mind, I spent the next few hours taking care of business at the inn.

Shelley nabbed me when I passed through the dining area. "I just took three pumpkin raviolis with sage sauce down to your office for lunch. Clementine is there with your grandmother."

As if she understood, Trixie stood on her hind legs and gazed at Shelley with desperate eyes.

"Don't worry, little Trixie. There's a doggie version for you, too."

Trixie wagged her tail and raced along the corridor toward the office.

"How could she know?" I asked.

Shelley shrugged. "Beats me. They understand a lot more than we realize. Or maybe she smells the food."

I joined Oma, Clementine, and Trixie in the office. The sun had burned through the clouds, turning it into a beautiful fall day. Lunch had been set up on the small terrace outside, complete with an orange tablecloth and matching purple napkins printed with orange jack-o'-lanterns.

Clementine was carrying Twinkletoes in her arms upside down, like a baby. I could hear her purring.

"I'm so glad you came!"

"I think I'm suffering from mommy syndrome. It's a treat for me to talk with adults. Not to mention to eat with people who don't throw their vegetables."

Oma placed a gentle hand on Clementine's arm. "Enjoy these years, liebling. They go all too fast."

"I'm sure they do. It's tough herding triplets, though. Especially two rowdy boys."

We were about to take our seats at the table when Mr. Huckle entered carrying a tray laden with beverages.

Clementine rushed toward him. "Mr. Huckle!" She waited until he set the tray on the buffet. But when he turned around she embraced him, sobbing.

Their affection for each other was so evident that my eyes welled up, too.

"Now, now, Miss Clementine. We don't make

scenes in public." But no sooner was his back to us than he reached into a pocket for a handkerchief to wipe his own eyes.

He served hot coffee and iced tea while Trixie ran in frantic circles, impatiently waiting for her food.

Mr. Huckle served Trixie and winked at Clementine before he left.

"I miss him so much." Clementine sniffled. "I think it broke Daddy's heart to let him go." She looked at Oma. "Thank you for giving him a job. At his age, not many people would have taken a chance on him."

"He is wonderful!" Oma gushed. "The guests love him. And he's very classy in his uniform. It takes the whole inn up a notch. Yes?"

We caught up a little bit, with Oma asking questions about Clementine's children. In typical nosy fashion, she asked in a matter-of-fact conversational way, "Your husband—he was having an affair with another woman?"

Ouch. Nothing like coming right out and putting it on the table.

Clementine speared a piece of ravioli. "That's all behind me now."

Deftly avoided, Clementine.

But Oma didn't give up. "Holly tells me that a man is following you."

"Oh! It's nothing."

Oma focused on her and waggled a finger.

"Your father is away, and you need our help. Now you be truthful with me, Clementina."

Clementine beamed at her. "No one has called me that in, gosh, over a decade!"

"Don't change the subject. What is the story with this man? Who is he and what does he want with you?"

Clementine glanced at me. I just grinned. She clearly wasn't used to Oma's no-holds-barred interrogation style. I took another bite of the fabulous ravioli. I wasn't about to step in to save Clementine from Oma, though. The man was following her, and that couldn't be a good thing. I waited for her response, concentrating on the creamy pumpkin ravioli filling, which didn't seem like it should go with a savory sage sauce, but the combination was delicious.

"Oma," said Clementine, "don't make a fuss. He's simply someone I used to date. You probably had a lot of admirers. You must know what that's like."

"I still have admirers."

We all burst out laughing. But I was thinking how cleverly Clementine had distracted Oma by turning the subject to her.

Oma sipped her coffee. "What is this man's name?"

Clementine blinked too many times before answering.

"Russell Lake."

Eighteen

Bad timing. I had just taken a swig of iced tea when Clementine lied about the name of her stalker. I choked and coughed.

Oma raised an eyebrow.

Clementine looked at me with alarm, and I knew it wasn't because she was afraid I couldn't breathe. I assured them I was fine, which gave Oma license to return to the subject of the mysterious Russell Lake—or Parker Colby—whoever he was.

"Why do you hide from this man?" Oma demanded.

"Oma, I have all I can handle right now. The divorce has only been final for a few months. The last thing I need is a romance. Is that jaded of me? Maybe I *am* a little bit sour on romance now. My children and my father come first."

"You are afraid of this Russell?"

Clementine paused too long.

"Then I will call Dave. You will stay here at the inn with us."

"I couldn't do that. Really."

"I have two bedrooms," I said. "I could bunk with Oma. You and the kids could have the run of my apartment."

"We couldn't. It's very kind of you to offer."

Oma gazed at Trixie. "Do you have a dog?"

"I do!" Clementine seemed relieved that the topic of conversation had changed. "Star Baby. She's from one of Babylicious's litters."

"Too bad you did not bring her with you today."

"Dad took her to the show."

Poor Clementine uttered those words without realizing that she had walked right into Oma's trap.

"Then you must stay here with us."

"Oh no!" I was so eager to help Clementine that it hadn't dawned on me that the inn wasn't the safest place for her. "Oma, I'm afraid *Russell* is a guest of the inn."

Oma's fork fell to the stone terrace with a clank. "What?"

Clementine turned toward me in shock and confusion.

I picked up Oma's fork.

Oma clasped her hands to her cheeks. "Nothing like this has ever happened before in all the years that I have run this inn. Nothing!"

Mr. Huckle appeared in the doorway with a fresh fork. "Begging your pardon, madam, but I will gladly go to stay with Miss Clementine and the children."

"But—"

He stopped Clementine before she could say more. "It would be my pleasure. You are like a daughter to me. I like to think that if I had had a daughter, she would have been exactly like you, Miss Clementine. I shan't leave you alone in your hour of need." He turned to Oma. "Shall I serve dessert now, madam?"

What a sneaky old fellow. I bet there wasn't much going on in the inn that he didn't know about.

Our lunch ended on a high note, but when Clementine took her leave, I made a point of escorting her out. Trixie went with us.

"Thanks for making up that story about Russell Lake staying here."

I laughed out loud. No wonder she was confused. "But he is. Under a different name."

Clementine's face flushed red when she realized she'd been caught. "Holly, I'm sorry I lied. Is he really bunking at the inn?"

"I'm afraid so."

"What's his name?"

"You honestly don't know?"

"Please, you saw right through that. Trixie is a Jack *Russell,* and we were sitting out near the *lake.* Russell Lake."

"I gather that means he's not an old boyfriend."

Clementine stared down the pedestrian zone. "You and Oma are dear friends. You can't imagine how much I hated lying to you." Clementine folded her arms across her chest. "I came back to Wagtail to escape something terrible. The kids and I need a fresh start. I don't want my personal troubles all over town. I don't want to be *that* woman. I don't want people feeling sorry for me or whispering when I pass by. And most of all, I don't want my children growing up and hearing the whispers and the rumors and living with the shame."

I could understand that. I wasn't one to broadcast all my personal problems, either. "It sounds like a terrible divorce."

She held one hand over her forehead. "You can't begin to imagine."

I let it go. I didn't want to pry. "He registered under the name of Parker Colby. Do you think your husband sent him?"

She finally met my eyes. "We'll be fine with Mr. Huckle. We'll be just fine."

I wasn't so sure about that. Mr. Huckle was a sweet old man, but somehow, I doubted that he was much protection.

She picked up my hand and gave it a squeeze. "This is why I came home to Wagtail. People look out for each other here." She gasped. "Isn't it ironic that I don't want people in town to know my troubles, yet I expect them to protect me and my children?"

She ducked down the little passageway lined with bushes and hopped into a golf cart driven by Mr. Huckle.

Trixie and I returned to reception. We had barely

entered when Oma said, "I know every guest in this inn. There is no Russell Lake. The guest who follows Clementine, is he a ghost hunter?"

"It's Parker Colby."

"Nooo!" whined Zelda. "It couldn't be. He's so dreamy. He wouldn't be that scuzzy. There must be a mistake."

Oma's lips pursed. "You always like the bad boys, Zelda. You should make a point of looking for nice men."

"Not all gorgeous men are bad to the bone," she protested.

"You and Felix make a cute couple," I said.

Oma glanced up from the computer. "You, my liebchen, have the reverse problem. You must break away from the boring studious types, like your ex-boyfriend. Has he called you yet?"

"No. I really don't expect him to call. It's over, Oma."

"Did he help you pack?"

"No."

"Hmpff. It's a good thing you broke off that relationship. I'm glad to see him go. Hmm, I have our Mr. Colby here. He is from New York City."

Zelda peered at the computer. "He doesn't sound like a New Yorker. If you'd said he was from Texas, I might have believed you."

"The three of us will keep an eye on him, yes? And I will notify Officer Dave."

"Oma, Clementine doesn't want that. She said

she came here for a fresh start and doesn't want the whole town knowing about her shameful troubles with her husband."

"Shameful? She has nothing to be ashamed of if her husband betrayed her."

"I think it might be worse than that. She doesn't want people feeling sorry for her."

"So it's like that, is it? An abusive husband, you think? That's still nothing to be ashamed of. However, I understand her desire not to be pitied. I would feel the same way." Oma looked from me to Zelda. "The first sign of trouble, and we notify Officer Dave. Agreed?"

The phone rang and Oma answered. When she hung up, she asked, "Would you mind giving Shelley a hand with the ghost hunters since Mr. Huckle has gone to help Clementine?"

"I'm on it!"

Trixie's nails clicked on the hardwood floor as she hurried along the corridor with me.

The Apparition Apprehenders had gathered in the Dogwood Room, the open sitting area next to the grand staircase. Felix was leaning back on a sofa with his eyes closed, but he held a mug on his lap. Brian perched next to him, jazzed and energetic. Casper lay quietly at their feet.

Eva walked Mrs. Mewer toward us. Twinkle-toes, who had been watching from the staircase, scampered toward Mrs. Mewer, hissed at her, and dashed away. Some feline ambassador she was!

Shelley handed me a pot of coffee. "The ghost hunters are having an impromptu breakfast meeting. They're all just getting out of bed, so they'll want lots of caffeine. I've set up a station with orange juice, cream and sugar for coffee, and a buffet server of bacon and scrambled eggs. So if you could keep their mugs filled, that would be a huge help. Oh, and I have a tray of breakfast breads that Mr. Luciano ordered. Would you carry that in for me?"

I was more than happy to help out. The tray of croissants, muffins, and sweet rolls was bigger and heavier than I'd have imagined. I hoped Trixie wouldn't run underfoot and trip me.

Happily, I managed to deliver it without catastrophe. I positioned the goodies near the orange juice.

Mr. Luciano stood by the fireplace speaking softly to Mark, whose gaze continually flicked over to Eva. Gina, the bulldog, sat by Mr. Luciano's feet, calmly taking everything in.

Twinkletoes jumped onto the mantel behind Mr. Luciano but kept a wary eye on Mrs. Mewer.

Most of the guys appeared to have dressed in two minutes, bothering only to don wrinkled T-shirts and jeans, but Eva was pulled together. A broad lavender hairband pulled her hair back, sixties-style. Her top matched the hairband, and her slim cropped trousers accentuated her figure.

Two cameramen were waiting to tape the meeting.

The chatter stopped when Mr. Luciano began to speak in his deep *Godfather*-ish voice. "You had a very successful night at the Wagtail Springs Hotel. Mark and I have been going over some of the footage and some amazing EVPs, which astonished us. I think you'll be very pleased."

Lillian Elsner was walking by. She paused and gazed at the collected group in the sitting room. "Oh my. Did I hear you say ghosts? They fascinate me. Is this a private group, or may I sit in?"

Mr. Luciano couldn't have been more gracious. With a grand sweep of his hand, he said, "By all means, Lillian, please join us."

She strode in and settled near Eva. I expected to see orbs on the walls reflecting off her dazzling earrings. An inch in diameter, they looked like balls cut in half and covered in diamonds. As before, large gemstones surrounded by diamonds graced her slender fingers. She plopped a casual designer handbag on her lap.

When GloryB's head popped out of it, Mrs. Mewer yowled her protest, which woke Felix.

His head jolted up, and he shouted, "Here!"

It didn't appear to upset GloryB, though. She gazed around the assembled group with great interest.

I poured coffee into Felix's mug. He smiled at

me, sat up straight, and self-consciously ran a hand through his mussed hair.

"Mark, would you play the EVP we discussed?" asked Mr. Luciano.

Mark reached forward and pressed a button on a recorder. At first we heard nothing but static. Suddenly, children giggled in the background. A child's voice spoke. *"I'm going to get you!"*

Eva frowned and sat forward. Everyone started talking at once, but a hush fell over them when Brian rewound it and played it again. *"I'm going to get you!"*

It wasn't as clear as if someone had spoken into a microphone. The child's voice was in the background with static over it, but even I couldn't mistake what it said.

Luciano waited until the talking and high-fiving died down. "But that's not all. Brian, would you do the honors?"

Brian played a different section. Again, it began with static. But then, underneath the static, a rattling sound emerged. I didn't know what a rattlesnake sounded like, but I'd have backed away from that and fast!

Brian replayed it for everyone. He tugged at my sleeve and pointed to his mug. I'd been so entranced that I had forgotten to do my job.

Finally, he played one last portion. Like the others, it began with static. The sound of footsteps running could be heard in the background. I'd been there for that one and had heard it with my own ears live, when it happened.

"Eva," said Mr. Luciano, "any impressions?"

She spoke with assurance. I could just imagine her in her classroom. "I can't tell you anything until I examine them more closely."

"How about this?" Mr. Luciano projected a video on the wall.

I recognized it immediately—the flashlight that had responded when Brian had asked Hiram to turn it on. We watched, spellbound.

Eva snorted. "I'm sorry, Mr. Luciano. I doubt there's a person in this room who isn't familiar with the flashlight trick. Brian is well known for this kind of performance. I've called him on it before."

Brian's mouth dropped open, and his hands curled into fists. "What did I ever do to you? Why are you trying so hard to ruin my reputation? This is my career, not some game. No wonder Mark dumped you."

Eva sucked in a deep breath. Her eyes opened wide, and she stared at Brian in horror.

It seemed like time stopped in those seconds of painful silence. Mark jumped to his feet. "Hey. Wait a minute. Don't go talking about things you don't know about."

Felix's eyes darted back and forth between Mark and Brian. "Now come on, guys. Brian, apologize to Eva. She's just doing her job."

"I notice she's not putting *you* down. Only me. It's always only me. You better beware, Felix. I'm sure you're next on her list of lives to ruin, like she has mine and Mallory's."

Mr. Luciano finally stepped in. "Just a moment. Let's not get heated. I believe you've over-stepped, Brian. Felix is right. I hired Eva to do exactly this. She's only analyzing the results."

"Yeah? Is that what she's doing? Well, try this on for size. There was a witness when Mallory died. I saw you, Eva. Yup, with my own two eyes. You can't disprove that." Brian pointed at her with a pudgy forefinger. "I saw you sneaking back into the inn the night Mallory died. Try to dodge that truth. Not quite as easy as pooh-poohing ghosts, is it?"

Eva seemed almost breathless. "I was not sneaking."

Brian didn't try to hide his joy. "So you admit it! Then you won't mind telling us what you were doing outside in the middle of the night."

Eva raised her chin. "Perhaps *you* could enlighten us. What exactly were *you* doing outside?"

Nineteen

"I couldn't sleep, so I went for a walk." Brian spoke smugly, as though he wasn't concerned by the implication that he might have had something to do with Mallory's death.

Eva's eyes narrowed with suspicion. "I don't suppose you happened to meet Mallory during this walk?"

Brian leveled a wicked look at Eva. "Mallory is gone. You can pretend you don't believe in ghosts all you want. But that won't stop Mallory from coming back for you. Just like Becca, Hiram, and Obadiah can't find peace." He leaned forward. "Mallory is looking for you."

They say emotions travel up and down the leash, meaning that your dog knows if you're tense or afraid. But I had no idea it worked that way for cats, too. In the instant that Brian stood up menacingly, Mrs. Mewer leaped onto his shoulder and clung to him.

Brian howled and turned in a frantic circle, trying to knock the cat off, but Mrs. Mewer sank her claws in deeper and held on like she was riding a bucking bronco.

If the implications of what they had confessed hadn't been so dire, the ensuing chaos might have been very funny—Brian turning and turning. Eva and Mr. Luciano reaching for Mrs. Mewer. Mark and Felix trying to help but getting in the way as the other three rotated. Casper, Gina, Trixie, and GloryB barking underfoot.

In the blink of an eye, Mrs. Mewer flew off Brian's shoulder, landed squarely on her feet and took off down the corridor with Twinkletoes in hot pursuit. The dogs couldn't resist a good chase, and they raced behind the cats.

Brian wiped his shoulder. When he turned his fingers up, I saw a tiny smear of blood.

He eyed Eva. "Bring it on now, devil woman. One more word criticizing me, and I'll sue."

"Calm down, Brian." Felix stood on tiptoe to see Brian's shoulder. "It's just a cat scratch."

"Yeah? Haven't you ever heard of cat scratch fever?" He turned menacingly toward Eva. "You better watch yourself."

He sucked in a deep breath, squared his shoulders, and said, quite calmly, "Felix, Holly, I'd like to speak with you, please."

Felix and I followed Brian outside onto the porch.

"Did the camera get that? See, I'm not really a jerk, Holly. Well, okay, sometimes I *can* be, but that's just because I can be stupid, but I'm not being stupid *or* a jerk right now."

I tried to follow his rambling, which seemed to be a disclaimer of some sort.

Felix gave him a dirty look. "You were a little hard on Eva, don't you think?"

Brian slapped him on the back. "You won't feel that way when the ratings come in."

"So you're not really angry?" I asked.

"Oh, I'm plenty angry." He sucked in air noisily. "Eva acts so superior, like she's some kind of genius, when she's the dope because she can't open her mind enough to see that ghosts exist. What I said was the truth. She really was outside the other night, and she sure hated Mallory."

I walked inside, much relieved that Brian had been putting on a show. I wondered if Eva knew that.

I helped Shelley clean up, expecting the dogs to return. When they didn't, I found them at the reception desk, where Zelda was using her psychic skills on them. Felix looked on in delighted amazement. I wondered if he really believed she could read their minds, or if he just thought it was a cute gag.

Zelda offered them tiny treats, and Trixie nearly knocked little GloryB over in her eagerness.

I hurried to correct her. "Sit, Trixie. We don't jump like that." Her little bottom barely grazed the floor in compliance before Zelda laughed and gave her a tiny corner of a biscuit.

Casper sat properly and raised a paw for his treat.

"That's a good Ghost," Zelda cooed to Casper.

A whirlwind rushed above us. Visible through the wrought iron railing on the balcony, Mrs. Mewer and Twinkletoes faced each other in a classic cat standoff.

Zelda handed me Mrs. Mewer's leash. "I took it off so she wouldn't get tangled on anything, and I put a Sugar Maple Inn GPS collar on her."

I sighed. Now she would be that much more difficult to catch.

As though she had read my mind, Zelda added, "Let her have her fun. Mrs. Mewer loves racing around with Twinkletoes. She says she never gets to play with other cats at home. She's not interested in going outside. She just wants to play."

"They don't look like they're having fun. They look like they're going to scratch and bite each other."

"They're fine," Zelda insisted. "They're batting around a turquoise mouse." Zelda lowered her voice. "But Mrs. Mewer is very concerned about Eva. She says she's never see Eva so upset."

A dreamy look came over Felix. He tilted his head and stared at Zelda with open fascination.

I never knew quite how to respond to Zelda's pronouncements about what animals were thinking. I didn't really believe that Zelda could read their minds or communicate with them. But she had an annoying habit of being correct. Of course, it didn't take a psychic to know that Eva was stressed out. "I'm a little worried about Eva, too. Make sure it's okay with her for Mrs. Mewer to have the run of the inn. Okay?"

Zelda's eyes shifted toward Felix. She gave him a little nudge and cocked her head toward me.

"Oh!" Felix straightened up. "Would you be able to show Grayson and me the way to your aunt's house this afternoon?"

I'd forgotten all about Aunt Birdie. "Why don't I just draw you a map?"

Felix and Zelda shared a look and laughed like they had a private joke.

Felix cleared his throat. "I believe her exact words were 'and bring my heartless niece with you or I won't open the door.'"

"Leave it to Birdie to extend a gracious invitation."

Felix and I left Trixie and Casper in Zelda's care. Wagtail might be pet-friendly, but I didn't have to ask to know that Aunt Birdie's home was off-limits to furry creatures.

Felix, Grayson, and I set off for her house, stopping briefly at Au Bone Pain, which Oma had recommended for baked goods.

The clerk recognized Grayson from his previous reality TV show. Giggling like a schoolgirl with a crush, she asked him to autograph a bakery bag.

He rose to the occasion, cleverly writing *The best buns in town! Grayson Gatewood.* He even posed for selfies destined for Facebook.

Felix tapped his watch. "Grayson, Aunt Birdie is waiting."

Grayson followed us out the door but turned to wave to his fans inside.

"Wow. Does that happen to you a lot?" I asked.

Felix laughed. "All the time. Makes me feel like the invisible man when I'm with him."

Grayson grinned. "Wait until the Apparition Apprehenders are on TV. You'll get just as much attention."

"Eva didn't want to come along?" I asked.

"She's back at the inn going over the EVPs," said Felix.

"Those were amazing," said Grayson. "Mark said he had never heard anything so clear. The owners ought to promote the place as a haunted hotel. Bet they'd do a big business. Who owns it?"

Felix sniffed the muffins. "Mark said it's a funny little guy named Wiggins. Think Birdie would be offended if we ate some of the muffins on the way?"

I pretended to whisk them out of his reach to protect them. Not that I blamed him. The aroma was mouthwatering.

We marched bravely up the walk to her home.

Aunt Birdie answered the door dressed for a business meeting. A prim white blouse peeked out the front of a red suit. Giant mobe pearl earrings flanked her face, which bore such an inhospitable expression that I immediately felt like a child who had been caught misbehaving.

I quickly introduced Felix and Grayson. "We brought muffins. I hope you like them. They smell heavenly."

She thanked us politely and invited us inside. She peeked in the basket. "Store-bought," she sniffed. "You couldn't bake something to bring to your only aunt?"

Felix glanced at me with wide eyes. "Holly hasn't had much time. We're keeping her very busy."

"Are you? How refreshingly chivalrous of you to come to her defense."

I meant to let it slide, really I did. But under my breath I muttered, "And you're not my only aunt."

"So Mrs. Dupuy," Felix said hastily, shooting me an annoyed look, "why do you think you have ghosts?"

"Miss. It's *Miss* Dupuy. And I don't *think* I have ghosts. I know I have them because I have seen them. I expect they'll be making an appearance now that Holly is in the house."

"And why would that be?" asked Felix.

"She hasn't been here in years. My only living relative can't be bothered to visit."

It took all my willpower not to point out that she knew very well that my mother—her sister—was very much alive and well and living in California. Not to mention their parents and my half siblings.

They were, however, wise enough to reside an entire country away from her.

Aunt Birdie must have thought my silence gave her license to continue in that vein. "But everything will be different now that she's living here. We'll have dinner together on Saturday nights, and Holly will take over care of the family graves at Wagtail Cemetery. I go there every Sunday after services, and I expect to see seasonal arrangements on the graves. See that you take care of that today, Holly."

I closed my eyes for a few seconds. How to handle *this?*

"Don't look like that. I've taken care of those graves for as long as I can remember. It's time your generation took responsibility for our ancestors."

To be honest, I had never given their graves a single thought. With the sole exception of my grandfather—Oma's husband—all my grand-parents were still alive. A flash of shame rolled over me. I sucked in a deep breath of air. Flowers at the cemetery didn't sound too terrible. After all, they deserved to be remembered nicely.

"I'll be glad to do that, Aunt Birdie. But I don't know what my schedule will be like yet, so we'll have to see about dinners on Saturdays."

She looked like I had slapped her. I swear the hollows under her prominent cheekbones grew deeper.

Felix jumped in. "Where do you see these apparitions, *Miss* Dupuy? Perhaps you could show us and tell us a little bit more about the circumstances?"

"What a nice young man you are. Married?"

Felix sputtered, "No-o-o."

"Isn't that lucky? My niece, my only living relative on this earth, is single, too."

Felix and Grayson both looked back at me as Birdie led us through her home. I rolled my eyes, held up my palms, and shrugged. Fortunately they both grinned.

I wasn't used to living near relatives. Up to now, I had done pretty much as I pleased, when I pleased. I hoped I could work something out with Birdie eventually. Living in dread of seeing her might be worse than catering to her once in a while.

"Right here." She fingered her hair. "This has always been the sitting room. My house has been in the family for four generations. Holly will inherit it one day." She gazed at Felix. "Did you hear that? Holly will be an heiress."

It was all I could do not to snort. Heiress? Hardly. Her sitting room surprised me, though. Definitely not modern, but not the stuffy, uncomfortable, Victorian-type room I remembered from my childhood.

Elaborate yet tasteful floral curtains with a bold yellow background swagged across the windows.

Pale yellow walls provided a backdrop for what appeared to be family portraits, including one of my mother as a child, holding a cocker spaniel. A window seat bore bright blue cushions, and a love seat was clad in the same cheerful fabric as the curtains. A Ouija board sat on a rather modern ottoman-style table that was clad in a coordinating yellow and white lattice print. Two additional chairs did seem a bit older and stuffier in style, but their faded blue fabric bore faint yellow roses that suited the room. A small table between them held an aged book.

I felt a little bit ashamed, actually. I had never given any thought to Aunt Birdie's financial situation. What did she live off of? This wasn't the time to ask. Oma would surely know.

"Uh, Miss Dupuy?" said Felix. "You haven't been playing with that Ouija board, have you?"

"You ask that as though it were a bad thing, young man."

Felix shook his head. "You really shouldn't do that, Miss Dupuy. You don't know who you'll get with a Ouija board. You could accidentally open the door to dark spirits."

He sounded so earnest. It was really very sweet.

Birdie rambled on about my great-great-grandparents and how she sometimes heard sounds at night in the sitting room. "Oh, here's Elmer now."

I gazed around the room. I didn't see anyone. Not even a mist or an orb.

"Miss Dupuy, are you by any chance a sensitive?"

Aunt Birdie beamed. "Yes, Felix. I have seen ghosts since I was a child. Don't *you* see Elmer? He's over there by the table with the book."

We turned to look in that direction, and for absolutely no reason the book flew to the floor.

Twenty

I gasped and scanned the area. None of us were anywhere near close enough to have influenced the book. It hadn't slid down. It hadn't fallen off. It had flown about three feet as though it had been tossed.

"Now, now, Elmer. Don't be upset. I'm sure they appreciated your effort to move the book." Aunt Birdie smiled at us. "Your great-great-grandfather always was a rascal. He hates it when people can't see him. He was a lawyer, and you know how they like to be the center of attention."

Uh-oh. Either Aunt Birdie had lost her marbles or she was as bad as Brian. Did she know how to rig a book so it would fly off a table? I stood perfectly still. I didn't feel anything moving—no motors or anything that might have jiggled the book. I eyed the little table. Could it be at a slant?

Grayson could hardly contain himself. "Oh, man! That was so cool. We have to come back at night. Would that be okay? Maybe we could shoot a second episode of the TV show? Whadda ya think, Felix? We have to talk with Luciano!"

"Mr. Luciano?" asked Aunt Birdie. "A rather distinguished gentleman? Snappy dresser? Has a bulldog?"

Well, well, well. Aunt Birdie certainly had noticed Mr. Luciano about town. Maybe I could introduce them and Birdie would focus her energy on Luciano instead of me. Only a month ago, Birdie, Oma, and Rose had tried to set me up. I shuddered at the memory. None of their attempts went very well, and it had been horribly embarrassing. Yet here I was thinking about doing the very same thing. I consoled myself by imagining it might be genetic.

I pulled myself together, picked the book up off the floor, and examined it. Bound in worn red leather with fancy scrolls that showed wear from age, the cover had been embossed with the names *Elmer and Lisette Dupuy*. I turned it over. No signs of wires or anything that might have launched it from the table. My eyes met Felix's.

He mashed his lips together, then said, "Just like in the castle."

Birdie frowned at us. "I suppose that's Elmer's way of telling me it's time I passed his journal on to you, Holly. It's not terribly interesting. Elmer was a decent but excruciatingly boring man. Still, he kept records. Lisette drew some sketches and stashed a few family photographs in it. I have a few other items to pass along to you as well."

The second Birdie left the room, Felix and Grayson descended on the book and examined the table.

I watched them, but they didn't come up with any cogent explanations for the flying book, either.

Aunt Birdie bustled into the room carrying a stack of ancient books. She handed them to me. "Take good care of these. They are the history of your family. If it weren't for me, we wouldn't have anything to hand on."

"Thank you, Aunt Birdie." Why did I have a funny suspicion she was really cleaning her house? No matter. I *was* glad to have them. And I would hand them on eventually, too. Maybe sooner than she thought, if I could dump them on my half siblings.

"Now then, about Mr. Luciano and your TV show—" Birdie stopped and turned to me. "Well? What are you still doing here?"

"I beg your pardon?" What was she upset about now?

"The flowers for their graves. Didn't you hear what I said? I want fresh flowers on those graves tonight when people view the cemetery. I will *not* have anyone thinking that the Dupuys don't honor their dead."

Hadn't she claimed my presence would bring out the spirits? But any excuse to leave sounded good to me. "I'll take care of it immediately. See you later."

I was hightailing it for the front door when it dawned on me that she would hate whatever I chose. I dashed back to the sitting room. "Excuse me. Sorry to interrupt. Which florist do you prefer, Aunt Birdie?"

Her bitter expression changed for once. Evidently she was thrilled that I had asked her advice. I made a mental note that she liked being asked for her opinion. Even if I didn't follow her suggestions, it might be beneficial to ask for guidance once in a while.

"Catnip and Bark," she said.

I waved and left so fast that my tailwind probably blew the ghosts out of the premises.

It was a gorgeous fall day. The nip in the air was as crisp as a ripe apple. I longed to be outside, but I hurried back to the inn, afraid to be away too long when I should be working.

I needn't have been concerned. Zelda, Oma, and Rose were chatting in Oma's office over tea and coffee. The sun shone through the French doors. Twinkletoes and Mrs. Mewer had stretched out in a sunbeam and didn't even twitch an ear when I entered.

Trixie and Casper jumped to their feet and greeted me like they hadn't seen me in years. I deposited the handful of books on the desk and squatted to pet the dogs.

While the dogs were happy, Oma, Rose, and Zelda wore worried expressions. "What happened? Why so glum?"

Oma's lips drew tight. "Officer Dave paid Zelda a visit."

Zelda cringed and bit into an éclair.

I guessed it had to happen sooner or later.

Zelda swallowed hard. "He was asking questions about the night Mallory died." She waved her forefinger as she spoke. "I knew she didn't drown by accident. I've been in that bath. It's like a big kiddie pool. There are deeper public fountains everywhere."

Rose shot Oma a fearful look. "It was an accident. Why won't Dave accept that?" She glared at me. "You too, Holly. Why can't the two of you concede that Mallory drowned on her own, without help from anyone else?"

I could feel the color rising in my face. "What if Holmes drowned in less than two feet of water in Chicago, and they wrote off his death as an accident?"

"Don't be ridiculous. That would never happen. And if it did, I'd be right there in a flash, demanding to know what had"—Rose's voice faded—"happened."

"Mallory was an orphan." I just let it hang there in the air.

"Now you're making me feel terrible. But that doesn't mean it wasn't an accident. I trust Doc."

At least Rose wasn't glaring at me anymore. I eyed the selection of pastries on the table, took a seat, and poured myself a mug of coffee, doctoring it with milk and sugar. Trixie edged toward me, watching my every move, no doubt hoping for a terrible accident that would land the entire pastry tray on the floor.

"Officer Dave had the nerve to imply that I killed her out of jealousy because she was flirting with Felix. I was afraid of this. He thinks *I* killed Mallory!" said Zelda.

I nearly dropped my coffee mug. Mallory's outrageous attention to Felix hadn't escaped anyone's notice. But to imagine that Zelda would be so angry that she would murder? Dave had gone too far. I recognized that he had to consider all the possibilities, but that seemed over the top to me.

Zelda lived with a clowder of cats. I didn't imagine they would provide an alibi for her. "I don't suppose you contacted anyone or sent any e-mails when you got home?"

"It was past two thirty in the morning!" Zelda put down her éclair. "I know Felix didn't kill her. He's much too kind. I mean, think about it. He's the only one of them who bothered to walk us home."

"You girls stop that now," said Rose. "Doc is so upset with Dave for undermining him. And you too, Holly. You and Dave aren't helping things by running around town asking questions that imply Mallory was murdered. I understand that Dave would like to do something more exciting than look for a lost dog, but honestly, you're making people think something worse happened than is the case."

I looked to Oma, who nodded in agreement. "Doc was very clear. There is no evidence of anything criminal."

"It's disrespectful, too," said Rose. "Dave is a sweet boy, but Doc has decades of experience that shouldn't simply be disregarded. Of course he knows more about these things than Dave."

Like Zelda, I bit into an éclair. I happened to agree with Dave, and Rose's little lecture didn't change that. But I knew when to keep quiet. I would have to be more discreet in the future.

"How did the visit with Birdie go?" asked Oma.

"As well as can be expected. Oma, what does Birdie do to make a living?"

"A number of things. She's an appraiser. Quite well-respected from what I understand."

"Real estate?"

"No, no. Things. Objets d'art. Crystal, historical documents, jewelry, old books, old gadgets."

"She writes columns for a few fancy magazines about that sort of thing," said Rose. "She used to transcribe manuscripts for a local writer before computers took over."

"I'm to take flowers to the graves of my ancestors."

"That doesn't sound so bad," said Oma.

"I *love* Wagtail Cemetery!" cooed Zelda. "It's like taking a step back in time. Except for the addition of new graves, I bet the church and cemetery haven't changed a bit in a century."

I glanced at her doubtfully.

"What?" asked Zelda. "A lot of people like grave-yards. Wagtail's is so cool and old-fashioned."

Rose asked, "You *are* coming to the graveyard party tonight?"

"Eww. Isn't that a little bit macabre?" I asked.

Oma groaned. "Loosen up, liebling. It's all in good fun."

"I believe Liesel is right. When did you become such a stick-in-the-mud, Holly?" asked Rose.

"Now just a minute. I like fun as much as anyone else. But isn't it a little bit disrespectful to party in a cemetery?"

"It's all the rage!" raved Zelda.

"Celebrations at cemeteries are nothing new," said Rose. "Years ago, people gathered at cemeteries for special occasions. They even took picnics. On some days, the whole town turned out to clean up the cemetery. I think it's wonderful that people take an interest in our cemetery. If it happens to be because of Halloween, well, that's just fine."

Zelda laughed. "And if a few ghosts show up, all the better!"

"Holmes will be there." Rose shot a coy glance my way.

"Holmes is engaged. Don't you start that again." I hurried to change the subject. "So what's going on here? Seems awfully quiet."

Zelda grinned. "No one checking in or out. Not even many questions. Just a bunch of handsome ghost hunters running around."

"You can spend some time unpacking. I hear your apartment is quite the mess." Oma didn't say it in a critical way, thank goodness.

"Now how would you know . . ." It came to me as I spoke. "Mr. Huckle. I think he banged into some boxes. Since it's such a beautiful day, I think I'll take the dogs for a walk. We can deliver the flowers to the cemetery and get it out of the way so Birdie won't complain about it."

But at that moment, Oma gasped, looking as though she'd seen a ghost.

Twenty-one

"I wondered where everyone was!"

We all swung around.

My old boyfriend, Ben Hathaway, loped through the doorway. His dimples flashed when he smiled at me. He would fit right in with the ghost hunters. He wore classic nerd glasses, with frames that were dark at the top and clear at the bottom. In spite of his studious appearance, he was actually fairly good-looking. He parted his dark brown hair on the right and wore it short. But like Holmes's fiancée, he was a city person, hopelessly out of place in Wagtail.

Gingersnap wagged her tail and kissed his hand, which he promptly yanked out of her reach. Trixie backed away from him. She had no reason to do that—well, other than the fact that he thought I shouldn't have kept her. But she couldn't know that, could she?

"Ben!" I jumped up. "What are you doing here?"

He held up a hand in greeting to the others. "Hello. I had to drive up here for business."

I would have been suspicious, but his very wealthy boss happened to have a fishing cabin in Wagtail. It wasn't out of the realm of possibilities that Ben really did come to work.

I hustled him out to the reception desk. "Where are you staying?"

The dimples made another appearance. "Here."

He said it with such cheery assurance that I thought he must believe he had a reservation. "But we're booked."

"I didn't think I had to pay for a room. I figured I'd bunk with you."

Oy. My head spun. "Ben, we broke up."

"Not really."

"Yes. Really. I packed up my life and moved here, remember?"

Two creases formed between his eyebrows as though he was perplexed. "You make a move sound so final. And anyway, we're still friends. Right?"

Oh boy. I had never considered anything like this. Why hadn't he called? "Well, I guess so." It wasn't as though we ended our relationship in a big snit. And I did have a spare bedroom in my apartment. "Okay, you can stay, but I have to warn you that I haven't unpacked yet." I handed him a spare key to my quarters.

Ben wrinkled his nose. "You've been here for days. What have you been doing?"

"Thanks, Ben," I said sarcastically. He had just helped me remember why we broke off our relationship. I ignored the confused look on his face but I wondered how he knew when I had moved. "Did you go by my house?"

He flushed red. "Your tenant was moving in."

Served him right. I hoped it shocked him to realize that I was gone. "Let me grab some books."

I hustled into Oma's office and hissed, "Did you have anything to do with this?"

Oma clutched her forehead with one hand. "Not the Ben again."

"Don't call him that!" I whispered. "Ben. Just Ben. Not *the* Ben."

"Ja, ja. How long does he have to stay?"

Zelda grinned. "I'd forgotten how cute he is."

"Ach, Zelda. Do not encourage her."

I grabbed the books Aunt Birdie had given me and bustled out to Ben. "Follow me."

When I unlocked the door to the apartment, Trixie, Twinkletoes, Casper, and Mrs. Mewer were waiting inside. They must have used the pet doors to scramble up the hidden stairway. Not one of them ran to Ben.

Trixie pulled her ears back and watched with worried eyes. Twinkletoes sat on top of the tallest packing box looking quite regal with her black tail wrapped around her white front paws. I hadn't known that sweet face could be so aloof and superior. Mrs. Mewer looked on, the turquoise mouse at her feet. Casper must have picked up on Trixie's concern, because even he wore an unhappy expression.

"Good grief, Holly! How many animals do you have? I thought there were only two."

"The other two are guests of the inn." I deposited the books on a bookshelf near the fireplace and showed Ben to the extra bedroom.

"This is much better. I can deal with this. Lucky you didn't let that mess migrate into this room, huh?"

I bristled. "Look, Ben, I'm not going to apologize. I moved a couple of days ago, and it's been busy around here. Besides, it's not like I was expecting company, you know."

"It's a good thing I came! I can unpack your stuff while I'm here."

I had to stop myself from screaming, *No, no, no!* Why was I so testy with Ben? He hadn't done anything. Okay, so maybe he'd been critical, but I could take that. Ohhh, but he hadn't done *anything*. He hadn't called. He hadn't given me a hand with packing or moving. He hadn't shown up to say good-bye. And now he had appeared like he thought he was a white knight riding to the rescue on his steed. I took a deep breath and exhaled. "No, thanks. This is my home. I'd rather not have to call you when I can't find my belongings."

"Of course. How can you stand to live in this mess?"

"Why aren't you staying at your boss's cabin?" Oops. That certainly sounded rude. He didn't seen to notice, though.

"He rents it out. Apparently all of Wagtail is sold

out right now. For Howloween, I guess? I saw the big sign when I rode into town."

Rode? Hade he really said *rode?* I must be imagining things. "I need to take care of a little chore. Make yourself at home. There are drinks and snacks in the fridge."

"I think I'll go with you, at least downstairs. Your pack doesn't appear very friendly."

I turned to find the two dogs and two cats sitting in a perfectly straight line just outside the door. There was no growling or hissing, but even Ben hadn't missed their wariness.

"Don't be so worried, guys," I said to them.

"Okay. You don't think they'll bite, do you?" Ben evidently thought I had directed my assurance to him.

"They can tell you don't like them." Good grief! Now I sounded like Zelda. "Get whatever you need and let's go."

"What's the big rush? I thought you moved here for the quiet life." He followed me into the sitting room.

"There's a celebration at the cemetery tonight, and I need to take some flower arrangements over before my Aunt Birdie throws a conniption fit."

"Ugh. There's charming chore. Is it a memorial for the girl who was murdered?"

"How did you know about that?"

"Gosh, Holly, I read newspapers, you know."

I didn't imagine for one minute that any of his

highbrow newspapers had picked up the story of Mallory's death. "No. It's a Howloween thing."

"What is this?" asked Ben. He held out the odd ball that Trixie had found at the Wagtail Springs Hotel.

"Not a clue. Trixie was carrying it around."

"It's kind of cool. Look, the stem that juts out is concave so it sticks to things." He popped it on his forehead.

It wasn't the first time he'd done something childish and fun, but it always surprised me when it happened because it was so unlike him.

"Can I have it?" he asked.

"If it's okay with Trixie."

He leveled a worried look at me. "Holly, she's a dog. Her brain is the size of a walnut."

"Oh, I think she'll know."

As if to prove it, she jumped high in the air as if she intended to snatch it off Ben's forehead.

"She's attacking me!" He stumbled backward.

"She's playing with you. You have her toy."

"Yeah?" He plucked it off his forehead and pitched it across the room.

Trixie ran for it and played coy when he tried to retrieve it.

"Some weird dog toy," he said.

Before leaving the inn, I checked to be sure Gingersnap, Trixie, and Casper were wearing Sugar Maple Inn collars so we could track them if they managed to take off.

I latched leashes onto them and set out on a leisurely stroll in the perfect weather.

Ben chatted about his boss and people we knew. He acted as though nothing had happened between us. It was sufficiently comfortable, and I soon found myself laughing with him.

We quickly found Catnip and Bark. Tiers of bright flowers surrounded the front of the store, making it hard to mistake it for anything else. Ben peeled off to pursue whatever he came for, and I entered the shop with the dogs. When I explained to the proprietor that I wanted *exactly* what Birdie Dupuy usually ordered for the family graves, he clapped his hands and said, "You must be Holly. I'm pleased to see that you take after your grandmother's side of the family."

Although he didn't come right out and say he was glad I wasn't like Birdie, I could read between the lines and grasped the implication.

"I've been expecting Birdie, so everything is ready. She's rather impatient and never phones ahead."

"Apparently I'll be doing this from now on. So go right on making the arrangements just as she likes them, and I'll drop by to pay for them and pick them up."

He nodded. "Sounds like a plan. And I don't mind telling you, I won't be sorry to see your smiling face instead of cantankerous Birdie."

He disappeared to the back for a few minutes

and returned pulling a giant wagon filled with flowers.

"What's this?" I had stupidly imagined there would be two or three little vases or bouquets.

"Birdie's standard order."

I thanked him, looped the three leash handles over one hand, and pulled the wagon with the other. The dogs walked like a team, three abreast, as though they had known each other forever. Six blocks later, I spied the cemetery across one of the main roads that ran along the outskirts of town. I dragged the wagon across the street and up the sidewalk that led to the charming old chapel.

The white building with a steep slate roof could have been in a children's picture book. Arched stained glass windows flanked the front door. A round stained glass window adorned the pitch just under the roof, and a small steeple acted as a bell tower. I remembered the bells ringing on Christmases before my family moved away. Giant pine trees flanked the church and dark woods provided a quiet background behind it.

The cemetery was less appealing. An old black iron fence bearing decorative spikes on top surrounded it. No one had raked the leaves recently. The gravestones varied from tall and notable pillars to some so small they were little more than the size of a book. Seemingly out of nowhere, a dark cloud covered the sun. The day grew chilly and a wind kicked up. Leaves flew through the air like whispers. If Brian were there, he would surely tell me spirits were present.

The dogs lifted their noses to sniff the scents, and without warning, Trixie barked.

I eyed the dense woods behind the church and the cemetery. I didn't see anyone or anything unusual. She probably smelled possums or squirrels. Casper appeared to be on alert. His tail was perpendicular to the ground, and his nose was quivering.

I turned my attention to the mass of flowers and lifted the first arrangement out of the cart. Golden sunflowers and chrysanthemums melded with pumpkin orange lilies, purple liatris spikes, and stunning gaillardia with their deep rust centers and bright yellow edges.

I'd played my hand wrong with Birdie after all, because I had no idea where the graves were, nor had I realized there would be so many arrangements. From now on, maybe we would make this our little get-together. I could pull the wagon for her, and she could count this as time spent with me. Maybe that would get me out of unpleasant Saturday night dinners.

I gazed at the grim cemetery. I didn't believe in ghosts, so why did it creep me out? The specter of death, I supposed. Sucking in a deep breath of air, I entered the ancient gate with the dogs leading the way. "To the Dupuy graves, please, puppies."

They charged ahead, sniffing the ground.

Okay, how hard could this be? I just had to look for graves with the name Dupuy. I concentrated on the names engraved on tombstones. *Richardson, Clodfelter, Pierce, Quinlan*—I recognized the names of local families as I walked. No Dupuys yet.

A fierce wind blew, whipping my hair into my face. It howled through the nearly leafless trees in the cemetery. I paused, trying to wipe my hair out of my face with my arm, when Trixie and Casper pulled away from me and ran, their leashes flying through the air behind them. Gingersnap wagged her tail and gazed up at me as though she wanted to run and have fun, too. Not a chance. I grabbed her leash.

"No!" I screamed. "No!" That was probably the wrong command in a hundred different ways. "Come, Trixie!" Who was I kidding? She hadn't been to training yet. Maybe Casper had. It was bad enough to lose my own dog, but someone else's? That was a nightmare!

"Come, Casper! Casper, come!" He paid me no attention at all. The dogs had stopped in the back corner of the cemetery. They pawed and sniffed and dodged in circles.

Relief flooded over me. The fence. They couldn't go any farther.

I let Gingersnap join them and promptly found Elmer's grave. I set the arrangement down. "I hope you'll like these. They're gorgeous."

I fetched the other arrangements and closed the gate behind me lest the dogs lose interest in the back corner. It wasn't until I had placed flowers on the third grave that I realized I had said something to each of my ancestors. Only half an hour ago, I had sounded like Zelda. "Now I'm as looney as Aunt Birdie."

I shook my head and used both hands to clear windblown strands of hair out of my face. "Oh, this is ridiculous. There's no reason to feel jittery or uneasy. It's just wind, and there are no such things as ghosts."

Leaves blew around me with such force that I felt certain Brian would have insisted the spirits were complaining about what I had said.

The dogs were still barking in the corner of the cemetery. I made my way toward them, pausing to see who warranted the ornate obelisk.

Swags of roses had been cut into the top. Beneath them, perfect folds of fabric had been carved in the stone, ending in ornate stone tassels. I peered at the name. *Dr. Ira Wraith.* His wife and son's epitaphs appeared there as well. The sun broke through the clouds, turning the giant cherub beside it golden. It was every bit as ornate as the obelisk. The chubby angel held one foot in the air behind him as though held aloft by his finely detailed wings. A wrap looped around his legs, and carved flowers cascaded down the pedestal on which he stood. *Rebecca Wraith.*

I was surprised that she hadn't been buried with the rest of her family.

Furious barking broke my concentration. I jogged among the headstones and nabbed the three leashes.

"All right, all right. Hush. Enough barking!"

They weren't interested in the grave, as I'd thought. They aimed their noses toward the woods outside of the fence. Moss grew on two plain tombstones that sat next to each other outside of the cemetery. I craned my neck to see the names. *Dr. Hiram Montacue* and *Obadiah Bagley.*

I stepped back, shocked. They had been ostracized. The people of Wagtail hadn't buried them among their own respectable townspeople. Hiram had been a murderer. I wasn't surprised that they wouldn't want him in their cemetery. But Obadiah had been his victim. Why had they buried him outside of the fence, and even worse, right next to the man who had killed him?

Gingersnap started another round of barking, which prompted Trixie and Casper to join in. "Shh. You're noisy enough to wake the dead."

At that exact moment, I caught a movement in the trees. A shiver shuttled through me. It was probably only a deer. But wouldn't I have heard a deer prancing away through the dry leaves? Only the youngest, most naive deer would stick around with this barking.

I was letting all the talk of ghosts get to me. Still, I felt as though someone was watching us. Many of the leaves had fallen, but the evergreens still provided a dense, dark thicket.

Nonsense. I was being silly because I was in a graveyard. Of course, that didn't explain the dogs' behavior.

"C'mon." Holding their leashes, I turned quickly and bounded through the cemetery as fast as I could go, watching my step and dodging around grave markers.

When we reached the gate, I glanced up and screamed.

Twenty-two

Holmes opened the gate for us. "You're running like you saw the devil himself."

"Where did you come from?"

He was as calm as a summer sky. "Across the street. I'm supposed to meet Doc Kilgore and some of the guys here to set up for the celebration tonight."

I peered at him. "Are you sure you weren't in the woods trying to spook me?"

His gaze shot over my head to the woods. "I would never do that."

"Yeah, right. So it *was* you."

"Honest, Holly, I just got here. It was probably a deer."

"That's what I thought too, but they have trouble not making any noise when they leap away."

Holmes couldn't hide his grin. "You're so skittish! The next thing I know, you'll be telling me you've changed your mind and that you believe in ghosts."

"Speaking of ghosts, do you know why Obadiah is buried outside of the cemetery?"

"Sure. He murdered Hiram."

"Duh. Obadiah couldn't have murdered Hiram, because he was already dead."

"Ah, but they saw the ghost of Obadiah delivering the snakes that killed Hiram, remember?"

"That's stupid. I'd rather not think our ancestors would fall for something like that."

Holmes laughed. A nice hearty laugh that always warmed my heart. "Shh. I wouldn't say that quite so loud out here in the cemetery where they'll hear you."

"Very funny."

Several golf carts drove up, laden with supplies. I waved good-bye to Holmes and turned to leave.

"Hey, Holly!" he called. "You're coming tonight, right?"

How could a girl turn down that kind of heartfelt invitation? "You bet. Wouldn't miss it." Not if

Holmes would be there, I wouldn't. Maybe it would be fun. Maybe Oma and Rose were right. I just needed to loosen up a little and enjoy the spirit of the season.

When we returned to the Sugar Maple Inn, I removed all the leashes from the dogs. They descended upon Eva, Felix, Mark, Grayson, and Ben, who were relaxing in the sitting room with glasses of wine.

"I see you all met Ben."

"They've been telling me about their ghost hunting adventures," he said.

Eva waved at me. "Look at this. Isn't it the cutest?"

She beckoned me to the huge window. Twinkletoes and Mrs. Mewer lay side by side, fast asleep. They weren't touching, but given a little more time together, they might even snuggle.

"I thought this might be a boring trip for Mrs. Mewer, but she's having the best time of her life. Who thought *she* would make a friend?"

"I'm just glad they're not hissing at each other anymore."

"Zelda told me about the GPS collar. Is it okay to let Mrs. Mewer run around the inn? I'll be out part of the night at your aunt's house."

"Sure. No problem. We'll look after her."

"If you see her in the library, you might want to shoo her out of there. She's been known to shred books and newspapers."

We tiptoed away from the sleeping kitties just in time to see Officer Dave arrive.

He looked straight at us. "Eva Chevalier? I'd like to have a word with you, please."

"Brian." She barely breathed his name. "This is Brian's doing."

Mark jumped up from his seat. "What's this about, Dave? Eva didn't do anything."

Dave kept a poker face, but his gaze locked on Mark for a hair too long. "I'd like to speak with you privately, Eva. Excuse us, please."

Eva and Mark exchanged a fearful glance.

Dave followed Eva to her room in the cat wing.

Mark's chest heaved with each breath he took. He kept his eyes on Eva. We all trailed behind Dave and Eva. When the door to her room closed, we waited in the inn library.

Ben whispered, "I feel like I missed something. What did Eva do?"

"Nothing!" barked Mark. In a softer tone, he repeated, "Nothing."

"Brian saw Eva outside the inn the night that Mallory was murdered," I murmured. Doc would be furious when he learned about this.

"Brian doesn't know what he's talking about," Mark snarled. "I never should have put him in the mix of ghost hunters. He's just retaliating because Eva caught him in some underhanded ghost tricks."

"Which you knew would happen," said Felix.

"Makes for good TV. People like conflict. But it's not fair of him to lie about Eva and imply that she was mixed up in Mallory's death somehow."

A little shuffle behind us drew our attention. A cameraman bounded in our direction. "Where are they?"

Mark held his hand up. "We're not shooting this."

Brian thundered toward us. "You just said conflict makes for good TV. Wish we could see her face. Was she panicked?"

"You're a worm, Brian. The lowest of the low." Mark seethed with disgust.

"Oh, it's okay to make money off *me* by putting me on the hot seat and wrecking my reputation? That didn't seem to bother you so much, Mr. High and Mighty. But now that it's Eva in the middle of the controversy—"

"You twit. This has nothing to do with the show. I will not allow it to become a sick drama about Mallory's death." Mark's eyes flashed with anger.

"Really, Mr. Big Shot Author? Why not? Where were you when your girlfriend was drowning?"

"I wouldn't be quite so bold about accusing other people if I were in your shoes."

"What's that supposed to mean?"

Felix stepped between them. "Hey, guys. Let's not start attacking each other. We're all friends. Okay? We need to stick together."

It was Brian who seemed the most put out.

Trixie placed her paws on his thigh and nuzzled his pocket for treats. He pushed her away. "What's wrong with your dog? I don't have any dog treats."

Mark kept a vigilant and worried eye on the door to Eva's room. Grayson had stayed out of the argument, but he stood by with his friends.

I excused myself, but before I walked away, Felix said, "Would you like to join us for dinner tonight? Ben is coming. Then we're going to walk over to the cemetery."

"Sounds great. I just need to check in with my grandmother." I walked toward her office with Trixie trotting ahead of me. I had risen early so I could get to work but I hadn't done a thing for the inn all afternoon.

Oma wasn't in the office, so I walked upstairs to her apartment. She answered the door in a chic pantsuit with a jacket reminiscent of Chanel.

"Wow. Where are you off to?"

Oma smiled coyly. "Dinner at the Blue Boar."

I suspected that the charming chef who owned the posh restaurant had a bit of a crush on my sweet Oma. "Is Rose going, too?"

"You would like to join us, perhaps? Doc will be coming when he finishes helping at the cemetery."

"Is it my imagination or is there a spark between them?"

Oma nodded. "It would be nice, no? Doc and Rose have been widowed for a long time. Like me, Doc has a daughter who lives in Florida and never visits. Such a pity. We miss them so much." She bestowed a beautiful smile upon me. "I'm so glad I have you, liebchen." She hugged me with a fervor that I knew came from deep within her. "So would you like to come with us?"

"And bring Ben?" I teased. "Thanks, but I thought I'd go out with some of the ghost hunters. I just came by because I feel so guilty for not helping out more here today."

"No? I didn't notice. Some days are like that. Other days will be so crazy busy you might regret your decision to move here. You have fun with the young people tonight, liebling. It will do you good. I will see you later at the cemetery?"

"Absolutely."

I left thinking I would make up for it tomorrow. It bothered me not to pull my weight. Still, I had only been here a few days—and what bizarre days they had been. Before long I would be in a boring routine, taking over so Oma could have some much-deserved time off.

I took a few minutes to freshen up in my digs. I filled two bowls with cat food, in case Twinkle-toes brought Mrs. Mewer home for dinner. I changed into a belted plaid skirt and a scoop-necked top in ivy. After running a brush through my hair, I pulled on boots and a suede jacket, then wrapped a long scarf around my neck. I grabbed my purse and Trixie's leash, and we were off.

Ben and the ghost hunters were still clustered where I'd left them. Casper nuzzled Trixie, glad to have canine company again.

"He's still questioning Eva?" I asked.

"Can you believe it?" Mark swallowed hard. His jaw muscles tensed.

The door opened, and Dave walked toward us. "Holly, could I speak with you?"

Eva emerged, looking none the worse for the interrogation. Under her breath Eva muttered, "I need a drink."

"You guys go ahead. I'll catch up," I said.

"We'll be at the barbecue place," said Felix.

Grayson ushered the group out.

Dave and I sat down on the window seat in the library.

He ran both his hands up his forehead and sighed. "Everyone had the opportunity and no one has an alibi. Did Eva say anything to you about a weird light in her room?"

"As a matter of fact, she did."

"I don't know what to make of that. She says she doesn't believe in ghosts, but then she tells me this crazy story about a light in her room. Doesn't that seem contradictory to you?"

"Not really. Sometime we see reflections of something. The day they checked in, an orb floated across the registration area. It had to be a reflection of some kind. I saw it myself. That doesn't mean I thought it was a ghost. It's her job to figure out stuff like that and prove it wasn't a spirit. It probably bothers her that she can't explain it."

Dave nodded. "Catch up to them and see what you can find out. One of them has to know something."

"What about Brian? He was outside that night too, or he wouldn't have seen her."

"Says he went for a walk. He could easily have killed Mallory. Know of any reason he would want to?"

"He said something about asking her out. I gather she turned him down and he was offended. It sounds like all of them, except Felix, knew her one way or another."

Dave stood up. "More than one person has a motive."

"Who? Who has motives?"

"I can't tell you everything, you know. Besides, I'm not sure. See what you can dig up."

"Rose and Oma chewed me out for asking questions that implied Doc is wrong and Mallory was murdered."

Dave's lips bunched up in anger. "I find it painfully ironic that Doc says I'm not letting him do his job but he cannot see that I have to do *my* job. The old guy made a judgment call and now he feels like he has to prove that he's right. He keeps telling me there's no evidence of an altercation. The way I see things, it's his job to determine the cause of death. It's my job to find the evidence. I hope that Doc doesn't try to interfere, because I'm not a little kid anymore. I have as much clout around here as he does. Maybe more."

We left the inn together, but Dave kept going when we reached Hot Hog. The entire group had gathered at a table with Mr. Luciano and the last person on Earth I ever expected to see there—Aunt Birdie.

She flushed like a young girl on a first date, raised one hand, and curled her fingers at me in a wave. Mr. Luciano appeared to be in his element. I said a silent little prayer that he would amuse Aunt Birdie and keep her away from me.

I gratefully accepted a chair near the opposite end of the long table, as far away from Birdie as possible, next to Ben and across from Mark and Eva.

No sooner had I been seated than Holmes arrived with a group of locals who had been working at the cemetery. It took him exactly one minute to say, "Mind if we join you?" He shoved another table up to the end of ours and took the seat beside me. Introductions flew around the table.

"Hey, Donna," he called to the waitress. "Barbecued shrimp and corn bread for the whole table?"

It was as though his mere presence transformed an ordinary dinner into a party. Beer mugs clinked against wineglasses in toasts. Not a single person around the table wasn't smiling or laughing. We shared the tangy shrimp and nibbled on warm corn bread with fresh country butter.

And I was stuck between my dream man, who had his arm slung around the back of my chair, and my former boyfriend. *Oh, joy.*

No one else seemed to notice. I decided Oma was right. I was too stiff and concerned about these things. I should relax and laugh and chatter with everyone else.

To my complete shock, Birdie regaled everyone with stories of Wagtail in the 1800s. "The interesting thing about Obadiah is that he really did cure snake bites. Probably not all of them—but the original snake oil salesmen sold tea tree oil or Chinese water snake oil, which really did have an effect on snakebites. It didn't take long for unscrupulous people to bottle any old thing and sell it as snake oil, and that's how snake oil salesmen got a bad name."

Platters of ribs, glistening with a deep ruby sauce, arrived, along with pulled pork, French fries, lightly charred grilled ears of corn, and little white ramekins that nearly overflowed with creamy coleslaw. The lively banter subsided as we dug in.

I did notice that Aunt Birdie skipped all the luscious, messy, sauced foods and primly ate her chicken breast with a knife and fork while the rest of us used our fingers.

Trixie, Casper, and Mr. Luciano's bulldog, Gina, ate the Nothing But a Hound Dog Special, which appeared to be pulled pork with kale, corn bread, and a few French fries as a garnish. They ate somewhat faster than we did.

We were too stuffed to order dessert, which worked out well, because it was time to head for the cemetery. "Dessert afterward," we declared.

During the walk across town, Eva sidled up to me. "I like Ben. He's a nice guy. He says you almost married him."

I wish I could have been more ladylike, but that caught me by surprise, and I snorted. "Did he mention that he texted me a six-letter proposal?"

Eva laughed. A hearty, warm, life-affirming laugh. "Oh no! Six letters?"

"*marE me?* It took me a few minutes to sound it out and realize it was a proposal."

"These geeky guys are just clueless. I love them to death, but they don't understand romance at all."

"Like Mark?"

She turned her head and pulled away to look at me. "Mark? Why would you say that?"

"No? I thought I was picking up on something between the two of you."

For a moment I thought I saw fear flash across her face. She recovered quickly. "Hah! What about you and that Holmes fellow? My goodness, but he looked like he was staking out a claim."

"No such luck. Holmes is engaged. We probably just seem comfortable together because we've known each other since we were kids." I tried to bring the subject to Mallory. "So most of the guys knew Mallory?"

"I guess so. Not Felix, though. I'm no shrink but I always thought Mallory's interest in Mark stemmed from her need to find a place where she belonged after losing her family. I wouldn't have coped with that well as a teenager, or even now. It must have shattered her."

"You mean because Mark is wealthy?"

"No. Look at them. Grayson is pretty, definitely eye candy, but he's a follower, not a leader. Felix is adorable, but he's a little shy and goofy. Brian is just a kid in a grown-up's body. Poor judgment, never thinks things through. Mark is the only one of them who is solid and dependable, takes action. He's the security that she lost when her family died. I've always thought she gravitated toward ghost hunters out of a need to believe that her family lived on somewhere else."

"Who could blame her for that? I'm like you. I would have been a basket case."

It dawned on me that Eva might be ready to spill some dirt about Brian now that he had reported her to the police. As casually as I could muster, I asked, "Did you see Brian outside on the night of Mallory's murder?"

Twenty-three

Eva shook her head. "I didn't see anyone. I went outside to look for the source of the strange light in my room. Now I wish I *had* seen someone, because then I'd have an alibi!"

I glanced ahead to be sure Brian wasn't in earshot and dared to come right to the point. "Do you know of any reason Brian might have disliked Mallory?"

Her head snapped toward me again, her eyes wide. "You think he killed Mallory?"

I shrugged. "He was outside in the middle of the night by his own admission."

Eva appeared to think for a moment. "Brian isn't the brightest guy in the world. That's why I'm often able to see through his tricks. If he killed Eva, I rather suspect he would have taken the easiest route and simply lied about being out at night at all. It would have been more like him to claim he was asleep in his room."

It was a well-considered response. Academic, not phony. "Unless," I said, "Brian thought someone caught him. Like you?"

"I see your point. I'm not sure he's that clever. Though that little drama earlier today leads me to believe he might be quick to anger."

"He claims that was staged for the show. Do you think Mallory upset him that night?"

"Who knows what goes through his boorish brain? She certainly made a production of her interest in Felix." Eva lowered her voice. "You know that he walked her home, right?"

"So I've heard." I still had trouble imagining that Felix could kill anyone.

We paused before crossing the street to the cemetery. Costumed children, adults, and dogs milled about the church parking lot. While I couldn't see any electric lights, beams behind fog machines created mists worthy of horror movies. Candles and lanterns flickered in the dark.

Holmes and crew had set up carved pumpkins along a broad path. They glowed with scary faces, sinister grins, polka dots, and some truly artistic depictions of witches and ghosts.

In the background, ghoulish moans and witchy cackles were interrupted by clanking chains. I hoped the very small children wouldn't have nightmares.

Scary guides with lanterns waited to take small groups of visitors into the foggy cemetery. One of Clementine's triplets ran screaming from a scraggly zombie in torn clothing.

I found the frighteningly pale gentleman in a ruffled shirt, formal coat, and top hat more intimidating. A woman in a simple country dress with a white apron might have been reassuring but for her white makeup and the dark circles around her eyes.

Clementine's boys were fascinated by the guide with an arrow through his head. They readily accompanied him, along with Mr. Huckle, Clementine, and her daughter, who carried the ever-present stuffed dog. Inside the graveyard, white mists floated across the aging headstones.

"Oh, look!" Eva prodded me gently. "They've set up the Ouija board. This could be good."

"A fun show, you mean?"

"Kind of. I'll explain when it happens."

"A trick?"

"Not exactly. I'm going in on the tour. Want to come?"

"I'll wait. You go ahead." I watched as she hurried over to join a group. Surely it wasn't a coincidence that she was in a rush to join Mark's group.

Right behind her, my own staid Aunt Birdie willingly joined a tour group with Mr. Luciano by her side. Unbelievable! She had a spark of fun in her after all.

Lillian carried GloryB and chatted with Grayson and Mark while they waited to begin.

It seemed like the whole town and all the tourists had turned out. A dog howled somewhere in the distance, setting off all the other dogs, including Trixie. Their melancholy group howl sent shivers down my spine.

One tour guide seemed very familiar. She wore

a red tulle skirt and a hooded cape. Red fabric lined the hood. I stared at her. It wasn't until she flashed her fangs at Felix and Brian that I recognized Zelda.

Laughing, I joined their group for the tour of the cemetery. Zelda regaled us with a mixture of spooky tales and lovely tributes to people who had lived in Wagtail.

The group ahead of us shrieked in horror. Zelda cautioned us and walked forward, swinging her lantern.

The light caught a coffin in the mist. Zelda had launched into the story of Hiram and Obadiah when we heard a creaking sound. The coffin opened with a slow screech to reveal a skeleton inside. Even Brian yelped and jumped back.

It was all in good fun, and before we knew it, we were back in the parking lot. Felix and Brian led the way to the card table that had been set up with a Ouija board. Five chairs circled it. Eva was taking a seat. Mark, Felix, Brian, and Grayson slid into the other chairs.

Rose whistled like a sailor. "Quiet, please! The tours will continue after this presentation."

The crowd hushed and clustered around.

"And now," said Rose, "we will try to bring back the spirit of Dr. Hiram Montacue through the use of the time-honored Ouija board."

Like magic, an eerie orange glow illuminated the table and the participants.

Ben ambled up next to me to watch.

In a singsong voice, Brian called out, "Mallory! Mallory! Tell us who murdered you!"

Mark slammed his open palm over the moving pointer. "I told you we're not going to disrespect Mallory that way."

Brian snickered at him. "What's wrong? Afraid she'll appear and tell the truth, Mark?"

Mark's Adam's apple bobbed. "Everyone agreed that it would be wrong to take advantage of her death by trying to contact her. What's wrong with you?"

Brian seemed chastened like a little boy.

Mark called out, "Hiram Montacue! Hiram Montacue! We invite you to join us in our celebration tonight. Are you here?"

Ten hands were poised over the Ouija board.

Four of the tour guides held lanterns and kept the crowd from closing in on the table.

The pointer moved slowly to *yes*. I heard a few gasps and saw some people looking up in the air as though they thought they would see Hiram hovering over us.

"Hiram, did you murder Obadiah Bagley?" intoned Mark.

They had placed the pointer back in the middle of the board, but once again, it moved to *yes*.

"Is Obadiah here with you?"

Another *yes*.

"Send us a sign of your presence, Obadiah!"

The participants placed their fingers lightly on the edge of the table. For what seemed an eternity, nothing happened at all.

There was some mumbling in the crowd.

And suddenly, the table lifted at an angle. Aunt Birdie screamed, along with some of the onlookers. The table wobbled slightly and fell back into place.

"How did they do that?" I whispered to Ben.

"Must be a trick of some sort."

The crowd fell silent in anticipation.

Mark spoke gently to Aunt Birdie. "Try not to scream this time, okay? It breaks our concentration."

Birdie flashed him an irritated look that I knew all too well. She didn't like being corrected.

Mark sang out again. "Becca Wraith, we feel for you. Send us a sign of your presence."

Once again, the participants poised their fingertips near the edges of the table. We waited in silence.

Just when I thought nothing would happen, the table lifted off the ground and moved so much that the participants had to stand up. The crowd shifted back to make room for them.

Murmuring arose and the table fell to the ground.

The crowd broke into applause. The ghost hunters staggered over to Trixie and me.

"That was exhausting." Felix rubbed his forehead. "I've never done that before."

Mark laughed, a bit giddy. "I'm just glad it worked. I wasn't sure it would."

"C'mon," said Ben. "There had to be a trick."

We were in the middle of the parking lot. There was nothing to which they could have tied strings.

I noted that I wasn't the only skeptic. Several people had turned the table over to examine the bottom. I heard one of them say, "That's impossible. There's not a thing here. It's just an ordinary card table like I have at home."

"Okay, Eva. How did you do that?" I asked.

"It's known as the Philip Experiment. A bunch of Canadian parapsychologists invented a character who never existed. They tried to reach him, which clearly couldn't happen since he was a figment of their imaginations. Yet to their surprise, the table where they gathered did exactly what you saw tonight. The general belief is that it's some kind of mind over matter thing. That the collective concentration of the group is able to make the table levitate."

Grayson nodded. "I wasn't sure it would work for us, but we were willing to give it a try."

"The original group was filmed, and the experiment has been reproduced by other groups," explained Eva.

"You're pulling my leg." There was no way that could happen.

Ben drifted over to examine the table for himself.

"No, no," insisted Felix. "It's true. It can happen. It's the collective subconscious."

"That's really scary. If a small group of people can raise a table, imagine what a crowd could do!" My head reeled at the prospect.

Several of them nodded.

I looked down at Trixie, who was listening in. "Do not try this with Casper to levitate treats off the counter!"

She wagged her tail as though she understood and was laughing. If Trixie ever learned how to levitate food, nothing would be safe.

She jumped up and pawed at Brian's pocket. "Wrong pocket, silly." He pulled a dog treat out of his other pocket and handed it to her.

Brian nudged me. "Who's the babe?"

I cringed a little. "Where?"

"The blonde."

Clementine. Not that I could blame him for being attracted to her. Her long tresses almost glowed in the dim light. "Clementine Wiggins. Fresh from a divorce, so tread carefully."

"Is that your way of telling me to stay away?"

I debated. It wasn't any of my business, really. It might give Clementine a boost to know someone besides Parker was attracted to her. On the other hand, she might not appreciate Brian's attention. "She's been through a rough time, Brian. I know she's not ready to date again just yet."

He didn't seem one bit put out. "How about the ghost woman giving tours?"

"I don't know her."

He wiggled his eyebrows. "Well, I *am* a ghost hunter." He sauntered in her direction.

The tours resumed while the ghost hunters helped eager little kids have their turn at the Ouija board. The spooky clanking of chains and unearthly moans resumed.

Before they wrapped up the events, Rose and Doc Kilgore prepared the graveyard for the official bone hunt. People lined up with their dogs. It was like an Easter egg hunt, but bone-shaped dog cookies were hidden around the fenced cemetery for dogs to locate with their sense of smell.

Clementine's daughter was turned away because her dog was actually a stuffed toy. I hurried over and asked, "Would you like to take Trixie on the bone hunt?"

She turned an eager face up to her mom. "Please?"

Clementine was not happy. I knew that look. But she acquiesced. "Don't drop her leash. I'll hold Lassie for you."

"I recognize that dog. Is that the same Lassie you used to lug around everywhere?"

The hint of a smile crossed Clementine's lips. "Can you believe it?"

Holmes must have overheard. He joined us and

said, "I remember teasing you because your Lassie was a cocker spaniel, not a collie."

"We've loved the fur right off Lassie's back, I'm afraid, but she's still holding up. My husband even took her to be re-stuffed and freshened up."

"Sounds like a nice guy. I'm sorry things didn't work out," said Holmes.

"Funny how you can live with a person and not know him as well as you thought you did. I seem to be making that mistake over and over." Clementine shot me a look of daggers.

"What's the problem?" I whispered.

Twenty-four

"Holmes, would you take the boys over to the Ouija board table?" asked Clementine. "They've been itching to play with it."

"Sure thing. C'mon fellas. Do you know any ghosts you want to talk to?" The twins ran to the table with Holmes on their heels.

Clementine crossed her arms, still clutching her old stuffed dog. "I trusted you, Holly. I can't believe you went to Dave and blabbed about my problems."

"Sorry, Clementine, but you're angry with the wrong person. I didn't say a word to Dave." I glanced over at Oma, but didn't rat on her. If I had to bet, I would put my money on the interim mayor of Wagtail running to the police about Parker Colby.

"You obviously told Holmes."

"Did not! Everyone knows that you're divorced. What's the big deal about that?"

A long sigh shuddered out of her mouth. "It's that stupid Parker Colby. He has me on edge. Look at him over there pretending he doesn't see us."

He was leaning against a tree, casual and unconcerned.

"Did Dave talk to him?"

"Says Parker has a clean record. Dave asked him to stay away from me."

"And Parker said?"

"Some kind of garbage about being attracted to me."

"You're still beautiful. Maybe he was serious."

"Oh, puh-leeze! Not you, too. I'm a divorcée with three small children and not a . . ." Clementine winced. "And more problems than anyone can imagine."

"Is there something I can do to help?"

"Find someone to rent the space where Putting on the Dog used to be. It's one of the biggest storefronts in town, just sitting there empty. If we had a tenant, it would produce a cash flow again, which would be such a big help."

"Parker said he was looking for an office for his dog magazine."

She shot me a dirty look. "I want him to *leave* town! Not to stick around."

All three of her children ran back to her clamoring for her attention. She addressed each of them, oohing and aahing in excitement with them.

Her daughter handed me Trixie's leash. "Trixie was very good. She was the first one to find a bone!"

Why did that not surprise me? "Thank you for taking such good care of her."

Clementine gave me a little wave. She joined Mr. Huckle, and they started across the street with the children.

"Who was that?" Ben had sidled up to me.

"An old friend, Clementine Wiggins."

Ben watched her fade into the night. "Very attractive."

And acting very peculiar.

Holmes loped up to us. "Ben, would you mind giving me a hand loading the coffin into Doc's golf cart? It's a little heavy for some of the scouts."

Ben readily agreed. I hoped the scouts were stronger than Holmes thought, because Ben had trouble lifting a heavy briefcase.

With the ghost hunters and scouts pitching in, we made short work of cleaning up.

The general consensus was that there wouldn't be sufficient time to stop for dessert at a restaurant, because the ghost hunters and their new pals, Ben and Holmes, had to be at Aunt Birdie's in about an hour and a half.

Holmes prodded me. "I bet there's dessert in Oma's magic refrigerator."

I bet there was, too. "Let's go back to the inn. I'm sure I can find something yummy."

Trixie shook like a wet dog when I removed her leash in the lobby of the inn. "Are you glad to be able to run around with Casper?"

She answered by trotting over to her new friend.

Eva crooked her finger at Ben. He followed her to the cat wing. Holmes saw them and hurried after them.

What were they up to? I couldn't help tagging along.

Eva unlocked her room.

"What's going on?" I whispered to Holmes.

"Eva promised to show us the flashlight trick."

Ohhh. I wanted to see it, too. It had been astonishing when I saw it live at the Wagtail Springs Hotel.

Holmes closed the door behind us, and Eva fetched a flashlight.

She held it out to us. "Care to examine it?"

Holmes opened it and looked inside. "Just a battery-operated flashlight. Looks ordinary enough to me."

"Are there any ghosts known to inhabit this room, Holly?" asked Eva.

"No. This is the new wing. It was built in the last few years."

Eva grinned. "Okay. I'm going to turn out the lights. Is everyone ready?"

She placed the flashlight on the dresser and turned off the overhead light. "If there is a spirit in this room, please acknowledge your presence by turning on the flashlight."

We waited. Seconds ticked by. Suddenly, the flashlight turned on.

Ben gasped, "Cool!"

I understood why—it was quite impressive.

"Thank you," said Eva.

The flashlight went out.

"Is your name Goober?" asked Eva.

The flashlight flicked on immediately.

When it turned off, once again she thanked the ghost. "Goober, have you ever murdered anyone? If so, please turn on the light."

This time it took a little bit longer, but the light turned on again.

Eva was laughing when she hit the switch for the overhead light.

"How did you do that?" asked Holmes. "It seemed like Goober was really here."

"Watch the flashlight," she said.

Oddly enough, it flicked on again. Eva picked it up and unscrewed the top. "There are two tricks here. The easiest is to screw the top on just enough to make a loose connection. The light is turning itself on and off because because the top isn't attached properly. The connection breaks and it goes out."

"What's the second trick?" asked Ben.

"Timing your questions right. Sometimes the light comes on faster than a ghost hunter expects. Of course, that's when he has to make a joke about the ghost being eager."

"Are there other tricks that are this easy?" Holmes tried the flashlight trick, screwing the top on and off until he thought it was just right.

"You'll probably see some tonight. Feelings are difficult to disprove. Sometimes I can find a draft in a spot everyone claims is cold because of a spirit presence, but it's nearly impossible to explain being touched on the shoulder or the sensation of being watched."

"I thought some people are more open to spirits," said Holmes. "Like my grandmother Rose. She's seen them her whole life."

Eva nodded. "Obviously, I can't see what they're claiming to see. It's fascinating to me that every culture has spirits and ghosts. Sophisticated cultures and primitive tribes—they all share in the belief of the supernatural."

"Doesn't that support their existence?" asked Holmes.

"There are a few things that everyone on this planet has in common. One of them is death. It only stands to reason then that all peoples need to develop a mechanism to cope with that."

I wanted to listen to more, but everyone was in a rush tonight to get over to Birdie's to hunt for ghosts at her house. "I hate to leave this conversation, but I have to find some desserts. Excuse me."

"I'll be there to help in a minute," called Holmes.

I walked through the dining area to the official inn kitchen. If luck was with me, I might find an entire cake or a platter of lemon bars. I opened the walk-in cooler to look around. Eureka! Cupcakes! Some had chocolate icing with candy corn pumpkins on top, others had white frosting with spiderwebs. A few even had black Halloween cats on them. I retrieved a cupcake stand and loaded it up, thinking that I hadn't seen the black Halloween cat toy in a while. Trixie must have lost it.

Holmes stuck his head inside the door. "There you are. What can I do?"

"Carry this into the sitting room for me? And then come back for the cups?" I loaded a tray with cups, saucers, dessert plates, spoons, and napkins, and added a couple of dog cupcakes and some fishy-smelling kitty treats for Twinkletoes and Mrs. Mewer. On another tray, I added creamer and sugar.

Ben wandered in as I was making coffee. He adjusted his glasses. "Holly, I think I might have been wrong about you moving here."

I looked over at him in surprise.

"I thought you were out of your mind to move to a remote place where everything revolves around pets. There's not even a Starbucks!—which I still think is nothing short of barbaric. But I'm really enjoying the ghost hunters. Maybe they're not typical Sugar Maple Inn guests, but they're smart and interesting. I guess I'm starting to see what you like about Wagtail." He looked around. "Where are your dog and cat?"

"They're not allowed in the official inn kitchen. It's the way Wagtail meets the state regulations. People food is prepared in kitchens where animals are not allowed."

He frowned at me. "I'll have to check on that. It doesn't sound right at all. They shouldn't be in dining areas, either."

"Leave it alone. They worked it out long before I came here. I mean it, Ben. Don't start trouble."

He nodded, albeit somewhat reluctantly. He brightened up. "Hey, are you coming with us to Aunt Birdie's tonight?"

Why did it bother me so much when other people called her Aunt Birdie? I guessed she must like that title, but somehow it made me suspicious. When had she gotten to know Ben that well? She'd made a point about being Miss Dupuy to Felix. "No, thanks. I need to get some sleep. While you guys snooze tomorrow morning, I'll be up and about."

I handed him the tray with the creamer. "Take this and give it to Holmes. He'll know where to put it."

"Like it's so complicated that I can't figure it out?"

I ignored his sarcasm, poured coffee into a pot and trailed along to the sitting room, where I made the rounds pouring coffee.

Ben surprised me by being so comfortable that he looked like he belonged to the Apparition Apprehenders. I watched him engaging Felix and Eva in a lively conversation. What happened to my boring ex-boyfriend? The one who didn't believe in ghosts? Suddenly he was eager to stay up all night and go with them to Aunt Birdie's house? The Ben I knew would have rather curled up with a book in the privacy of his own home.

And then it hit me. Maybe *I* was the staid one. All these people were excited about staying up most of the night to search for ghosts. I had seen my own great-grandfather's book fly off a table at Aunt Birdie's house for absolutely no good reason, yet I was much more interested in going to bed. But I cut myself some slack because I hadn't had more than a few hours' sleep since I arrived.

Tomorrow I would lighten up.

After they left for Birdie's, I dutifully lugged everything back to the kitchen, loaded the dishwasher and turned it on so the cook wouldn't have to deal with dirty dishes in the morning.

When everything was tidy, I took Trixie out to the doggy potty.

Stars shone bright in the velvety sky. There wasn't a sound in the night. No wind, no voices, no ghosts, no cars, no barking. Just a peaceful night in the mountains.

We headed upstairs to our quarters. Twinkletoes and Mrs. Mewer were waiting for us, watching TV. I'd been here for days, and I still didn't know where the remote was. I used the button on the TV set to turn it off and headed straight to bed.

With the ghost hunters entertaining Aunt Birdie and no one screaming in the middle of the night, I finally managed to get a decent night's sleep. In the morning, I was uncharacteristically energetic and ready to get going.

Trixie opened her eyes briefly before rolling over to continue snoozing. I peeked into the kitchen, where steaming tea awaited me. With a bite of chocolate croissant in my mouth, I opened the cat door for Twinkletoes and Mrs. Mewer.

I popped in the shower, blew my hair dry, and pulled on a black-and-white houndstooth dress. I fastened the narrow black belt at the waist and slid into black suede flats. I stepped outside on my balcony while I fastened silver earrings on my earlobes.

The sun shone on Wagtail. The usual early birds ran or walked with their dogs and cats. A few people sat on park benches enjoying coffee. In spite of Mallory's death, I was brimming with happiness at being in Wagtail.

When I went inside, I found Ben lounging in one of the cushy chairs, drinking coffee and noshing on chocolate croissants. Trixie sat on the huge footstool trying out all her best begging faces. She raised a paw, but it had no impact on Ben.

"How can you sleep with all these animals around?" Ben grumbled. "The cats clawed at the door until I opened it. Then they jumped on the bed, over the bed, over me, played tag, ran through the apartment, and returned to stare at me. Kind of like they're doing now."

Twinkletoes and Mrs. Mewer sat on the hearth. Mrs. Mewer yowled a loud complaint.

"They were trying to tell you to feed them."

"Ohhhh."

They shot to the kitchen ahead of me and rubbed against my legs while I spooned Cheesy Chicken into two bowls.

Trixie ran back and forth between them and Ben, unsure where she might score a snack.

I coaxed her away from the cats with a crunchy dog biscuit.

"Does that old fellow bring you coffee every morning?"

"Mr. Huckle delivers tea to me. And he's off two days a week, so it's not every morning."

Ben yawned and scrubbed his face with his hands. "I thought you were insane to move here. But you've got it pretty cushy. This apartment is four times the size of my place. And you never have to cook. You just walk into a kitchen and help yourself."

I bit back the temptation to say *don't get too comfortable.* I didn't have to worry. He would notice all the boxes again when he recovered from the surprise of pre-breakfast room service.

"Did you see any ghosts last night at Birdie's?"

Ben licked his fingers and frowned.

I perched on the arm of the matching cushy chair with my steaming mug of English Breakfast tea. "Did something happen?"

"I went along with them for fun, but by the end of the night, I have to tell you, Holl, I was reconsidering. Aunt Birdie said you saw a book fly off a table?"

I nodded. "It was—" I broke off as I searched for it on the shelf. "That's odd. I put it right here."

"Elmer's diary?" asked Ben.

"How did you know?"

"It was on the floor yesterday. Did you know Elmer was a lawyer, like me? Pretty interesting guy." He eyed the big footstool. "That's odd. I left it right there."

"It'll turn up. Anyway, I've examined it. I didn't see anything that would make it fly through the air."

"It happened when we were there, too. Holly, I looked at the book myself. There were no strings and it wasn't weighted. Like you said, it just flew through the air. Birdie said Elmer likes to toss books around."

"They probably slide off the table. Don't you think?"

"How about the Ouija board demonstration? That was the weirdest thing. They all had their hands above the table, yet it lifted."

"They told you about the melding of minds thing, right?"

"Are you kidding? I looked it up right away. I don't know—after talking with Felix, Mark, and Grayson, I have to wonder if I was too quick to jump to conclusions. They're pretty bright guys. I wrote off ghosts as preposterous without much consideration. I'm going to have to give this some thought. It sure felt like someone was at Aunt Birdie's place last night. I could swear someone touched my arm."

I almost fell over. Ben? Believing in ghosts?

He stretched and yawned again. "I expected the caffeine to wake me up, but I'm pooped. I'm going back to bed. Good night."

"Good night." I watched him stumble toward the guest bedroom and thought it was very decent of me not to remind him that it was morning.

After a quick trip to the potty for Trixie, we headed for breakfast. I was beginning to look forward to the fabulous breakfasts at the inn every day.

Oma was already sipping coffee in the quiet dining area. Gingersnap lay at her feet and wagged her tail when she saw us.

I pecked Oma on the cheek and said good morning. Stroking Gingersnap's broad red head, I slid into a chair. Due to the early hour, only a scant handful of non-guests had showed up for breakfast. With the ghost hunters asleep after a night of work, Shelley didn't have much to do yet. She brought mushroom and spinach crepes for Oma and me and spinach crepes for the dogs. At Oma's invitation, she retrieved another crepe for herself and joined us for breakfast.

We gabbed about Wagtail until Mr. Luciano arrived. Oma immediately invited him to join us as well. Shelley shifted into waitress mode just long enough to fetch coffee, orange juice, and a stack of pumpkin pancakes with pork sausages on the side.

"You are up early," said Oma.

Mr. Luciano waved his hand. "I don't stay up all night with the ghost hunters. No, no. Mark is in charge of them during their investigations, and I get my sleep!"

Mr. Luciano cleared his throat. "Liesel, our stay at the Sugar Maple Inn has surpassed all expectations. Except for one small item. Has anyone ever suggested that you have a poltergeist?"

Oma's eyebrows lifted. "This is a very old building. A few guests have reported ghost sightings over the years."

Shelley stopped eating. Her gaze darted around the room. "Your team is seeing ghosts in the inn?"

Twenty-five

"Nothing like that," Mr. Luciano directed a reassuring smile at Shelley. "It seems things are being moved. Small items. Felix reported leaving a package of crackers on the nightstand of his room. When he returned, the bed had been made but the crackers were gone. He found them later on the seat of a chair."

Oma tsked. "I shall ask our housekeeper to be more careful. She probably moved them to dust."

"They are such insignificant things that I wouldn't normally mention them at all." Mr. Luciano speared a piece of pancake with his fork. "It sounds like a poltergeist. Brian left a pen on the dresser and found it in the bathroom. One of the cameramen seems to think someone went through his duffel bag."

Duffel bag? How would anyone know? They weren't like suitcases where everything would be orderly. Just picking up a duffel bag could dislodge an item.

Oma frowned. "Is anything missing?"

"No, no. You don't have a thief on your hands. Are you sure no guests have mentioned a possible poltergeist before?"

While they chatted, my mind wandered. First someone tried to sneak into the inn through the back door. Now items were being moved around? Luggage searched? Could there be a connection? A thief who was looking for something?

Oma nudged me. "Holly! Mr. Luciano asked you a question."

He graced me with an indulgent smile. "I hope you'll join us today at one o'clock when we discuss our findings from our investigation at Birdie's house. Your charming aunt will be there."

Charming wasn't exactly the word I would have used to describe Birdie. But then, she probably hadn't awakened him in the middle of the night to see if he would come to her rescue. "I would love to attend. Are we serving breakfast again?"

Shelley nodded. "I can't wait to hear what they found. That Ouija board demonstration last night was something else."

"Speaking of poltergeists, Mr. Luciano, when the ghost hunters checked in, a most mysterious orb floated across the wall. You wouldn't have had anything to do with that, would you?" I asked.

Mr. Luciano roared. "That was fun. A most appropriate greeting for them, don't you think?"

"How did you do that?" I asked.

"It was easy. I arrived a few days early and Lillian was kind enough to help me experiment. All you need is a flashlight and a good hiding place. The balcony overlooking the reception area proved ideal. I could stand back far enough to be out of view from anyone downstairs. I simply turned on the flashlight, pointed it at the wall and let it travel around the room. The beam makes a perfect glowing orb! I'm told it can also be done through a window, though I suspect that might work better in the dark."

After breakfast, I spent the morning with Oma, working out my responsibilities and setting up a schedule that would give her plenty of time off.

I grabbed a quick lunch of crab cakes and salad with Shelley, then helped her set up the breakfast buffet for the Apparition Apprehenders in the sitting room.

I hadn't seen Ben all morning. Now that he was a converted believer in ghosts, surely he wouldn't want to miss the Apparition Apprehenders's meeting. I dashed up the grand staircase, gasping for breath at the top.

Trixie beat me there but showed no sign of being winded.

I unlocked the door and strode in—to a mess! As if it weren't bad enough that boxes still cluttered the floor, someone had spread shredded newspaper all over it. I hurried to the guest room and opened the door. "Ben?"

He rolled over and covered his eyes with his forearm. "Mmm."

"What happened here?"

"Hmm? Sleep." He turned to his side.

"Mr. Luciano is about to start his discussion of the findings from last night."

Ben sat up fast. "Why didn't you say so?"

"What's with the newspaper?"

"What newspaper?"

"Out here." I left him alone to dress.

He was pulling a shirt over his head when he stumbled in and saw what I meant. "What happened?"

"Don't you know?"

"I was asleep."

He had the decency to help me gather the newspaper shreds and deposit them in the trash.

Trixie and I left him and rushed back downstairs to work.

Eva arrived first, carrying a cup of coffee. She wore a turquoise dress with a boat neck and a brown leather belt that cinched her waist. The skirt flared out in generous folds. She kept her eyes glued on the mirror where we had seen Mallory's face, but she must have noticed me. "Any more appearances by Mallory?"

"Not that I know of. Have you seen Mrs. Mewer this morning?"

Eva dared to turn her back on the mirror. She cocked her head and smiled. "She was so cute. She came to my room and mewed outside the door. When I opened it, she walked in proud as could be, holding her tail high. And your darling Twinkletoes followed right behind her. They jumped on the bed and snuggled down with us for a nap. They were adorable."

Us. Did she realize she'd said *us?* Or was her relationship with Mark common knowledge now? Did Dave know about it?

Eva smoothed her skirt, settled on a sofa, and patted it. "Could we talk for a minute before everyone else arrives?"

I sat down next to her. "Sure. What's up?"

She lowered her voice. "Has Ben ever done anything that made you wonder if you didn't know him as well as you thought?"

"Funny timing. Just this morning, he said—"

She leaned over and whispered, "I'm afraid Mark killed Mallory." She covered her mouth with both of her hands. "I can't believe I said that out loud. It's been weighing on me for days!"

A shiver started at my head and zigzagged down to my toes. "Why would you think that?"

Eva heaved a huge sigh. "Mark and I were engaged once, but Mallory came between us." She set her coffee on a side table and fingered the fabric of her skirt. "I couldn't bring myself to forgive him for the longest time. I hated Mallory.

I had been ready to marry Mark when she came along and ruined everything. Part of me blames Mark, of course. He didn't have to fall for her, to be seduced by a little vixen. But Mallory used people and knew how to stroke a guy's ego. She latched on to him like a tick. And suddenly, my future changed. No marriage, no Mark. I took a job in another town."

She sipped her coffee. "After a few months, Mark tried to get in touch, but I ignored him. I was too hurt. There was no amount of explaining that could ever help me overcome what had happened between us. But as time went on, my thoughts kept coming back to him, like we were destined to be together. When he contacted me about the Apparition Apprehenders, I thought he was trying to mend fences. I was ready to see him again. To find out if there was still a spark between us after all. We e-mailed back and forth, and honestly, it was like those years had never passed."

Now it was beginning to make sense. "So you were expecting a romantic reunion with him."

"Exactly. But when I arrived, Mallory was here." Her eyes met mine. "I was shocked to see her. It tore me apart to know she and Mark were still an item and that everything he'd said had been a big lie. You can imagine how furious I was. No, it was more than that." She closed her eyes briefly in pain. "I relived all the dashed hopes that I experienced at my broken engagement. I thought

Mark lured me here under false pretenses, hoping to spark the existing animosity between Mallory and me for the show. I *hate* that petty fights boost ratings. I was having none of it. I will not be used for such base sensationalism."

But hadn't I seen her sneaking off with Mark? "You changed your mind about Mark's intentions?"

Eva blinked hard. "I was mistaken. It wasn't easy convincing me that he and Mallory weren't an item. I'm not that foolish. I'm not a young girl eager to believe sweet talk. I guess that's obvious. I'm not easily duped. But there's no question that Mark still has feelings for me."

I didn't want to give her cause to reconsider, but the words slipped out of my mouth. "Then why was Mallory staying with him?"

Eva heaved a sigh. "Yes, that disturbed me as well. Mark is a kind soul. I gather that in her quest to snare Mark, romantically speaking, Mallory made several surprise visits to Wagtail. During her last visit, she agreed to participate in the ghost walk this week but failed to reserve a room. Then she came back and there wasn't a room available in town, so Mark capitulated but told her this was the very last time she could bunk at his place."

I didn't know Mark the way Eva did but I would be suspicious. Oma had said the whole town was booked solid. Still, if I were in Eva's shoes and the woman who had been the cause of my broken engagement appeared to be shacking up with my boyfriend again, I don't know that I would have bought that story.

"I . . . I'm still in love with him. I'm surprised. Deep inside I hoped our reunion would play out with a happy ending, but I never thought I would feel this way. It's still there. We were meant to be together."

Oh no. I really liked Eva. But didn't that admission put her first in line for murdering Mallory?

Eva released a shuddering breath. "Mallory was such a pill. Mark was afraid she would come between us again. And then Mallory was murdered. It's like she's haunting me."

I nudged her in a friendly way. "But you don't believe in ghosts."

She turned her head to glance at the mirror again. "I don't have to see her. I can't get her out of my head. Maybe that's the reality of ghosts. Maybe they live in our heads."

"I don't follow."

She held her arms out as though she were embracing the world. "There's so much input around us. Sounds and smells and sights—everywhere we look, there are a million details to take in. Our brains compensate by filling in the blanks. That allows us to capture what we need at a glance. Maybe when someone dies, and we're thinking about them, our brains fill in blanks by adding them for a moment." She brightened. "That would account for sightings where the ghost is gone in an instant."

"But I saw Mallory in the mirror, too."

"That's right." She scowled. "So much for that theory. Oh no, here they come. Please don't mention this to anyone?"

Why did people keep asking me to keep their secrets? Especially when danger was involved? I didn't know Eva nearly as well as I knew Clementine, but if Mark was a murderer, then Dave needed to know.

I stood up in a hurry, eager to avoid promising anything.

Casper bounded in with a moccasin in his mouth. Trixie ran to him to sniff his score. Felix carried an oversized mug, which I promptly filled with coffee. His eyes were barely open but he politely murmured, "Thanks," before nestling on the sofa.

"Is it okay for Casper to chew on that shoe?" I asked.

"Huh?" Felix moaned. "Give me that!" He hustled over to Casper and took the moccasin away from him.

The rest of them staggered in slowly. Even energetic Brian viewed me with bleary eyes and a giant yawn. "Your aunt is a hoot."

I poured coffee for him. "Really? I don't know that side of her."

"Aw man, she's so into spirits. Wish I had an aunt like her."

I bit back my desire to beg him to take her.

Mr. Luciano turned up, looking rested and pleased. Gina trotted along beside him.

Lillian Elsner and Aunt Birdie arrived simultaneously from different directions. Their eyes met, and I could almost hear Western-style dueling music. Walking as fast as she could, Birdie collided with Lillian, elbow to elbow in her eagerness to be the first to reach Mr. Luciano.

Lillian won. She straightened the riding blazer she wore over a blue button-down shirt and smoothed her trousers. GloryB joined the other dogs. Polite canine sniffing protocol ensued.

Aunt Birdie's thin lips rolled into an angry slash as she watched Lillian greet Mr. Luciano.

Eva's words, *two can play this game,* echoed in my head as Birdie slid into the seat next to Mr. Luciano. The very seat in which Lillian, no doubt, had planned to sit.

I saw it coming before it happened. Not realizing that Birdie had slid into the chair behind her, Lillian sat on Birdie's bony knees. Birdie jerked up, sending Lillian to the floor.

I set the coffeepot on a table and rushed to Lillian's aid. "I'm so sorry! Are you all right?" I held out my arms to her.

Birdie rose to her full height. In her very best Southern lady voice, she trilled, "Mercy me!

Dahlin', a heifer has to be careful where it plops its hindquarters."

I wanted a hole to open in the floor and swallow her. I wasn't that lucky, though. "Lillian, let me help you up."

Grayson beat me to it. I scooted out of the way, and Lillian looped her hands over his shoulders.

But if Birdie thought she'd won, she was dead wrong.

Mr. Luciano offered Lillian the coveted chair next to him.

Birdie turned paler than Becca Wraith's ghost. "Maybe you should go," I whispered.

"I will do no such thing! They're going to talk about *my* ghosts. If anyone has a right to be here, it's me."

I hoped she realized that her game had backfired and she'd lost the battle for Mr. Luciano.

Birdie lifted her scrawny chin. Holding her head high, she strode across the room, took the seat next to Grayson and patted his hand.

Lillian was as sweet as could be. "Now don't fuss about me. I just took a little spill is all. I seem to be doing that a lot lately."

I cast a dirty look at Aunt Birdie, who turned away.

When everyone had calmed down, Mr. Luciano asked Eva if she'd had a chance to analyze the EVPs from the hotel.

One cameraman turned in her direction, and the

other focused on Brian, who scooted to the edge of his seat.

I hoped he wasn't gearing up for another outburst like the one yesterday.

Eva cleared her throat. "While almost anything can be achieved these days through technology, I'm unable to find any evidence of tampering with the recording. EVPs can be a little bit tricky, because the sounds are so full of static that they're often unrecognizable as words until the words are imputed and the power of suggestion comes into play."

Eva paused for a moment. "You will be happy to know that in my years of listening to EVPs, these are the most remarkable ones I have ever heard. There is no doubt that a child's voice is saying, *'I'm gonna get you.'*"

A cheer went up among the ghost hunters. Mr. Luciano applauded and grinned.

When the noise subsided, Eva continued. "Unless the recorder picked up a child's voice from another location"—she lifted her forefinger as though suggesting caution—"which is possible, what with baby monitors and the like, I cannot explain away this particular EVP."

The guys high-fived and the dogs danced among their feet, joining in the excitement.

They settled down to discuss their plan to return to the hotel that night to see if they could catch more EVPs or even contact the child.

"Birdie," said Mr. Luciano, "are you aware of any children who died at the Wagtail Springs Hotel? Mark's research hasn't turned up anything involving children."

Birdie sat up straight, clearly proud to be considered an authority. "I don't know of any child ghosts at the hotel, but I'll go through some of my books to see if I can find any mention of children dying there."

"And finally," said Mr. Luciano, "we thank you, Birdie, for a fascinating night at your home. Our ghost hunters caught images of your flying books on tape. Perhaps the most startling moments were when Birdie channeled her deceased relatives and told us what they had to say. It's not every day that we meet a psychic medium."

Birdie blushed. "Now, now. I'm not anything special. The ghosts just live in my house, and I talk with them."

"Eva, what's your take on the haunting of Birdie's house?" asked Mr. Luciano.

"With all due respect to Birdie, of course, I cannot enter her mind to hear and see what she perceives as a ghost."

"That's right," said Birdie. "*You* can't see or hear them."

Eva smiled. "There are several theories that may apply. Automatism certainly comes to mind. It's an altered state of mind, not unlike sleepwalking. People enter a spontaneous fugue in which they can spirit write or speak to spirits. Most likely, however, the thoughts and drawings actually stem from their own memories and thoughts."

Birdie snorted. "They do *not!*"

"Another popular theory, which has been scientifically verified, is the presence of low frequency vibrations. The human ear only captures certain sounds but there are other sounds around us, caused by weather, movement, all sorts of things. Not everyone is affected but some people, like Birdie perhaps, are more in tune with them and they tend to hear or see things that are actually caused by the low frequency vibrations."

"Maybe ghosts are the source of these low frequency vibrations!" Birdie was miffed.

"And lastly, I have to say that I saw some definite apophenia."

"I do *not* have apophenia!" declared Birdie. "What is that?"

"It's when we attribute significance to insignificant or unrelated things. Like last night when the book fell off the table, for instance. You said Elmer must have thrown it. Then the wind blew and the curtain billowed. You claimed Elmer was walking around the room and had made the curtain move. Later on, you tripped in the dark and claimed Elmer was at fault. The truth of course, is that there was simply no connection between any of those events. The book sliding off the table, I'll grant you was odd, but I am confident there is a slope or some underlying low frequency vibration that caused it to fall. The curtain blew because of the wind, not because of Elmer. And you tripped because it was dark and the floors in your lovely old house are uneven."

"Why, never in my entire life have I heard such a load of hogwash! The only true thing you said was that you can't see or hear what I see and hear. So there!"

"Miss Dupuy, do you have gas in your house?" asked Eva.

"Yes, of course. I only cook with gas. I don't know how anyone can stand electric stoves."

"You might want to have your house checked for low levels of carbon monoxide. It's been known to induce hallucinations."

"Were you raised up in a barn, child? No one has ever insulted me like that, except, of course, for my only livin' relative, Holly Miller."

Me? What did I do now?

Thankfully, Mr. Luciano wrapped things up. When he finished, Felix raised the shoe that had seen better days before Casper gnawed on it. Holding it in the air, he asked, "Uh, who does this belong to?"

Most of the guys glanced at him, but no one claimed the shoe. "Huh." Felix lowered his arm and examined the moccasin. Casper tried to take it from him. "I'll make you a deal. If no one comes looking for the shoe by tomorrow, you can have it. Okay?"

Casper didn't seem pleased by the bargain, but what choice did he have?

"Uh, Felix, if you and Casper don't mind, maybe I should stash that in the lost and found box at the reception desk."

"Oh, sure!" Felix handed the moccasin to me.

Casper's sad expression reminded me that I had to find a replacement for the toy dinosaur that Gingersnap and Trixie had de-stuffed. I retrieved my wallet and a leash and paused on my way out to place the shoe in our lost and found box and let Oma know where I was going.

Trixie and I took the walkway through the grassy green center of the pedestrian area. Little pumpkins still lined the meandering path. Toward the middle, we cut over to the stores on the right. But before we hit the sidewalk, I caught a glimpse of Parker Colby up to no good.

Twenty-six

There wasn't a place to hide and spy on him. I pretended to walk in the opposite direction, but quickly paused to admire a store window display. Why hadn't Dave gotten rid of this creep yet? I knew he was busy with the murder investigation,

288

but there were laws against stalking. It was time Dave took some action.

Out of the corner of my eye, I saw Clementine and her children leave a store. Parker ambled along behind them. Once again, Eva's words echoed in my head. *Two can play this game.*

I hurried toward him. "Parker! Parker, hi!"

He kept going.

I tried again. "Par . . . ker!"

By now everyone was looking at me. Everyone except Parker. I could see the tension in his shoulders. He finally turned toward me. I rushed up to him and started babbling to give Clementine time to get away.

"Hi! I thought you didn't hear me. Isn't it a glorious day? How is your search for office space coming?"

Parker stared at me blankly. Aha! Caught him.

He recovered, though. "Very well, thanks." He pointed in Clementine's direction. "I'm just on my way to an appointment."

"We'll walk with you." I grinned at him and hoped he would think I was flirting. "Where are you headed?"

But before he could answer, I heard a sweet little voice shout, "Trixie!"

Clementine's daughter, Emily, ran toward us. Trixie tugged at her leash, wagging her tail.

Emily dropped her stuffed dog and wrapped her little arms around Trixie, who licked Emily's face.

It would have been a heartwarming scene if big mama bear Clementine weren't standing a few yards away shooting daggers at me with her eyes.

"Emily! Come this instant. Emily!" shouted Clementine.

I bent over to Emily. "Honey, I think your mom wants you. Maybe you can play with Trixie later on."

"Emily, right now." Clementine's voice held a no-nonsense note that even I recognized.

Emily stood up. "Bye-bye, Trixie." She ran back to her mother, who hustled her children around the corner and out of sight.

All I had to do was engage Parker for a few more minutes. "Have you rented a place, then?" I picked up Lassie, the stuffed dog Emily had forgotten in her haste.

"Not yet. Excuse me, but I have to hurry."

I stepped in front of him. "Nonsense. You're in Wagtail. Life moves at a different pace in the mountains. Don't you think that's one of the nicest things about it? I moved here from Washington, D.C. Everyone was always in such a rush. It's nice to be laid-back, you know?"

"Still, I shouldn't be late . . ."

"Of course not. Don't let me keep you. Was it this way you were going?" I strolled on, straining to think of things to keep asking him to slow him down. "So have you signed a lease? What's the name of your magazine?"

"I really have to go. Excuse me." Parker bounded off and turned in the direction Clementine had gone.

Trixie and I dashed after him. We slowed at the corner and I peered around it. Parker stood in the middle of the street, his hands on his hips.

They'd lost him. Yay! Feeling pretty darned good about myself, I gazed around at the stores.

The dark storefront of Putting on the Dog looked like a gaping hole among the cheerful show windows. I was surprised no one had grabbed it. Puppy Love was a much smaller store, but I popped in, hoping they might have a dinosaur toy. They didn't, but the lovely clerk sent me to Pounce & Fetch.

The second we walked in the door, Trixie went into wagging overdrive. She wriggled from her nose to her tail.

I asked if they had a Halloween black cat toy for dogs, but they didn't. Trixie wasn't too upset about it, though. She snuffled her way through an aisle of amazing cat toys. I made a mental note to bring Twinkletoes with me one day. She would love the remote control mice, catnip toys, and incredible cat trees to climb. I picked up a crinkle tunnel for her.

Trixie led me to the selection of balls—from tiny ones no bigger than a golf ball all the way to special soccer balls made with creases so dogs could pick them up. Trixie kept going, though. In the stuffed animal aisle, she zeroed in on a squeaking fuzzy yellow duck. It was a little too big for her, but I didn't care. She loved it and carried it around the store as I searched for a dinosaur. And there it was—a green stegosaurus with triangular purple spikes on its back. Just like the one Trixie and Gingersnap had destroyed.

I took my items to the register and paid for them.

Pointing at Emily's stuffed dog, the clerk asked, "Shall I add the other doggy to the bag too, so you don't have so much to juggle?"

"Great idea. Thanks." Armed with our bag of goodies, Trixie and I left the store and bumped into a very weary-looking Dave. His haggard appearance softened my resolve to let him have it about Parker Colby.

"How about I buy you a cup of coffee?" I asked.

His face brightened briefly. "You have information for me?"

"Come on." I bought two pumpkin spice lattes, a big box of Frankenstein brownies with green faces, big white eyes, teeth, and screws in their necks, and a bat cookie for Trixie.

Dave led the way to a bench on the path in the green. He popped off the top of his coffee and swigged half of it.

"Don't you ever stop to eat and drink?"

"Maybe you haven't heard. There was a murder in town."

I ignored his sarcasm. "Does that mean it's officially a murder now?" My pulse quickened, and not from the coffee.

He grunted unhappily. "Murder, no. Drowning, yes. Doc was dead on. The official autopsy report is back. Cause of death was drowning. She had a bruise on the back of her head and another on her back. Not inconsistent with a fall. No sign of strangulation. No scratch marks. Nothing of interest under the nails."

"You're not buying it."

"Are you?"

"I want to. The ghost hunters are all so nice. I really want to think that they're innocent." I sighed. "Did you know that Mark and Eva were engaged and Mallory came between them?"

Dave sat back against the bench. "Yeah. Sure gives both of them motive, doesn't it?" He bit into his brownie.

I felt like a traitor. "Mark seems nice. I'm still not sure why he didn't report Mallory missing."

"He was at the inn with Eva until early in the morning."

"Then he could have killed Mallory on his way home! I can't quite figure out why Mallory was staying with Mark if they weren't a couple."

Trixie cocked her head at me as though she was wondering if she would ever get a bite of her cookie. I broke off a piece for her.

"You still seeing that guy Ben?"

That was a major change of topic. "No. We broke up. We're done."

"I have it on good authority that he's staying with you."

"Well, yeah, but he's in the guest room . . . Oh, I get it. Mark told you she was staying there but they weren't involved?"

"Apparently it was her habit to arrive unannounced. This time he agreed to let her stay because she had signed on to play the role of Becca Wraith in the ghost walk. He called around to find another place for her to bunk, but all the rooms were booked for Howloween."

"But that doesn't make sense. I'm not sure I believe him. Mallory was dreaming of their wedding. She wanted to be married right away. A girl doesn't usually do that unless there's some flame to the fire."

"Maybe *dreaming* is the right word. Sometimes one person is more involved than the other. People have been known to be delusional and not give up on someone whom they loved."

I'd forgotten about his rotten experience with his last girlfriend. "Did you give up?"

"This isn't about me. Focus, Holly. Anything else?"

"How about Parker Colby?"

Dave drew back and looked at me. "What does he have to do with Mallory?"

"You tell me. Didn't Oma complain to you about him stalking Clementine?"

"Oh, that. Yeah. I'll have another talk with him."

"How can you be so calm about it?"

"He checked out okay. Clementine hasn't said a word to me about him. Are you sure she's upset?"

"She's running from him, Dave!"

"Okay, okay."

The sound of rustling leaves drew our attention. It was Trixie, digging in them frantically. She turned over a piece of broken pumpkin and continued to dig.

"What is that?" asked Dave.

"Just pumpkin. When I came through here the other night one had broken. I guess that's a leftover piece."

"I hate it when kids do that. They come to Wagtail for Howloween because it's fun and all decked out but then they go and vandalize the things that make it special. Hey, she found something else."

Dave rose and picked up a small item.

Trixie didn't take her eyes off it when he brushed off the leaves and dirt.

"A penknife. Pretty nice one, too."

I watched him turn it over. "Aren't you going to fingerprint it?"

A red flush crept up his neck to his ears. "Aw, Holly. You've been in the city too long. Some guy probably sat at this bench, and it fell out of his pocket. Besides, Mallory wasn't stabbed."

"Well sure," I said sarcastically, "because her killer dropped his knife."

Dave dutifully pulled a plastic bag out of his pocket and slipped the red knife inside. "You do realize that almost every male resident of Wagtail owns one of these? This isn't going to be a clue." He held the bag between his hands and stared at the knife. "I wish it was. I could use some help with this case."

He sat down beside me again.

"So you'll talk to Parker? Can't you just run him out of town or something?" I knew what he was thinking—that he had a bigger problem on his hands with Mallory's death. "How can you be so sure that Parker didn't kill Mallory?"

Dave picked up his brownie with a napkin and ate the rest of it instead of answering me. "We don't live in the wild West, Holly. I'm on top of it. You're as pushy as your grandmother."

"Thank you."

He suppressed a grin. "There has to be something I'm overlooking."

Trixie's lips brushed my fingers when she tried to nibble the cookie that I held in my hand.

I broke off another piece for her. "We know that Brian and Eva were outside of the inn that night."

"It always comes back to the same people, doesn't it? Brian and Eva, Felix and Zelda, and Mark."

"You can't be serious about Zelda?"

Dave took a deep breath. "Just doing my job, Holly. Please. I'm getting enough flak from Rose and Doc and their crowd. They're fighting me tooth and nail on this. Don't you start on me, too." He stood up. "Thanks for the snack. If you learn anything else, let me know." He turned to leave.

"Hey, Dave?"

He paused and looked back at me.

"Do you know where Mark lives?"

He grinned at me, and I suspected I was in his good graces again. "Over on Elm, on the west side of town. It's a white Cape Cod with the brightest blue door you ever saw. You can't miss it." Dave left, ambling along the path lined with pumpkins.

I wanted to believe Doc. There was only one problem—I didn't. From the beginning, I had thought someone had a hand in Mallory's death.

I watched Trixie dig in the leaves, tossing them every which way. Mallory's death was driving a wedge between generations in this town. The older folks sided with Doc and his belief that Mallory's death had been an accident, while the younger crowd suspected foul play.

I stretched and stood up. Well, no one could be upset with me for walking Trixie, could they?

We struck out for Hair of the Dog. At the tables in front of the bar, I checked my watch. At a leisurely pace, we walked the six blocks to the pedestrian zone, crossed it in the most logical location and walked the couple of blocks to Zelda's house.

The ancient home suited Zelda. A short stacked stone fence surround the property. Carved pumpkins sat atop it, flanking the walkway to the house. Ivy climbed the walls. Stone covered the first story, and dark, weathered wood clad the upstairs. Diamond pane glass accented the dormer windows. Out front a sign announced her pet psychic business. A black cat sat on the front stoop, eyeing us warily.

Zelda had capitalized on the natural gingerbread appearance of her home by placing a black kettle near the front door, along with witches' brooms and old black boots. A collection of witches' hats hung on a coatrack. Spiderwebs draped the doorway, and skulls lay about helter-skelter.

I checked my watch. Twenty minutes. On to Mark's place. Elm Street was only two blocks down. It was a typical Wagtail street with lots of trees, tidy yards, and an odd combination of house styles, reflecting the years they had been built. Three blocks later, the bright blue front door of a Cape Cod indicated that we had arrived. I checked my watch again. A mere twelve minutes from Zelda's house.

Trixie and I headed back to the inn. Another fifteen minutes. By my calculations, Felix would have been back at the inn just before three in the morning. And that didn't even count the amount of time Mallory would have needed to change into the Becca Wraith costume. Of course, it was largely useless information, because no one had noted the exact time of Felix's return to the inn. Still, had he drowned Mallory, he would have returned much later and might have been seen by Eva or Brian, both of whom would have surely mentioned something by now.

I had barely stepped inside when Shelley called out, "She's here!"

Zelda peeked out of Oma's office. "Where have you been?"

"Walking. What happened?"

Shelley motioned for me to follow her into Oma's office. "We can't talk about this when your grandmother is present. Hurry!"

Casey was lounging on the sofa with a cup of coffee. Holmes sat on the other side. He waved to me and smiled.

"Didn't you bring any leftover goodies, Shelley?" asked Casey.

Trixie sprang onto the sofa and nestled under Holmes's arm. She gazed up at his face as though he were the most wonderful person in the world. Not that I blamed her for feeling that way.

I set the box of Frankenstein brownies on the table. "Will this do, Casey?" I plopped my shopping bag on the floor next to a cushy chair.

"Hey, cool!" He snatched one up.

Zelda poured coffee into a mug and handed it to

me. She cracked the door ever so slightly. "So I can see if anyone is out there," she explained.

I added milk and sugar to my coffee and settled into my seat.

Shelley spoke in a low voice. "We're all worried about Zelda because of the rumor. We thought if we brainstormed and worked together, we might be able to figure this out. But"—she looked from me to Holmes—"no blabbing to the older set in Wagtail, specifically your grandmothers."

I felt like I had missed something. "What rumor?"

Zelda choked on her coffee.

Holmes spoke up. "That three people left Hair of the Dog together that night, and one of them was dead in the morning."

My initial reaction was to spout, *Nonsense!* and say how silly that was. But then it dawned on me that the rumor, no matter how ugly it sounded, was true. "Ugh. That's really rough."

"It *is!*" whined Zelda. "It's totally unfair. Just because we left with her doesn't mean we killed her."

"Of course not," I said as soothingly as I could. It didn't look good for her, though. Anyone could see the logic in that dreadful rumor.

Shelley cleared her throat. "So let's talk this through, okay? I don't dare leave Mr. Huckle alone too long serving afternoon tea. I've made a list. Zelda aside, because we know she didn't do anything, I figure it has to be one of the Apparition Apprehenders because so few people in Wagtail knew Mallory."

"Let me guess," said Holmes. "Mark is first on the list."

"Of course he is." I ticked off items on my fingers as I spoke. "Mallory wanted to marry him. She was staying with him. She had already come between him and Eva once before. And he was planning to reconcile with Eva this weekend. At least that's what Eva thought."

Holmes frowned at me. "Look, I know Mark a little bit. He's a good guy. What you're saying doesn't make sense unless he was two-timing them, and honestly, I don't think he's the type who would do that."

I held up my hands. "Just saying—he and Eva are an item now."

Shelley spoke as she checked off little boxes on her list. "Mark had a motive to get rid of Mallory, and apparently he had the opportunity."

"Which brings us to Eva," said Zelda. "She doesn't even deny being outside later that night. So she has motive and opportunity, too."

"They could have done it together!" said Casey.

"What about Brian?" I asked. "I still don't know what he was doing outside in the wee hours of the morning. At least Eva concocted a story about a light in her window. Brian said he went for a walk."

"Hmm, opportunity—but did he have a motive?" asked Shelley.

"He kept hitting on Mallory at the bar, and she was pretty brutal in her rejection of him," said Zelda.

"He wouldn't kill a girl for that, would he?" I asked.

"Are you kidding?" Casey helped himself to another brownie. "It's hard being rejected by girls all the time. The poor guy probably flipped out."

"It's not like it hasn't happened before," said Shelley. "What about that Felix guy? I'm sorry, Zelda, I know you like him. I do, too. But he *was* the last person seen with her."

Zelda shook her head. "Impossible. I saw him leave Mark's house."

"I just walked it. We can count out Felix and Zelda."

Zelda beamed at me. "Why didn't I think of that?"

"He could have doubled back," offered Casey.

"In that case, we're not any more suspect than anyone else," Zelda protested. "Brian could have just as easily walked over to Mark's house while he was out on his walk. Besides, Felix doesn't have a motive."

"That we know of," Casey muttered.

"I think he might be true-blue," I offered. "He was upset that Mallory was flirting with him in front of Mark. You know, when she introduced herself to Felix, Mallory said *she* had written *Haunting Horrors of Wagtail*."

"I've heard that, too. Taking credit for his book is motive number two for Mark." Shelley made another note on her list.

"Felix could be putting on an act in the hope that Zelda would be blamed for the murder," said Holmes.

Zelda gasped. "Nooo." She gazed around at us. "I'm sure that's not the case!"

"That leaves Grayson." Shelley flicked her pad with her pen.

"Seems pretty nice," I said. "When we stopped to buy some muffins for Birdie, the ladies in the bakery went wild over him. He was very sweet about it."

Shelley sighed. "They all had opportunity. We might as well just accept that. Any one of them could have left the inn and come back."

"That unobserved front door is a bad idea." Casey's mouth twitched. "I check it just about every hour now to be sure no one left it unlocked. It's a pain."

"Someone could sneak in so easily." I shook my head. What had Oma been thinking when she moved the registration desk to the side entrance? I had to take up that subject with her.

"I saw *you* coming back that night." Casey grinned at me. "You were wetter than a dog after a swim."

I gazed at him in shock as I realized what we had all overlooked. "Maybe none of our guests killed her."

They turned their attention to me.

"I was soaked through. Whoever drowned her must have held her down. The water isn't deep but that's all the more reason her killer would have had to be in the water. Whoever it was must have been wet—at least his or her feet and legs. Probably arms, too."

We fell silent.

"That's the missing link," said Holmes. "Even after walking back to the inn, his shoes probably would have left wet marks on the floor. Has anyone talked to the housekeeper? Maybe she noticed wet clothes or shoes."

In a calm voice, Shelley said, "It had to be Mark, then. He was the only one who didn't have to come back here. He went home and changed clothes. No one else was there to notice. He could have washed everything that night, and no one would have been the wiser."

Shelley's plan to find the culprit and eliminate Zelda as a suspect had backfired. There was one other person who could have gone home soaking wet and no one would have been the wiser—Zelda. In my heart, I knew she couldn't, wouldn't, have killed anyone. But she could have gotten away with it just as easily as Mark could have.

"I'll talk with the housekeeper," I offered. "All of us need to do some snooping to find out if Felix or Grayson had a motive."

Shelley nodded. "I fear most of the evidence is pointing straight at Mark, but it wouldn't hurt to be sure."

The bell rang at the registration desk. Zelda flew to the door.

Lillian cocked her head and smiled. "I wondered where everyone went."

The rest of us rose to leave.

"Casey," I said, "the ghost hunters are making a return visit to the Wagtail Springs Hotel tonight. If you want to go along, I'll fill in for you."

The sleepy kid came to life. "No kidding?" His mouth hung open. "That's so great! Oh man! This is the opportunity of a lifetime."

Shelley grabbed his shirttail. "Don't forget to do some snooping about Grayson and Felix's connection to Mallory."

"Yeah, yeah," Casey agreed, still excited about the ghost hunting expedition.

"How long are you staying in town, Holmes?" I asked.

"Just through the big Howloween bash tomorrow night. I'm flying back to Chicago the next morning. Right now, I'm headed over to help Grandma Rose. Wanna come along?"

A rustling noise caused us to look down.

Trixie had buried her nose in the bag I set on the

ground and was pulling out the stuffed dog that belonged to Emily.

"No!" I took it from her. "Not this one." I dug around for the yellow duck. "Here. Drool and chew on this all you like."

I looked at the loved-to-death dog in my hand and had visions of Emily crying and Clementine retracing her steps for it.

"I think I'll pass, Holmes. I'd better get Lassie back to Emily before Clementine mounts a statewide search for him."

"There's a major crisis," he teased. "Call out the National Guard!" Holmes left with Shelley.

I called Clementine from the phone in the office.

No answer. Not even the ubiquitous voice mail picked up.

"Wanna go for a ride?" I asked Trixie. She wagged agreeably. We walked outside to the golf carts. Trixie carried her yellow duck the entire way.

She hopped into the golf cart as though she'd been riding in them her whole life. She'd adapted quickly to life in Wagtail and had been surprisingly well-behaved. I was beginning to think she might not run off again. I tucked the shopping bag into the black storage compartment of the cart, and we were off.

The drive to Fireside Farms was gorgeous. Most of the leaves had fallen, leaving bare branches exposed, but the reddish gold carpet they created on the ground was stunning. The air held a nip in it, just enough to suggest that winter would be on its way, and we ought to enjoy the sunshine while it lasted. An occasional cloud drifted over the sun, and in one of those moments, I felt cold and wary. Without sunbeams, the leaves seemed drab and lifeless, and the wind whispered through the bare limbs of the trees.

The white fence of Fireside Farms came into sight. We turned and chugged down the long driveway. But we had only made it midway when a scream pierced the air.

Twenty-seven

Trixie leaped off the golf cart and sped toward the barn, yelping.

I parked the cart and ran after her. At the barn door, I paused. Trixie barked furiously at a man bending over something—or someone. Clementine!

I glanced around for a weapon. Anything I could slam over his head or back. Where was a pitchfork when I needed one? I grabbed the only things nearby, a saddle and a rope horse halter connected to a lead.

I flung the saddle on his back to weigh him down, straddled it, looped the halter over his head and pulled it tight. "Clementine! Clementine!

Are you all right? Say something, Clementine!"

Trixie danced around them, continuing her relentless yipping.

"Clementine!"

A feminine hand waved near the ground.

I yanked the halter, stepped off him, and kicked the saddle away. "Get up!"

That didn't turn out quite so well, because Parker towered over me and could have easily strangled me with his bare hands. Instead, he loosened the tight halter at his throat and choked out a whispered, "Can't breathe."

Clementine rolled over and sat up slowly, her hands around her throat. She waved at me, flicking her hand down, but I didn't understand her gesture.

Parker seized the halter lead, and with one quick jerk it was out of my hands. I backed away and tried to call Dave, but couldn't get a signal on my phone.

"Clementine, are you okay? Where's your gun?"

She leaned over, pulled it out of a pocket, and handed it to me.

Oh swell. A toy. I pointed it at Parker anyway.

He backed away a step, his hands turned up with palms facing me. "I should get some credit here. Clementine, tell her."

Clementine nodded. Her voice was raspy. "He's okay."

I was thoroughly confused.

"Trixie," I said, "that's enough barking."

She followed her nose to another door, still emitting an occasional yip.

Parker spoke calmly. "Please put down the gun."

"Not a chance." Did he think I was some kind of idiot? As long as he didn't get too close, maybe he wouldn't figure out that it was plastic.

Parker rubbed his neck. "What did that guy want?"

"What guy?" I asked.

"The one I pulled off of her."

Clementine staggered to her feet. "What did he want?" she rasped. "The same thing you want!" Her voice gained strength with her anger. "I don't have them! I don't have them! I don't have them! How many times do I have to tell people that I don't have them?" She broke into a hacking cough. "The phone rings all day long," she wheezed. "I don't even answer it anymore. People are sneaking around, scaring me, frightening the children. For pity's sake, can't you leave us alone? I *don't* have them!"

Parker stared at her. He mashed his lips together and frown lines creased over his nose. After a long moment, he nodded his head. "You know, I believe you."

"Then, please, leave me alone."

Why did I feel like I was on the outside of this conversation? I didn't dare interrupt, though.

"Hey!" he protested. "Is this any way to show

your appreciation? I just saved you from that creep. Tell her to put the gun down."

Clementine held on to me as though she didn't have strength in her legs. "Thank you," she said bitterly. "You'll forgive me, I'm sure, if I'm not overwhelmed with gratitude to someone who has made my life miserable."

Parker inhaled. "If you'll pardon my saying so, I don't think *I'm* the one who did that."

Clementine bit her upper lip and winced. "Would you *please* get off my property?"

Parker blinked at her. "Am I the only one who understands that you were just attacked? You could use my help. What if he's still around here?"

I finally butted in. "You'd better come stay at the inn, Clementine."

"I'm not leaving the house."

"I'm calling Dave." I pulled out my cell phone again and walked toward the huge barn door.

"You won't get a signal here," said Clementine. "You can use the landline in the house."

"Let's go then," I whispered.

We stopped at the door to the barn and looked around.

"When I say *now,* run for the side door," instructed Clementine. "Now!"

Clementine, Trixie, and I ran like our lives depended on it.

Parker strolled, as if he hadn't a worry in the world. "Where are the kids?"

Clementine shot an angry look at him. "They're not here." She pulled a key from her pocket, but her hands shook so hard that she fumbled with the lock.

"Give me that." Parker took the key from her and unlocked the door.

In a split second we were inside with Parker. I wasn't sure if that was a good thing or not. After all, he did save her. But he shouldn't have been there in the first place.

I picked up the wall phone, dialed 911, and told the dispatcher that Clementine had been attacked. A small tabby wound around my legs. She clenched a turquoise mouse in her mouth, much like the one Twinkletoes and Mrs. Mewer had played with.

When I hung up, Clementine and Parker were going at it.

"If I had wanted to hurt you, I could have. But it wouldn't do me any good to kill you, would it?"

Clementine pumped her fists on her hips. "You have no business intruding on my life."

"I don't know about that. I think you were plenty lucky that I happened to be here. Do you know who he was?"

"Not a clue. You're not the only one, you know."

I was completely out of the loop again. "Did her ex-husband hire you?" I demanded.

Parker looked at me in complete surprise. "Man,

you're really out of it." He hitched his thumb in my direction. "She doesn't know?"

Clementine sagged into a chair.

She looked so wan that I hurried to the fridge for something sweet, like orange juice, but it was nearly empty. Seriously empty. Like my refrigerator looked when I was getting ready to go on a long trip. There was milk for the kids in a glass jar. No label. Did they have a cow, I wondered? A bunch of spinach from the garden, four apples, and a block of cheese.

I put the kettle on for tea. I hoped she had that. "What's going on, Clementine?"

"Have you ever heard of Ron Koontz?"

"Heard of him? I nearly lost my job because of him."

She cringed. "How much money did you lose?"

"None. It wasn't like that. He made anonymous donations through my company. I was a fund-raiser."

Clementine closed her eyes and massaged her temples. "Is there no end to the people he hurt?"

Parker slid into a chair at the kitchen table. "Sounds like Ron."

"I don't get it." I opened empty cabinets in search of tea. All I found were dried chamomile blossoms in a pickling jar. I located a Royal Stafford bone china teapot with a bold red rim and lacy gold detail. It was far more ornate than we needed, but I placed a sieve on the top anyway and filled it with chamomile. I poured boiling water over the chamomile and brought the whole contraption to the table with mugs, napkins, spoons, and a sugar bowl.

Clementine looked me straight in the eyes. "My husband was one of Ron's associates."

"What?" She couldn't be serious! But she was.

"I'm sorry. What they did was horrible." Her eyelids fluttered. "Stealing from people by promising them huge returns on their investments—I still can't bear to think of it. I asked Dad not to say anything to anyone. You can't imagine the guilt. But now I've lied to everyone I cared about. I hope you understand, Holly. I didn't want the pain and the shame following us here."

Parker raised an eyebrow. "Like you didn't know what your husband was doing? Give me a break."

Clementine threw him an ugly look. "We lived so well, but I never thought to question it. The nannies, the housekeeper, the exotic trips on private jets with Ron. Now that I look back, I don't understand how I could have been so blind." She studied her fingers. "I trusted my husband."

"Your husband went to prison with Ron for the pyramid scheme?"

Clementine nodded. "I divorced him, of course. I turned everything of any value over to the feds. *Everything.* The house, the jewelry, the cars. It's been a huge adjustment for the children. I didn't think anyone would mind if I took the cats, but I had to sell some of my horses."

"Where are the horses?" I asked. I hadn't seen any in the barn.

"I took them over to another farmer for safe-keeping. They're grazing on his land. I couldn't leave the house without being afraid someone would steal or harm them." She wiped a strand of hair out of her face and winced. "I never imagined anything like this could happen. I only kept what I brought into the marriage and gifts from my parents. It's one thing to lose your money because you make a poor investment. I know all about that from raising horses. But to steal other people's hard-earned money! They were relying on it for their retirements, for their kids' educations, for their dreams. And we squandered it. *We* even gave huge donations. Isn't that the worst? We got credit for being soooo generous"—she closed her eyes briefly—"and it was all with other people's money."

Parker leaned back in his chair and watched her.

"I'm so ashamed, Holly. I didn't want everyone in Wagtail to know. I just wanted to slink back here and lead a quiet life. Raise my children and try to recuperate. If it's any consolation to the people they stole from, I'm broke. Flat-out, completely broke. I'm bartering with the French teacher. Riding lessons for her kids in exchange for French lessons for mine. I can barely scrabble together enough change for a couple of cans of cat food. If this weren't farmland, we wouldn't have anything to eat. Don't ask me what I'm going to do come winter. I didn't get here soon enough to plant a big garden or put up preserves this year."

I reached for her hand. "Oh, Clementine! Don't worry about food. We'll take care of you."

She grimaced. "We're living in this big fancy house and still have all the trappings, but between Dad's investments with Ron and the spending habits of his last wife, he's nearly wiped out, too. We own the two most useless properties in all of Wagtail—his ex-wife's empty store and the Wagtail Springs Hotel. There's no money for us to make a go of either one of them, and no one is interested in buying or renting. We're a mess, Holly."

Parker had made himself useful by pouring tea into mugs and passing them around.

I eyed him suspiciously. "If her husband didn't hire you, who are you, and why are you stalking Clementine?"

"*Stalking* is an awfully strong word for it, don't you think?"

At exactly the same time, Clementine and I said, "No!"

"It's common belief that your friend here has some items of great value. Namely, the frustratingly elusive ghost diamonds worth millions."

I sucked in a deep breath. We were having tea

315

with the enemy! "You're here to steal them?"

Clementine leaned forward and waved both hands in the air. "How many times do I have to tell you that I don't have them?"

"The story goes that mastermind Ron and his patsy, Clementine's husband, saw the big crash of their pyramid coming and invested in a tidy nest egg that they could sell on the black market if necessary—the ghost diamonds. Except the feds can't find them. All we know is that Clementine's husband was heard to say that he hid them in something Clementine would never give away."

"Holly, I swear I don't have them. Didn't know a thing about them, don't know where they are. I even sold my engagement and wedding rings and gave the proceeds to the feds. But horrible people like Parker have been swarming to Wagtail in the belief that the diamonds are here. The other night I found a crazy woman in my closet who demanded I turn them over to her because her boyfriend lost all his money, and he wouldn't marry her if he was poor. Can you imagine? Like I'd hand them over to a lunatic stranger? If I had them, I'd give them to the feds. Then she asked for my Hermès handbag. Can you believe her nerve? I gave it to her and told her the truth—she could have it if it would make her feel better, but my boys stashed their crayons in it and left it in the sun on a hot day. If it weren't damaged, I'd have sold it and turned the cash over to the feds."

Parker tilted his head at her. "And her clever husband knew Clementine would also turn over the diamonds. So where did he hide them? As diamonds go, they're huge, but they're still little bitty things that could be stashed anywhere. It's a mystery. Unless, of course, Clemmie knows and isn't saying."

"Don't call me Clemmie," she uttered through clenched teeth.

"So you're following her around in the hope that she'll—what? Go to a safe-deposit box in a bank? Visit the diamonds in a hay bale?"

"There are people who want them."

People? What did that mean? I imagined a lot of people would want them. Then his meaning dawned on me. "Someone hired you? You're not here because *you* lost money?"

"Hey, I'm a private investigator, okay? It's an honorable way to make a living."

"Not very good at it, are you?" muttered Clementine.

"If I had made the effort, you never would have seen me tailing you. The ones you'd better worry about are the ones you don't see." He faced me. "I'm not doing anything wrong. May I once again point out to you that I saved Clemmie today? If you'll pardon my saying so, you ought to be treating me like a hero right now."

"Frightening Clementine and her children, and disrupting their lives is wrong. By the way, here's your gun, Clementine." I handed it to her.

Parker leaned over for a better look. "A toy?" He frowned at Clementine. "You cannot tell me your father doesn't have guns. I know he's a hunter. Why aren't you carrying a real gun for protection?"

The corners of Clementine's mouth twitched. "We sold them to pay for his trip to the dog show."

I sucked in a deep breath and stared at Clementine. No wonder dark bags hung under her eyes. I doubted that she was getting much sleep between watching out for intruders, protecting her children and horses, and worrying about money. "If you sent the horses away, why are you out in the barn all the time?"

She whispered, "I'm afraid my stupid husband hid the diamonds here somewhere. He knows the one thing dad and I would never sell is this land. If I could just find them and turn them over to the feds all this terror would end. People like Parker would go away." She released a huge sigh. "I'm beginning to think it was a huge lie perpetrated by the person who really has the diamonds. That would be the worst thing for me. The ghost diamonds have been missing for decades. There isn't a reason in the world to think that Ron and my husband bought them. They could remain lost, and my life would be a never-ending misery, because people would think that I have them."

Clementine opened the clip holding her hair back in an untidy mess. Masses of straight blonde hair spilled over her shoulders. She would be a natural to play Becca Wraith.

Of course! Clementine wouldn't even need a wig. She was clipping her hair back up haphazardly when I asked casually, "Have you been staying at the Wagtail Springs Hotel, Clementine?" As soon as the words slipped out I wondered if I should have asked her privately instead of in front of Parker.

She blinked at me. "How do know that?"

Parker frowned. "When did you do that?"

I played coy. "I hear there have been quite a few sightings of Becca Wraith there lately. I saw her myself."

Clementine licked her lips. "I went there a couple of times. Like the night I found the woman in my closet. After the bonfire. I thought the hotel might be safer. Out here, no one would hear our screams."

Parker slumped in his chair and chuckled. "I can't believe it. Clementine is nothing if not a creature of habit. Every day at five in the afternoon, she locks up tight. I never dreamed she might be slipping out after dark."

"Because monsters like you are lurking outside. I have to lock my doors behind me when I step outside for anything. Otherwise people walk in and snoop around."

They were getting off the subject. "So after the woman broke in—"

"She didn't so much break in as walk in unnoticed. I guess she wandered through the house."

It *was* a pretty big place. "You threw her out and went to the hotel?"

"Right. Why are you questioning me? There's nothing wrong or illegal about it. My dad owns the Wagtail Springs Hotel."

I had to tread carefully. "I'm not suggesting you did anything wrong. You were there the night Mallory was murdered?"

"Murdered? Doc told me her death was an accident," said Clementine.

"I'm not so sure about that. You were so close! Didn't you see anything? Did you hear anyone scream or argue outside?"

"Murder? Are you sure?" Clementine pressed her hand against her forehead. "I thought she was drunk and fell into the water. Holly, she's the woman I found in my closet."

I sat back in my chair, stunned. "The one who said her boyfriend lost all his money?" She must have meant Mark.

"That's the one. I'm just horrified that someone killed her." Clementine's chest heaved with each breath. She coiled her fingers into fists. "I couldn't sleep, of course. Most of the night I paced. You know, worried about money, and

Parker, and people breaking into the house because I wasn't there. It was really pretty quiet that night. I don't recall a scream. Maybe a few boisterous voices when the bars closed, but nothing worrisome." She held up a finger. "I do remember seeing someone run by. I thought he might be looking for a dog or something."

"Would you recognize him?"

She held her palms up. "It was dark. He was nothing but a shadow. Could have been a woman, for that matter. The only thing I remember was a distinctive gait. It was awkward. Maybe an old person, or someone who wasn't used to running. Like his feet or legs hurt."

That didn't sound like anyone I could think of. "You need to tell Dave when he gets here."

The diamonds put a whole new slant on Mallory's death. What if another diamond hunter had killed her? I turned to Parker. "What about you, Mr. Nosy Pants? Where were you that night?"

"I grabbed a bite at the barbecue place and then I went back to the inn." He studied his hands for a moment. "If you must know, I took a long, hot bath."

I couldn't help but grin at the thought of macho Parker indulging in a bath. "With bubbles, I hope?"

"Hey. I've been standing around in the cold watching Clemmie. A guy's allowed to warm up, you know. My room has one of those old-fashioned claw-foot soaking tubs."

"Stop calling me Clemmie!"

Unless I was mistaken, Parker seemed to have formed a fondness for Clementine. What if he was lying? Or worse, what if he killed Mallory so he wouldn't have competition in the search for the missing ghost diamonds?

I must have looked at him funny, because he asked, "What? May I remind you that I saved Clemmie? What would have happened if I hadn't been here? Huh?" His eyes narrowed. "What I don't understand is why that guy wanted to kill Clementine. If she's gone, no one will find the ghost diamonds."

Twenty-eight

"Did he say anything to you?" asked Parker.

Clementine winced and gently massaged her throat, but shook her head. "Not a word. Did you get a good look at him?"

"There wasn't much to see," said Parker. "A guy in black wearing a beagle mask."

Clementine gasped. "A beagle? Are you serious? That changes everything."

"You mean because your dad breeds beagles?" I asked.

"Too odd to be a coincidence, isn't it?" Clementine's brow furrowed.

Trixie barked, and a moment later when someone knocked on the door, we all jumped.

"It's Dave, Clementine," he called from outside.

I rose to open the door.

Dave entered, clearly surprised to see Parker.

"I want you to come stay at the inn, Clementine," I said. "There's safety in numbers."

"I can't. They'll ransack the house. It's all we have left. I'm not leaving."

Dave sat down at the table. "Suppose you tell me what happened?"

I had other ideas. Now that Dave was with Clementine and Parker, she'd be okay. I hoped so anyway. I said good-bye, called Trixie, and hurried back to the inn.

I hadn't had a moment to open a bank account, but I had a nice little wad of cash stashed in my quarters. I retrieved it as fast as I could. With any luck, Mr. Huckle would still be at the inn.

Trixie on my heels, I ran down the stairs and into the dining area. Mr. Huckle was just getting ready to leave. I asked him to wait a moment and dodged into the inn kitchen. "Any leftovers today?" I asked.

The cook pointed at a stack of containers. "I was about to put them in the fridge."

"Thank you." I could barely carry them. Nevertheless, I stopped by the pantry where we kept a stash of cat and dog foods on hand for people who preferred to feed their babies what they were used to eating. I nabbed a few cans of the food I had seen Clementine buying for her cats and staggered out to Mr. Huckle. "Would you please take these to Clementine?"

I helped him carry them to his golf cart and then I dug in my pocket and handed him the wad of cash. "Stop by the store to pick up whatever Clementine needs. She won't take it if she thinks it's from me, so tell her that her dad sent money or something."

Mr. Huckle planted a kiss on my cheek. "You're just like your grandmother, bless you both."

I dashed back to the inn and asked Oma and Zelda, "Anyone know where Holmes might be? He said he would be helping Rose."

Oma grinned so wide that I had to add, "It's nothing romantic, okay?"

"Ach. Too bad. I think he is with Rose on the front porch. Tonight is trick-or-treating night for canines, felines, and children in Wagtail. Does Trixie want to go with Gingersnap?"

Trixie's ears perked up at the sound of her name.

Zelda laughed. "Trixie would love to go. She says she'll do anything for treats."

Yeah. Like we didn't already know *that*.

I barged out to the porch where Holmes was helping Rose organize for the trick-or-treating event.

Placing a gentle hand on Holmes's arm, I spoke softly so other people wouldn't hear and be alarmed. "Someone attacked Clementine in her barn. She's afraid to leave the house and refuses to come to the inn. Would you mind staying at her place tonight? I know she'd appreciate it."

Rose shuffled over. "What's going on?"

"It's Clementine, Grandma," said Holmes. "Someone attacked her. Is she okay?"

"She'll be fine. But she's unnerved. And for good reason."

Rose gasped. "What's going on in Wagtail?"

"I'll round up some of the guys, and we'll keep watch over our Clementine. Nobody messes with her."

Rose whispered. "Do you think there's a connection to Mallory's death?"

I was stunned that Rose had begun to have second thoughts about Doc's theory that the death was accidental. I decided to honor Clementine's wishes to keep her business private. If she wanted Holmes to know, she could tell him herself. She probably would. "I don't know. Dave is with her now."

"Grandma, have you got everything under control?" asked Holmes.

"My goodness, yes. You go right on and help Clementine."

"I'll be here if Rose needs a hand."

"Thanks for telling me about this, Holly. It's

good to have you back in Wagtail." He bounded off the porch in two giant steps and took off running along the sidewalk.

"Wish I could say the same," I murmured.

Rose overheard me. "Me, too. He's not going to be happy with that prissy fiancée of his. I can't tell him anything, though. Who am I? Just his granny. Why would I know anything about love or life?" She flashed me a little wink. "Don't you give up on him."

"Rose, that ship has sailed. You and Oma have to face it." And so did I. "I have one quick thing to do and then I'll come assist you now that I've stolen your helper."

Thanks to the late nights that the ghost hunters kept, the housekeeper was working afternoons instead of mornings. I'd barely seen her since I'd been back and had never really talked with her.

Trixie followed along, sniffing the hallway on the second floor. The cleaning cart stood outside Grayson's room.

I peeked inside. The petite housekeeper was tucking a fresh sheet under the mattress. Her long black ponytail swung as she worked. She wore a simple white T-shirt with the Sugar Maple Inn logo on it, a pair of white slacks, and running shoes.

"Hi! I'm Holly." I extended my hand. "We've never been properly introduced."

She smiled at me and shook my hand. "Marisol."

I pitched in and helped her make the bed. "Are you happy to work afternoons for a change? No early mornings?"

She smiled. "It's okay. I like getting up early."

I was helping her turn back the sheet when a black tail whooshed by my legs. Twinkletoes?

"Your kitten likes to help me. She's very, how do you say? Nosy!"

I watched as she knocked a tube of lip balm off the desk and spun it into the bathroom.

Mrs. Mewer slunk through the door, her body low to the ground like a wildcat on the hunt. She spotted the lip balm on the bathroom floor and knocked it back into the bedroom. I should have realized. Twinkletoes and Mrs. Mewer were our poltergeists. Silly kitties.

"So, Marisol, do the guests wash their clothes sometimes? Have you noticed any wet clothes when you're cleaning?"

She blinked at me as though I had asked an odd question. I guessed I had. I could have phrased it more delicately.

"Mostly the ladies. Mrs. Lillian and Miss Eva. But sometimes men do, too."

"Oh? Like who?"

Marisol gripped fresh towels in her hands. Her dark eyes rose to meet mine. "This is about the dead girl?"

I might as well tell her the truth. "Yes."

"Mr. Felix is very tidy and hung some things in

the shower to dry. Also Mr. Grayson and Mr. Brian."

Felix! I never seriously suspected him.

We finished making the bed. I gazed around the room. Grayson's clothes lay on a chair as though he had changed in a hurry. I peeked in the bathroom. Male toiletries cluttered the counter. It was a large, old-fashioned bathroom with a charming claw-foot tub.

"Thank you, Marisol," I said. "If you need anything, let me know, okay?" I walked to the door.

"Holly?"

I turned to look at her.

"Zelda couldn't kill anybody. She is much too kind."

"I know, Marisol. Thanks for sticking up for her."

An hour later, Dave marched through the front door. I knew trouble was brewing when Twinkle-toes arched her back like a Halloween cat and hissed at him.

She dashed up the grand staircase and watched him. Mrs. Mewer followed her cue, eyeing Dave with wary suspicion. She let out a bloodcurdling yowl.

"Is Eva here?" Dave asked.

My breath caught in my throat. I nodded. "In her room, I think."

Dave strode through the library. I could hear him knocking on her door.

Felix, Mark, Grayson, and Brian clustered around me.

"What's going on?" asked Felix.

Before I could answer, Eva and Dave emerged and walked toward us.

Eva reached out to me. "Will you take care of Mrs. Mewer?"

"You're arresting her?" asked Brian. A gleeful smile played across his face.

Dave was carrying a clear plastic bag in his hand. A chill shook me when I realized that Mallory's lavender necklace nestled inside it. There wasn't a reason in the world that I could think of for Eva to have the necklace in her possession.

"No!" Mark stepped forward. "No. She didn't do it. I killed Mallory."

"Aww," moaned Felix. "Don't do this, Mark."

"Shh," Mark hissed. In a gentle voice, he said, "I can't let you take the blame for this, Eva."

Oh no! Had they both been in on it?

From her spot on the stairs, Mrs. Mewer lived up to her name by emitting complaining meows.

"Mark, stop it!" Felix pushed his way next to Mark.

Mark held Eva's hands and stared into her eyes. "Leave me alone, Felix."

"But you didn't . . ." Felix looked at Dave. "He didn't kill Mallory."

Dave drank it all in without a word.

"Okay," said Felix, "if you killed Mallory, how did her necklace end up in Eva's room?"

"I hid it there after I killed her."

Oh no. That didn't sound good at all. Poor Eva. She had been right about Mark all along.

"Mark," Eva whispered. "Why?"

He squeezed her hands. "I won't let you take the blame, Eva." He looked into her eyes with love.

"You're ready to confess?" asked Dave.

Mark nodded.

Dave escorted him out the door. Behind them, Felix protested, "Mark, don't do this. Don't believe him, Officer. Ask him for details! He won't know the answers."

Eva scooped up Mrs. Mewer and held her so tight that Mrs. Mewer complained. Eva released her grip but didn't let go. She sat down on the sofa in the sitting room, still clutching Mrs. Mewer. The other ghost hunters clustered around her.

Grayson released a long breath and shook his head. "Lillian warned Mark about Mallory."

"Warned Mark? What do you mean?" Seemed like it should have been the other way around.

"I came up a few days early," said Grayson. "Lillian is friends with Mark's parents, so we went out to dinner a couple of times. Mark didn't want Mallory to come with us, but every time, she showed up at the restaurant uninvited, like she was following us. Lillian said Mark needed to be really careful, because that was obsessive behavior. 'Unbalanced,' I think Lillian called her. She was really worried about Mark letting Mallory stay at his place. Hey, where's Ben? Mark needs a lawyer. Ben?" He raised his voice. "Ben? Felix, hand me your phone, I'll call his room."

"Bet you'll be glad to get your new phone." Felix glanced at me. "Can you believe it? Grayson dropped his in the tub."

Had he? I squinted at Grayson. I had just been in his bathroom and the tub was nowhere near anything. Unless he was talking on the phone while bathing, which I doubted, I didn't quite buy that story.

Felix sat on the sofa with his elbow on the armrest and his forehead in his hand. "He doesn't need a lawyer anyway." Felix glanced at his watch. "I bet he's back here in less than two hours, and that includes driving time."

Brian frowned at him. "Are you psychic now?"

"No. I don't have to be psychic. Mark didn't kill Mallory. He just said he did to protect Eva. When Dave starts questioning him, he's going to get stuff wrong and the police will realize that he had nothing to do with Mallory's death."

"To protect me?" Eva wiped her face with her fingers. "What do you mean?"

"From the beginning, Mark was afraid *you* killed Mallory. She's the reason that you broke off your engagement to Mark. He knew how much you hated her."

"He thought I killed her? How could he imagine for even a second that I would do anything so heinous?"

Funny. She had suspected the same thing about Mark.

Felix groaned. "Are you kidding? He's so crazy mad in love with you that he's willing to take a murder rap for you."

Eva gulped air and sniffled. "Why did Mallory have to show up and ruin everything? Felix, are you sure they'll bring Mark back? Maybe Grayson is right, and we *should* send Ben to help him."

Ben happened to be ambling down the stairs, and heard his name.

Felix made quick work of filling him in.

Seemingly in deep thought, Eva sat quietly, stroking Mrs. Mewer's silky fur.

I liked Eva. If Mark had confessed to a murder he didn't commit just to protect her, then her trip to Wagtail had turned out better than she initially thought. She had Mark in her life again. In a way, I envied her. Ben wouldn't have protected me. He would have turned me in.

And that brought me to another horrifying thought. What if Mark made that huge sacrifice because Eva really did murder Mallory? She certainly had motive. We knew she had been outside of the inn that night, not only because Brian saw her but by her own admission. Her claims of the strange white light could have been nothing more than a story she invented. After all, she knew better than anyone what could and couldn't be proven.

"Eva, did you ever see that orb in your room again?" I asked.

She gazed at me in surprise. Eva set Mrs. Mewer gently on the sofa and crooked her forefinger at me. I followed her to her room.

She walked over to a recorder. "Listen to this."

She switched it on, and I heard the usual static of an EVP. I shrugged. But then I heard it. Little more than a whisper. *"Eva. Evaaa!"*

She played it again. *"Eva. Evaaa!"*

Maybe it was because of Halloween. Maybe it was because I had been immersed in ghost lore all week. But the disembodied voice creeped me out. If there were such a thing as a ghost, that soft breathy voice, almost like a wind whispering in the trees, was how a ghost would sound. Goose bumps perked up on my arms.

"You're the only one I can talk with about this, because you don't believe in ghosts," she said.

The past few days had loosened my conviction that ghosts didn't exist. I had learned about a lot of tricks, but the book on Aunt Birdie's table had opened the door in my mind just a crack, even if there were low frequency vibrations that we couldn't feel. I laughed aloud on purpose to break the tension. "You're the expert."

"Mark thinks it's real." Eva strode to the sliding glass doors and looked outside. "It's as though everything I knew for certain, all that was so clear to me has suddenly been turned upside down. Do you think it was Mallory?" She didn't wait for an answer. "Of course you don't. It couldn't be, that's ridiculous. Would you listen to me? I'm no better than anyone else, allowing emotions to cloud my judgment. It's impossible that Mallory would have come to me as an orb when she died. Or that this could be her."

"I did see her in the mirror."

Eva turned around. "Mark thinks Mallory is haunting me."

Twenty-nine

Haunting? The mere thought knocked the air right out of me. It was preposterous, of course. These people lived in a perpetual atmosphere of Halloween with notions of ghosts and goblins and otherworldly things in their heads. I responded carefully, though, so I wouldn't offend her. "Do *you* think Mallory is haunting you?"

Eva rubbed her upper arms as though she was cold. "A few days ago, I would have laughed at the mere thought. But strange things have happened since Mallory's death. The unexplained light in this room. Mallory's spirit in the mirror. Believers think that mirrors are portals for ghosts. Now the EVP with my name. I don't have an explanation for Mallory's necklace being in my room, either."

I couldn't help wondering if guilt played a role. Could it be that Eva expected to be haunted by the woman she murdered? "Why would Mallory haunt you?"

"Because I have what she wanted. I have Mark. I have his undying love. I can't believe he was willing to go to jail for me."

I would have felt so much better if she had mentioned her innocence.

"I won," said Eva. "In the end, I won."

And Mallory had lost something much bigger than Mark or his love. She had lost her life. I was getting a little bit uncomfortable. "Oh, Eva! You're the ghost debunker. You're supposed to see through these things and explain them away."

"That's just it. There are too many things I can't explain on this trip."

There were a few things I couldn't explain, either. Like who killed Mallory, and who attacked Clementine. But I wasn't planning to blame ghosts. I planned to find out who the perpetrators were. Even if one of them turned out to be Eva.

I left her room perplexed. Had Mark tried to

take the blame because he knew Eva had killed Mallory?

Back in the lobby, Ben was joking around with Felix, Grayson, and Brian. "Want to join us for dinner at Chowhound?"

"Sure. What about Mark? I thought you were off to help him."

"I phoned," said Grayson. "He'll be back in about an hour."

Oma and Rose breezed by us, unaware of what had transpired.

"Does everyone have a costume for tomorrow? It's Howloween, you know!" said Rose. "We wear them all day in Wagtail."

The ghost hunters joked about dressing like ghost hunters. But Ben pulled me aside. "Maybe I should buy a mask. To be in the spirit of things."

It was a nice gesture. I wasn't used to this side of Ben. Back in Washington he always turned down fun ideas.

"We'll meet you at Chowhound," I said. I dashed upstairs to retrieve my wallet. Ben, Trixie, and I strolled to All Dressed Pup, where I had seen costumes for people in the window.

While Ben looked around, it dawned on me that Clementine might not have costumes for the children. If I didn't have any money, a costume was the last thing I would buy. "Hey, Ben. If you were a five-year-old boy, what kind of costume would you want to wear?"

I knew the answer before he said anything. The adult pirate costume he held in his hands was thoroughly boyish and loads of fun. He adjusted his glasses. "Can a guy wear glasses over an eye patch?"

"Absolutely. Try it out." I hid my smile. Maybe Wagtail brought out the best in all of us.

A saleswoman hurried toward us to assist him. Meanwhile, I found two pirate costumes for five-year-olds. I wasn't sure about Emily. Banking on the notion that most girls liked princess clothes, I picked out a tiara, a pink dress, matching shoes that sparkled, a wand, and a white veterinarian coat. There weren't any rules that a princess couldn't be a doctor, too.

Clementine said she had sold everything. I wondered if she had something fun to wear. I thought about a witch costume, not unlike the one I planned to wear, but when I saw the not-too-revealing I Dream of Jeannie costume, I dared to purchase it for her. With her hair pulled up in a ponytail, she would make a perfect Jeannie. Besides, she could use a little magic in her life. She could always exchange it if she hated it.

Armed with our purchases, I borrowed a Sugar Maple Inn golf cart. It was still daylight when I headed for Fireside Farms with Ben and Trixie.

Ben exclaimed as the long white fences came into view. "This is quite a place. Is that really a chandelier in the stable?"

"We call it a barn in these parts. And yes, it is a chandelier."

Golf carts cluttered the driveway. The minute I stopped, Trixie jumped off and raced for the side door of the house. Ben and I followed her.

I knocked and tried the door handle. It was locked.

Parker let us in. Chaos reigned in the house. It looked and sounded like a huge party. Mr. Huckle offered us drinks.

"Thank you, but we're not staying," I said. "What's going on here?"

"It seems that Holmes took your request to guard Clementine and the children quite seriously. Half of Wagtail is in the living room. They're doling out shifts at the moment. Shall I tell Holmes or Clementine that you are here?"

"No, thank you. I'd rather you didn't." I handed the shopping bags to Mr. Huckle and whispered that they contained costumes for Halloween.

He nodded. "Very kind of you, Holly. I'll see they get them in the morning."

"Maybe you shouldn't tell her who brought them. Just say they were delivered."

Mr. Huckle smiled. "By the Howloween fairy, perhaps?"

"Works for me." I didn't want Clementine to feel indebted.

We left in a hurry so she wouldn't see us there.

We arrived at Chowhound just as Eva and Mark

338

walked up. His arm circled her waist. Mrs. Mewer and Twinkletoes accompanied them on leashes.

I scooped up Twinkletoes for a big hug, but she was more interested in the faux crows that were staring at us.

Trixie didn't mind the crows or the cobwebs and spiders that decorated the restaurant, but she jumped back in shock and yipped when the animated skeleton seated by the door spoke to her.

We joined the others at a large table.

The events of recent days had been wild and stressful, so when the waitress took drink orders, I dared to try a Voodoo Witch's Brew. The names of the other drinks had us all laughing—Black Widow Martini, Once Bitten, Bewitched, and Hocus Pocus.

Small wonder that Ben's staid request for a beer brought boos from our table. He sheepishly changed to a Killer Bloody Mary.

For dinner, I ordered the Vampire's Curse, which was shrimp and pasta in a potent garlic sauce. No garlic for Trixie, though. Goblin eyeballs made of ground chicken and rice served on a bed of gold coin cooked carrots sounded better for her.

Twinkletoes insisted on sitting on my lap for a better view. She stretched her neck and gazed around with big alert eyes. I ordered Evil Pirate Booty for her from the feline menu. She would like the locally caught catfish.

Twinkletoes and Mrs. Mewer jumped into a bay window outfitted just for cats. It was decorated for the season, with skeletons resting among glowing pumpkins and mock tombstones. The cats explored and looked out at passersby.

Mark regaled us with the story of what he called his "arrest," putting a humorous spin on what had undoubtedly been an unnerving experience.

"So, um, what did they ask you?" inquired Felix.

At that moment, the drinks arrived. Black, orange, red, and glow-in-the-dark blue. Black sugar rimmed some of the glasses. Dry ice caused fog to float off of others. When we recovered from our amusement, Mark finally answered.

"The same old stuff about Mallory. In a way, I can see why it sounds odd to them. Mallory is . . . was . . . kind of childish. At first her attention was flattering. She was like a ghostie groupie. It didn't last long, though. For more than a year we had no communication at all." He rested his elbows on the table and tented his fingers. "She appeared on my doorstep here in Wagtail without advance warning a few months ago. She had heard about the Apparition Apprehenders and the TV show. I informed her we had filled the positions and there was no room for her. My big mistake was letting her stay the weekend. She kept coming back. And then she went and promised Rose she would play the part of Becca Wraith. When Mallory showed up this weekend I told her she had to find a room someplace else, but everything was booked for Howloween. I didn't want to let Rose down, so I agreed that she could stay with me. I wish I had never done that." Mark closed his eyes. "If she had gone home, she'd be alive right now."

Felix broke the silence. "It's not your fault, Mark. You don't know what might have happened if you had turned her away. She might have died sooner."

"Yeah," said Grayson. "Hindsight always makes us wish we would have done things differently, but we don't know what might have happened instead."

Eva took Mark's hand and squeezed it in a show of solidarity.

"Do they have any leads?" asked Brian, looking straight at Eva.

"Like they would tell me?" Mark sipped his drink and then shook his forefinger. "But here's something bizarre. They asked me if any of us had a leg injury. What do you think that means?"

I suspected I knew. Clementine must have told Dave about the person with the odd gait. I wasn't about to spill those beans, though. I scanned the people at the table. No one appeared upset by the revelation. What if the killer hadn't been a ghost hunter at all? Maybe a total stranger had killed Mallory.

Over an hour later, we groaned after polishing off a six-layer Deadly Devil's Food Cake with orange frosting and a scarily decadent chocolate ganache poured over the top and sides. Felix, Eva, and I still had time to get a little trick-or-treating in for Trixie, Casper, Mrs. Mewer, and Twinkletoes.

The entire group came along for fun. In the plaza in front of the inn, a witch was handing out maps and paper trick-or-treat bags imprinted with the word *Howloween* and an adorable dog and cat wearing witchy attire.

The witch rested a scraggly black fingernail against the wart on her nose. She gazed at the faces around her, causing several children to shriek and hide behind their parents. But every single one of them peered out at the witch. The toes of her shoes curled upward, and I suspected that the green stars on her stockings glowed in the dark.

She cackled gleefully and threw her head back. The black hat with large white polka dots and a giant black-and-white bow stayed on her head, but the spider that hung off the bent tip swung through the air, eliciting more screams of fright.

"You, my little one." She pointed a gnarled forefinger at me and crooked it. "Come here, my dear," she said in a singsong voice. "I've been waiting for you."

I shuffled through the crowd as though I had no will of my own and was under her power.

A dachshund dressed as a skunk yelped a

warning at Trixie as we approached the witch. But the scary woman didn't fool Trixie for a minute. She knew Rose by scent and wagged her tail with joy.

Rose cackled at a boy who was pretending to be cool and bored with the whole thing.

He jumped back and stuck closer to his dad, never taking his eyes off Rose.

She raised her arms dramatically and whispered to me.

Thirty

"Go by Doc's house and see if Birdie is there, will you? Mr. Luciano went out to dinner with Lillian. If I know Birdie, and I suspect I do, she's chasing Doc again."

I tried not to giggle about the small-town romances and jealousies. "What does Doc's place look like?"

"It's down Cedar Street. You can't miss it. Skeletons are crawling out of the upstairs windows."

I pretended to be entranced and walked away from Rose with my arms raised and pointing straight forward, like Frankenstein. Little kids parted before me, skittering back in fear.

The ghost hunters fell in step, Felix and Grayson

copying my awkward walk, and we marched toward the residential area on the east side of Wagtail.

We soon broke into giggles and relaxed. The residents of Wagtail had outdone themselves again. Porch lights glowed, illuminating skeletons, witches, and, on one porch, a headless couple dressed for a ball. Children raced around the streets comparing their loot and pointing out the houses that were doling out the best booty. Costumed dogs and cats were either excited or wary in the midst of the commotion.

Mark shouted, "Look, a bat!"

We all turned our attention overhead. Indeed, a tiny bat flew along the street, swooping up and down.

Twinkletoes and Mrs. Mewer froze in ready-to-jump positions. If it came back our way and swooped too low, one of them might snag it.

Screams arose and children rushed back to their parents. A few of the dogs yelped and tried to chase it.

We visited a few houses, collecting an assortment of made-in-Wagtail dog and cat treats.

Brian collected people treats at each house. We made fun of him until we hit a home where a sweet lady was handing out homemade chocolate chip cookies. Even thought we'd eaten dinner and had full stomachs, the scent wafting out the door almost induced drooling. Each of us politely accepted a soft cookie full of melting chocolate.

At the house across the street, a fog concealed much of the porch. In the mist we could make out a man holding up a lantern in one hand and lifting off his head with the other. Upstairs, skeletons crawled out of the windows. Doc had gone all out for Howloween.

Even though we knew it was make-believe, the headless man caused us to approach the house with caution. Doomsday music played when Mark rang the doorbell.

The door opened slowly with a frightening creak, and a black dog in a Batman costume dashed out, wagging his tail. He ran straight to Grayson, who rubbed his head with both hands.

"Hey, Siggie. How's my pal?" asked Grayson.

Doc stepped out holding bowls of treats.

There weren't many lights on inside the house. I shuffled over to get a better look. No sign of Birdie or any other female company.

I went out on a limb and whispered, "Doc, Rose is afraid Birdie is visiting you."

He laughed heartily. "Not to worry, I'll see Rose a little bit later on tonight. Birdie seems more interested in Luciano these days."

"I'm sure you don't mind that."

Doc raised his eyebrows. "Don't sell your aunt short, Holly. She's a very bright woman."

That took me completely by surprise. Aunt Birdie drove some people bananas, yet had ingratiated herself with others. I thanked him for the cat and dog treats and scuttled down the stairs of his front porch.

On our way back to the inn, I sought out Rose to assure her that Birdie hadn't been visiting Doc. I needn't have worried. Doc was already with her.

"Holly!" called Rose. "Did Holmes find you? He said you have the wrong shoe."

"Wrong shoe?"

"That's what he said. For a costume, maybe?"

I shrugged. I had no idea what he was talking about. "I'll find him. Thanks, Rose!"

Back at the inn, I phoned Holmes, but his number rolled over to voice mail.

At eleven o'clock, Oma retired to her quarters, and I filled in for Casey behind the registration desk. Silent tranquility had settled over the inn. The Apparition Apprehenders had all gone over to the Wagtail Springs Hotel for a final investigation. Mrs. Mewer and Twinkletoes were nowhere to be seen.

"Looks like it's just the two of us, Trixie."

She wagged her short tail and aimed her nose at the treat jar on the counter.

"You're lucky you're so cute." I indulged her with a tiny Sugar Maple Inn cookie.

I tidied up a little bit, replenishing brochures and tucking away items that needed to be out of sight. The shoe Casper had carried around and chewed on was still in the lost and found box. One of the ghost hunters would probably realize that he had lost it after he checked out, went home, and unpacked.

I brought the bills up to date on the computer, an easy task because Mr. Luciano was footing the expense for everyone except Lillian Elsner and Parker Colby. By midnight, I realized why Casey often napped on the love seat. My eyelids were growing heavy and precious little remained to be done.

The registration area Oma had built made sense for arriving and departing guests. But at this hour, I felt as though anything could be happening in the hotel without my knowledge. I would have to talk to Oma about making a change.

To be on the safe side, I took a cue from Casey and walked through the silent hallway to make sure the front door was still locked. It was. But it wouldn't hurt to put on a pot of coffee. Without caffeine, I would drift off to sleep.

Trixie pricked her ears and turned in the direction of the registration area. Uh-oh. What if someone was looking for me?

I jogged along the hallway behind Trixie, whose nails clicked against the floor as she ran ahead. A gust of cold wind blew into the room as the automatic doors slid closed.

"Hello?" I called.

No one answered. I peeked in the office. Empty.

I couldn't help thinking it was eerily reminiscent of the day the Apparition Apprehenders checked in. Someone had said it was a ghost when the doors opened on their own and wind blew through the room.

Against my better judgment, I looked up at the wall where we had seen the orb. Perfectly normal. "I've been hanging around ghost hunters too long, Trixie. I'm beginning to think there *are* such things as ghosts."

Trixie followed a scent on the floor. She sniffed upward and, for a moment, I thought she was smelling the treat jar, but she balanced on her hind legs and overturned the lost and found box with her front paws.

"Trixie!"

I knelt on the floor and gathered the items. A child-sized red and blue mitten, a sheer pink blouse that made me wonder how the owner lost it, three dog toys, and a thin camera. Replacing the box where it belonged, I said, "Don't do that again."

She wagged her tail as though I had said she was the best dog in the world. I leaned over and hugged her.

And then I realized that the gust of wind had definitely not been a ghost. As far as I knew, ghosts were not in the habit of stealing shoes.

Thirty-one

In case I was wrong about that, I knelt on the floor again, just to be sure the shoe hadn't slid under the desk or been overlooked. It wasn't there.

"Who would steal a shoe from a lost and found box?"

Trixie knew, of course. She had smelled the scent on the box. But she wasn't telling. Where was Zelda when I needed to read Trixie's mind?

I hit the button to lock the doors. From now on at least I would know who came in or out. Suddenly, I wasn't quite so sleepy anymore. I pulled the box out from under the counter and took everything out. There was no question about it—the shoe was gone. But why? To be on the safe side, I made an inventory of the contents before putting them all back into the box.

Casper had picked up the shoe somewhere. Most likely he found it inside the inn. Felix would have noticed Casper carrying it around if he had discovered it outside. It had been a quality shoe of soft leather. Casper had left some scratches on it, but the shoe hadn't been wet. Of course, it could have dried in the days since Mallory's death. Didn't leather become stiff after being wet?

Would Casper's chewing have softened it up? The leather had still been supple.

If the shoe had been worn by the killer, then he probably was staying at the inn.

Nonsense. I was being silly and leaping to conclusions. One of the ghost hunters had probably griped about his missing shoe, and when Felix said it was in the lost and found box, he ran back to the inn to retrieve it.

There were serious flaws in my logic. Why not pick it up when he returned? Why take it back to the haunted hotel with him? Ugh. There must be some logical and perfectly innocent reason that someone barged in at midnight to swipe that shoe.

I wondered what size the shoe had been. Why hadn't I paid attention? Such an obvious detail.

At one in the morning, Mr. Luciano, Lillian Elsner, and GloryB returned from the ghost hunt and rang the bell to enter. I pressed the button under the desk and the door slid open.

"How's it going over there?" I asked.

"No sign of any child ghosts. They're all a bit disappointed," Lillian said.

"I'm exhausted." Mr. Luciano wiped his brow. "Ah, to be younger again and think nothing of carousing in the wee hours."

"It's amazing how many people are still milling about in the pedestrian zone." Lillian smiled at Mr. Luciano. "We considered stopping for a nightcap, but"—she clasped a hand just below her neck—"we changed our minds."

I thought I could read her mind. "Aunt Birdie?"

"Goodness, but she can be a pest," Lillian said, laughing. "I believe she thinks I'm chasing our dear Mr. Luciano! Isn't that cute? We met here at the inn for the first time a few days ago. We're becoming good friends but nothing more."

"Your aunt is a lovely woman but a bit possessive," said Mr. Luciano in a very dignified and polite way.

A bit obsessive, too, if you asked me. "Perhaps *I* could offer you a nightcap? Birdie's not here, so I think you'll be safe from her claws."

"That would be delightful. Thank you, Holly." Mr. Luciano peeled off his jacket and helped Lillian with hers.

Lillian pushed her hair into place. "I don't think it's a typical nightcap, but the ghost hunters have talked about it so much that I'm itching to try a Zombie Brain. Would that be too much trouble?"

"No trouble at all," I assured her. "Mr. Luciano?"

He laughed. "Make it two."

They settled on the love seat, and I dared to leave them alone while I dashed to the kitchen. A quick call to Hair of the Dog and I had Val's super easy recipe. When I poured the Rose's Sweet Lime on top of the Bailey's, it sank through the Bailey's in small greenish clouds.

Definitely spooky—and a little bit repulsive.

I set the small glasses on a silver tray and added a plate with a few of the pumpkin whoopie pies in case they wanted a little nosh.

When I returned, I overheard Lillian talking.

"—I never expected to love Wagtail so much." She took the drink and napkin I held out on a tray. "Thank you, Holly." She sipped her drink. "Oh, it's strong!" Taking a breath, she continued. "I lost my husband a few years ago. It was a bigger adjustment than I could have imagined. I didn't realize how much our lives revolved around his career."

"That would have been Congressman Elsner?" asked Mr. Luciano. At her nod, he smiled. "A virtuous man."

Lillian threw her head back and laughed with glee. "You should be a politician. Such a delicate way of putting it. I loved the man, but he was draconian. Rigid and punctilious. Heaven forbid a hair be out of place. My gracious, but he was fussy." She flipped back a tendril of hair. "Now that I have no need to live near Washington anymore, I've been looking for a place where I can be myself. Be a little more relaxed." She leaned forward and spoke in a stage whisper, "Wear a T-shirt and get dirty in a garden!"

When we stopped laughing she said, "Mark's parents raved about Wagtail. I thought it would be a nice little vacation for GloryB and me. But now

I think I might want to buy a cabin in the woods. It's just so relaxing here."

"You knew Mark before you came here?" I asked.

"Oh sure. Since his I-will-not-wear-clothes days when he ran around buck naked."

Mr. Luciano grinned. "I hope that wasn't recently."

"I think he was about two or three," she assured him.

"Did you have a chance to visit with Mark before"—I stopped short of saying the ugly truth, *before the murder*—"before he got so busy with the ghost hunting?"

"I did. I had a couple of lovely dinners with Mark and Grayson. The only damper on this trip has been the death of that poor young woman Mallory. I warned Mark about her. I knew she was trouble. It breaks my heart to think that Mark is under suspicion."

"Indeed," said Mr. Luciano. "He's a fine young man. I hope things will blossom between Mark and Eva. If I'm not mistaken, I believe I've seen a twinkle in his eyes when he looks at her."

Mr. Luciano and Lillian headed off to bed, leaving me to take care of paperwork in the office and contemplate Mark. Everything seemed to point at him. His involvement with Eva was especially concerning. We all thought Mallory had a lot of nerve taking credit for his book. But what if he did the research, and she wrote the book? Had he given her credit? We probably had a copy. If I knew Oma, she would have purchased it.

I scrambled to my feet and hurried to the inn library. Yesterday's newspaper lay on the hardwood floor, shredded. Assorted books had been knocked from the shelves, the pages clawed.

Trixie had been with me the whole time. Gingersnap had retired to bed with Oma. Casper was out hunting ghosts with Felix. But this mystery wasn't quite as difficult to solve. Two furry rascals had the run of the inn. While I'd been working, they had been, too.

"Twinkletoes!" I called softly.

Trixie made a mad dash for Eva's room. She'd left her door ajar. I knocked out of habit, pushed the door open, and switched on the chandelier overhead. Mrs. Mewer and Twinkletoes sat on the bed looking as innocent as little kittens. A telltale shred of a page clung to one of Mrs. Mewer's claws. I closed the door so they wouldn't attack any more books.

There was no point in scolding them. But Twinkletoes's new friend had taught her a very irritating trick.

I returned to the library, cleaned up the newspaper, and reshelved the books. Only three had to be replaced. Oddly enough, one of them was *Haunting Horrors of Wagtail*. No mention of Mallory on the cover. I flipped it open to the title page. Only Mark's name was listed. The copyright was in Mark's name, too. I read the dedication. No mention of Mallory whatsoever—not even thanks for her assistance.

I started back to the registration desk with the damaged books in my arms. As I passed the front door, someone knocked eagerly and peered inside.

I unlocked the door. "Brian. Hi!"

He rubbed his arms as he lumbered in. "Brrr. It's cold out there! Thanks for letting me in, Holly."

"Are you through for the night?"

"Uh, not completely. I just came to get some, um, batteries for the recorder."

"Lillian said you're not picking up children's voices tonight."

"It's a bummer. But sometimes we don't hear the voices and sounds until we play them back. So far no running feet, though. Nothing exciting like that." He headed upstairs.

I put on a pot of coffee in the private kitchen and poured myself a mug to stay awake. Assuming Brian had left, I locked the front door. Trixie turned her head to look up the stairs. I didn't see anyone, but she wagged her tail as though she anticipated someone's imminent arrival.

"Come on, Trixie," I called. There wasn't a good place to conceal myself. I did a one hundred and eighty degree turn and reentered the private kitchen. I scooped up Trixie so she wouldn't give me away. With the door cracked just enough to see, I peered out.

Brian stole down the stairs, glanced around, and headed for the library carrying a purse.

When I thought it was safe, I followed him. On the other side of the library, he opened the door to Eva's room and disappeared inside.

It was a tough call. Confront him or let him carry out his plans? If he had killed Mallory, he could be violent, and I could be in serious danger.

I opted to return to the kitchen and wait until I saw him pass by in the other direction.

Seconds later, he unlocked the front door and left. If he was carrying batteries, I didn't see them. They could have been in a pocket, I supposed.

I stepped out on the front porch into the night air. Brian jogged along the empty sidewalk.

For a long moment, I considered what to do. It wasn't right to snoop in a guest room. But what if Brian had put something dangerous in that bag? There was no question that his behavior had been highly suspicious. I returned to the lobby and locked the front door securely behind me.

With some trepidation, I opened the door to Eva's room. The cats lounged on her bed.

I spotted the purse right away. The handle stuck out from under the dressing table, as though Brian wanted it to be discovered.

Taking a deep breath, I pulled it out from underneath the furniture. It was an Hermès Birkin bag—the signature purse of outrageously wealthy women who could plop down cash for a handbag that cost as much as a car. I had seen plenty of them at my old job as a fund-raiser but had never actually held one. It was made of exquisite light blue leather with gold hardware on the front.

I opened it with caution, leaning back in case something fizzed out of it. Nothing happened. I peered inside. It was empty. The interior was oddly stiff. A colorful mosaic that melded into strange hues covered the bottom. Surely this was not how a pricey handbag was supposed to look inside.

I stifled a gasp. One sniff and I knew the truth— it was Clementine's handbag.

Thirty-two

There was no mistaking the smell of crayons. What were the odds that there would be two expensive Birkin bags in Wagtail in which someone had melted crayons? Zero to none, that's what.

Clementine had given the bag to Mallory. I wanted to imagine there was a good reason for Brian stashing it in Eva's room. I could only come to one conclusion, though. He must have taken it from Mallory and wanted to frame Eva for

Mallory's death. That would explain the presence of Mallory's necklace in Eva's room, too.

I jogged to the registration desk and phoned Dave.

He sounded groggy. "I'll be right there."

Ten minutes later, Dave stood in the lobby with me, examining the purse.

By four in the morning, Clementine had confirmed that it was, indeed, the handbag she had given to Mallory, and with Brian's permission, Dave was searching his room.

Oma, Mr. Luciano, and Lillian had awakened and joined the crowd of ghost hunters downstairs. I ran around answering questions and offering hot cider. Oma rustled up some platters of cheese and crackers, as well as cookies.

Eva glared at Brian, whose face had turned crimson as the fall leaves. "Why?" she demanded. "Why would you do this to me?"

He squinted at her. "Are you kidding? Do you not know how mean you are to me? You act like I'm a big, dumb galumph. My teachers used to treat me that way, like I was the stupidest blockhead of a kid they'd ever encountered. This is payback, baby! You run around so cocky and full of yourself with your nose pointing up in the air. *This is how Brian manifested a ghost out of thin air and bamboozled the public.*" He held up his hands and gestured in a prissy manner when he mimicked her.

Eva held a hand to her throat and swallowed hard. If Brian wanted comeuppance, he'd just achieved it.

Dave ambled down the stairs carrying a laptop and a cell phone. "I'd like you to come with me, Brian, so I can ask you some questions."

"About what? All I did was play a few innocent and harmless pranks to make Eva think Mallory was haunting her. Nobody got hurt."

"Did you find the other shoe?" I asked.

"No. But there are a few photographs of Mallory on your phone and computer that I'd like to talk about."

"That's not against the law."

"Some of the images are disturbing."

I gasped. "Are they kind of warped?" I glanced at Eva. "The image in the mirror!"

"My personal favorite." Brian took a bow. "Heard you both saw that one. It was pretty spooky, huh?"

"Where was the projector?" asked Mark.

Brian shook his head. "I'm not giving away all my secrets." But the way his glance flashed over to the decorative mummies gave me a clue. Trixie had sniffed around the base of them. I should have paid more attention to what her nose found interesting.

"The recording of a ghost saying Eva's name?" Mark asked.

"Also me. Pretty convincing, eh?"

"The light in Eva's room the first night you were here?" I asked.

"Guilty. But none of that was illegal. Just harmless fun."

He was admitting everything.

"Where did you get the jewelry and the purse?"

Brian grinned as if he was proud of himself. "From Mark's house, the day we went over to express our sympathy. I dropped them out a window and collected them later. No biggie. I was just borrowing them."

Dave calmly said, "I'd like to talk with you further back at the station, okay?"

"Wait!" I cried. "Did you try to break into the kitchen door on the lake side of the inn?"

Brian's brow wrinkled. "Nope. Had nothing to do with that. Sure, I'll go with you." He sneered at Eva. "Because *I* haven't done anything wrong. *I* have a clear conscience."

The moment Dave and Brian left, chatter filled the inn. To a person, everyone speculated about Brian killing Mallory. Only the dogs and cats seemed bored.

Eventually everyone straggled up to bed, except for Ben and me. I thought about Brian and Mallory while we cleaned up.

Mallory must have gone to Clementine's house while the ghost hunters were eating dinner. I thought back but didn't recall Mallory carrying a handbag when I saw her at the bonfire. She probably dropped the purse off at Mark's house. Then she joined the ghost hunters for drinks at Hair of the Dog and walked home with Zelda and Felix. At that point, for some unknown reason, she changed into her Becca Wraith ghost outfit. Had Brian sneaked out to Mark's house? Mark wouldn't have known, because he was here at the inn with Eva.

I stopped in the middle of washing a pot. A shudder ran down my spine as I considered how cleverly Brian had stolen the handbag and the necklace and planted them in Eva's room. Maybe he wasn't as dumb as Eva thought.

Ben brought the last tray into the kitchen.

"Will Brian's admissions be enough to charge him with murder?" I asked.

"Not a chance. They probably have enough for petty larceny, but that's all."

"Those purses have price tags in the five-digit range."

"What kind of idiot would pay that much for a handbag?"

"That's not the question."

"Okay"—he shrugged—"grand larceny. But I didn't hear anything that tied him to Mallory's murder."

Neither had I. Someone must have seen or heard something helpful that night. I stopped in my tracks. But someone had. Clementine had seen someone running with an odd gait. And that merchant from town said his wife saw the ghost of the black panther.

Well, that didn't help at all!

Ben went up to bed. I held down the fort until Frankenstein showed up at the glass doors of the reception area. My breath caught for a moment, but Shelley, dressed as a cheerleader, arrived right behind him. I buzzed them in, and Frankenstein took off his head long enough for me to realize he was the cook.

Halloween Day had officially arrived.

I was thrilled when Zelda showed up to replace me dressed as a cat. She had drawn whiskers on her face, accented her eyes with makeup, and wore ears and a tail.

I stumbled upstairs to my apartment, brushed my teeth, pulled on a nightshirt, and fell into bed thinking that I would never volunteer for another all-nighter. I dozed off with Trixie at my feet.

At one in the afternoon I returned to the living. No hot tea or chocolate croissants awaited me in the kitchen. I had missed breakfast, too. A shame. I had come to enjoy them.

While I showered, I considered what costume would be most comfortable to wear during the day. I had a witch costume planned for the gala in the evening. In which box might I have packed my costume for Dorothy from *The Wizard of Oz*?

I threw on my bathrobe and rummaged through

boxes. Twinkletoes jumped into them and Mrs Mewer stretched up to peer in at her. They made it into a game and chased each other.

The costume turned up in the fourth box and was surprisingly unwrinkled. I'd had the sense to pack shoes together but had to dig down to find the ruby slippers, which were pumps covered with red sequins. Even the bows just above the toes glowed with sequins. Trixie sniffed around the box.

"You're a terrier, but not exactly Toto." I cupped my hands around her ears and kissed her forehead. There was no rule that said Dorothy didn't have a thing for Tootsie Rolls. I slid the costume over Trixie's head. She seemed quite comfortable in it.

I pulled on my own white blouse and slipped the blue and white gingham pinafore dress over it. I braided my hair and tied it with matching gingham ribbons. White socks, the fabulous ruby slippers, and I was ready to go.

Trouble loomed before I made it all the way downstairs. Dave strolled in the front door of the inn, looking grim. There was no mistaking his police uniform for a costume.

I smiled at him anyway. "Good morning!"

"Living in a different time zone, Holly? It's afternoon."

Uh-oh. He seemed a little bit grumpy. "What's going on? How's Brian?"

"Brian will probably be back soon. I'm looking for Mark."

I glanced around the sitting room and the dining area. "Try Eva's room."

"Thanks."

I grabbed his arm. "You're not going to tell me why?"

Dave looked dead tired. He shrugged. "You can tag along, *Dorothy*."

Eva answered the door in a trim pink suit, pillbox hat, and white gloves. Jackie Kennedy for sure.

"Afternoon, Eva. Is Mark here?" asked Dave.

Eva's eyes widened with fear, and she backed up. "Mark?"

He strolled toward us barefoot, wearing a Sugar Maple Inn bathrobe and a towel around his neck. His hair stood at odd angles, as though he had just towel dried it. "Hi, Dave. Holly."

"Mark, do you own a penknife?"

"Yeah."

"Can you describe it?"

"Sure. It's one of those Swiss models with all kinds of cool stuff on it. Did somebody find it? I've been looking everywhere for that thing." His eyes narrowed. "My name isn't on it. How would you know it belonged to me?

Dave ignored his question. "When is the last time you saw it?"

"I had it when Grayson got here. We went over

to Wraith Hollow and hiked up the mountain. I took it with me then. After that I couldn't find it. Turned the house upside down looking for that thing."

"Did Grayson use it?"

"I don't think so."

Dave focused on Mark intensely. "Why would Mallory's fingerprints be on it?"

Thirty-three

I'm not a psychologist, but Mark's surprise seemed as genuine as my own.

"Mallory?" asked Mark.

"Mallory?" I echoed.

"Maybe she borrowed it," said Mark.

And just like that, my suspicions about him faded. Mark was calm as a lake on a Sunday morning. He could have used a word like *swiped* or *stole,* but he showed his true colors when he said *borrowed,* as if it were a natural act between friends, and she would have returned it to him.

But I was reeling from the revelation. Someone, presumably Mark or Mallory, since their fingerprints were on the knife, had lost it exactly where the pumpkin had been smashed.

"When did you hike with Grayson?" I asked.

Mark's forehead wrinkled. "A couple days before everyone else arrived."

I waited for Dave to continue with his questions. I shouldn't have butted in.

While Dave and Mark spoke, I was calculating. It seemed perfectly reasonable that it might have fallen out of Mark's pocket. But it happened during a very narrow window of time, which made it suspect. It had landed there sometime in the last few days. It was lying under a piece of the pumpkin, so one might even draw the conclusion that it happened before or when the pumpkin smashed, making the potential time frame still narrower. But I couldn't see how it tied into Mallory's death.

"Where else did you go?" asked Dave.

"When?"

"That day. Before hiking or after hiking?"

"Grayson met me at my house. We walked over to Wraith Hollow and hiked, then I went home to shower and change before meeting with Rose at Café Chat."

"Thanks." Dave turned toward me. "Could I have a word with you privately?"

"Sure." I led the way to the kitchen.

"Someone called the chief of police to lodge a complaint against me. There's a remote chance that they'll pull me off the Wagtail detail."

"No! You're part of the fabric of Wagtail. We'll stage a protest."

"Don't you dare. I don't want a big fuss. Don't say a word to anyone else, okay? I'm on my way to meet with the chief. I'll keep you posted."

"No, it's not okay. We're not going to let that happen to you. Who complained?"

Dave sighed. "One Birdie Dupuy."

"Why would she do a thing like that?" What was I thinking? She was crazy enough to have gotten me out of bed on false pretenses and timed my response.

"She's been chasing Doc a long time. He only has eyes for Rose. I'd guess she's trying to ingratiate herself."

"Say no more. I'll call your chief and tell him she's a nut."

"Thanks, Holly, but that's not necessary. This business with Brian, the attack on Clementine, Mallory's fingerprints on the knife"—he shook his head—"I don't know how it all ties together yet, but at least the chief will know I'm not out of bounds by suspecting murder. Don't worry. I'll still be around. They could assign me somewhere else, but I live in Wagtail, and they can't make me move."

I hugged him. "Good luck. Let me know if I can help. Okay?"

Dave smiled at me. "Don't call anybody on my behalf yet. I'll be in touch after I meet with the chief."

No sooner had we left the kitchen than Holmes flagged me down.

In dark jeans with bloodred stripes up the sides, tall boots, a cream-colored captain's shirt with a V-neck, and a black utility vest, he looked fairly normal, but the mock blaster pistol he carried gave his costume away—Han Solo.

"Good morning, Mr. Solo. I'll be right with you. I think it's Mr. Huckle's day off. I'd better give Shelley a hand setting up for the ghost hunters."

With Holmes pitching in, the breakfast buffet in the Dogwood Room was ready to go in a matter of minutes. The Apparition Apprehenders trickled in, groggy after being up all night. Brian showed up as the Incredible Hulk. Felix and Casper wore coordinating Batman and Robin outfits. Grayson looked dashing in a trim Star Trek uniform. Mark appeared comfortable and normal in khakis, a tan shirt, and a leather jacket, but there was no mistaking Indiana Jones's hat and whip.

When they settled in, I made a quick round of pouring coffee.

"I need a mug of this," I whispered to Holmes.

"I could use one, too. I'm not used to staying up all night. How did I ever pull all-nighters in college?"

We headed for the coffee station, where I made a fresh pot and poured the rich, hot liquid into mugs for us.

"How did it go at Clementine's last night?"

"Great. It was more like a party than anything else. She told everyone about Ron Koontz and her husband. She'll be okay. Clementine has always been a trouper." He smiled. "She's just not the wealthiest girl in town anymore. Did you get my message about the shoes?"

I glanced down at my ruby slippers, which were beginning to pinch my feet. "Rose said we have the wrong shoe?"

Holmes laughed. "That's my grandma. I love her like crazy, but she has so many projects going on that she doesn't listen. I didn't say 'the wrong shoe.' I said, 'We're wrong about the shoes.'"

"How so?"

"Because when you go to the gazebo, you take off your shoes and dangle your feet in the water. The killer's shoes wouldn't have been wet."

"It's October! It's cold out, and it was the middle of the night."

"You're not following me. When a guy goes there with a girl with romance in mind, they take off their shoes. You know, play footsie with the water."

I poured sugar and milk in my coffee and stirred it. "What makes you think there was romance?"

Holmes leaned against the counter. "Mallory must have set up a rendezvous with someone. Otherwise, she would have been asleep at Mark's house. What other reason would she possibly have for being out in the middle of the night after everyone else had gone to bed?"

"So you think Felix dropped her off at Mark's place, and she changed into her Becca Wraith costume to meet some guy she was hot for? Give me a break. You don't know women, Holmes. Who would put on white makeup and black goop around her eyes to impress a guy? Not exactly sexy."

"Think about it, Holly. The most likely killer was one of the ghost hunters. Wouldn't they think it was cool if she showed up as a ghost?"

The wonderful aromas from the kitchen were making my stomach growl. "Want some lunch?" I walked over to the serving counter and rapped on the window hatch.

The cook opened it.

"Hi! You're making something that smells heavenly."

He grinned, obviously pleased. "For two?" He walked away but returned quickly with three plates. "No garlic in Trixie's dish. Enjoy!"

Holmes and I cracked up when we saw what appeared to be meatballs with olive eyes staring back at us on a bed of spaghetti in a bloodred sauce. Breadsticks shaped like dog bones accompanied our meals.

We settled at the corner table. I was as famished as Trixie usually was. She snarfed her meal immediately.

"So here's the thing, Holmes. If we're wrong about the wet shoes, then why did someone swipe a shoe from the lost and found box last night?"

His hand held a fork full of spaghetti, but it stopped in midair. "Whoa! Someone must have thought the shoe would give him away. Are you certain it was a man's shoe?"

"I think so. A women could wear it, but Eva wouldn't be caught dead in a shoe like that."

I slipped off my own shoes while we ate. They weren't as comfortable as I remembered.

"The thief only swiped one shoe? Then where's the other one?"

"My thought exactly." I looked down at Trixie, who perked her ears, no doubt in hopes of a bite of my lunch. "Where did Casper find that shoe?" I asked her.

If she knew, she wasn't telling.

"Casper? Maybe the shoe belongs to Felix."

"Then would he have asked to whom it belonged? He could have just tucked it under his arm and walked quietly away with it."

"That shoe must mean something if the owner saw him offering it to everyone and didn't claim it as his own."

"That's what I think—not to mention that it was sufficiently important to steal it from the lost and found box."

"But what would be so special about a shoe? If

I left one of my shoes here today it wouldn't point a finger at me. No one would know it was mine. I don't get it."

I didn't, either. I filled Holmes in on Brian and the purse that belonged to Clementine.

"That's really creepy. You think Brian murdered Mallory?"

"Eva thinks he's not very bright. Yet he was clever enough to have her wondering why Mallory was haunting her. Maybe that big dumb galumph thing is just an act."

"I feel for Mark, though. The pyramid scheme affected a lot of people. He say anything about it to you?"

"No. I'm not sure he knows about Clementine's connection."

"I bet he does. He could be the one who attacked her. Maybe the attack didn't have anything to do with the ghost diamonds. Someone who lost all his money might be inclined to attack out of anger."

I didn't want to imagine that Mark could be so cruel to Clementine. Just an hour ago, I was convinced that he hadn't killed Mallory. Yet here I was wondering if he was so depraved that he killed Mallory and intended to eliminate Clementine, too.

The afternoon flew by. I itched to change into my costume for the gala, because the ruby slippers were torturing my feet. At four o'clock, the ghost hunters, Mr. Luciano, Lillian, Rose, and Oma clustered in the lobby.

"Holly!" Oma beckoned me. "Hurry!"

I limped over to join them. "What's going on?"

"Shh." She pointed to the Dogwood Room.

Thirty-four

Mark knelt before Eva on one knee and swept off his Indiana Jones hat. Something sparkly dangled from a bow on Mrs. Mewer's collar.

"Eva Francine Chevalier, would you do me the honor of becoming my wife?"

Eva's pillbox hat tumbled off when she crouched to pull Mark into a big smooch.

The group in the lobby cheered and applauded. Mrs. Mewer recoiled at the noise.

Mark managed to grab her before she took off. He untied the bow on her neck and slid a ring on Eva's finger. Even from a distance I could tell it was a whopper.

Oma must have had advance notice, because Shelley arrived with a tray of champagne glasses.

Mr. Luciano raised his glass. "Long live true love!"

Eva blushed, but her happiness shone through.

Lillian whispered to me, "I helped Mark pick

out the vintage 1960s engagement ring. I knew she would flip for it."

An oval diamond appeared to be set in a platinum. Three-tapered baguette-cut diamonds flanked it like fans on both sides. "It's lovely."

"It was such fun shopping for it," chirped Lillian.

I glanced at the ring again. Diamonds were pricy. Hadn't Mallory told Clementine that Mark lost his money to Ron Koontz? I whispered to Lillian, "Didn't Ron Koontz steal Mark's money, too?"

"He lost quite a bit, but I don't think he was wiped out." Lillian grasped Mark's hand and pulled him toward us. "What with the TV show and the book, things are looking up for him. Aren't they, Mark?" She pecked him on the cheek.

"Hey, I would have hocked everything I have to buy that ring for Eva! I'm glad I didn't have to. I was sucked in by Koontz, though. I should have known he was offering a deal that was too good to be true. Luckily, I didn't invest everything. I have a little nest egg left—but I know a lot of people who took a bath."

Surely I hadn't misunderstood. "Did you tell Mallory that you were broke?"

Mark winced. "It seemed like a gentle way to make her lose interest in me. Mallory had issues, and the security of a well-padded bank account was important to her."

Lillian raised her glass. "I think most of us can relate to that desire."

Mr. Luciano cleared his throat. "May I have your attention? I have good news. Based on early viewings of your work, I am very pleased to announce that the Apparition Apprehenders are being offered a nine-episode TV deal to be shot at various locations yet to be determined."

Cheers rose, along with a lot of high-fiving all around.

I congratulated Eva and edged away, eager to change clothes and ditch the shoes that hurt my feet. "C'mon, Trixie."

Gingersnap trotted along with us. Casper came too, carrying his dinosaur.

I was hobbling toward the elevator when Oma saw me.

"What happened to you? You're walking like an old woman."

The funny gait Clementine had seen! Maybe the killer wore only one shoe or his shoes didn't fit. "I'm going up to change clothes. Do we have someone to mind the inn while we're all at the gala?"

"I have taken care of that. You have fun with the ghost hunters. They should be in good spirits tonight with so much to celebrate."

I took the elevator up to the third floor, hoping my witch boots were roomy. All three dogs met me at the door. I unlocked it, kicked off the miserable shoes, and collapsed into one of the big cushy chairs.

An hour later, I woke to the sound of Ben ranting.

"Look what your cats did to Elmer's book."

It was a shame, really. I didn't dare show it to Aunt Birdie. The beautiful leather was intact, but they had ripped the inside of the cover. "Maybe I can repair some of the damage. Mrs. Mewer is going home tomorrow, so I think the wild behavior will probably cease."

Ben sat down in the other chair and plopped his feet up on the ottoman. It would have been rude to ask, *How long must you stay?* Besides, he'd been kind of fun this week. Not at all like the staid fellow I knew. "So what kind of work brought you here?" He didn't seem to have been doing much of it, whatever it was.

"I came to see *you*."

I couldn't have been more shocked. "Why?"

"I didn't think you would really move. It's not the same without you, Holl. I miss you."

I didn't know what to say. "Why didn't you call me? Why didn't you come by the house during the month I was packing? You acted like I was already gone."

"It didn't seem real. I expected you to come to your senses and go back to your old job, and everything would fall back in place again."

"So I messed with your comfort zone. My departure disturbed the status quo for you."

"It seemed so final. Like you had dropped off

the face of the Earth." He gazed around at the mess of boxes. "Most of your stuff is still packed. You could move back."

I rose to put on some coffee. "I thought we put this behind us. I like it here. I love Trixie and Twinkletoes. And Oma. I'm sorry, Ben. This is my home now."

He didn't say another word.

I retreated to my room to dress. The horizontally striped orange and black tights had always been favorites of mine. I slid the dress over my head and zipped the side. It had been for a formal Halloween event and featured spiderweb lace across the top. The long, flowing sleeves were made of the same spiderweb material. I pinned on a large black spider brooch that sparkled when I moved. The dress came to mid-calf to show off the fun stockings. Rhinestones glimmered on the pointy hat and the spiderweb lace trailed around the brim, like a veil.

I hurried toward the coffee and gulped it. While I waited for Ben, I fed Twinkletoes and Mrs. Mewer a dish our cook had named Black Cat Indulgence. It smelled like liver. They lapped it up.

When they finished and began to wash their faces, I said, "Now that you've damaged Elmer's book, may I recommend that you make yourselves scarce while Ben is here? We'll be leaving any minute, and you can come back in here then."

Just like typical cats, they didn't care. I scooped

them up and carried them into my bedroom. They seemed quite content to continue with the washing ritual there.

Hmm, I should have bought Trixie a matching witch costume. No matter—I found shears, snipped a bit of the lace off the hat, and tied it in a bow around her neck.

"You're probably happy to be out of that Tootsie Roll costume, aren't you?"

Ben finally emerged from the guest room dressed as a pirate and looking sheepish. "Maybe I should just wear a T-shirt and jeans, like Mark did today."

Ahh, the shy, boring Ben was back. "Not a chance. I think you're quite the dashing swashbuckler. And your glasses work great over the eye patch!"

Someone rapped softly on my door. Trixie ran to it barking.

I opened it to find Marisol, the housekeeper, holding a shoe. A lot of men's shoes looked alike to me, but I would know those anywhere. It matched the shoe that was stolen from the lost and found box.

"I am sorry to disturb you," said Marisol, "but I found this shoe in the trash today. I don't know what to do. Is a good shoe. Maybe it falls in garbage can by mistake?"

I could hardly breathe. "Do you know which room it came from?"

"Yes. Mr. Grayson's room."

"Grayson!" I should have considered him more seriously. Hadn't a woman accused him of getting rough with her at his previous TV gig?

I thanked Marisol, took the shoe, and assured her I would take care of it. I closed the door and shoved the shoe into a bag. "Let's go. I need to find Dave. Grayson murdered Mallory!"

I dialed Dave's number as we walked down the stairs but got his answering machine. Oma, Rose, and Doc were in the lobby. I told them what happened. "Marisol found the missing shoe. Steer clear of Grayson. I'm trying to reach Dave." I hoped they hadn't taken him off Wagtail detail yet.

Rose sagged with relief. "I just saw him over at the Wagtail Springs Hotel."

"We're headed straight there. C'mon Ben."

We took a large golf cart to the gala. On the way, Ben said, "I don't understand why you think this shoe is evidence of murder."

"Because Clementine saw someone running with an odd gait that night. Then someone stole the matching shoe from the lost and found box. There has to be a connection."

Ben was silent for a moment. "I hate to disappoint you but in the first place, there's no evidence that the person with the odd gait committed murder. And in the second place, that shoe isn't tied to Mallory in any way that I know of. Sorry, Holly, but I think you're making a big fuss over nothing."

The road leading to the hotel was already packed with golf carts. We parked and walked a short distance, giving me time to consider what Ben had said. I hated to admit that he was probably right. The shoe wasn't really evidence of anything. "Maybe Grayson won't know that, and Dave can use it to get a confession out of him."

As we approached, the notes of "Monster Mash" were so loud that we could hear the music outside. The grand old place had come alive for the night.

A live band performed in the ballroom. Zelda spun on the dance floor in a white dress. She made a perfect Marilyn Monroe.

Clementine was a knockout in the I Dream of Jeannie costume. "You came!" I said.

"The people of Wagtail are truly wonderful, Holly. Oma called and insisted that Dave would be here to keep a watchful eye over us. Then Dave arranged for an off-duty cop to stay at the house. Everyone has been so kind and thoughtful." Tears welled in her eyes.

"Don't cry! You'll ruin your makeup."

Parker walked over and extended his hand. "Come on, Clemmie, you know you want to dance."

"Don't call me Clemmie!" She smiled, though, and accompanied him onto the dance floor.

I pressed through the crowd in search of Dave. Where was he? If he was off duty, he might have worn a costume. I scanned people as they danced past me. After half an hour, I tried calling him again but to no avail. I spotted Holmes wearing the gross Obadiah costume again, complete with the awful latex mask over his head and the snakes attached to his hands. Yuck. He couldn't find anything better to wear?

I had lost Ben, but down the hallway, Obadiah waved his hands at me. The plastic snakes swung wildly. Holmes. He must be hot in that mask.

I walked toward him. "Really? You couldn't do better than this for a costume? It's so gross!"

He disappeared into infamous room three, where Hiram had died. Trixie walked beside me, jumping up to nip the pocket where I had stashed treats. We followed him into the room.

"What are you up to now?" I asked Holmes. "Are you going to make me listen to ghostly rattles?"

He slammed me from behind with such force that I flew forward and sprawled on the floor facedown. The bag containing the shoe arced through the air. Trixie sniffed my head. I tried to scramble to my feet but the turned-up toes of my witch's boots slipped and slid on the floor. I flipped over onto my rear but he quickly loomed over me. My skirt twisted around my legs.

Okay, clearly not Holmes! He was too tall to be Felix and not chunky enough to be Brian. "Pity that you couldn't just mind your own business. This is a warning. Do you understand?" He picked up the bag with the shoe in it. "Your grandmother would be devastated to find you dead. You wouldn't want that, now, would you?"

He was insane! I scooted backward on the floor, struggling to recognize the voice that was distorted by the mask. "Grayson?"

He clucked at me. "We do just about anything for family, don't we? Though you could be kinder to your aunt Birdie."

I looked around for a weapon in case he came at me. There wasn't much in the room. The chair. I inched toward it. "Why? Why did you kill Mallory?"

"Leave it alone. Stop poking your nose into everyone's business, or next time, you'll be the one floating in the water."

Trixie growled and jumped over me, right at his face. "No, Trixie, nooooo!" I grabbed the seat of the chair and pulled myself up. "Trixie!"

Thirty-five

The man caught Trixie by her neck. She snarled, her legs clawing at the air. "You wouldn't want to see your little dog hurt, either."

Nobody messes with *my* dog! I grabbed the

chair and slammed it into him with all my strength.

Releasing Trixie, he fell to the floor.

I scooped her into my arms, ran for the door, unlocked it, and swung it open. "Help! Help!"

The music blared, far too loud for people to hear me. Trixie barked nonstop. Gingersnap, Casper, GloryB, and a host of other dogs charged down the hallway to her aid, with Dave in hot pursuit.

I pointed my shaking hand at the man. Even my legs shook. I hoped they would hold me. "He threatened me."

The man lay on his back, groaning. "I think she cracked my ribs."

"Who is it?"

"Grayson, I think."

No sooner had I spoken than the ghost hunters barreled into the room. I looked up into Grayson's eyes.

"If you're here, then who . . . ?"

Dave eased the mask off the man's head. Doc looked up at us, his eyes angry.

"Noooo!" Grayson wedged past everyone, sat on the floor and held Doc's head gently.

"What's going on?" asked Felix.

"He attacked me!" I howled.

Grayson winced. "Oh, Gramps. Why?"

"You killed Mallory?" asked Mark.

"No." Grayson blinked hard. "No, I didn't.

Aww, Doc. I just found you, I can't lose you now. Someone call an ambulance!"

No one moved.

"Doc is your grandfather?" asked Felix. "I thought you didn't know your grandfathers."

"I knew one of them lived here."

Doc raised a hand and patted Grayson's hand. "I'd have done anything for you, son."

Everyone spoke at once.

Dave placed two fingers in his mouth and whistled. "Here's how we're going to do this." He pointed at us as he spoke. "Holly, Doc, Grayson, and I are going to the inn to see if we can figure this out. I want all of the ghost hunters back at the Dogwood Room pronto. We're going to leave quietly, two by two, and we're not going to attract any attention to ourselves or disrupt the party. Got it?" Dave held out a hand to Doc. "Get up, Doc. Let's go."

Doc winced. "I don't think I can. She cracked my ribs."

Dave licked his lips. "When I was a kid, I broke my leg at the top of Wagtail Mountain. Do you remember what you said to me?"

Doc sighed. "Tough it out?"

"You betcha. Now get up."

"Dave, maybe you should call an ambulance," I whispered.

A slight smile danced across his lips. He shook his head. "He's fine. I know Doc and his little tricks."

While Dave accompanied Doc from the room, I sat on the bed, checking out Trixie. She seemed fine and insisted on licking my face over and over.

I looked for Holmes when I walked out but didn't see him anywhere. Trixie, Felix, and I took the golf cart back to the inn.

Thirty-six

The ghost hunters who had walked back trickled in slowly. Mark and Eva, Grayson and Lillian, Brian and Mr. Luciano.

When everyone was present and seated, Dave stood up, very much in command. "Okay, I think we have established that Doc is Grayson's grandfather. Is that correct?"

Doc nodded. "Imagine me opening my front door a few days ago and finding baby Grayson there, a full grown man. I nearly burst my buttons with pride on seeing him."

"That was why I arrived early," Grayson explained. "I knew he lived around here. But it took some guts to finally knock on his door."

Dave crossed his arms over his chest. "Grayson, what happened the night Mallory died?"

"Stop. You don't have to drag them through this. It's my fault that Mallory died." Lillian raised her chin and spoke with a soft yet determined voice.

Everyone in the room turned to stare at her.

"That night, while everyone else was out at dinner, someone snatched GloryB and left a note under my door saying to meet them in the middle of the night and threatening to harm little GloryB if I told anyone, especially the police." Lillian stroked the little dog on her lap.

"That's why you were pacing through the inn that night," I exclaimed.

"I thought the person who took her might have locked her in a guest room. I was walking the halls, listening for her."

"Lillian! Why didn't you tell me?" Grayson asked. "I can't believe it. That explains so much."

I was glad it clarified things for him, because I sure didn't understand.

"It was Mallory who snatched her," continued Lillian. "Apparently she overheard me when I warned Mark about her. She wanted to make a deal. If I did *not* encourage Mark to marry her and praise her to his family, Mallory would cause me and my rather prim and proper deceased husband great embarrassment by revealing to the press that Grayson and I are involved in a romantic relationship."

I nearly fell off my chair. From the wide-eyed looks, I wasn't the only one caught by surprise. Lillian had to be fifteen years his senior.

Brian snickered. "A cougar!"

Grayson smiled, somewhat smugly.

386

"You cheated on your husband!" accused Brian.

Lillian recoiled. "I did *not!* He's been dead for years." She scowled at him. "Anyway, I tried to grab GloryB from Mallory's arms. We tussled a little and both fell, breaking one of those beautiful pumpkins that line the walk. I took off running for the inn with GloryB in my arms. When I heard Mallory was dead the next day, I thought she must have hit her head on a rock or something when she fell. I should have reported it. I'm so sorry. I . . . I felt I couldn't reveal the truth about Grayson and me without a public scandal. Even though my husband is deceased, I try not to bring shame to his memory. It was silly of me to feel that way and wrong of me not to come forward." She rose to her feet. "I'm ready to accept the consequences for my actions."

Grayson reached for her hand and clasped it in his. "You didn't kill her, Lillian. If anyone is to blame, it's me."

"You? Oh, Grayson, don't do this, honey. I have to suffer the consequences for not helping that poor girl." Lillian sank into her chair.

"Listen to her, son," said Doc. "Don't say anything. Not a word. I'll get you a good lawyer."

Grayson smiled at Lillian. "I'm not being heroic. I had a run-in with Mallory, too. Lillian didn't want to see me that night. Now I know why. But at the time, I was depressed and didn't understand the sudden cold shoulder. I thought I had found someone special in Lillian. Someone mature who wouldn't pull stunts and lie. I couldn't sleep, so I went for a walk and saw the ghost of Becca, clear as could be. Of course, it turned out to be Mallory. She was agitated and asked me to let her in the back door of the inn. When I asked her why, she said she wasn't staying at the Sugar Maple Inn, so she didn't think Casey would unlock the door for her. Apparently she had tried to break in earlier that evening."

I let out a little shriek. "I scared her away by turning on the kitchen lights!"

Dave scribbled a note on a pad.

"Mallory hedged and was evasive about why she needed to go inside," said Grayson. "I thought she might be meeting one of the ghost hunting guys, but if that was the case, why didn't he let her in, you know? I finally got it out of her. She was planning to murder Eva."

Eva's eyes flew open wide, and she gasped for breath.

"Eva!" cried Mark. "She's hyperventilating!"

I dashed to the kitchen, found a paper bag, and ran back to her with it.

Eva breathed into the bag, her chest heaving. "I never expected that," she choked.

Mark shook his head. "Mallory had some issues. Who wouldn't, after all she had been through? But I never would have thought her capable of anything so heinous."

"She finally realized that you weren't interested in her, and she was out of her mind jealous that you might reconcile with Eva," said Grayson.

"And then?" prompted Dave.

Grayson continued. "Mallory said something about stabbing Eva with Mark's penknife. But she couldn't find it. She rummaged through the pockets of that big dress she had on and was getting angrier by the moment."

My eyes met Dave's. That explained Mallory's fingerprints on the knife. It must have fallen out of her pocket when she and Lillian struggled. Trixie had found the penknife near the smashed pumpkin, corroborating their stories.

"I took out my phone so I could call Mark and Eva to warn them. Mallory pulled a stick out of the bonfire remnants and chased me. I ran to the gazebo near the hotel and was trying to get a phone signal when Mallory knocked it out of my hand."

"Ohhh," uttered Felix. "So it didn't fall in the tub."

"Exactly. It fell into the water. I hopped in to pick it up and when I bent over that crazy woman jumped on my back and tried to push my head under water so I wouldn't inform Eva and Mark. It was insane. I'm bigger and stronger, so I was able to wriggle out of her grasp. I left her there and took off. I guess she drowned after I left."

That did not sound good to me. I watched

Dave's expression. He blinked hard once. I guessed he might be thinking the same thing as me, that Grayson had murdered Mallory. We would probably never really know the truth about that. From everything I had heard tonight, it was abundantly clear that Mallory was conniving and devious, but Grayson could very well be shaping the story to sound better for him.

"How does Doc fit into this equation?" asked Dave.

Grayson swallowed hard. "I came up here a few days early, just to try to get myself back together after the scandal at my last show and . . . to find Doc. I knew he lived up here and figured it was fate that we would finally be in the same place. Destiny, you know?"

Thirty-seven

"You went to Doc for help?" asked Felix.

"No. He found me sitting on a bench, wondering what to do. I'd gotten in hot water on my last TV show when a girl claimed I got rough with her. It was a bald-faced lie. I never even touched her. And it seemed like it was happening all over again. If I called the police, would they believe me? Or would they believe Mallory when she turned the tables and said I had attacked her?"

"Exactly what were *you* doing out that night, Doc?" asked Dave.

Doc moaned. "I couldn't sleep thinking about all the years I'd lost with Grayson. Siggie and I went for a walk. We found Grayson on the bench, just like he said. I thought we better check on Mallory. But when we reached the gazebo, Mallory was dead."

"You just left her there? Of all people, you should have called me."

Doc closed his eyes. "Doc would have called you. But Gramps had to help his grandson. I saw the stick. It wasn't too hard to figure out what happened."

"But I told you I didn't drown her," insisted Grayson.

Dave sighed. "You started the fire again? I should have known it was you. But why?"

"Wasn't me," grunted Doc. "You think I'd start a fire and leave it unattended? I don't want to burn down the whole town."

He had to be lying. There was no stick in the gazebo when I found Mallory. "But you were the old man who was running with a funny gait," I said.

"I told you Clementine saw us," Doc said to Grayson.

"That was probably me," said Grayson. "Doc said I would leave tracks in the inn if my shoes were wet, so he swapped shoes with me. I kind of staggered back to the inn because his shoes were too small for my feet."

"Which one of you swiped the shoe last night?"

Grayson frowned at me. "I don't know anything about that. Doc was freaking out about the shoes, though, so I tossed the other one."

"Who attacked Clementine?" asked Dave.

Grayson seemed surprised. "Oh, man. Doc, what have you done?"

Doc started choking. "That wasn't me."

"I don't believe that for a second," I protested. "You had no problem attacking me!"

Dave ignored my outburst. "Did you falsify the medical reports?"

"Didn't have to. Mallory died from drowning. And there was a bruise consistent with falling."

Lillian inhaled sharply. "That must have been from when I grabbed GloryB and Mallory fell."

Dave handcuffed grandfather and grandson before transporting them to police headquarters on nearby Snowball Mountain.

Holmes, who had very sensibly dressed as a vampire, not as Obadiah, barged in with Ben.

We filled them in on what had happened.

Lillian leaned toward Ben. "Are they going to arrest me, too? She must have hit her head when she fell. That's probably why she drowned."

Ben attempted the local accent but it came out totally Texan. "That's not murder, that's just a killin'."

I glared at him. "Have you been reading Elmer's diary again?"

Felix scratched his head. "I don't follow."

Thankfully, Ben returned to his normal accent. "You need intent for murder. Or recklessness that any normal person would have known would lead to death, like running a bulldozer over somebody. You're going to be fine, Lillian."

Holmes wrapped an arm around me. "You okay?"

I nodded, even though my back was beginning to ache. "More importantly, so is Trixie." I scooped her up into my arms. "You tried to protect me tonight, didn't you?" I kissed her sweet little head and held her tighter than she wanted.

No one had the heart to return to the party at the Wagtail Springs Hotel. Holmes was kind enough to help me carry nuts, chips, dip, mugs of hot cider with cinnamon sticks, cinnamon apple pie, apple dog cookies, and salmon chips for the cats into the Dogwood Room. We sat there talking for a long time.

Eventually, one by one, the folks from the ghost hunting crew drifted off to bed. I cleaned up with help from Ben, Holmes, and Felix.

When we were done, Holmes bid me good night on the front porch. "I have an early flight out tomorrow, so I probably won't see you again."

"When are you coming back?"

He kissed my cheek. "Whenever you need me." And he loped off into the night.

Ben was waiting for me just inside the open door. "Nice guy. I'll be heading home tomorrow, too."

I locked the door, and we trudged up the stairs. "Back to the old grind, I guess?"

Ben opened the door to my apartment. "I have to tell you, this town could use a good criminal attorney."

"You've never practiced criminal law a day in your life."

"Might be an interesting switch."

I went into my room, changed into a nightshirt, and wrapped the big, comforting Sugar Maple Inn bathrobe around me. Ben had figured out how to turn on the fire. I poured us both Zombie Brains and was about to sit down, but found Elmer's book open on the cushy armchair.

"Did you leave this here?" I asked.

Ben scowled. "I put it up there where the cats couldn't reach it." He pointed to a high shelf where Twinkletoes and Mrs. Mewer sat, gazing down at us with feline superiority.

Mrs. Mewer yowled. Twinkletoes didn't say anything, but her fluffy black tail curled around her, and the tip waved below the shelf as though she was impatient about something.

When I picked up the book, the torn inside cover flipped open, revealing a fragile piece of paper. I sat down, sipped my drink, and extracted it. "Ben! You will not believe this." I read aloud.

My Dear Mr. Dupuy,
Thank you for your very kind invitation to speak at the renaming of the road leading into Wagtail as Wraith Way, in honor of my late father. I understand your plea that it will be unseemly if I am not in attendance. Not only will I not attend but I beg of you to reconsider such a high honor in his name.

As the attorney who has tended to matters for the Wraith family for many years, I trust you will keep this information in strictest confidence. It has weighed heavily on me for most of my life, and it is only at the behest of my mother to remain silent that I continue to suffer under the burden of the truth. Perhaps there will come a day when the Wraiths have long left this Earth and their shame can be revealed. I trust that to your hands, because no Wraith shall ever step forward to admit the abomination that is the Wraith legacy.

While all of Wagtail labors under the belief that Hiram Montacue murdered Obadiah Bagley, the truth is quite different.

My father, an arrogant and pretentious man of extreme pride, insisted I marry Hiram Montacue, another physician, equally prideful and with a cockiness that bordered on imperiousness. The two of them made a bargain for my hand over my objections. It was Obadiah Bagley who captured my heart. My father would not hear of my affections for this tender and decent man because he deemed Obadiah's status as a lowly snake oil salesman as beneath the station of his daughter.

My parents moved forward with their wedding plans for my marriage to Hiram. I refused and planned to elope with Obadiah. It was my father, Dr. Wraith, who brutally murdered gentle Obadiah with the help of Hiram Montacue. In an argument the following day, Hiram threatened to make my father's sin public. A foolish bluff, as he knew of my father's vainglory. For this he was rewarded with a deadly rattlesnake bite at the hands of my father—a gruesome and miserable death. The irony, of course, was that Hiram himself had aided in the murder of Obadiah, the one man who possessed the ability to save him from certain death.

There are those who think I lost my mind because of the deaths of Hiram and

Obadiah. Perhaps so. I have chosen to retire to my own devices among the animals who need my help. Unlike the ridiculous pomposity of my father and Hiram, they ask for nothing and give their hearts in pure love. I find solace in their company and hope in their goodness.

I beg of you not to honor my father. I trust you will find an adequate excuse to abandon the plans for naming the street in his honor.

Faithfully,
Rebecca Wraith

"Unbelievable!" Ben reached for the letter. "Pretty impressive that old Elmer sat on this information. It almost died with him." He sat back. "Makes me wonder how many huge secrets have died with the lawyers who knew the truth. But Elmer kept the letter. He must have thought he might need it one day."

"Poor Becca and Obadiah," I said. "I'm going to take this to the interim mayor—I have an in with her, you know—and ask for Obadiah's remains to be moved inside the cemetery. It's time people knew the truth."

"I suspect you're right," said Ben.

The sun shone on Wagtail on November first. I walked out on my balcony and gazed down at the town. People were walking their dogs and cats as if nothing untoward had transpired.

I dressed in a salmon colored turtleneck and a pleated skirt. My feet still ached from the ruby slippers, so I wore comfortable Keds—not exactly a fashion statement. I missed the tea and croissants that Mr. Huckle usually delivered, but their absence today would only make me appreciate them more tomorrow.

Twinkletoes rubbed against my ankles in the kitchen. I picked her up for a quick good morning snuggle. Mrs. Mewer meowed at me for food. I fed them a creation called Harvest Halibut, which they ate with great gusto.

After all the late nights he'd had, I didn't have the heart to wake Ben.

Trixie zoomed out of the door ahead of me and scampered down the stairs. She waited by the door to be let out.

Minutes later, we headed for breakfast. Oma and Dave were already sitting at a table with Gingersnap at their feet. "Mind if I join you?"

"Of course, liebchen." Oma stood up and hugged me fiercely. "Oh my. What you went through last night! Are you sore? Dave tells me Doc hit you quite hard."

"I'm a little achy and bruised." An understatement if ever there was one. "It's nothing that won't go away."

Oma placed her warm hand on top of mine. "I

was friends with Doc. I believed him when he said Mallory's death was an accident. I'm ashamed to say that I was also angry with you because you did not believe him. Ach. When I think what could have happened to you." She clasped her hand over her mouth in horror. "There I was, going out with Doc and Rose. All the time, he was calculating to harm my granddaughter. I am sick when I think of this."

"It's okay, Oma. We all hoped Doc was correct and it was an accident." I peered at their plates. "What's for breakfast?"

"Crab Cakes Benedict." Dave sipped his coffee. "And I recommend it."

It must have been Shelley's day off. Her replacement took my order.

"Did Grayson reveal anything of interest last night?" I asked.

Dave leaned back in his chair. "He's being very cooperative. Lillian bailed him out. He's already back at the inn. I was just telling your grandmother that it appears it was Mallory who tried to break into the inn. She meant to lie in wait for Mark and Eva to return. When that didn't work, she went to plan B."

"Do you know why she dressed as Becca Wraith?"

"It's only a guess, but I would assume so that anyone who saw her would think she was Becca's ghost."

Oma dabbed her mouth with a napkin. "She put a lot of thought into her evil intention."

The Crab Cakes Benedicts arrived, along with hot tea for me.

Trixie snarfed her breakfast before I had finished adding sugar to my tea.

For once, I didn't feel guilty eating a rich, wonderful breakfast. I tried to eat slower than Trixie, though. I unfolded the letter Becca Wraith had written to Elmer and handed it to Dave, who read it aloud while I ate.

"I never would have imagined such a thing," gasped Oma.

"Dr. Wraith got away with two murders. Incredible." Dave flipped over the letter and examined it.

Oma bestowed a smile on him. "They didn't have Dave Quinlan on the job."

I set my tea down. "Oma, do you think we could move Obadiah's remains? Maybe next to Becca's grave?"

"Holly, I like this idea. It is the right thing to do. We will make it an event and honor them. Yes?"

The Apparition Apprehenders trickled in for breakfast. Mr. Luciano and Eva arrived first. Eva wore an autumn gold dress with long sleeves and a matching headband. Her engagement ring glittered on her left hand. Lillian, Grayson, and GloryB soon joined them. It wasn't long before Brian, Felix, Casper, Ben, and Mark arrived.

I whispered to Oma, "Do you think Aunt Birdie has a chance with Mr. Luciano?"

Oma looked aghast. "Please. Mr. Luciano is a very fine man. Let us hope he can escape from Wagtail today without Birdie running behind him."

Trixie evidently realized that food would soon be coming for the other dogs. As soon as their breakfasts were served, she tried to help them eat. Casper gave her a little snarl that sent her to GloryB's bowl.

I had brought the leash, just in case, and I latched it on her until the other dogs had finished. The way she whimpered and cried, you would have thought she was starving. I felt terrible and kept giving her teensy bits of cookies.

When their bowls had been removed, I took off the leash.

Oma patted my arm. "She will learn soon."

Not soon enough.

Brian sat near us, and Trixie would not leave him alone. She kept trying to bury her nose in his pocket.

"I'm so sorry." I tugged her away and told her to sit.

She did. For two minutes. And then she went back to Brian's pocket. She placed her paws on the edge of his chair and wriggled her nose into the pocket opening. By that time, everyone was laughing.

"What have you got in there, Brian?" asked Felix. "Dog treats to snack on?"

Brian lifted his hands. "I don't know what she wants."

Trixie was obsessive.

I latched the leash on her and picked her up. But this time, she had what she wanted—the black cat toy she had found near the bonfire. "Where did you get this? I've been looking all over for one."

"I brought it with me. It's my good luck charm."

With dread, I lifted my eyes to meet Brian's. "Hasn't been very lucky for you, has it?"

"Sure it has."

"You lost it." It was a statement, not a question.

"Yeah. And I found it out on the porch. Must have dropped it there."

He might have found it there, but I knew good and well that wasn't where he lost it. "You *did* see Mallory the night she died."

His face flushed as red as the raspberry jam on the table. "What are you talking about?"

Maybe I was overstepping. He could have lost it at the bonfire without knowing it. Or he could have returned to the bonfire later, maybe with a stick he wanted to burn. "It was you who started the fire again."

"You're out of your mind. Are you in love with Grayson too, and now you want to get him off the hook by blaming me?"

"You burned the stick to get rid of the evidence.

402

Grayson didn't kill Mallory. You did. And you tried to pin it on Eva. How could we be so blind? That was the real reason for the handbag and the jewelry in Eva's room. You didn't even hide it well, because you wanted it found. You were trying to pin the murder on Eva."

Eva's coffee mug landed on the table with a thunk. "Nooo," she breathed.

"Brian, what have you done?" cried Felix.

Brian glanced around furtively, as if in search of an escape route. He jumped up and dodged through the tables with Dave in hot pursuit.

Sensing excitement, GloryB, Trixie, and Casper ran toward Brian, who stumbled and fell over the dogs.

Dave caught up to Brian, latched handcuffs on his wrists, and helped him to his feet.

Felix walked over to his friend. "Aw, Brian. What happened?"

Brian swallowed hard. "Mallory said she was coming to my room that night and that I should watch for her and let her in. I stupidly thought she was finally interested in me. But she never showed." He glared at Eva. "As soon as I saw Eva here, I knew this was my chance to get back at her. To make her change her mind about the existence of ghosts. For once, I wanted the upper hand. I wanted to discredit her. After I tricked Eva with the light, I walked over to the Wagtail Springs Hotel to see if I could find any ghosts, and there was Becca Wraith. Man, was I excited. Except it turned out to be Mallory. She was really nice to me and invited me to dangle my feet in the water with her. But then she tried to talk me into helping her murder Eva by bludgeoning her with a stick."

He looked down at his hands and his voice sounded almost like a little boy's. "She had my good luck cat and my *I'd rather be ghost hunting* cap. She must have taken them when we were at the bar. And I realized that she planned to pin Eva's murder on me. I know I'm not always the brightest guy, but this time I saw through her. That was why she wanted me to open the door for her. She didn't like me or want anything to do with me. She just wanted to be rid of Eva and have me take the blame."

Brian's demeanor changed. His eyes blazed. It reminded me of the way he acted the night Mrs. Mewer jumped on his shoulder. The amiable guy was gone.

"I wasn't going to take the rap for Mallory. I hate Eva. Man, I hate her. It was tempting to imagine her dead. But I knew what would happen. Mallory would pin Eva's murder on me. She was only being nice to me to manipulate me. No one ever cares about me. Mallory thought I was just a big tubby dummy. Well, I'm not! I showed her!"

He stopped shouting. The room was completely silent. He scanned our faces. "So I used Mallory's death as a reason to get rid of Eva. After all, they had a history. I borrowed Mallory's purse and necklace and planted them on Eva. If she was in jail, she wouldn't be mean to me anymore."

He looked at me. "How did you know?"

"Trixie found your good luck cat at the bonfire and carried it back to the hotel. I thought it was a dog toy."

"I must have dropped it when I threw the stick on the fire."

"So Doc wasn't lying about that."

Lillian grasped Grayson's arm. "Mallory was still alive! That proves Grayson didn't kill her."

Grayson's shoulders relaxed. "Holly, I'm so sorry that Doc attacked you last night. He was convinced that I had killed Mallory and wanted to protect me."

"Why did you try to conjure Mallory's ghost with the Ouija board? If you really believe in ghosts, weren't you afraid she might reveal your involvement?" I asked.

Brian's face contorted. "Why does everything think I'm so stupid? I was going to make sure it spelled out Eva's name!"

"Brian, did you attack Clementine?" asked Dave.

Brian took a deep breath. "I heard she could identify the killer."

"Let's go." Dave crooked a finger at Brian.

Brian gazed down at Trixie. "Two more hours and I would have been out of here, and no one would have ever known."

Grayson swung Trixie into his arms and Lillian fussed over her, promising to buy her the biggest dog treat she could find.

Trixie wagged her tail, thrilled with all the attention.

"I guess word will soon be out about your relationship," said Eva.

Lillian squared her shoulders. "It's just as well. I could never have stood on pride to Grayson's detriment." She smiled at him. "And now we won't have to sneak around."

I couldn't help thinking how different Becca's life would have been if her father had valued her more than his own self-importance.

At mid-morning, Eva stopped by the office. "I thought I'd go over to the hotel for a few minutes. Would you and Twinkletoes like to come with Mrs. Mewer and me?"

"Sure. On one condition. Would you mind if we took a golf cart? My feet are sore, and I'm a little bruised from Doc slamming me to the floor last night."

"Of course. That must have been awful!"

Trixie and Gingersnap joined us on our outing. This time I didn't latch leashes onto them. They hopped into the golf cart, and we were off.

When we arrived at the Wagtail Springs Hotel, Clementine and Parker stood outside. Clementine's sons were chasing each other, but her daughter looked as though she might burst into tears.

"What are you doing down here?" I asked.

"Now that Brian is indisposed, I'm feeling a lot safer. Parker invited the kids for ice-cream cones to cheer up Emily."

"What's wrong with Emily?" I asked.

"We lost Lassie a few days ago."

"Lassie! Emily, I have Lassie. I forgot all about him. Wait here."

I handed Twinkletoes's leash to Eva and walked back to the golf cart as fast as I could. Did I have the right golf cart? I peeked into the storage bag. And there it was—the bag containing Lassie.

I grabbed it, hurried back, and handed it to Emily.

She looked inside and screamed. Emily pulled Lassie out of the bag and hugged her. "Look, Mommy!"

"I see!" said Clementine.

"She dropped him the day I was trying to help you lose Parker. I'm so sorry. I forgot all about Lassie."

"Thanks a lot." Parker might have said it with a snarky tone, but he grinned. "Tell her what happened, Clemmie."

"Someone called this morning about leasing the hotel. It's like a miracle. After all this time with no one interested, a call came out of the blue. And Lillian Elsworth wants to rent the store!"

"The curse has been broken."

We turned around to see Felix and Casper.

"Come on, Felix. You know that's nonsense," scoffed Eva.

"No, really. I saw the letter you found, Holly. Hiram said the Wraiths would never know true love, and they would lose their money. *Misfortune and misery shall be the lot of the Wraiths until the day the truth be known.*" He looked at Clementine. "Are you a Wraith?"

Her eyes grew large. "I don't believe this. My father is a descendant of Becca's brother's daughter. That's why Dad bought the hotel. He felt like it belonged in the family."

"It's all coincidence." Eva chuckled. "There's no such thing as a curse."

Felix wobbled his head to the side. "I wouldn't be so sure about that, Eva. Facts are facts. Brian's black cat didn't bring him luck, but in a way, Brian might have saved your life."

It was good to hear them bantering again. I sucked in the clear mountain air. It was just about here that Eva had said *two can play this game.* Mallory and Brian had been playing games, trying to pin things on other people, and look what came of it.

Clementine's boys zoomed around us with their arms outstretched, buzzing like bees, but I suspected they were supposed to be airplanes. Odd little balls like the one Trixie had found at the hotel were stuck to their foreheads. They zeroed in on Trixie, chasing her.

Emily scolded them, but when they persisted, she dropped Lassie and ran after them.

"What are those things on their heads?" I asked.

"Kids' toys. They stick to each other and make all kinds of shapes."

One of the boys tried to stick one on Trixie. She grabbed it in her mouth and ran from him. He chased her in a huge circle, and his brother and sister joined in.

Trixie sped by us, the children in hot pursuit, shouting, "I'm gonna get you. I'm gonna get you!"

Eva shrieked, "The ghost children! No wonder the recording was so clear."

I gasped as things came together in my mind. "You were in the hotel the night the ghost hunters were investigating."

"I thought we would be safer there. I was so absorbed in my own problems that I'd forgotten all about the ghost hunters. I shuttled the kids into the room that locks. The one where the snakes killed Hiram? I locked the door and rattled one of the kids' toys when they tried the doorknob."

"That explains the ghostly rattle." Felix sighed. "Bummer. I guess those were your footsteps we heard, too?"

"Probably. I'm sorry if we ruined your investigation."

Emily screamed. "Lassie!"

Gingersnap and Casper had hold of Lassie and played tug with the ancient stuffed dog. Trixie sprang to join them, leaping up to grab one of poor Lassie's paws.

I ran to them. "Drop! Drop!"

They didn't care what I said. None of the dogs wanted to give up the toy. I seized hold of Lassie and asked, "Who wants a treat? Sit!"

All three dogs sat like it was a magic trick. I rewarded each of them with a treat.

"I'm so sorry, Emily. Will you let me take Lassie to the vet for stitches?"

She nodded somberly and reached for her dog.

I handed the dog to her.

She cocked her head. "Mommy, Lassie has rocks in her tummy."

We peered over Emily's shoulder as she pulled a small bag out of Lassie.

Clementine took it from her, opened the draw-string, and shook sparkling diamonds into her hand. Her eyes opened wide. "I don't believe it! Thank goodness all this nonsense will come to an end. I'm going to make sure the press is there when I turn these babies over to the feds. I want photographic evidence in all the newspapers so the diamond hunters will leave us alone."

Parker smacked his forehead and moaned. "Your ex said he hid them in something you would never give away. How could I have been so stupid?"

"He was a complete louse but he called this one right. I could never have parted with Lassie. I guess he had this done when he took Lassie to be re-stuffed." Clementine burst into a fit of giggles. "The ghost diamonds were with us the whole time."

Except for all those nights they spent in the golf cart. But I thought I'd better not mention that.

Parker raised an eyebrow.

"Don't even think about it." Clementine quickly reinserted the diamonds and closed the bag. "Could I leave these in the vault at the inn until the feds can pick them up?"

"Absolutely."

"We'll talk over ice cream," said Parker.

"I'm not as easy as my children."

"Tell me about it, Clemmie."

Clementine handed me the bag. "Would you mind? I don't trust anyone who calls me Clemmie."

I whispered, "You seem awfully chummy with Parker."

Clementine smiled. "Maybe the curse *has* been broken. We'll see how it turns out." She called the children, and the five of them strolled away.

"How about you, Felix? Any future for you and Zelda?"

Felix blushed. "I don't know yet. Zelda says there's a community college over on Snowball Mountain. Maybe I could get a job there. If they're not all taken by Mark and Eva."

"At this point," said Eva, "all I know is that I want a spring wedding at the Sugar Maple Inn."

"That's great!" I hugged Eva. "It will be so much fun. And Mrs. Mewer can come back and see Twinkletoes again. I'm sorry, Felix," I said. "It must be disappointing to learn that the sounds weren't from ghosts. I guess the old hotel isn't haunted after all."

"Are you sure?" whispered Felix. He aimed his phone's camera at the hotel. "Look. The Ghost and Mrs. Mewer see them."

Casper, the ghost dog, and Mrs. Mewer were staring up at the second-floor balcony of the hotel, exactly where I had walked in the Becca Wraith costume. Two woman in filmy white gowns looked out at us. One wore a wreath of black roses in her long white hair. I thought I recognized a softer, gentler Mallory next to her.

Eva murmured, "Becca and Mallory!"

Trixie barked at them, and they were gone.

Recipes

One of my dogs suffered from severe food allergies that did not allow him to eat commercial dog food. Consequently, I learned to cook for my dogs and have done so for many years. Consult your veterinarian if you want to switch your dog over to home-cooked food. It's not as difficult as one might think. Keep in mind that, like children, dogs need a balanced diet, not just a hamburger. Any changes to your dog's diet should be made gradually so your dog's stomach can adjust.

Chocolate, alcohol, caffeine, fatty foods, grapes, raisins, macadamia nuts, onions and garlic, salt, xylitol, and unbaked dough can be toxic to dogs. For more information about foods your dog should not eat, consult the Pet Poison Helpline, at petpoisonhelpline.com/pet-owners.

PUBLISHER'S NOTE: The recipes contained in this book are to be followed exactly as written. The publisher is not responsible for your specific health or allergy needs that may require medical supervision. The publisher is not responsible for any adverse reactions to the recipes contained in this book.

Chunky Cheesy Chicken

For dogs.

1 cup diced cooked chicken breast
1 cup cooked carrot slices
1 cup cooked barley
¼ cup shredded cheddar cheese
1 cup minced raw apples

Combine and warm slightly before serving.

Apple Chunk Muffins

For people.

½ cup butter
1 cup walnuts
1 cup flour
¾ cup sugar
1 teaspoon baking powder
½ teaspoon baking soda
¼ teaspoon salt
½ cup applesauce
1 teaspoon vanilla
2 eggs
1 peeled apple, chopped

Preheat oven to 350. Melt the butter and set it aside to cool. Line a cupcake pan with paper liners.

In a food processor, mix the walnuts with the flour, sugar, baking powder, baking soda, and salt. Pulse until fine. Set aside.

Whisk the eggs for one to two minutes, add the applesauce and vanilla and mix in butter. Pour the flour mixture on top and fold with a spatula. Do not overmix! Add the chopped apples and mix gently.

Spoon into the cupcake liners, distributing evenly. Bake 23-25 minutes or until the muffins are a light golden brown on top.

Pumpkin Whoopie Pies

For people and dogs (only a tiny portion
for dogs, please). Substitute plain
cream cheese for dog filling.

1½ cups flour
1 teaspoon baking powder
1 teaspoon baking soda
½ teaspoon salt
½ teaspoon cinnamon
½ teaspoon ginger
⅛ teaspoon cloves
2 eggs
1 cup packed dark brown sugar
1 teaspoon molasses

½ cup vegetable oil
1 cup pumpkin
1 teaspoon vanilla

Preheat oven to 350. Line a baking sheet with parchment paper. Mix the flour, baking powder, baking soda, salt, cinnamon, ginger, and cloves together in a bowl and set aside. Beat the eggs, sugar, and molasses. Add the oil, pumpkin, and vanilla and beat until smooth. Slowly beat in the flour mixture. Drop by heaping tablespoon on the parchment paper, trying to make each about the same size. Smooth the tops a bit. Bake 10-13 minutes. Cool on a rack. NOTE: The dough does not spread when baking. If you wish to carve out ghost shapes, make them larger. A ¾-full ¼ cup measure works well for the larger size. Use a miniature ghost cookie cutter to cut out the shape and pipe extra filling in the middle.

Marshmallow Crème Filling

1 stick unsalted butter (room temperature)
1 jar marshmallow fluff
2 cups powdered sugar
1 teaspoon vanilla

Beat the butter with the marshmallow fluff. Beat in vanilla, and gradually beat in the powdered sugar.

Pumpkin Cake with Cream Cheese Frosting

For people and dogs
(only a tiny portion for dogs, please).

Pumpkin Cake

2¼ cups flour
1½ teaspoons baking powder
1½ teaspoons baking soda
¾ teaspoon pink sea salt
2 teaspoons cinnamon
1 teaspoon nutmeg
¼ teaspoon cloves
¾ cup sugar
1 cup dark brown sugar, packed
¾ cup vegetable oil
1⅛ cups canned pumpkin
3 eggs, room temperature
2 teaspoons vanilla

Preheat oven to 350. Grease and flour a 9x13 inch pan. In a bowl, mix together the flour, baking powder, baking soda, salt, cinnamon, nutmeg, and cloves. Set aside. Beat together the sugars, oil, and pumpkin. Beat in the eggs one at a time and add the vanilla. Add the flour mixture ¼ cup at a time. Pour into prepared pan and bake 30 minutes or until a cake tester comes out clean. Cool before frosting.

Cream Cheese Frosting

1 stick (8 tablespoons) butter (softened)
6 ounces cream cheese (softened)
1 teaspoon vanilla
2 cups powdered sugar

Beat the butter with the cream cheese. Add the vanilla and beat. Add the sugar ½ cup at a time, beating in between.

Mini Meatloaf Mummies

For people and dogs.

2 eggs
1 cup shredded zucchini
½ cup shredded carrots
⅓ cup plain bread crumbs
1 pound lean ground beef or turkey
1 teaspoon salt
1 tcaspoon dried oregano or Italian seasoning
   mix

3 rounded tablespoons Parmesan cheese
¼ teaspoon pepper
6 ounces sliced white cheese (like Monterey Jack or Asiago)

Preheat oven to 350. Mix all ingredients **except the sliced cheese** in a bowl. Shape into mummies. Bake 45-50 minutes or until done. Drape sliced cheese over the meat as mummy wrap. If necessary, return to oven for a couple of minutes to melt the cheese.

Pumpkin Pancakes with Chocolate Chips

For people and dogs
(only a tiny portion for dogs, please).
NOTE: For dogs, OMIT CHOCOLATE.

1½ cups flour
2 tablespoons dark brown sugar
1 teaspoon baking powder
½ teaspoon baking soda
1 teaspoon cinnamon
½ teaspoon ginger
¼ teaspoon cloves
¼ teaspoon nutmeg
1 cup buttermilk (or 1 cup milk mixed with 1 tablespoon vinegar)

1 egg, lightly beaten
¼ cup pumpkin
2 tablespoons melted butter
¼ cup chocolate chips (OMIT FOR DOGS!)

Mix the dry ingredients in a bowl. Stir in the other ingredients. Grease a griddle or pan. Cook until puffed, then flip and cook the other side. Serve with maple syrup.

Spider Eggs

For people.

1 dozen large eggs
mayonnaise
mustard
salt
small black olives

Place the eggs in a pot. Cover with water and put the lid on. Bring to a boil. Turn the heat off. Leave the lid on and let stand for 20 minutes. Pour out the hot water. Add cold water and ice cubes to shock the eggs.

Peel the hard-boiled eggs and slice in half lengthwise. Scoop out the yolks, mash, and add mayonnaise, mustard, and salt to taste. Spoon into eggs.

Cut the olives in half lengthwise. Place one half on the center of each egg. Cut some of the halves into ¼ inch thick slices. Place four on each side of the spider's "body" as legs.

Hair of the Dog's Zombie Brains

For people. Use a small glass for this, like a miniature martini or a cordial glass.

1 ounce peach schnapps
½ ounce Bailey's Irish Cream
Rose's Sweetened Lime Juice

Fill half the glass with peach schnapps. Top with ½ ounce Bailey's Irish Cream. Gently add a couple of drops of Rose's Sweetened Lime Juice on top to drizzle through.

Voodoo Witch Doctor

For people.

½ ounce Bacardi 151
½ ounce spiced rum
½ ounce Malibu Coconut Rum
½ ounce peach schnapps

½ ounce banana rum
splash grenadine syrup
cranberry juice

Combine the first six ingredients in a highball glass. Fill glass with cranberry juice.

Center Point Large Print
600 Brooks Road / PO Box 1
Thorndike, ME 04986-0001 USA

(207) 568-3717

**US & Canada:
1 800 929-9108**
www.centerpointlargeprint.com